BLAKE COLLEGE

Other Books by Dan Armstrong

Taming the Dragon
Prairie Fire
Puddle of Love
The Open Secret
Chain of Souls
The Eyes of Archimedes Book I
The Siege of Syracuse
The Eyes of Archimedes Book II
The Death of Marcellus
The Eyes of Archimedes Book III
Zama
Cornelia: The First Woman of Rome

BLAKE COLLEGE

A Novel

Dan Armstrong

Mud City Press
Eugene, Oregon

To Josh,
Keep at it.
Write everyday!

Dan
8/8/2019

Blake College
Copyright © 2019 by Dan Armstrong

Published by
Mud City Press
http://www.mudcitypress.com
Eugene, Oregon

ISBN-978-0-9993219-2-8

Printed in the United States

To Sean

NARRATOR'S NOTE

The story I tell happened fifty years ago. It involves a series of unusual events that all witnesses swore never to mention outside their immediate circle—because the events could not be proven by any material evidence and seemed so unlikely that anyone describing them would be stigmatized. Due to the passage of time, I can't be certain that portions of this story have not been repeated somewhere, sometime, but as someone who was there, I see no reason to maintain the silence any longer. To keep my telling of the tale as objective as possible, however, I have decided to remain anonymous and narrate in the third person. You will not know which character I am or what part I played until the end of the story when my name is given. Call it a mystery within a mystery.

"If the doors of perception were cleansed, everything would appear to man [and woman] as it is, infinite."

-William Blake

"Though for the most part entirely unconscious of it, we pass the whole of our lives in the midst of a vast and populous unseen world. During sleep or in trance, when the insistent physical senses are for the time in abeyance, this other world is to some extent open to us, and we will sometimes bring back from those conditions more or less vague memories of what we have seen and heard there."

-C.W. Leadbeater, *The Astral Plane*

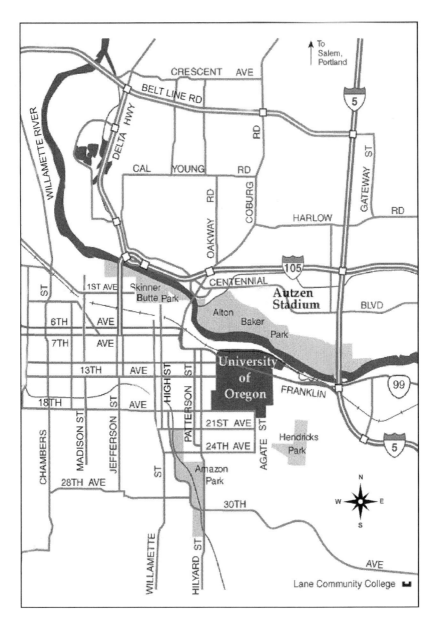

Eugene, Oregon

PROLOGUE

In the late 1960s and early 1970s, Eugene, Oregon, a small college town in the western part of the state, gained national recognition through the success of the University of Oregon track and field team. Their innovative coach Bill Bowerman led the team to four national championships between 1961 and 1972 and helped send thirty-one runners to the Olympics. Eventually dubbed Tracktown, USA, Eugene blossomed during these years of attention, and many foresaw a bright economic future ahead. After the summer Olympics of 1968, the city fathers and the university leaders made a push for Eugene to host the next men's Olympic Track and Field Trials, scheduled to take place in June of 1972.

The Trials were a highly popular, nationally televised competition for track and field athletes vying to win a place on the United States Olympic team. Since 1952, the Trials had been held in Los Angeles four times and outside San Francisco at Stanford University once. Holding the Trials would be a prestigious honor for Eugene and would add to its image as an up and coming city in as beautiful a natural setting as any in the United States. Getting the Olympic Trials became a motivating factor for the entire city. When the Olympic officials came to visit, everything was done to promote the healthy outdoor lifestyle that was Eugene. Hunting, fishing, hiking, cycling, jogging, this was the banner that flew over Eugene. Come west young men and women! You've not lived until you've experienced the Northwest!

At the same time, something quite different was happening across the United States. A counterculture was forming out of the anti-war, civil rights, and feminist movements of the 1960s, and in response many of America's youths hit the road to find a new American dream. While California, particularly San Francisco, was the most popular destination, Eugene was also a major stop on the winding road of American wanderers. Backpackers with bedrolls, hippies jammed into wildly painted Volkswagen buses, college dropouts, bicycle enthusiasts, war veterans, war protesters, motorcycle freaks, that class of modern day gypsy from a retired Colonel and his wife in a Winnebago to some kid on the bum for the first time were all part of the crowd that filtered through the small college town at the south end of the Willamette Valley. Some of these travelers merely passed through, some stayed for extended periods, some attended the University of Oregon, and some eventually made their homes in the region. A pleasant little city of fifty thousand, surrounded by farmland and framed by luxurious forests, was suddenly attracting young people as though it were the Promised Land. The once quiet street life of Eugene percolated with long-haired youths with little money in their pockets and a sense of revolution in their heads. Eugene was the place to be. It was hip. It was happening, and as a bonus the Merry Prankster Ken Kesey lived a few miles outside of town.

Roiled into this was the anti-war movement that gripped nearly all the college campuses in the United States. The University of Oregon, like many other schools, had its chapter of the SDS, its proponents of Black Power, and its outspoken feminists, but with the influx of the itinerant young people into the community, the street life was as alive with activism as was the campus.

The spring of 1970 marked the height of political activity at the University of Oregon. One of the bitterest issues was the presence of the Reserve Officer Training Corps (ROTC) on the campus. On April fifteenth, four days after the launch of Apollo 13, the U of O faculty, under pressure from the student senate to make a statement, voted 199-185 to keep ROTC on the campus. That night between fifty and one hundred students stormed the ROTC offices in French Hall, ransacking the building, starting fires in waste baskets, and breaking windows. The Eugene police were called in. Seven students were arrested. Four were accused of inciting a riot, and Oregon Governor Tom McCall put the National Guard on alert.

April twenty-first, the day before the first Earth Day, Emerald Hall, a U of O administration building, was firebombed. Two days after that three hundred students and activists occupied the ROTC offices and refused to leave. Following a three-day standoff with the police, sixty-one protesters were arrested. Two weeks later, on May fourth, four students were shot and killed at Kent State University in Ohio, prompting a two-day student strike at the U of O. The following week there was a third attack on French Hall.

With the escalating anti-war protests and violence, the summer break could not come soon enough for the city of Eugene. When the students left the campus at the end of the term, the movement to oust ROTC lost focus. Throughout the summer city and university officials worried that the temporary quiet would be broken by anti-war activists when the students returned in the fall.

CHAPTER 1

In 1966 Arthur Kotke, a frustrated history professor at the University of Oregon who had been caught up in the early throes of the counterculture movement, went on an extended sabbatical with a vision to start an experimental school to study "anything"—a school without walls, as he would say. Arthur bought a large, run-down Victorian house on two acres along the Willamette River, less than four miles from where he had spoken at a podium in a university lecture hall for twenty-one years.

Nine months after buying and partially restoring the house, Kotke printed a catalogue for *William Blake College* and began working to establish accreditation for his school. Applications peaked at twenty-one in the second year and then fell to two in the fourth, after being denied accreditation for the third straight year. Without a word, Kotke packed up his belongings and left Eugene in the spring of 1970. He left no forwarding address and made no provisions for the sale or management of his property. He may as well have been abducted by visitors from outer space so complete was his departure. Arthur Kotke's failed effort was the first incarnation of Blake College.

The first person to notice that Arthur had left was a twenty-two-year-old woman, Adrienne Stephens. Adrienne, a small, pretty woman, with long, dark brown hair, had dropped out of the U of O halfway through her junior year to learn organic gardening from the ground up. She bought a pickup truck for a hundred dollars and a lawn mower for ten and started her own one-girl yard maintenance company. Her first regular job was taking care of the grounds at Blake College, which she did for over a year. After mowing the lawn three times during the spring of 1970 without seeing Arthur or being paid, she realized he was gone. When May passed with no further word from Arthur, Adrienne, who lived with her dog Moxie in a converted garage for twenty-five dollars a month, moved into the old Victorian with her black and white terrier mix.

Her second week of camping out in one of the five upstairs bedrooms, she took an evening to smoke a joint and sort through the stack of unopened mail that had accumulated beneath the mail slot in the front door. In a stoned fit of naïveté Adrienne decided to use every penny she had to pay the overdue utility bills and mortgage payments, with the intent of staying in the house indefinitely. If Arthur returned, they would work something out. If he didn't, she would do whatever was necessary to hang onto the house. In her mind, paying the mortgage was the same as paying rent. As long as she paid the bills, no one would bother her.

Adrienne took to the place as though she owned it. She made a garden for vegetables and flowers. She planted fruit trees that she had received in exchange for pruning work at a local nursery, and thus began the long process of relandscaping the entire place. She lived for plants and gardening, and for her this was paradise. But her only source of income came from mowing lawns, and she was short on cash when it came time to make the next mortgage payment. That's when Rain Adams moved in with her calico cat, Lena, to contribute to the expenses.

One of the senior members of the Eugene counterculture, Rain was eight years older than Adrienne and highly respected for her knowledge of plants and environmental issues, which was why Adrienne was drawn to her. Rain, an attractive and remarkably serene woman with stunning auburn hair, supported herself drawing astrology charts and driving out to the forests and pastures of the Willamette Valley in her VW bug to wild craft herbs and mushrooms. She dried what she found and sold it on Saturdays at Eugene's brand-new street market—known as Saturday Market— under the banner of *Naturally Wild.*

One night, a month after Rain moved in, the two women stayed up late, sipping from a bottle of wine with a man Rain had recently met at Saturday Market. Tai, who used no last name, had arrived in Eugene in June after two years of world travel, investigating various forms of experiential religion. He was two years older than Rain and fashioned himself a cowboy mystic as a means of meeting women. He had already spent two nights at the house with Rain and had no extended plans beyond spending the evening with her again. He was tall and handsome, with blond dreadlocks—something rare in Eugene at the time.

As the two women combed through the mail to determine if they could make the next month's mortgage payment, Tai, a big talker, entertained them with stories about going to Nepal to find the best hashish in the world, trekking into the Amazon basin of Peru to try the hallucinogen ayahuasca, spending two months on the Fiji Islands drinking the provocative juice of the kava, and visiting the Navajo Indian Reservation in Chinle, Arizona to take part in a tribal peyote ceremony. "Two summers back I was at Timothy Leary's mansion in Millbrook, New York," said Tai, as the women opened the mail. "Took so much LSD I think my pupils are permanently dilated." He laughed at the thought of it.

While Adrienne tallied the bills, Rain, her cat in her lap, sorted through all the other mail that had arrived since Arthur's departure, much of it addressed to Blake College. Although the school no longer existed, the experimental college was still listed in a few college catalogues, and Rain discovered several applications for the coming fall in the pile of unopened mail.

"Did you see this, Adrienne? People are still applying to Blake College."

Adrienne shook her head. "No, never looked at that stuff."

"I've found six applications so far." She handed one, then another to Tai.

"What's Blake College?" asked Tai, after reading through the two applications.

Adrienne told him the story that most of the young people in Eugene already knew.

Tai found it fascinating. "Maybe you should restart the school."

"What do you mean?" asked Rain.

"Start accepting students."

"And then what?" was Adrienne's response.

"Resurrect Blake College. Instead of charging tuition, turn the school into a co-op and share the expenses and housework."

"But we have no teachers, no curriculum," said Rain.

"Adrienne can teach organic gardening," said Tai, "and how to cook out of the garden. You can teach wild crafting and astrology. I could do a class on shamanism."

Adrienne wasn't so sure.

But Rain perked up. "I know an older woman in town who could teach yoga and meditation. You know Gloria, Adrienne—Glorious Gloria. I think she needs a new place to live."

Just the mention of her name made Adrienne smile.

Tai took a swig from the bottle of wine and handed it to Rain. "I spent several years throwing pots. If we could find a pottery wheel and build a kiln, I could teach ceramics. How cool would that be?"

"Yes, yes," said Rain, getting excited. "Compared to what Arthur was doing, with all his emphasis on seminars and the great books, we could do the real thing. We could teach people how to live."

"Maybe we could use it as a way to hang onto the house," said Adrienne, warming to the idea.

Tai withdrew a small soapstone pipe and a black plastic film container from his shirt pocket. He placed a nugget of Lebanese blond in the pipe, got it started, and passed it to Rain. The second incarnation of Blake College was underway.

CHAPTER 2

Over the next month, Rain, Adrienne, and Tai accepted six students to Blake College and began gearing up for the school year. They added Rain's friend Gloria, the yoga teacher, to the faculty and turned the college into a cooperative, in which the students and teachers would share the living expenses. Three of the six potential students sent in the five hundred-dollar enrollment fee in August, with classes slated to begin September ninth. The first student arrived in the middle of the day on the eighth.

Van Hammond had taken the train from Youngstown, Ohio and walked the ten blocks from the Eugene train station to the school. He did not identify with the counterculture movement and could not have looked straighter in his chinos, button-down shirt, and college cut. He appeared on the front porch of Blake College on a sunny afternoon with a suitcase in one hand and a backpack hanging from his shoulders. Sweating heavily, he knocked on the door of the old Victorian and got no answer. He tried the door. When it opened, he stuck his head in and shouted, "Hello"—again with no response. He continued into the house. Weaving through the maze of Salvation Army furniture and empty wine bottles, he wondered if he were at the right address.

Still carrying his belongings, he returned to the front porch to verify that the house number matched that on his letter of acceptance—which it did, so he wandered around to the back of the property hoping to find a member of the faculty. Van spotted Adrienne in the garden, levering a shovel into the soil with her foot, and wearing nothing but a pair of rubber boots, work gloves, and a deep bronze tan. Her hair was collected in two braids that reached down past her waist. Eighteen-year-old Van, who had not experienced naked hippies in Ohio and whose sexual experience in high school had involved nothing beyond a kiss, was awed to silence by the sight of the young goddess. When Adrienne saw him standing there wide-eyed, she stood her shovel in the dirt and greeted him without the slightest show of modesty. She recognized him from the photo that had accompanied his application. "You must be Van," she said, smiling with welcome and extending her hand.

Van, embarrassed at his own embarrassment, took her hand without allowing his eyes to drop below her collar bone and muttered weakly, "Is this Blake College? I'm looking for an Adrienne Stephens—the admissions director."

"Yes, that's me. Have any trouble finding the school?"

"No...no, not at all."

"Come on. Let's go inside. I'll show you your room."

Adrienne led the way to the back door, her long braids swishing back and forth across her bare behind. They entered the house through the kitchen. Bright-yellow cabinets hung above an L-shaped counter covered with gray marble Formica from an era gone by. A collection of ceramic bowls and plates were stacked on the kitchen table—a matching slab of Formica on legs of chrome tubing, surrounded by four mismatched chairs. An array of large knifes and wooden spoons dangled from nails pounded into the wall above an electric stove missing one element. Two fifty-pound sacks of brown rice lay against each other beside a vintage Frigidaire. A two-foot by three-foot Quicksilver Messenger Service poster from Winterland and a small black and white photograph of Meir Baba were taped to the walls. *Revolution Now!* was painted in big red letters across the ceiling.

Sensing Van's discomfort, Adrienne took a cotton dress off the back of one of the chairs and slipped it over her head. The faded flower print fabric fell to the tops of her rubber boots and was so thin it revealed the silhouette of her body when the sun was behind her. "Just so you know," she smiled. "This is not a school for nudists. It's just me. I like the freedom when it's as warm as it is today." She pulled her braids out of the neckline of her dress and dropped them over her shoulders. "Want some tea?"

A large mason jar sat in the window brewing rose hip tea in the sun. Van nodded.

Adrienne poured them both a glass of the red beverage over ice. "Let's take your stuff to your room, and then I'll give you a tour of the grounds. The rest of the faculty will be here before too long."

Two more students arrived later that afternoon. Both were women. Seventeen years old according to her application, Janice Holden was from San Diego, California, and eighteen-year-old Marsha Lee came from one of Seattle's wealthier suburbs. Both identified with the counterculture and had applied to Blake College because it was in Eugene. Adrienne showed them to the room they would share on the second floor.

That evening the faculty of four and the student body of three made dinner together and ate at the big table in the dining room that would serve as a meeting place for all school discussions. After devouring a huge salad from Adrienne's garden and a stack of bean and rice burritos, they went around the table with brief introductions.

Adrienne, her braids undone, sat at the head of the table. "Welcome to the first gathering of Blake College." She was as excited as anyone to start the school. "As I told all of you, we run Blake College as a co-op. Students and faculty share the cost of housing, food, and utilities, and we'll take turns making the meals and tending the garden and doing the other chores. This school will be like no other you've attended. Learning how to work together is at the core of our hands-on, fully engaged teaching method. I teach organic gardening, cooking with fresh vegetables and grains, and the art of composting. Be prepared to get your hands dirty." Adrienne turned to Van sitting to her left.

By appearance Van was out of place. He had short, fair hair, pushed to one side in the front, and the faintest hint of blond facial hair on his chin that he shaved once a week. "My name is Van Hammond. Aside from a trip to New York City with my sophomore class in high school, I'd never been out of Ohio until this week." He blushed with his smile, then firmly said, "I applied to Blake College because the school's name attracted me—and no grades seemed like a good thing."

Janice was next. "I'm Janice Holden. I come from Southern California." Janice looked like trouble waiting to happen. She was a blue-eyed, somewhat stocky beach girl with a round face and short, loosely curled platinum blond hair—and didn't appear to be a day over fifteen. She wore very short, cut off blue jeans and a faded, pale green Hobie surfboards t-shirt ripped off below her breasts, leaving her midriff bare. "I'm here because I needed to get away from my parents, and it's as cheap a place to go to school as I could find," were her curt and slightly antagonistic reasons for being there.

Rain sat at the end of the table opposite Adrienne and beside Janice. "My name is Raylene Adams. Call me, Rain," she said with a disarming natural grace. An intelligent and educated woman with a degree in Botany from Swarthmore, she wore a long Indian print dress overlaid with veils. A scarf, bright with colorful flowers, was tied gypsy style around her head, wisps of auburn hair could be seen at her temples and the back of her neck. A trace of freckles ran across the top of her cheeks. "I will teach you the art of wild crafting herbs and forest treats." Her eyes sparkled with the radiance of fresh-cut emeralds. "We'll go into the local forests and pastures to collect herbs, while also learning how to harvest them in such a way that allows them to proliferate." Beneath the table, Tai, sitting to her right and next to speak, patted Rain's thigh in support. They currently shared one of the bedrooms.

Nearly six-three, with strong facial features and a wild starry look in his pale blue, almost white eyes, Tai attracted women like iron filings to a magnet—and he knew it. "I go by Tai," he said with a crooked grin. He wore a white cotton Mexican peasant shirt, open down to the middle of his well-foliated chest. He had woven bracelets on both wrists and several talismanic necklaces around his neck. Dangling amid the necklaces was the tiny bleached skull of a bat. "I'm a medicine man. You will learn more of what that means in my shamanism class. We'll use the herbs that nature gives us to explore Native American and Asian mysticism. I also teach ceramics. One of our first tasks will be to build a kiln." He turned to Gloria sitting beside him.

"My name is Gloria Freeman," said the fifty-six-year-old yoga teacher. Her brown hair was streaked with strands of gray and wound up in a bun at the back of her head. "I teach yoga and meditation." Her smile was full of warmth and blessing. "I'm completely thrilled about the opening of this school." Her eyes twinkled with excitement. "I will begin my yoga class at sunrise each day—starting tomorrow with a cup of tea, after which I will introduce you to a few basic poses."

Janice frowned. "That's too early."

Gloria smiled knowingly. "We're not a military school, Janice. The day is yours to manage. Be there if you like."

Marsha was last. "My name is Marsha Lee." She was a petite Chinese woman with long, straight black hair that was pulled back in a ponytail. She wore wire-rimmed glasses, hip-hugging, bell-bottom blue jeans, and a red and blue horizontal striped t-shirt. "As a senior in high school I only applied to Stanford University. By the time I learned that I had been turned down, it was too late to apply to any other school but Blake." She grinned self-consciously. "It took me two weeks to convince my parents to let me enroll. Everything I've heard here tonight is really far out."

After the introductions, they moved into the living room to lounge on the floor or the threadbare furniture. Tai, the only one standing, drew a joint from his shirt pocket and lit it. "From Panama," he said, passing it to Rain. Rain took a deep drag and passed it to Janice. She took a hit as though she'd been smoking for years. Van declined and passed the joint to Adrienne, who took a tiny toke, and gave it to Gloria, who deferred, and passed it to Marsha, who took a tentative puff, and gave it back to Tai to begin a second round.

An old TV sat on the floor in the corner. Tai took a hit off the joint, passed it to Rain, then plugged in the TV. "How about a little philosophy demonstration for our first night?"

"You've got the stage," said Rain, handing the joint to Adrienne.

Tai turned the television on. "All religions start with God." A grainy picture of a woman pushing Tide laundry soap filled the TV screen. "Here we have the American God."

Gloria groaned.

"Philosophy begins where religion ends." Tai turned the TV off. "God is now officially dead." He bowed to a chorus of boos and chuckles.

Marsha had the joint. She looked at it in her hand. "This is strong stuff," she said, then dared a second toke. As she handed the joint to Tai, the sound of someone playing a harmonica came from the porch. The front door creaked and swung open.

An older black man sauntered into the room with a red bandana around his neck and a well-traveled guitar slung across his back. "Man, that smells like some good herb. It took me a while to find this place, but I know I'm in the right place now." He winked at Adrienne as he slipped the harmonica into his hip pocket. "The name's Crow." He had a big afro and a beard dotted with curls of gray. "Here for my first day of college," he laughed as he ambled into the room, confident and easy going, gathering everyone's rapt attention.

"What brings you to Blake College, Crow?" asked Rain, glancing at Adrienne, knowing the man had not applied or sent in an entrance fee.

"I never made it past the eighth grade. I thought it might be time for a little higher education." He lifted a bone pipe from the pocket of his battered blue jean vest. "Got something we might put in here?"

"No need for that, Crow." Tai held out the half-smoked joint. "This one's already lit."

Blacks were a rarity in mostly white Eugene and highly welcomed by a hippie culture that valued diversity. Application or not, enrollment fee or not, there was never a second thought about letting Crow stay. Tai gave him a Black Power handshake, then the joint. The Blake College school year had officially, in its unofficial way, begun.

.

CHAPTER 3

Saturday morning, two weeks after the opening of Blake College, a sun-faded mint green and white 1961 three-quarter-ton GMC utility truck with built-in tool boxes bounced across the ten-acre field of rye grass adjacent to the Army Reserve Armory and Training Center on Thirteenth Street, three miles west of the university. The truck, towing a rough-looking trailer made from the bed of an older pickup, pulled up between two long-abandoned Quonset huts. The cab doors swung open, and two men in blue jeans and t-shirts climbed out ready to work.

The older of the two men, thirty-one-year-old Jack Spikes, walked the other man, Ray Harper, ten years younger at twenty-one, around the two badly rusted tin buildings. "Check'm out. Aren't they beauts!" Spikes laughed, loud and unrestrained. "We get them down and hauled away by tomorrow night they're mine."

Ray Harper, who had been working for Spikes all summer, appraised the buildings with skepticism. "And then what are you going to do with them?"

Spikes laughed again. "Man, these are free warehouses. You've seen all the shit I've got piled up around my rental properties. I need a place to put that stuff before the rain starts."

"Seems like a lot of work for a couple of marginal buildings."

"You've got no imagination, Ray. This is a cinch. Nothing but a bunch of bolts holding these things together. With two impact wrenches, we'll have one of these babies down by lunchtime."

This was a typical project for "Something-for-nothing" Jack Spikes. Spikes was an army vet four years back from two tours in Vietnam. The ex-sergeant, who had grown up poor in Roseburg, Oregon, had one goal in life—to make a lot of money. He, like many of the movers and shakers in Eugene, believed that the city was on the verge of a long-term surge of growth and that real estate was as close to a sure thing as any business venture in Oregon. Spikes used his severance pay from the army and a VA loan to buy two run-down properties in the student rental portion of south Eugene. He worked his ass off fixing them up, doing everything himself—plumbing, electrical, sheetrock, woodwork—then hired two college students at five dollars an hour to paint them. In thirty weeks, he had two crappy little rentals bringing in seven hundred dollars a month. He lived in an outbuilding at the back of one of the properties for the next two years, putting every nickel he made into more student-oriented rental properties, generally working without building permits and stretching building codes to suit his pocketbook. He also took advantage of any cheap or free building materials he could find and stored them in piles wherever there was space on his properties—that now numbered ten—all with highly leveraged mortgages. Beyond the trashy look his stash of used materials gave the rentals, he did need weather resistant storage for all the windows, doors, toilets, kitchen sinks, and lumber he had acquired during his four years of remodeling in Eugene.

Set out in the open field beneath a brilliant sun, the Quonset huts were little more than curved sheets of corrugated tin, bolted to a series of extruded metal ribs, and anchored to two, forty-foot by twenty-five-foot slabs of concrete. The idea was to unscrew the bolts and take them apart one sheet of tin at a time. Spikes and Ray would load them onto the trailer, and then drive them across town to the location Spikes planned to pour new concrete pads and rebuild the Quonset huts. The problems for this something-for-nothing enterprise began right away.

Spikes pulled two ladders off the utility truck's lumber rack and leaned them against one of the buildings, while Ray ran across the field to the armory with two, hundred-foot extension cords. When Ray returned, Spikes gave one impact wrench to Ray and he took the other.

"Here's how it works," said Spikes. He had already fitted both tools with the proper socket for the bolts. An Oregon version of Paul Bunyan, Spikes was a big man, maybe six-one, thick and strong, still lean in the midsection, with short brown hair and a big walrus mustache that completely covered his mouth—except when he laughed. He leaned up against the Quonset hut, pushed the socket onto a bolt, and gave it a whirl. The bolt was so old and rusted the wrench just spun around on top of it. Spikes lifted socket off the bolt and bent over for a closer look. "Well, shit. I just stripped the corners off that bugger."

Ray didn't say a word as Spikes spun the corners off two more bolt heads. "Mother fuck!" screamed Spikes. "Get that can of Rust Buster. It's on the dashboard. That'll fix it."

Ray got the aerosol can of solvent out of the truck and gave it to Spikes. Spikes gave two squirts to five more bolts. He applied the wrench to the first one and again spun the hex-head into a cylinder. The same thing happened to the other four, each time lifting the volume of Spikes' curses.

Spikes could be as fun as any man when things were going well, but he could melt down quickly when he thought he was losing money. Ray felt his boss heating up now and was smart enough not to say anything.

Spikes grinned through clenched teeth. "There's a grinder in the tool box. Get it."

Ray opened four of the tool boxes before locating the grinder. The only grinding disk available was on the tool. Ray plugged it in and handed it to Spikes. Spikes spun the grinder up to eighteen hundred rpm and pressed it against a bolt head. A shower of blue sparks streaked off the disk as Spikes leaned into the bolt. It took close to a minute to buzz the head off. Spikes used a hammer and a punch to knock the bolt through. "There—that'll work, but we need another grinder. Here take this." He gave the grinder to Ray. It was heavy, maybe twenty pounds. "See what you can do. I'll go to Rent-All and get a second grinder."

"You might get a few more discs, too."

"Good idea. Let's see you do one."

Ray repeated the process. It took some effort, but it wasn't long before he'd punched through another bolt.

"Good. I'll be back as soon as I can."

As Spikes turned away, Ray commented, "I've made a rough estimate of the number of bolts on these babies."

"Yeah?"

"About twelve hundred each. At a minute a bolt that's three days of work per building for one of us."

Spike grimaced. "With fresh discs, it'll go faster. I'll bet we can do it in two days if we work a few extra hours."

"You're dreaming, Jack."

"Not yours to worry about. I'm paying you by the hour. Get to it." Spikes pulled a pair of dusty safety googles from the truck cab. "And put these on." He tossed them to Ray. "I don't want to be paying for one of your eyes."

Spikes hopped into his pickup and wildcatted across the field at three times the speed he should have, pulling the empty trailer behind like a child dragging a doll. Ray shook his head, put on the safety goggles, then went at the bolts one at a time, starting with bolts he could reach from ground level.

Ray powered through ten bolts, then stood back to flex his arms and shoulders. Ray wasn't the size of Spikes, but he'd played football in high school and was plenty used to hard work. At eight bucks and hour, two days of this would be a ball buster.

"What the hell," he muttered to himself, then leaned into another bolt. The spray of sparks shot to his left into the dry rye grass. With the goggles restricting his vision, Ray didn't see the flames until the bolt head popped off. Then he was running around in the grass, frantically stomping out the fire. It didn't get away from him, but it made him considerably more cautious. He buzzed off two more bolts, then sparks from the next one got the grass going again.

Ray was stomping out this second fire when Spikes came roaring across the field in his pickup. "Christ," he shouted, jumping out of the cab, "can't I leave you alone for a few minutes? What's going on?"

Ray scowled at Spikes. "The sparks are setting the grass on fire. This ain't gonna work."

"Bullshit. Let me at it." Spikes put a fresh disk on the grinder he had rented and went at it with a fury. He knocked off five heads with Ray standing beside him.

"Get to it, Ray. I'm not paying you to watch."

Then they were both at it. They buzzed off enough bolts to remove one sheet of tin—of eighty—from the building. "Now we're cookin'," chortled Spikes, as he threw the eight-foot by two-foot sheet of tin aside.

Ray was already at the next bolt, but again the sparks set the grass on fire, and suddenly they were both stomping out the little blaze.

"Keep at it," snarled Spikes. "We've got to have these things down by Sunday night or I have to pay for them."

The two men continued with the grinders, knocking off bolt heads, and periodically putting out little grass fires. One by one they pulled off the sheets of tin and stacked them in the trailer. But when they got on top of the Quonset hut, things got sketchy. If the grass caught fire, they had to scamper down the ladders to put it out, meaning the fire had more time to burn.

The third time this happened, they were too slow in noticing. By the time they hit the ground, the fire had spread out in three directions. Spike went one way, Ray the other, but the remaining flames raced unchecked toward the pickup and trailer.

"Shit!" Spikes screamed, stomping out the flames just a little quicker than they were spreading. "Quick, Ray, grab the sheets of tin from the trailer and throw them on the fire. I'll move the truck."

Ray dashed to the trailer and quickly threw four sheets of tin onto the flames. But the tin was curved and he had to jump on them to smother the fire. Spikes joined him, rocking the sheets back and forth, smudging out the flames. It was all they could do to keep the fire from spreading across the field into the surrounding neighborhood.

Afterward, they dropped to the ground in exhaustion, Ray gasping for breath, Spikes filling the air with fucks, shits, and god damns. After a few minutes, Spikes climbed to his feet. "Look. This can't happen again—or we'll be in real trouble."

"Maybe if we mow the grass it won't flare up so badly."

Spikes was pissed, but he liked Ray's idea. "Yeah, there's a mower in the shed at your house." Ray lived in one of Spikes' rentals. "You've got the key. Go get it—and be quick."

Ray welcomed the break. He took the pickup and made the trip back and forth in fifteen minutes, during which time Spikes had removed another sheet of tin.

Ray mowed a wide swath around the two Quonset huts while Spikes continued with the grinder. With the mower and grinder going, neither of them heard the siren until the fire engine came screaming across the field.

"Oh shit!" groaned Spikes, as Ray cut off the mower. "Now we're fully fucked. Don't say a word."

The fire engine pulled up alongside the Quonset huts. The driver got out and his sidekick in tall black rubber boots and suspenders climbed down from the passenger's seat. The driver confronted Spikes. "We got a call about somebody starting fires out here." He eyed the patches of scorched grass. "What's going on? You know there's an active fire warning for Lane County, right?"

Spikes hated being talked to like this. He bristled badly but knew he was in the wrong. He told the man the entire sorry story, refraining from a single vulgarity. The fireman gave him a ticket, fining him five hundred dollars for an open fire within the city limits. Spikes bit onto his tongue and turned purple. Then the firemen did him a favor. They used their truck's water supply to hose down the grass around the Quonset huts.

"Finish your job, Mr. Spikes. And if you plan to be here tomorrow, give us a call before you set the city on fire. It's easier spraying water on an open field than putting out wildfires."

CHAPTER 4

Across town to the east, the Eugene street market where Rain sold her dried herbs was in full swing. For four months now, on Saturdays, a parking lot at Tenth and Oak in downtown Eugene became a vibrant food and crafts fair with close to sixty vendors under ten-by-ten, pop-up canopies, invariably drawing the entire menagerie of Eugene street life to the center of town. Anyone who was hip or even pretending to be made a point of wandering through the market at some point in the day to make a connection of some sort or another. Like a city of nomads staging a circus, Eugene's Saturday Market radiated good spirit from nine in the morning to four in the afternoon, with colorful people in colorful clothing believing this was the dawning of the Age of Aquarius.

And this Saturday was no different. The smell of grilled onions, steaming curried rice, street side pizza, and burning herb filled the air. Buskers sat on the curb with their guitars on their laps and their guitar cases open, singing for spare change. Mime artists staged performances anywhere they could draw a crowd, and jugglers filled the air with all manner of tumbling objects from colorful frisbees to flaming torches. The carnival street life of San Francisco in the 1960s had been transported to the south end of the Willamette Valley for the 1970s.

Three-quarters of the market was made up of craftspeople, individuals who wanted to earn a living on their own, no boss, no forty-hour week, just a commitment to their craft. They made jewelry or clothing or wooden toys, tie-dyed t-shirts, pottery, candles, leather crafts, roach clips, dream catchers, whatever people would buy. They would come each Saturday until the end of October, hoping to save enough money to make it through the winter without taking a straight job.

Another fifteen or so vendors were fledgling farmers. The back-to-the-land faction of the counterculture came bearing lovely organic fruits and vegetables. Like the craftspeople, these farmers were also seeking a way to live outside the ordinary economy, determined to create an entirely chemical-free food system for the new age. Nearly religious in their fervor, they had decided that growing organic produce was their way to save the planet. Many had never farmed before, but they wanted to grow good clean food—at a time when most of the United States didn't even know what organic was or that it was a choice one could make about their food.

Yes, there was something different in the air in Eugene, and on Saturdays the street market was where you could see and feel it. The counterculture had created a separate, and to some extent independent, economy within the existing economy of Eugene. For every business in the straight world, there was an alternative version in the counterculture, usually smaller, locally oriented, and family or cooperatively owned. It was the same experiment in lifestyle that was being played out all over the United States, and in Eugene, it had taken hold.

But that's not to say all was peace and love. A division existed in the market between the craftspeople and the farmers. Despite their mutual selling location, and the synergy created by having crafts and food together, they struggled among themselves about what the market was and who it represented.

Linda Sheedy was Saturday Market's manager and an east coast transplant who had found a home in Eugene. She was very sharp, totally committed to the women's movement, and had a degree in business from the University of Pennsylvania. Upon graduation she had headed west, landed in San Francisco, then bounced from Seattle down to Eugene. Now at twenty-seven, she worked for almost nothing running the non-profit organization that oversaw Saturday Market.

During the hours of the market, Linda occupied the information booth at the corner of Tenth and Oak. People came to the booth throughout the day asking for the location of this or that vendor. She also dealt with the various controversies that arose on a regular basis when you had scores of highly individualistic entrepreneurs competing for every dollar in a crowded, highly spontaneous setting.

Just after noon, John Walters, who ran the first organic dairy in Oregon with his wife Joyce, approached the information booth and rapped on the wooden sill to get Linda's attention. John, known in the community for his straight talk and intelligence, was a tall man in his early thirties. He wore a straw cowboy hat and sported an overgrown, blond mustache. "Linda, you got a minute?"

Linda respected John but thought he was a bit pushy. She put on her best smile. "I'm right here, John. What's on your mind?"

"We need more space."

Linda was an attractive woman, big and square boned. Her dirty blond hair was pulled back out of her face and tucked beneath a pink beret. In her usual sweatshirt and overalls, she appeared to be downplaying her beauty. "Everyone needs more space, John." The market had grown steadily since its first week, and space had become the biggest issue and the biggest bone of contention between vendors. "This half-block is all we have."

John looked off at the sea of white pop-up canopies then faced Linda. "We have a waiting list of farmers that almost equals what we have here each Saturday. We need more space."

Linda knew this was coming. It had been in the air since the beginning of August. She took a deep breath and reminded herself to be calm. "I hear what you're saying, John, but you know as well as I do, we assign spaces as needed with no prejudice to the vendor—and we have many more craftspeople than farmers."

John nodded his head slowly, kind of chewing at his lower lip, not at all happy with her response. "Look out there, Linda. How many of those craftspeople are selling anything of value? I walked through the market this morning. Half of them are selling trashy little trinkets and pot pipes. My people are selling the best produce you can find in Oregon. There's no comparison."

"That's bullshit, John, and you know it. We're all trying to make a dollar any way we can. And there's no extra space."

John wouldn't let it go. "You could easily cull out a quarter of your vendors simply by the poor quality of what they're selling. The farmers are providing good healthy food, saving the environment, and doing what's right. We don't come here stoned, and our clientele is as dedicated to us as we are to them. If we can't work something out, I'll go to the City Council to demand a space of our own."

Linda was furious. The farmers might need space, but there was no call for John's overbearing attitude. Still she maintained. "That would be a big mistake, John. They charge us nothing for this space. We start fighting over it, and we'll lose it or end up paying for it each week. Here's the deal. We have a board meeting coming up. We're putting together a plan for next year. We're going to ask the City for use of the four park blocks. That would give us twice the space we have here. That's the only way to get more vendors into the mix."

John frowned. "That doesn't help us this year. Do something now or we're forming our own organization." He turned away abruptly.

Linda was seething and called out after him, "Be at the board meeting if you've got a grievance!"

CHAPTER 5

It was seven-thirty Saturday evening before the first Quonset hut was unassembled and the last piece of tin was unloaded at Spikes' empty lot. Both Ray and Spikes were exhausted. Their wrists and shoulders screamed from the long hours of grinding bolts. They climbed into the truck cab that served as Spikes' mobile office. The dashboard was covered with several layers of opened envelopes, sandwich wrappers, dead flashlight batteries, pencils, pens, and pieces of candy bars melted by the sun. The well on the passenger's side of the cab was much the same—mid-calf deep in pop cans, beer bottles, fast food wrappers, and paper coffee cups from a life lived in a hurry. Spikes drove to his favorite watering hole, the Vet's Club. He used a phone booth to call his girlfriend who lived out of town. He told her about the grass fires and that he was staying at his place that night to get an early start in the morning.

Spikes and Ray sat at the bar in the dark little lounge that was by no means just a hangout for vets. It had the cheapest mixed drinks in town and brought in anyone with a thirst. To the right of the bar was a little bandstand that featured an aging country swing band on Sunday and Thursday nights. Dark stained, plywood booths lined two walls and part of a third. Little wall-mounted lamps gave a sense of cozy to what daylight revealed to be a forgettably dingy bar. Spikes bought a shot of tequila and a beer chaser for Ray and himself. They threw down the shot then both ordered burgers and fries.

Spikes didn't say anything for a long time. Ray had a lot of respect for Spikes because he was a vet—Ray had gotten lucky in the first draft lottery and had never served—but he was also intimidated by the man. Spikes had a sense of the unchained about him. As though he could erupt in a fury at any moment. Ray had never seen him go south, but it seemed to be part of Spikes' oversized-personality. Loud, forceful, and given to a laugh filled with bravado, Spikes had a twenty-two rifle in the gun rack of his pickup and a six-inch army knife strapped to his leg beneath his jeans. Once he lost his sense of humor, you needed a little courage to engage him. After downing his burger, Ray tried being positive.

"Should be a lot easier tomorrow, Jack. We've got the system down and won't have the fire problem."

Spikes turned to Ray and glared at him. "I just spent five hundred dollars on something I thought I was getting for free. Looking at the shape of that tin we took down today makes me want to vomit. If I didn't know the guy at the armory, I'd fucking blow it off. I ain't looking forward to tomorrow in any way at all."

As Spikes threw down the last of his beer, a clean-cut man of the same age came up and put a hand on Spikes' shoulder. "Something-for-nothing, Jack! How's it going?"

Spikes' best friend Bob Yates, also a vet and an officer in the Eugene Police Department, sat down next to him with a big shit-eating grin. "A report came in from the fire station about somebody starting fires on the west side."

"Fuck you, asshole. Buy me a drink. I need it."

Yates was a forthright fellow in his own right. Over six-foot but not as thick or rugged as Spikes, he shook his head. "I'm the one that needs a drink. That bitch I once pledged my life to got the house yesterday. You only lost a few hundred bucks today. I put twenty grand into that place. You're the one who ought to be buying the drinks." Then he laughed and punched Spikes in the shoulder. "How fucked can it be, anyway?"

"As fucked as a pregnant whore!" Spikes exploded with a loud laugh. "Let's stretch this ugly night out into tomorrow."

Yates appraised Ray. "Who's this dipshit? Your brother?" He laughed at his own humor and waved his hand to get the bartender's attention.

"You've met Ray before," ragged Spikes. "He was out there helping me start fires today. He's splitting the fine with me."

"No way," snapped Ray. "It's your gig."

Spikes roared with laughter.

Ray was not fond of the Vet's Club or Yates, whom he had met several times before. Ray smoked pot, and officers of the law made him nervous. He had long, bushy sideburns but didn't have the long hair most of his friends did. He finished his beer in a single swallow. "You guys have fun tonight. I'm beat." Ray looked at Spikes. "I'll get my bike out of the truck. What time tomorrow?"

"Dawn," grimaced Spikes, as the bartender set two more shots of tequila on the bar.

CHAPTER 6

Ray Harper, like many of the young people in Eugene, had come to Oregon from somewhere else. His girlfriend since high school, Laura Schneider, whom he had always expected to marry, dumped him during the second semester of his sophomore year at the University of North Carolina. She told him she had been liberated and needed to know more than one man. Ray took this as an indictment of his virility and was devastated. Instead of jumping out a window, he skipped the last five weeks of the semester, and without going home or saying a word to his parents, hitchhiked west with no other plan than getting away from his broken heart.

Three days into this impossible task, Ray decided Southern California with its warm weather, beaches, and bikini bathing suits would be his landing spot. Stuck outside Lawrence, Kansas on Interstate Seventy, he smoked a joint with a fellow hiker by the name of Cory. With the remarkable candor of strangers, they both admitted that a woman was the reason they were riding their thumbs.

"Probably half of America's on the road this summer because of women's lib," concluded Cory soberly. Only nineteen, he wore his sun-streaked hair in a long ponytail. Three strings of beads adorned his neck and chest. With no shirt, he was brown as dirt from the sun and hard traveling. Four tokes into the joint he grew philosophical. He stared at the ground for a moment then looked up at Ray. "Don't get me wrong. Women's lib is right on. My older sister's a feminist. She's totally cool, but as she says, this free love thing cuts both ways."

"Too true," sighed Ray. "I just wasn't ready for it."

"No one is. But you know the best way to cure a broken heart?"

"A pint of whiskey?"

"A new girlfriend."

"That's prettier than the last."

"And with bigger tits!" They both laughed at their mutual predicament.

While they recounted their women troubles, Corey told Ray that Eugene was the easiest place in the world to get laid.

"Then why'd you leave?"

"I got crabs!" They both honked again with laughter.

That's when Ray decided to go to Eugene instead of Southern California.

Ray arrived in Eugene with two hundred dollars in his pocket and all his belongings in a backpack. He went to the university bulletin board in the student union looking for a room for less than sixty dollars a month. He wrote down the addresses of four potential places, bought a used bicycle for fifteen dollars, then pedaled around Eugene the rest of the day checking out rooms. All of them were in houses shared by students or other young people. He met Spikes at the third place he visited. The house was rented by five students, but one had recently left. Ray took the empty room, put a few things in the refrigerator, and took his dirty clothes to a laundromat.

Spikes came by the rental off and on to paw through the collection of used plumbing parts he stored beneath an electric blue tarp behind the house. One day Ray helped him move a claw foot porcelain bath tub. A week later he did some painting for Spikes, then some rough carpentry. Two months of part-time work later, Ray decided he wanted to do what Spikes did. To hell with going back to school, he'd buy and remodel houses for a living. Now, five months after his arrival, he worked nearly fulltime for Spikes and did his best to learn everything he could about construction.

Ray left the Vet's Club that night but didn't go home. He smoked a joint as he rode his bicycle ten blocks east to a little tavern he found more to his taste. Max's was a hangout for university students, hippies, and assorted lowlifes. He locked his bicycle to the bike rack out front and waded into the smoke-filled dive.

If any place in Eugene most exemplified the subterranean nightlife of the times, it was Max's Tavern on Saturday night. Classes at the university had begun a week earlier, and the place was so packed on this warm September evening that the crowd spilled out onto the sidewalk. A little bluegrass band played in the back corner, barely audible over the laughter and carrying on. Ray stood up to the bar and had to shout to get the bartender's attention. He was so stoned he dropped his wallet on the floor trying to get out a five. A young woman standing in the crowd behind him picked it up and handed it to him.

"Much appreciated," he mumbled, recognizing the woman as someone he'd seen in Max's before. He had been captured from afar by her long brown hair, startling big brown eyes, and shapely caboose. He'd had no intimate contact with a woman since his break up with Laura. Only the spontaneous nature of the moment allowed him to overcome his battered self-image. "Can I buy you a beer?"

The woman gave him an appraising look, tossed down her half-glass of beer, and slammed it on the bar. "Why not," she grinned, cocky like a lot of the hippie women in Eugene, "this one's empty."

When the beers arrived, the woman slid onto the stool beside Ray. "Got a name?"

Ray chuckled. "Why, don't you?"

The woman laughed. "What do they call you—wise guy?"

"Ray works pretty well. How about you?"

"Adrienne," she said, looking him over a little more closely. His face was streaked with soot from the fires, and his t-shirt and jeans were worse. "Looks like you just climbed out of a ditch."

Ray laughed. "Work can get a little dirty. Today especially." He took a slug of beer.

A long-haired man in his late thirties with tattoos on his forearms and rings in both ears pushed up to the bar beside them. "Hey, Adrienne," he slurred, waving his empty glass at the bartender. "I got a booth over there." He pointed with the glass. "You wanna join me?"

Adrienne smiled. "No thanks, Johnny. I'm good here at the bar."

The man got his beer, gave her a wink, and staggered off.

"That a friend of yours?" was Ray's loaded question.

Adrienne wagged her head. "Kinda. He's in here a lot. I've talked to him a few times."

"I've seen you in here before, too. Always wanted to introduce myself." He lowered his eyes. "Didn't get the chance until tonight."

"I've seen you also." Even with no makeup, wearing a faded pair of blue jeans with grass stains on the knees and a pale-yellow sweatshirt with the sleeves torn off at the shoulders, Adrienne was a radiant, back-to-nature beauty who would have looked good in a burlap bag and a straw hat. Her smile radiated beams of light. "I like your sideburns."

She would have seen Ray blush if it hadn't been so dark in the place. A woman's scream shrieked from the back, followed by the sound of breaking glass. A deep voice called out to the bartender for a towel.

A motorcycle that was loud enough to hear over the general barroom din pulled up to the curb outside the tavern's front window. Adrienne and Ray watched the rider lift the big bike onto its kickstand, dismount, and meander into the crowded tavern. He was a curious looking fellow, very tall and thin, with wire-rimmed glasses. He wore a black vest over a white t-shirt, suspendered black Carhartts that were about two inches too short, red Converse high tops, and an antique leather motorcycle helmet with its goggles lifted over his forehead. Several people seemed to know the man and nodded to him as he edged up to the bar beside Ray. The bartender delivered a beer to him before he even asked. When the man reached for his wallet, the bartender waved him off.

Before the motorcycle rider took a drink, he withdrew a tobacco pouch from his vest pocket and set to rolling a cigarette between some seriously brown-stained fingers. A man with a thick, untrimmed beard and grease on his hands and his t-shirt slipped out of a nearby booth and sidled up to him as he lit his smoke. The two men leaned over the bar and exchanged a few words between themselves, then the bearded man returned to his booth, where he huddled with two other men, one in a stained buckskin shirt with fringe hanging from the sleeves, the other in a ragged set of dark blue mechanic's overalls.

"He's a printer," whispered Adrienne, nodding at the man beside Ray. "I've seen him around. Seems to know just about everyone in town."

The man wasn't much older than Ray. He pulled off the leather head gear and replaced it with a black, short-brimmed cloth cap. His hair was short and brown, but he had a tuft of fair hair on his chin and the hint of a blond mustache across his lip.

"Yeah," said Ray. "I've seen him in here many times. I think his name is Tim. That motorcycle out there is a classic." The big maroon bike leaned against the curb. It had a full fender skirt on the rear wheel and the profile of an Indian in a feathered headdress emblazoned on the gas tank.

While they appraised the motorcycle through the window, an older man rolled up to the tavern doorway on a stingray bicycle. He laid the bike flat on the sidewalk and wedged into the bar, listing a bit to the left.

The man had a white shock of hair that stood up straight up from his forehead and a large, bulbous, drinker's nose. He wore a dark green custodial uniform with the name of the company, Eugene Sanitary, embroidered in red above the breast pocket. He eased up to the bar where the printer was sitting. "I thought I might find you here, O'Malley."

Tim O'Malley opened up with a genuine smile. "Hey, Stoopid. Can I buy you a beer?"

"Not tonight. I'm headed to work."

"You've got a job?"

"Graveyard at the university. I'm a janitor twenty hours a week. Even a dedicated communist like myself has to eat."

Ray and Adrienne couldn't help over hear the conversation.

"I found that Schwinn springer front end you and Gino were looking for. That's why I came by. It's at my place. It's yours for the taking. Catch me any time I'm home."

Tim nodded, very pleased. "Nice. What condition?" He took a drag off his cigarette.

"Better than average. You'll love it." He looked out the door. "I've got to go. Could I leave my newsletters with you?" An olive-green canvas satchel hung from a strap draped over his shoulder. "I doubt they want me passing out socialist literature at work."

"Yeah, sure, leave them here," said Tim, exhaling smoke. "They'll be stashed at the print shop."

The old man placed the satchel on the bar, then patted Tim on the back before heading out the door. "Drink one for me," he called out over his shoulder.

"How about two?" laughed Tim in response.

Ray and Adrienne watched the man climb onto his bicycle and pedal off into the dark. Ray couldn't resist. He turned to Tim beside him. "Did you call that man stupid?"

Tim smiled. "That's his name. He spells it with two ohs. Stoo-pid."

"Really? He named himself Stoopid?"

"He's a street philosopher. He's nearly seventy years old. Been pushing socialist tracts on the streets since the thirties. I met him years ago in San Francisco."

Adrienne leaned into the conversation. "Wow, that's impressive."

"Yeah, it is." Tim took one of the eight-page newsletters out of the satchel and handed it to Adrienne. "Writes this himself. I do the printing for free. Doesn't really get the respect he deserves, but I'd say he's one of the heroes of this community."

Adrienne opened the newsletter and began going through it. Ray read over her shoulder.

"This isn't bad," said Adrienne, looking over at Tim, noticing for the first time that he had a dime-store sheriff's badge pinned to his vest.

"He's a smart man. Just isn't into capitalism." Tim took another long pull off his cigarette.

"That's not all bad," said Adrienne with a grin.

"Hell no." Tim exhaled. "I'd call it right on."

Adrienne closed the newsletter. "Want this back?"

"No, keep it," said Tim. "That's why we print them—to give them away."

"I'll take it, Adrienne." Ray folded it over twice and put it in the pocket of his jeans, then finished off his beer. He raised his glass in the direction of the bartender and looked at Adrienne. "You need another?"

Her smile nearly knocked Ray off his stool. "No, I'm still nursing this one."

Thirty minutes later, a mass of people ran down the street out front of the tavern screaming and yelling. Everyone at the bar, except Tim, stood up to watch. A woman stuck her head in the door. "Somebody bombed Campbell Hall!" Then she took off down the street toward the university.

About twenty people in the tavern, including Ray and Adrienne, went outside to see what was happening. Blue revolving lights sped toward the university from all directions. A fire engine sirened past, red lights flashing, followed by an ambulance. The light from the flames fanned out across the sky in the east like the aurora borealis. A bunch of the people started walking in that direction. The others went inside, leaving Adrienne and Ray standing alone on the sidewalk. Adrienne looked at Ray. A spark of mischief flashed in her eyes. "I'm going over there."

Ray's inclination was to stay as far away from the fire as possible, but Adrienne had his full attention. "I'm game."

They walked the five blocks to the university then across the campus until they could see the flames. Several squad cars and two fire engines provided a perimeter. A big crowd had already gathered, mostly students and others like Ray and Adrienne who had come in from the surrounding neighborhood looking for excitement on a Saturday night.

"I wonder if this was anti-war inspired?" said Adrienne. They stood about thirty yards from the burning building.

Ray shrugged. "Kind of feels that way—especially after last spring."

"I hope it was. I'm not that political, but I'm against the war. Vietnam is all about money, and in my opinion it's immoral."

"I haven't thought about it a whole lot." Ray had avoided campus politics at the University of North Carolina. He would have joined the Navy if he hadn't gotten a high lottery number.

"Look!" Adrienne pointed to the building. Someone had spray painted *Fuck ROTC* on the doors. "I bet that was tonight. Good for them."

Ray didn't agree with this kind of vandalism and violence, but he was impressed by the conviction in Adrienne's voice and didn't feel strongly enough to confront her on it. Besides, she was the most beautiful woman he'd ever met and didn't want to foul things up with politics. "Looks like they've got it under control. Doesn't seem to be that much damage."

With four hoses dousing the fire, the excitement lasted longer than the flames. The police worked quickly to break up the crowd. It was nearly midnight when Ray and Adrienne walked back to Max's Tavern.

On the way, Ray mused aloud, "Do you remember when that printer first arrived at Max's? That other man whispered something to him, then when the woman shouted into the bar, he didn't seem to react at all to the bombing. Think he could have had something to do with it?"

"I don't know," replied Adrienne. "He's a known radical."

Out front of the tavern, Ray went over to his bicycle. "I've got work early tomorrow, Adrienne. I better get going." As he unlocked his bicycle, he ventured a glance at her. "You have a phone number or some way I might get a hold of you? Like tomorrow?"

Adrienne shook her head. "No phone yet. Hope to have one next week. How about meeting back here about eight tomorrow night?"

Ray couldn't keep from grinning. "That would be great."

"I've got a truck if that would save you some time getting home."

"You've got a truck? Really?"

"Yeah. Just down the street."

Ray walked his bike alongside Adrienne to a well-battered 1954 Ford pickup parked on a side street. A lawnmower, a gasoline can, a couple of rakes, and a mound of grass clippings lay in the bed.

"Wow! What a beaut," said Ray. "Whose mower?"

"Mine," beamed Adrienne. "I have my own lawn service." Even with Blake College up and running, Adrienne had to mow lawns to make ends meet. "Check it out." *Easy Does it Lawn and Garden* was hand-painted on both of the truck's doors.

"Decent."

"Throw your bike in the back. I'll get you home—if this dang thing starts."

They climbed into the old beast. The upholstery was the original and badly torn. Ray used his finger to delve the springs beneath the seat. "How'd this lawn service begin?"

"Unexpectedly," Adrienne grinned. "I spent three years at the U of O studying American Literature. I took one class in botany and fell in love with plants. I want to learn to garden organically. I think it's important." She put the key into the ignition. Three grinding cranks of the engine and the old V-8 powered up. It was an easy five-minute drive to Ray's house. Ray lifted his bike out of the pickup, then leaned into the driver's side window. The streetlight illuminated Adrienne's face like Ingrid Bergman's in Casablanca. "Appreciate the ride. I'll see you tomorrow."

Adrienne kissed her forefinger and touched it to Ray's cheek. "I'm looking forward to it." She powered up the old Ford and motored off.

Ray watched the one working taillight fade into the night, then went into the house, fell onto his bed, and stared at the ceiling. For the first night in many months he wasn't thinking about Laura Schneider. Now it was Adrienne who was on his mind. He had been seriously smitten by the little hippie girl in the big pickup. Man, oh, man, had he been smitten.

CHAPTER 7

Eugene's Mayor Les Anderson got a phone call at one a.m. that morning from the Eugene Police Chief Hugh Wilkerson. "A stick of dynamite was ignited in Campbell Hall tonight," said Wilkerson. "Judging from the graffiti, it was anti-war protesters."

"We can't have this," screamed Anderson, suddenly sitting up in bed, his wife Maureen lying beside him.

"A janitor got caught in the fire. He's at the hospital in the burn unit as we speak."

"A man in the hospital. Christ! Didn't we have enough of this last spring?" Anderson raged. "These people are dangerous—and they're cowards. Call in the FBI. Tell them they'll have our full cooperation. Damn it! This stuff puts our bid for the Olympic Trials in jeopardy." No one wanted the Trials more than Anderson. They were still a year and a half off and were the first thing on his mind when he woke up in the morning.

Anderson entered his office in City Hall five hours later with Eugene's newspaper, the Register-Guard, tucked under his arm and a scowl on his face. His secretary, Sally Mayer, and the City Manager, Rudy Laslo, were already in his office waiting for him. Sally was on the phone with Robert Clark, President of the University of Oregon, a man who had spoken out several times already against the violence, though he himself was against the war.

Anderson threw the paper on his desk. The headline was printed in red—*University in Flames*. Beneath it was a color photograph of the damaged portion of Campbell Hall. "We simply can't have this," he shouted loud enough for Clark and anyone within a mile to hear. "God damn SDS! Not only are they a menace to the university, they're fucking with our chances to get the Trials."

The secretary put Clark on the intercom. "I'm as furious as you are, Les. I had hoped we'd seen the last of this. It's destroying the university—and will likely get me fired." You could almost feel him shaking through the phone line. "And you're right about the Trials. The university needs them as much as the city. I'll do whatever it takes to rout these renegades out. I think some of them are members of the student senate!"

"I told Wilkerson to call in the FBI. This cannot—cannot—happen again."

"When are they making the decision on the Trials?" asked Clark through the speaker.

"Damn, I wish it had been last month," stormed Anderson before turning to his secretary. "When is it, Sally?"

Sally was in her mid-sixties and had worked for Anderson at several different jobs. "It's a year off, Mayor. I think we're still safe. They haven't even formed the selection committee yet."

"Christ!" shouted Anderson to the heavens. Getting the Trials would be the crowning achievement of his first term as mayor. "If this continues the way it did last spring, we won't even make the short list."

"And what about all the hippies downtown?" reminded Laslo. "The whole damn city looks like it's been taken over by freeloaders."

"Almost all of them are against the war," added Clark.

"Round them up and put them on buses," muttered the city manager.

Anderson shook his head. "Fuck! We're going to need a damn miracle for this one."

CHAPTER 8

Ray didn't sleep a wink that night he was so excited about his upcoming date with Adrienne. He and Jack would need every minute of daylight to get that second Quonset hut apart if he were going to meet her at eight. He got so anxious he gave up on sleep and went to the worksite well before sunrise. Ray was laying on the ground with the sun fully up when Spikes' pickup and trailer rattled across the open field toward the Quonset huts.

Spikes climbed from the cab badly hungover and immediately vomited. He had a big plastic jug of water in one hand. He washed out his mouth then drank a long swallow. He spit out the last of it as Ray angled over to him.

"Fuckin' agitators blew up a building at the U of O last night," he snapped. He hadn't shaved in two days. Some of the vomit was still stuck in his over-sized mustache. "Traitors. That's what they are. They need to spend some time in Nam." He took another slug of water, then used the back of his hand to wipe the last of the residue off his face.

Ray decided not to tell him he'd been at the site of the bombing.

The ground was still wet from the day before, so they went right to it—buzzing off bolts one after another. The fire department came at ten to saturate the grass a second time. Spikes and the firemen, who had been at the blaze the night before, jawed on unmercifully about the bombing and how they blamed it on the pot smoking, derelict hippies. Ray stuck to the work, determined to get it done, but heard much of what they said. He wasn't a hippie. He wasn't anti-war, but he still didn't like the way the men talked, especially when he thought about Adrienne and the opinions she had expressed the previous evening. He liked her gumption. He liked her gumption a lot.

CHAPTER 9

The first two weeks at Blake College had been uneven. Except for Gloria's yoga class in the morning and Adrienne's afternoon session in organic gardening, there had been no other "formal" classes. Most of the work at the school had focused on organizing the daily tasks and facing basic needs as they came up.

Sunday morning after the bombing, Adrienne started the day at ten o'clock with a bowl of granola. She sat at the dining room table with her dog Moxie on the floor at her feet. She had no lawn mowing planned for the day and had slept late—like everyone else at the school, except Gloria who had gotten up at dawn for her daily salutation to the sun.

Moxie woofed twice at the sound of someone coming down from upstairs. Adrienne put her hand on his head as Rain and Tai came into the dining room. Tai wore no shirt or shoes or socks, just a pair of faded jeans with enough patches to be a quilt and several necklaces and leather bracelets. He joined Adrienne at the table while Rain, in a lovely second-hand Japanese kimono, boiled water for tea and coffee.

When Rain came into the room with coffee for Tai and green tea for herself, Adrienne spoke up, "Someone bombed Campbell Hall last night."

"Good," said Rain with defiance. She considered herself a leftist revolutionary and had attended almost every anti-war demonstration in Eugene. "Do they know who did it?"

Adrienne shook her head. "Most likely radicals at the university. Maybe something will be in the newspaper. I got there after it happened and watched the fire fighters put out the blaze."

"I ran into a lot of unhappy GI's in my travels," said Tai. "I wasn't far from Vietnam."

"How'd you avoid the war?" asked Crow, who came in from the den where he slept.

"I was drafted when I was eighteen and served two years. But there was no war back then. I spent six months in Germany."

Tai produced a joint from behind his ear and lit it. He passed it to Crow who took a hit as did Rain and Adrienne. It went around two more times before Crow slipped into the kitchen to make himself a cup of coffee.

"Damn, that's some strong weed," said Adrienne suddenly. "Where'd that come from?"

"Cambodia," said Tai. "Won't find anything better in Eugene." He extended the joint to her.

She waved it off with her hand. "No more for me."

Van was the next to come downstairs. The smell of marijuana filled the lower level of the house. "Boy, you sure start that stuff early."

Tai lifted the roach from the table. "You want some?"

"No, thanks."

"Me either," said Marsha, now drifting into the room. Only Janice was still asleep. She had shown a penchant for sleeping well past noon. "I take it Gloria already did yoga."

Adrienne bobbed her head. "Long before I got up. I think she's out in the garden saying hello to the slugs."

"It's one of her meditations," said Tai, eliciting some chuckles.

"And a good one," said Gloria, coming in through the kitchen, causing even greater laughter. Crow followed her in with his coffee.

"I didn't mean that to be nasty," said Tai.

Gloria smiled. "I didn't take it that way. I thought of it as profound."

"As it should be," said Crow.

"You know," said Adrienne. "We've talked about building a kiln, but what we need more is a greenhouse. Could you do that, Tai?"

Crow spoke up before Tai could answer. "I could. I've worked half my life doing construction. We should go out there and pick a spot, then we need to think about getting some materials—and some tools. What do we have to work with?"

"Mostly rakes, shovels, and clippers," said Adrienne. "Maybe a hammer and a handsaw."

"That's something we should focus on," said Rain. "Building a collection of tools. Too much of what we want to do here involves construction of some kind."

"So, everyone, when you're out and about," said Adrienne, "look for used tools—cheap or better yet free."

"Hey, it's Sunday," said Tai. "We should organize a little trip into town to hit garage sales. What do you think, Rain? Want to take the van into Eugene?" Tai had a Ford Van that he had driven up from LA. A mural of the desert was painted on the sides, replete with coyotes, rattlesnakes, and cactus.

"While you're at it, look for used lumber or old windows," said Crow. "If we're building a greenhouse, we'll need some glass."

The toilet upstairs flushed.

"Blondie has risen," said Tai, always first with a quip.

"And a little earlier than usual," said Gloria.

Janice tromped down the stairs and entered the dining room in what had become her usual attire—super-short cutoff jeans, a loose, white blouse, and very obviously no bra. She sat down at the table without a word. She had already gained a reputation as a sour puss in the morning. Everyone stayed quiet, waiting for her words of wisdom for the day.

Janice saw the roach lying on the table with Tai's lighter beside it. She picked up the roach and lit it. She smoked it down to a nub, then laid her head sideways on the table. Everyone else exchanged a glance.

Adrienne got up. "Crow, let's go out back. I'm excited about building a greenhouse."

As Crow and Adrienne walked out through the kitchen, Tai piped up, "Rain, you up for finding some tools?"

"Yeah, I could do that. Marsha and Van, want to come with us? You haven't really seen much of Eugene yet."

Both Marsha and Van perked up, eager to go.

Janice raised her head from the table. "Anyone want to make me a cup of coffee?"

"I will, Janice," said Gloria. "But afterward, I want a chance to introduce you to yoga."

Janice frowned. "I just want some coffee, Gloria. I wasn't trying to make a deal."

Gloria came over to the young woman and put her hand on her shoulder. "Neither was I. We can talk it over while you drink the coffee."

This was how things proceeded each day—weekend or weekday. People took each need—a greenhouse or tools—as they came up and applied themselves to the task. Any sense of a great plan or even a curriculum did not exist. Everything was worked out organically as it happened—and often that was stoned.

CHAPTER 10

The City of Eugene sits along the Willamette River between two small mountain peaks—Skinner's Butte at the north end of the city and the somewhat larger Spencer's Butte a couple of miles out of town to the south. A small public park extends from the east side of Skinner's Butte to the river. A hundred and seventy years ago it was a landing for boats and barges moving up and down the Willamette. In 1970, a lightly populated neighborhood of smaller homes was scattered around the butte and the edges of the park. A sprawling red house with white trim and a small garage occupied an unkempt lot on the south side of this neighborhood. The landlord had remodeled the place multiple times, each time extending a wall or two to add another rentable space. The eight odd-shaped bedrooms were rented at fifty dollars a month to an ever-changing array of college students and itinerant hippies. Rain Adams had lived there before moving in with Adrienne.

Tim O'Malley rented one of the eight rooms and ran a small print shop out of the garage, which he rented separately. He owned a massive Harris LTG printing press, an antique letter press, and an AB Dick Offset 360, all crammed into the tiny shop.

Tim had dropped out of high school at sixteen and lived on the streets of Haight-Asbury until he got a job as an apprentice in a print shop. Three years later, when the drugs of choice on the streets of San Francisco became heroin and speed instead of pot and LSD, he moved north to Eugene, as did a lot of the folks from the Bay Area who wanted to get away from the ugliness that had blossomed after the Summer of Love.

One of the first things Tim did when he arrived in Eugene was buy a used printing press—the AB Dick. Now he made a modest living printing for the alternative community in Eugene—Saturday Market, two organic grocery stores, six neighborhood food co-ops, the Grower's

Market, a women's newsletter *Gorgons and Gargoyles,* the People's Café, the alternative newspaper *The Augur,* the SDS's political rag *The Statement,* plus whatever odd jobs he picked up. After the bombing of Campbell Hall, many in the city pointed to Tim as a potential culprit. It was no secret he did the printing for the SDS and had run off ten thousand copies of *Prairie Fire* for the Weather Underground the year he arrived in Eugene. He was a known radical, though by his own admission he rarely went to protests and never wrote anti-war manifestos; he just did the printing and did it cheap or for trade or, as in Stoopid's case, for free. A bushel of potatoes and a crate of organic apples might get five hundred flyers for the Saturday Market.

Tim's shop was one of the hangouts in Eugene, along with Max's Tavern, Saturday Market, Lucky's Pool and Tobacco downtown, the People's Café, and the Odyssey Coffee House at the north end of Willamette Street, Eugene's main drag.

Sunday afternoon, Tim and his friend and occasional printing assistant Gino Gregor were printing the latest edition of *The Augur.* Tim had promised to deliver two thousand copies to the Augur office by eight the next morning. At five they took a break to share a quart of Old English malt liquor and a joint. The back door rattled.

Gino shot a glance at Tim. "After that bombing last night, it could be the pigs."

Tim shrugged and called out as he always did, "It's open. Come on in."

Dave Berman, the head of the SDS chapter at the U of O, and also the Student Senate President, slunk into the room in his usual paranoid skulk. He had extremely long, wavy black hair that was more or less pulled back in a ponytail and loosely held together with a leather cord. A black Fu Manchu mustache wrapped around his mouth, making him appear much more menacing than he really was. He wore tinted, wire-rimmed glasses over a pair of intense, brown eyes. Today he had a blue bandana tied around his head. Tim handed him the joint. Dave took a toke and passed it to Gino.

Berman was always in stealth mode. He fashioned himself an extreme radical and he was. "Need a poster printed quick, Tim," he said, stalking around the cramped print shop. "A thousand. Real quick." Three R. Crumb posters and two SDS anti-war flyers decorated the partially paneled walls. Several smaller black and white photos of racing motorcycles added to the decor.

"We plan to work all night on *The Augur*. When do you need them?"

Dave carried a black leather satchel with a big brass buckle. He opened the satchel and produced the original for the fliers he wanted. "Wednesday by midnight."

"No chance, man. After tonight, we might be gettin' outta bed by then," chuckled Gino, a small, wiry, twenty-three-year-old street freak stoner, who never stopped moving, cocking his arms, or spinning on his heals. He handed the joint to Tim.

Dave ignored Gino and spoke directly to Tim, who was six-foot five and weighted about one-sixty. "Got to have it, Tim." He glanced around as though someone might be listening. "And I ain't got no *money*." He looked like a weasel when he accented a word to make a point.

Gino laughed. "Then we don't have to worry about printing it."

Tim remained attentive. "What's the hurry?" Tim passed Dave the joint.

"We want a quick follow-up after what happened last night." He took a pull off the joint and passed it to Gino. "Gotta strike while the iron's hot!"

"With no money?" Gino took a hit from the joint and stubbed it out on the layout table.

Berman grinned. "But this might interest you." He wore GI fatigue pants and a red t-shirt with a big black star on the front. He withdrew a match box from the large pocket on his left thigh.

Tim and Gino moved in close. Berman dramatically slid open the box so they could get a look. "Straight out of Owsley's lab. Eighty hits of blotter."

In the years prior to 1968, when lysergic acid diethylamide was legal, LSD entirely infiltrated Haight-Ashbury. It was the drug of the moment, even more so than pot. For all the testing that had been done on the drug in university and government labs, the real experiment took place on the streets of San Francisco, where for a short period of time it was freely used by thousands of young men and women. Most of the people who tried it never did it more than a few times. It was a strange, deeply psychological experience, that was wearing and often unsettling. Bad trips happened, and not everyone was willing to take that chance. But it also had a powerful truth-seeing quality and taking it became a kind of counterculture initiation—the Acid Test. To see oneself with all pretense stripped away took a fair amount of courage and, to some, was the first step to self-realization.

Others believed that the drug was like a steroid for the brain. That it made you smarter if you could manage the high anxiety of the psycho-activating, hallucinatory experience. Some learned to navigate day to day on the drug and thought it made them more perceptive, almost magically so.

The relationship of LSD to the radical left was not so clear. Half the radicals wanted no drugs, the other half thrived on them and believed that LSD, specifically, allowed an individual to strip away all the political propaganda that had been ingrained during one's youth and open his or her mind to a different, if not greater, reality.

Tim O'Malley saw it in all of these ways. He took a sheet of the acid out of the match box and studied it closely. The sheet was divided into eight squares, perforated on the edges so that they could be easily separated. Each square was a single dose. The image of Mr. Natural was printed in red in the center of each hit. Tim handed the sheet to Gino, who sniffed it. He nodded and handed it back to Tim.

The two men grinned and simultaneously said, "Deal."

Dave nodded his approval. "Have the flyers at the SDS office by midnight Wednesday." He glanced around suspiciously, then whispered, "Tim, you have any idea who bombed Campbell Hall?"

"No, I thought it was you guys."

"Not unless one of our people did it on their own. We thought of painting the ROTC building pink one night. But we were never close to explosives. Wow, I wonder who did it?" Then he shrugged. "Maybe it's better not to know." He started to leave then stopped. "You hear about Stoopid? He was working in Campbell Hall last night."

"No. What happened?"

"He got caught in the fire and was badly burned. He's in Sacred Heart Hospital right now. If he dies, they'll attach a manslaughter charge to the bombing."

Tim shook his head in disbelief. "I saw Stoopid last night just before he went to work. He had a bike part for Gino and me."

"Oh, man," muttered Gino.

"Yeah, pretty heavy." Dave looked at Tim and gave a half-hearted shrug. "Flyers by Wednesday." Then he walked out.

"That's awful about Stoopid," said Tim, showing more emotion than he usually did. "Maybe we ought to do some detective work. I'd hate to think one of our own bombed the building with him in it." He hung his head thinking about it.

"At least we got that acid," grinned Gino.

Tim and Gino were acid freaks going back to San Francisco where they'd met. For them, being high on acid was like being able to see through walls. But even with that said, Tim found little comfort in Gino's offhand comment. He was worried about his friend.

CHAPTER 11

Sometime around six that evening, Spikes and Ray were stacking the last of the tin panels and steel ribbing from the second Quonset hut onto Spikes' trailer.

"Damn," said Spikes, as he began lashing the material to the trailer, "the way I felt this morning, I didn't think there was a chance in hell of getting this done. You worked your ass off, Ray. You carried me."

Ray, who had said little all day, finally gave in to his own excitement. "I've got a date tonight at eight. I had to make it happen."

"Hey, you've been holding out on me." Spikes grinned as though he could see into Ray's mind. "Who's the lucky girl?"

Ray yanked hard at one of the ropes to cinch it tight. "Someone I met last night after I saw you. Had a beer with her. We agreed to meet again tonight."

"Where?"

Ray looked down at his shoes. "Max's Tavern."

"Oh, so you're really doing it up big. That place is the worst dive in Eugene. You couldn't drag me into that place. Nothing but fucking hippies." He shook his head in disdain.

Ray just took it.

Then Spikes broke out into loud laughter. Ray could never read Spikes. He could sound angry as hell, then suddenly burst out laughing as though it were all a joke.

It was shy of six-thirty when everything had been loaded onto the trailer and the site cleaned. Spikes and Ray headed across town to leave the trailer at the empty lot and to eat at a dirty spoon on Willamette Street called Dan's Hamburger Heaven. On the way, Spikes detoured into a little neighborhood south of where they had been working. Spikes pulled the pickup into the driveway of an abandoned house on Eighteenth Avenue.

"This is our next project, Ray." They both climbed out of the cab. Spikes led Ray around the house. "We're gonna pick this house up off its foundation and move it to that double-lot I have at Twelfth and Jefferson."

Ray knew the location. They'd reroofed the house on the adjoining lot earlier that summer.

"We'll start tomorrow at eight," continued Spikes. "We'll crawl under the house and map out a strategy for jacking it up."

"Why move it?"

"Because the owner's going to tear it down and build something nice. I get the house for free if I take it away."

"Like the Quonset huts?"

Spikes frowned. "I've got four months to get it off the foundation and ready to move."

They returned to the front of the house and climbed into the pickup.

"Moving a house across town—that's gotta cost something?"

"Five grand." Spikes pulled out into the street. "A friend of mine does it for living. He'll ram some big timbers beneath the house, lift it onto a gurney, and tow it down to Chambers, then right on Thirteenth, then left on Jefferson. Easy as pie."

"No way can you do that. Not a whole house."

Spikes grinned big. He loved the idea of moving a house. "Just wait. We'll post signs a week ahead to get the cars off the street for a four-hour period in the morning. We'll roll it right through town with me on the peak to lift the telephones wires as we go. It'll be a kick. And I'll get a whole house with all the parts for five thousand dollars."

"But you'll have to build a foundation to drop it on, right?"

"Yep, that's the other thing we'll be working on. Some hard work ahead, Ray. Be prepared."

"This is what I want to learn about, Jack. You do what I want to do. I'm looking forward to it."

"How about tonight?" prodded Spikes, pulling the truck around a corner a little too fast. "Must be looking forward to that. Gonna get ya some?" he sneered with a leer.

Ray looked out the side window, trying to ignore the question.

Spikes burst out laughing. "Man, you are! I can tell you're thinking about it. Probably already got a boner. Whooo-wee!"

CHAPTER 12

Adrienne was as excited to see Ray as he was to see her. She liked to work hard and that's what she saw in Ray. His coming to the bar completely filthy from work was perfect for her. She wanted to be an organic farmer. Right now she did lawns and had a lot to learn but digging in the dirt and getting sweaty was her ideal. Ray seemed cast from the same mold. He was lean and well-muscled and good looking and kind of quiet. That fit Adrienne's wants just right.

That afternoon, while Rain, Tai, Van, and Marsha toured Eugene garage sales, Adrienne washed her hair and brushed it out so that it shone. She put on a three-button, printed cotton dress she'd gotten at the Goodwill and wore nothing underneath. With her lustrous complexion and no makeup, she looked more like a farm girl than a hippie. During dinner she was briefed on the used tools that had been acquired, then she excused herself without saying where she was going.

Ray had gone home and showered after the meal at Dan's. He wore clean blue jeans and a black t-shirt with a profile of Bob Dylan stenciled in white on the back. He saw Adrienne's pickup parked in front of Max's as he rolled up on his bicycle. She sat at the bar in the same location as the previous night.

"Hi, Adrienne. Hope you haven't been waiting long."

"No, not at all. Haven't even ordered a beer yet. Can I buy you one?"

"Well, sure. Shouldn't it be me buying the beer?"

"You bought mine last night. It's my turn."

Ray smiled into her eyes—totally smitten. "Can't argue with that. I like Budweiser."

The place was not as full as it had been on Saturday night. When the bartender placed two glasses before them, Ray suggested they move to an open booth across from the bar.

"How'd the job go today?"

"Good. We finished what had to be done. Took apart a couple Quonset huts. Hard ass work."

"But you got cleaned up tonight. You look good, Ray."

The color rose in Ray's face. "So do you. You look really nice in a dress."

Adrienne's smile made her even more beautiful. Neither one of them were big talkers, Ray less than Adrienne.

"You from Oregon?" she asked between sips of beer.

"No, North Carolina. Came to Eugene on a whim in the spring." Ray took a gulp from his glass. "You're not from Oregon are you?"

Adrienne smiled. "Vermont. I came out here to go to the U of O. By the third year I had become so excited about being in Eugene and all that was going on, I dropped out to get into gardening." She glowed when she spoke about gardening. "What turns you on?"

"I like construction. I'm working for a guy who's not much older than I am, but he does everything himself and I'm learning a lot. He owns a bunch of houses. That place you dropped me off at last night is one of his rentals."

They were both excited to learn about each other. They finished their beer quickly, and Ray ordered a pitcher. He refilled their glasses, and they continued to pour it down. Somewhere in the back of both of their minds was the end of the night. The counterculture had opened the door on dating. A month of courting was no longer a necessary prelude to sex. They both knew this and were slightly nervous about where they were headed at the end of evening—Ray more than Adrienne, so he was drinking even faster than she was. They finished off the pitcher and Ray bought another. A quiet man grew steadily more talkative. Ray told her about playing football in high school, his year and a half at the University of North Carolina, and working for Coca-Cola during the summers. "Kids out here work in the woods during the summer break. It's pretty cool. Setting chokers or working at a mill on the greenchain."

"I worry about them cutting down too many trees."

Ray laughed. "Well, sure, we need the trees, but in western Oregon lumber pays the bills. That much I do know."

"But we can't cut them all down," said Adrienne. "They're the lungs of the planet. Only thing more important than the trees is the soil."

Ray wasn't sure if she was right, but he nodded anyway. More than that, he sensed that Adrienne was smart, and it impressed him. He refilled both their glasses, emptying the pitcher. He took a big gulp and grinned. "This kid I met hitchhiking told me Eugene was the easiest place in the world to get laid. Do you think that's really true?" He would never have asked this question if he hadn't had so much to drink.

Adrienne lifted her head as in thought. "I don't know about any of the other women, but I'm pretty easy." She winked at him. Drilling him right in the heart with a burst of warmth that traveled all the way down to his balls.

Adrienne turned the pitcher upside down. "Let's get out of here. I wanna show you where I live. It's even cooler than my pickup."

Neither of them were big drinkers, but they had gone at it hard. Ray staggered as he threw his bike into her pickup, then climbed into the cab. The engine started on the first try, drawing a big smile from Adrienne. "That's a good omen."

Adrienne made two wrong turns before getting to the old Victorian. It was almost eleven when they arrived, but there was half a moon and enough starlight to show off the hundred-year-old house.

"Wow, Adrienne! This is your place! I love these old houses. They're all over Eugene. This one reminds me of the Addams Family. You don't own it do you?"

Adrienne grinned like an elf and shook her head. "A friend of mine abandoned it. Me and a girlfriend just kind of took it over."

"Took it over?"

"We pay the bills and hope nobody comes by to hassle us."

Ray laughed out loud. "That's brazen."

"We've turned it into an experimental college."

"What?"

"Yeah, we've got four students. And four faculty. I'm the director of admissions."

"No way!"

"Yeah, come on in. Maybe some of the others will be around."

When they stumbled in, Rain and Tai were sitting at the dining room table. A single candle and a nearly empty bottle of wine stood between them. Tai picked a half-smoked joint off the table and lit it.

"Who's your friend, Adrienne?" queried Rain, a little loose herself.

"This is Ray," she said with an over-sized smile. "Ray, meet Rain and Tai. They're two of the teachers at the college."

When Ray reached out to shake Tai's hand, Tai extended the joint. Ray didn't hesitate and took a long drag. He offered it to Adrienne.

She shook her head. "Not that Cambodian. It's way too strong for me."

Ray sucked in another deep hit and handed it back to Tai. Adrienne took hold of Ray's hand and with no subtlety at all dragged him upstairs to her bedroom, where the only furnishings were a mattress on the floor, an orange crate subbing as a bedside table, and a bunch of cardboard boxes that contained her clothes. The windows had no curtains, and two dresses hung in the doorless closet. A poster of the Doors was taped to the wall. Adrienne lit a candle as Ray closed the door behind them. Adrienne lifted her dress over her head. Ray's mouth fell open at the sight of Adrienne's body. He stripped off his t-shirt, then dropped down on the mattress ass first to pull off the work boots he wore all the time. That's when he realized how strong the marijuana was. The room—even with Adrienne standing naked before him—wavered in the candlelight, then began to spin. He managed to pull off one boot and one sock, then he leaned over and threw up into his boot. "Uh, what was that about a good omen, Adrienne?" he muttered, then fell back on the mattress out cold.

Adrienne went down the hall to the bathroom to wash out Ray's boot, then filled a glass with water and brought the glass and a towel back to the room. She drank half the water then cleaned Ray up with the towel. She pulled off his other boot and sock and his blue jeans. She almost pulled off his boxer shorts but decided that was inappropriate. She straightened him out on the bed, lay down beside him, and pulled the blanket over them both. She was out before her head hit the pillow.

Ray woke up when the first streaks of sunlight crossed the bed. It took him a moment to remember what had happened. He saw Adrienne beside him and the glass of water by the bed. He quickly gulped down all the water to quell his thirst and get the stale taste out of his mouth. Adrienne's eyes opened. She gave him a sad smile. "You okay?"

"A little hungover, but mostly embarrassed. I apologize. That pot was strong and on top of the beer—a very dumb idea."

"I should have stopped you. That was a lot of beer for me, too." Adrienne sat up, and the covers fell below her navel. She was deeply tanned all over. Her breasts were small but stood out unsupported with pert pointed nipples.

Ray had seen her remove her dress the night before, but that had been lost to the blur of the evening. In the clarity of the early morning she was as beautiful as the sunlight coming through the window. "I guess I really fouled up our first date," said Ray, gazing at her with growing arousal.

"You know," said Adrienne, "I'm glad we didn't do it last night."

Ray cocked his head.

"It's much better to do it sober the first time, so we can really appreciate each other." She leaned over and kissed him lightly on the cheek. "How about now?"

Ray's smile was her answer. Adrienne pushed away the sheets as Ray slid his boxers off. They embraced and kissed passionately. Mid-kiss, Ray mumbled, "I've got a condom."

"No need," grinned Adrienne. "I'm on the pill. Let's do it *au naturel!*"

The first time didn't take very long. But the second was more fulfilling. Afterward they went downstairs. Gloria, Van, and Marsha were at the dining room table finishing breakfast. Adrienne introduced them as Ray realized how late it was. He took a couple slurps of coffee and raced for the door.

"Want to get together again?" he called over his shoulder.

"Come by after work. I'm making dinner tonight."

"Perfect!" He stopped halfway out the door. "Thanks for cleaning my boot." Then he was gone, pedaling his bicycle across town as fast as he could.

CHAPTER 13

Tim and Gino finished printing *The Augur* at six that morning. They had each taken a hit of Dave's acid to keep them awake through the night. Still buzzing, they put the alternative newspaper in a couple of bicycle trailers and pedaled downtown to the Woodmen of the World Meeting Hall, a leftover from the Conservation Corps of the 1930s. Now known as the Wow Hall*, The Augur* and several other alternative groups shared the rent. All the furniture in the building was second-hand or handmade. Anti-war and rock band posters hung on the walls, and four banks of dusty florescent lights lined the ceiling of the central room, a forty-by-fifty conference room and auditorium.

The Augur office was on the second floor. No one was in yet, so Tim and Gino left the pile of newspapers in front of the door. They took twenty of them into the basement where the Saturday Market had its offices. Linda Sheedy was at her desk when Tim and Gino came in with the short stack of *Augurs*. She looked up, and though clearly bothered by something, smiled. Seeing the Mutt and Jeff duo of Tim and Gino did that to people.

Tim was one of the most respected individuals in the counterculture community. There could be no revolution without a printer, and Tim made every effort to fulfill the needs of the community, cutting prices and making trades. Gino had a less favorable reputation. Gino was a natural born cutup, with a silly comment for just about every occasion, especially when he was high and giggly. His nonsense and bad manners ran counterpoint to Tim's remarkably business-like approach to everything—even when soaring a hundred feet off the ground on psychedelic drugs.

"What's the matter, Linda? Looks like you swallowed a mouse," jazzed Gino, who probably didn't weigh one-twenty-five soaking wet. He was wearing his customary black tuxedo pants with suspenders and a sleeveless, white guinea shirt. A brown felt pork pie hat, curled up in the front, sat on his head. Add his yellow-tinted shooting glasses, and he looked like a pint-sized New York hood.

Linda ignored Gino's comment and spoke directly to Tim. "I need a favor, Tim. We've got way too much tension down here in the basement. Maybe you could help."

Tim wore pretty much what was his everyday uniform, a black vest over a t-shirt, black work pants, a black printer's cap, and his red high tops. "What's the problem?"

Linda got up and closed the door. "The fucking farmers."

"What'd ya mean?"

"They're jerks. John Walters and his wife Joyce are threatening to pull the farmers out of Saturday Market and start their own market."

"What's the issue?"

"They want more space—and they're fucking organic and damn purists. Most of those folks don't drink. Some get uptight around weed. And they treat us like a lower life form."

"Then Tim ain't gonna be much help," cracked Gino. "He lives and breathes acetone."

"You're the lower life form, Gino," snapped Linda before turning back to Tim. "You've done some printing for them. They know you. You willing to try a little diplomacy?"

Tim squirreled up his face thinking. He could be just as goofy as Gino when he was high. He scratched at the little patch of hair on his chin. "A little busy right now. How about I bring it up the next time I do some work for them. You know, kind of casually, as though I'm not on a mission—just a thinking citizen."

"Thinking citizen. Man, that's pretty funny." Gino laughed and did a little jig.

Tim gave Gino an elbow in the ribs. "What should I say?"

"We're going to make a push for the park blocks in the off-season. Make sure the farmers know there's power in numbers when we talk to the City Council. Plus, it's far more efficient to have a single organization than two, and, damn, the synergy between the farmers and the craftspeople helps us both. We need each other. United we stand, divided we fall."

Tim bobbed his head like he always did. "Okay. I'll talk to them."

"Bottom-line, Tim, it's just good business for us to stay together. Other than that, the whole mess of those organic freaks drives me nuts."

She stared down at the papers on her desk and shook her head. She looked up. "Just do it as soon as you can."

As Tim and Gino made their way out of the building, a tall black woman came out of an office on the first floor. She hustled after Tim and caught him on the sidewalk. "Tim, hold up. Can we talk?"

Tim and Gino spun around, their pupils dilated thrice their ordinary size. They grinned like banshees when they faced Rebop Rodriguez, who was close to six feet tall with short nappy hair that was died a bright chartreuse. She wore black tights with a long sleeve, black turtleneck. "You still have a press for me, right?"

Tim nodded quickly several times. "Oh, yeah, Rebop. It's up at my shop. Just gotta get it down here." He had agreed many months earlier to help set up a women's press. Rebop was a lesbian poet and a writer and the impetus behind the project.

"And you'll be there for the first couple of runs, right?"

"Oh, yeah. I haven't forgotten. Just a little busy right now. We'll need all the manpower we can get to move it. It's a big one."

Rebop was a Cuban who had grown up in the Bronx. In 1965, she graduated from the School of Journalism at Columbia University. She stood number two in her class and took a job with *The New York Times* three days after graduation. She was straight then and planned to marry a New York lawyer, but a series of revelations regarding her place as a woman with *The New York Times* and the shallowness of her fiancée's love caused her to re-evaluate her life. In 1967, she quit her job with the *Times* and broke off her engagement. Nineteen-sixty-eight found her yet another east coast transplant in Eugene.

No one who had known her in New York would have recognized her now. With her dyed hair, widely flared nostrils, thick sensual lips, and dark, almost purple complexion, she looked more like an androgynous visitor from outer space than a publisher. She was at once entirely primitive and ultra-modern. As unusual as she could seem at first glance, her appearance was a singularly attention-grabbing beauty—if you dared rest your eyes on her long enough to absorb it. Though her demeanor was subdued, aloof, and confusingly sensual, she was the center of attention wherever she went. She was too personally dynamic, too unique-looking to be missed. "You set a day," she said, "and I'll get all the help you need."

Tim didn't keep a calendar. There was today, tomorrow, and yesterday. He was in such high demand he just did whatever had the highest priority at any moment—like the printing for the SDS. He looked at Gino. Gino exaggerated a shrug, then grinned sideways.

"How about Tuesday morning?" said Tim.

Gino shook his head no.

"That works."

"Be at the print shop at eight-thirty."

"Great. Thank you." She lowered her voice. "You know anything about the bombing of Campbell Hall?"

"Nothing."

"Not the SDS?"

"Not according to Dave."

Rebop tilted her head in thought. "Guess it doesn't matter, but I can't help being curious."

"It does matter, Rebop," said Tim. "Stoopid was working in the building that night and got caught in the fire. He's in the hospital now. I'd like to know who did it."

"I heard that, but I didn't know the man other than by sight."

"Just one of our brethren, trying to make a buck on the night shift."

"I understand. I'll keep my ears open."

"Thanks. He's a good friend of mine."

As Tim and Gino walked away, Gino looked up at his friend. "You said *manpower*." He grinned. "You meant womanpower."

"What we really need it some kind of super power. We'll be lucky to be half done with the SDS job by Wednesday night. We've got to get a move on."

"Yeah, I couldn't believe you said Tuesday. Fuck." Gino wagged his head. "Talking about super power. We do have that acid." He grinned showing his teeth, which were not the prettiest pearly whites in town.

They pedaled to the People's Café, a cooperative that opened at seven a.m. They got a breakfast of coffee, eggs, and home-fried potatoes, then headed over to Sacred Heart Hospital hoping to see Stoopid.

They went to the information desk and were told that Stoopid was in the burn unit and not available for visitors. Tim's old girlfriend, Prairie, worked in the hospital so he had her paged.

Prairie came down to the information desk in her scrubs and gave Tim a hug, knowing his friend was in bad shape. When she hugged Gino, he put his hand on the right buttock. She pushed him away angrily. "Can't you ever be serious, you idiot?"

"I only squeeze the prettiest buns in town, baby," said Gino, trying not to smirk. "Consider it a compliment."

"I can do without. Next time, you little turd, I'll kick your ass from here to Portland." And she meant it. She was a good three inches taller and twenty pounds heavier than Gino.

"Can you get us up to see, Stoopid?" asked Tim. "We don't have to talk to him. I just want to see how he's doing."

Prairie, a runaway farm girl from Missouri, had her brown hair pulled back in a braid for work. She looked at the floor and then at the other nurses and doctors coming and going in the hospital. "Okay," she whispered, "but this could get me fired. Stay close and don't say a word."

Prairie led Gino and Tim to the staff elevator and took them up to the fifth floor. Prairie peeked out when the doors opened. No one was there. She motioned to Gino and Tim to follow her. They weaved through the back hallways and entered the intensive care wing of the hospital through the nurses' changing room so that no one would see them.

Prairie led them to the burn unit and a large window that let them see into Stoopid's room. "We can't go in there. There's a huge concern for infection. But you can have a look, and then we've got to get out of here."

Tim and Gino pressed up to the window. The seriousness of the situation sobered even crazy Gino. Stoopid was lying in a bed, hooked to every kind of body monitor available. His face, except for his eyes, was covered with bandages. His hair had been burned off. The rest of his body was under a blanket. Gino tapped on the glass. Prairie snagged his hand and pulled him away from the window. "Fuck!" she whispered as loud as a scream. "Cut that out. My ass is on the line!"

But Stoopid heard the tapping and slowly turned his head. His eyes met Tim's. Tim made a fist with his right hand, symbolizing unity and strength. Stoopid might have smiled with his eyes, but it was difficult to tell. Then Prairie quickly ushered Gino and Tim, who was fighting tears, back through the halls and down the elevator to the ground floor.

"Thanks for doing that, Prairie," said Tim, as they prepared to part. His voice trembled with emotion. "It doesn't look good. Does it?"

Prairie hugged him again. "No, we should all be very worried about Stoopid. He's an older man, and he got badly burned—head to toe."

CHAPTER 14

Spikes arrived at the house he planned to move at seven-forty-five. After surveying the inside, he walked around the outside checking the cinderblock apron that served as the foundation. He looked to the street hoping Ray might arrive, then pulled the screen off the crawl space and bellied alligator style beneath the house to see what it looked like. He was squirming out of the opening an hour and a half later when Ray rolled up on his bicycle. Spikes was covered with dirt and spider webs and was more than mildly upset by the amount of dry rot he'd found—and he hadn't inspected the north end of the house yet! It was not a good day for Ray to be late.

"What the fuck, dude? I asked you to be here at eight. It's almost ten. You want a job or not? You gotta be on time if nothing else."

Ray hung his head but was so ecstatic from the morning roll in the hay that he couldn't stop a smile from leaking onto his lips.

"You think it's funny, Ray?"

"No," Ray muttered, staring at the ground to hide his joy.

"Are you fucking stoned or something? Might as well leave now if that's the case. Fucking weed is not on my menu." Spikes was pissed.

Ray looked up at him. "No, I'm not stoned."

"Then what the fuck is going on? Where have you been?"

Ray couldn't contain it any longer. He smiled big and wide, knowing he had an answer that would be perfect for soothing his raging boss. "Between the legs of the sweetest thing I've ever met in my life."

Spikes started to sputter more angry words—then caught himself and burst into his own big grin. "That date last night! Of course. I should'a known." He laughed in his bold way, completely blowing away the anger and tension of the initial encounter. "Sweetest thing ever! That sounds like love to me." Spikes howled with laughter.

Ray grinned and glowed red.

"HA! You're in fucking lust! Now I know I've lost my best worker."

"A minute ago, you were going to fire me. Now I'm your best worker."

"My only worker!" Spikes laughed. He really did like Ray. He'd been great help all summer. "Come on. Follow me under the house. I'll show you what we've got to do."

The house sat twenty-four inches above the ground on three courses of cinder blocks, with two openings for access, each covered by a wood framed, removable screen. The one Spikes had removed had a large hole in it. Their task was to jack the building up high enough to slide four big timbers underneath. The timbers would allow the house to be lifted onto a wheeled carriage and towed across town. Spikes had twenty-four jacks and fifteen, four-by-eight beams that he would use to lift the building. The first thing they needed to do was finish assessing the existing beams and floor joists for dry rot.

They got down on their bellies, and each carrying a flashlight, crawled beneath the house, avoiding nails, spiders, puddles of water, rat shit, and the random junk that accumulates beneath a house over the course of forty years. For Spikes, it seemed the perfect place to tease his young friend.

"So, tell me about this girl?"

Ray grunted as he pulled himself forward under the house, pretending he didn't hear the question.

"Come on, what's she like?"

Ray cursed as he squeezed beneath a floor joist where the ground was a little higher. "Tight and stinky like this fucking place," he snapped.

Spikes laughed. "She one of those hippies with hairy armpits and doesn't take baths?"

"Fuck no, I was making a damn joke, Jack. This place stinks. She doesn't stink at all."

"But she's tight!"

"Not one word will I utter to disrespect this woman. She's the best thing I've ever met. I want to marry her."

Spikes stopped crawling and looked back at Ray. "No way. You've known her all of, what, two days? Marriage is more trouble than you need, no matter how hot she is. You didn't get her pregnant, did you?"

"Fuck no. This girl is smart. Works her ass off and knows more ways to turn me on than I knew existed. I'm not letting her get away."

"Well, damn, Ray. When do I get to meet this woman?"

Before Ray could answer, a snarl came out of the darkness to their left. Spikes quickly turned his flashlight to the northeast corner of the foundation. A gray fox glared at them, growling and showing its teeth. Two little kits, the size of kittens, huddled behind the adult.

"Shit! That mama's angry," hissed Spikes. The fox snarled, made a rush at Spikes, and snapped at him—just missing. "Backup, Ray, quick! This girl's dangerous."

They both scooted backward as fast as they could. The fox rushed at them two more times but stopped short of biting either of them. When they climbed out from beneath the house, Spike announced his plan. "We need a trap."

Ray went to Blake College for dinner that night. Adrienne made the meal with Marsha, and he sat down at the table with all the members of the school. Ray was not a big talker, but he enjoyed meeting the unusual collection of people. The hot topic of the night was Janis Joplin. She had died the previous day of a heroin overdose at the age of twenty-seven. Two weeks earlier Jimi Hendricks had overdosed on sleeping pills. They lit a candle for both of them to begin the meal.

After dinner, as had become the habit, Tai passed a joint around the table. Gloria and Van didn't smoke. Adrienne took only one hit, and Ray, being careful, had two. In the conversation that ensued, Adrienne asked Ray if he would help them build a greenhouse. He had access to tools and materials that the school didn't. Fully under Adrienne's spell, Ray readily agreed to come over one weekend to help begin the task.

Ray slept with Adrienne that night. They woke up at seven-forty-five with Ray due at work at eight. He skipped breakfast and coffee and raced across town on his bike, only to be fifteen minutes late. Spikes let it go, but Ray felt bad about it.

CHAPTER 15

Eugene Mayor Les Anderson, U of O President Robert Clark, and the City Manager Rudy Laslo were in Clark's office, 110 Johnson Hall, at eight-fifteen Tuesday morning. It was the first time they had met since the bombing. The president's office was large and lined with shelves filled with big books. He stood at his desk facing the other two men, who sat in black leather chairs. Behind Clark, the office's large window framed an expanse of green lawns and red brick buildings.

The Mayor, despite a large, narrow nose, was a handsome middle-aged man, dressed in an expensive suit, with dark hair showing gray at the temples. Clark was close to seventy, distinguished, and also dressed in a high-end suit. Laslo, in his thirties, wore slacks that were too tight and a sports coat. His hair was fair and razor-cut. They were waiting for Todd Bascomb, the FBI agent who would lead the Campbell Hall investigation, and Hugh Wilkerson, the chief of police. Bascomb and his team had arrived Monday afternoon.

They expected the two men at any minute when Bluto Harris, one of the wealthiest developers in Eugene, with several large projects in progress, including a massive mall north of town, stormed through the door in a huff.

"Damn it, Clark, can't you get a grip on these radicals? What are you waiting for? Toss their asses out of the university before things get any further out of hand." Bluto matched his name. He was large, close to three hundred pounds, sixty plus years old, with a big round face and well-thinned, once red hair turned white. He hadn't been invited to the meeting, but had gotten word of it through Laslo, and decided to show up to express his opinion, something he valued highly and was always ready to share. Bluto, as much as anyone, was concerned about Eugene's image—and getting the Olympic Trials.

Clark didn't like the intrusion or the language. "Mr. Harris, please leave my office. If you want to talk to me, make an appointment."

"Laslo invited me." Laslo looked up at the ceiling. "And now that I'm here, I'd like to stay. I've got as much at stake here as the university—and you know it."

Clark glared at the overbearing businessman. "Fine. Stay. Pull that chair in the corner over here in front of the desk." Laslo offered Bluto his larger softer chair, then got the one in the corner for himself.

Bluto dropped into the chair as though he were in his own living room. "So, what's going on? What are you going to do?"

Anderson looked at Clark. Clark sat down in his chair. He didn't like Bluto, but the man had made several large donations to the university in recent years and could not be ignored. "We're waiting for the lead FBI agent. He'll have a plan.

Bluto sat up. "FBI?"

"And don't say a word to anyone. Anyone. I have a list of suspects to give him." Clark looked at Anderson who nodded.

"Can't you just arrest the entire SDS? It had to be them."

"That's not quite the way we do it in the United States."

Bluto puffed up. "I don't see why not. Those kids are a bunch of Communists. Burning our flag and their draft cards and defaming the nation. They're traitors. Plain and simple."

"Americans have the right to protest," said Anderson. "They have to commit a crime to get arrested."

"They just bombed a building!" snarled Bluto. "And they all smoke pot! Arrest them for that. Get the police to search the SDS office."

"That's not a bad idea," followed Laslo. "Did you talk about drugs with the FBI, Mayor?"

Anderson nodded. "Yes, of course, these men are professionals."

Bluto always seemed to be charged up. "I've got everything I own wrapped up in this town, Clark, and I've bet it all on Eugene becoming a big deal. The Trials would be the icing on the cake. Don't let this stuff fuck that up."

The intercom on Clark's desk buzzed. A moment later Bascomb and Wilkerson came into the office, Bascomb, tall and thin, in a black suit, Wilkerson, thicker and shorter, in his uniform, carrying his cap.

Introductions were made, and two more chairs were brought into the office. Clark described what had happened. Bascomb made a few notes, then looked up. "Any idea who could have done it?"

"Not really," said Clark. "But it must be connected to the anti-war movement. The Mayor, the Police Chief, and I have put together a list of the most notable radicals in the city." Clark lifted a piece of paper from his desk and handed it to Bascomb.

The FBI agent read through the list of names and descriptions. "This includes the entire membership of the SDS?"

"As we know it."

"And these others?"

"There's a strong anti-war contingent in our community that's not associated with the university. They're in with the drug dealers and hippies. Eugene is a haven for the so-called counterculture."

Bascomb nodded.

"What are you going to do?" asked Bluto.

Bascomb glanced at the heavyset man before facing Clark. "I'll run these names through FBI headquarters in D.C." He turned to Anderson. "The Chief and I will share everything we learn. I've got a man at the scene of the bombing right now. He and I will conduct interviews with the people on this list."

"No arrests?" pushed Bluto.

Bascomb looked to the police chief then back to Bluto. "When the time comes."

"How many men did you bring?" asked Anderson.

"I have a team of four. Myself and my partner Franklin, and two more men on the street. It's going to take some time."

"You can't let it happen again," snapped Bluto.

"We'll do what we can, sir."

One of Clark's phone lines flashed. He picked up the receiver. He listened to a voice at the other end then hung up, his face drawn and serious. "The janitor caught in the fire has been transferred to intensive care. They're afraid he's going to die."

Bluto swelled up and then exploded, "Fuck! That'll be murder!"

"More likely manslaughter," said Wilkerson. "The FBI will be investigating the bombing. Terrorism is a federal offense. The Eugene Police Department will investigate the injury to the janitor. He was a university employee and that's our jurisdiction. We'll work independently but share our findings. In the end we're both looking for the same person or group of persons."

Bascomb agreed. "I'll get back to you, President Clark, and you too, Mayor, after I get some feedback on this list."

CHAPTER 16

Of all the diverse people who passed through the Northwest, an unusually high number of young, free-thinking women from the first wave of the feminist movement stayed in Eugene to live. This was the modest beginning of a growing pro-women culture in the small college town. It was a slow and haphazard process, but the result seemed some wildly conceived sociology experiment, as small women-run businesses—some taking part in Saturday Market—gradually became a significant part of the local economy.

Little by little, these women began to sense the uniqueness of the situation. Never before had so many individualistic women with so much in common freely accumulated in the same location. Their unity came as an afterthought, and because of this, it became a totally spontaneous, awakening community of women.

This was not obvious to any but the women themselves. The percentages of those in better jobs still favored the males, as did the pay. A newcomer to Eugene might notice those rare women carpenters or plumbers or the firmness of eye and brisk step of the up and coming woman on the street, but the women's influence was most apparent behind the scenes, amid the political and social workings of the alternative community.

Perhaps the least visible but best organized faction of the women's movement in Eugene was the lesbians. In this era of free love, many women were open to bisexuality, but the more radical lesbians were something else. They cropped their hair and wore working class clothing and stood firmly on political grounds, many espousing a form of Freudian-Marxism. From a distance, it could be difficult to differentiate the sex of these women. In blue jeans and black leather jackets, they could appear remarkably masculine, though some espoused a detached resentment or indifference to men.

For all their rough appearance, these women were often quiet left-wing intellectuals. Although radical bohemians should be surprised if they get any respect at all, the lesbians did have the support and respect of many of the other women and the more aware males in Eugene. Unfortunately, however, the older working-class males—those the lesbians' working-class philosophy could have embraced as brothers—found these women the most revolting element of the counterculture and a favorite target for abuse. They laughed and hooted whenever they saw these rough-looking women walking together arm-in-arm in men's clothing.

Rebop Rodriguez was the leading proponent of radical women's politics in the city. She wrote, edited, and published a women's newsletter and arts monthly called *Gorgons and Gargoyles*. Its appearance was strictly stylized Black Panther. So was Ms. Rodriguez. Tim O'Malley had done her printing since the newsletter's origin, but now she wanted to own a press and do the printing herself. Only in that way could she achieve the complete independence she desired.

Rebop was at Tim's print shop at eight-thirty sharp Tuesday morning with five other women—the five strongest women she knew. They had a large press to move, and they came ready to work. Rebop knocked on the print shop door and got no response. She peered in the window and didn't see anyone inside. She told her friends to wait outside. She went into the house, put some water on to boil, and climbed the stairs to the second floor where Tim had a room. She found him in bed sound asleep. She knelt beside the bed and gently shook his shoulder. He rolled over. She shook him again. He pushed her hands away, then kind of squinted at her. He reached down to the floor and located his glasses. After taking a moment to pry his eyes open, he slipped them on.

"It's eight-thirty, Tim. Time to move the press."

He nodded. "Got some folks with you?"

"Outside."

Tim stood up out of bed. He was fully dressed including his shoes. "I need some coffee."

"I've got water on the stove."

While Rebop made coffee, Tim went out to the street to wake up Gino, who lived in his panel truck which he kept parked in the print shop driveway. Tim knocked heavily on the back doors of the truck, then pulled them open. Gino and a young woman were asleep inside.

Tim grabbed Gino's bare feet and dragged him out of the truck, blankets and all; only the weight of the woman kept the foam pad bed from coming out with him. The five women who had come with Rebop stood back watching. Tim pulled the covers off Gino so that he twirled around once and nearly fell down. He wore not a stitch and had a hardon. He scrunched up his face, saw the women staring at him, covered himself with a blanket, then snapped at Tim, "Why the fuck did ya do that?"

"We've got a press to move, Gino. Coffee's in the kitchen."

Gino looked back inside the truck at his sleeping partner, none other than Janice Holden of Blake College, now sitting up and scowling at him. He turned to Tim. "I got some shit to take care of. I'll be right with ya."

Tim went inside where Rebop had a hot cup of joe waiting.

"Gino will be here shortly," said Tim, who rolled a cigarette and a joint between sips of coffee.

"Late night, Tim?" Rebop, like everyone else, loved Tim because he was smart as a whip, crazy as hell, and dead set on making the counterculture a working community in Eugene.

"Gino and I were printing posters for Dave until who knows when last night."

Rebop knew Dave and had nothing but respect for his radical politics, which included full support of the women's movement in Eugene.

"Had a couple beers after that." Tim fired up a cigarette and took a long drag. One of his legs, draped over the other, ticked up and down. "Feel like shit right now. But I'll be fine once I get this coffee down and smoke a joint."

Gino staggered in wearing his black pants and suspenders, no shirt, no shoes, no socks. He snatched the cigarette out of Tim's hand and took a drag, then traded it back to Tim for the joint he'd just lit.

"What's this we're doing?"

"Moving the Harris down to the WOW Hall."

Rebop gave Gino a cup of coffee. He took a sip then again traded the joint for the cigarette. "How we gonna do that? It's close to five thousand pounds."

"You saw our help out there."

Gino ran his hand through the rat's nest of his hair. "You're kidding, right. We couldn't move that thing with ten more people."

"Yeah, we can. I got a plan," said Tim, taking another drag off the joint before offering it to Rebop, who declined.

Gino sidled up to Tim as the group of them headed outside. He knew they had a long day ahead. "Got any more of that acid?"

Rebop overheard him. "Fuck you two. You're gonna screw yourselves up permanently the way you take that stuff. It ain't candy, you know."

Tim took the little matchbox out of his vest pocket. "It makes us smarter."

"Right." Rebop shook her head. "I've done it before. That stuff is dangerous. Two times is all I was good for. It makes people goofier with every trip."

Gino laughed. "But when you're sitting up here where we are," he used his flattened palm to suggest a height above his head, "it looks like everyone else is walking around with their eyes closed."

The other women moved up close to listen.

Tim withdrew two hits of acid from the matchbox. He handed one to Gino, put the other in his mouth, then turned to the women. "I got more if you want some."

"If it takes us where you guys are," said one of the women, "I think we'd best skip it."

This sent Gino into hysterics. He slapped his knee and turned to Tim. "Let's see what they say after we get that press down to Rebop's place. They'll know they're working with real geniuses." Gino frowned. "How we gonna do it, anyway? We haven't got a truck big enough. Or a decent lift."

But Tim, as he said, had a plan. He put it in motion by telling Gino to move his panel truck, where Janice had fallen back to sleep, so he could open the print shop's garage doors. Everyone came in close as he pulled back the doors. The Harris sat there in the opening. It was a huge press—six feet long, five feet wide, and five feet high. It was made in 1914, had a 22-inch by 17-inch plate, and weighed 4670 pounds. It sat on the concrete slab of the garage floor. Beside it, leaning up against the wall, were four sheets of one-inch plywood and eight steel pipes, six feet long and two inches in diameter, and another six shorter pipes of the same diameter.

Tim turned to his audience. "We're going to roll it down the street."

Gino broke out laughing. "That's twenty blocks, man. Rebop's right. You are getting crazier every day."

Tim grinned. "Watch."

Tim had four heavy duty jacks. He positioned them at the four corners of the press and assigned Gino to one, Rebop to another, Florence, one of the other women, to one, and he took the fourth. Tim synchronized the jack operation to slowly lift the press twelve inches off the concrete. Tim and Gino slid a sheet of plywood beneath the press, and using four bolts, attached the plywood to the bottom of the press— to act as a smooth, stable surface. With the press still jacked up, they placed a second piece of plywood on the floor beneath the press, then laid six of the six-foot steel pipes across the plywood to act as rollers. With Tim supervising, they lowered the press onto the steel pipes, so they were sandwiched between the two sheets of plywood. With the bottom piece of plywood acting as a flat surface, Tim demonstrated that they could roll the press forward or backward on the steel pipes.

Tim instructed the women to lay the other two sheets of plywood on the driveway—which had a slight downward grade—and told Gino to be ready with the two remaining six-foot pipes to place them in front of the press as it rolled forward.

"Okay," said Tim, when everything was in place. "This'll be a piece of cake."

Seven sets of skeptical eyes stared at him. But Tim knew what he was doing. Tim and Rebop pushed the press out of the garage, while Rebop's five friends acted as brakes to keep it from rolling down the driveway too fast. Gino leapfrogged the steel pipes freed-up at the back of the press to the front as it rolled forward. It came to a stop at the edge of the road where the surface was level. They leapfrogged the plywood that had been in the garage down to the other end of the ramp, so they could roll the press into the street. Once in the street, they used the shorter steel pipes to swing the press around ninety degrees, parallel to the direction of the street. Using the leapfrog method of pipes and plywood, they took on twenty blocks of mostly level city street, much as the Egyptians had moved large blocks of limestone to build the pyramids. It looked as crazy as it was laborious; a team of women led by exotic Rebop and scarecrow Tim and his tuxedoed sidekick Gino rolled the huge press down the street. They slowed one lane of traffic down to about half a mile an hour and pushed the press across town to the WOW Hall, making one left turn and one right turn by using the shorter pipes to swing the press around.

They used the jacks to lift the press up to the floor level of the building, then rolled it into the main lobby. Fortunately, the *Gorgons and Gargoyles* office was on the first floor. Tim removed the door and door frame and some of the surrounding dry wall, so that they could roll the monster into the office. All told it took six hours.

Afterward, Tim bowed theatrically. Stoned on the blotter acid, he grinned like the man in the moon. "Sure, none of you ladies want a hit of Vitamin A?"

Gino cracked up giggling, but all six women declined for a second time. Tim and Gino spent the rest of the afternoon rebuilding the doorway to Rebop's office.

CHAPTER 17

The entire time that Tim and his crew were moving the press across town, they were being watched by Bascomb's undercover FBI agents. The previous day, agents Patrick Ball and Christopher Mathers had rented a house with a garage in the Whitaker neighborhood in north Eugene, considered one of the hippest parts of the city. Both men were in their twenties, had long hair, and had dressed down to the level of street life in Eugene. They immediately began converting the garage into a bicycle repair and resell shop—to serve as a front for their FBI work. Making money in any backstreet way—selling crafts or pot—and not having a real job was the counterculture ideal, and selling used bikes was as good a way as any to infiltrate Eugene.

Tim O'Malley's name was at the top of the list of suspects compiled by the University of Oregon and the Eugene Police Department. Ball and Mathers had staked out Tim's print shop Monday afternoon, shortly after they'd arrived in Eugene. Tuesday morning, they were riding through the Skinner's Butte neighborhood on ten-speed bicycles when Tim, Rebop, Gino, and the others rolled the press out of the garage onto High Street. They watched the process from a distance then pedaled on. They circled back, stashed their bikes in an alley, and using a Polaroid camera, documented the entire six-hour odyssey.

Rebop took Gino and Tim to Max's that evening to celebrate moving the press. They sat in a booth at the back of the tavern. It was happy hour and Rebop bought a pitcher of beer. After one beer, Gino refilled his glass and moved to another booth to introduce himself to two young women. Rebop waited for Gino to survive his opening line, then leaned across the table to Tim and said softly, "See the two guys up there by the door. They arrived about ten minutes ago."

Tim slid to the edge of the booth to get a look. One man had a long brown ponytail, the other a red goatee and a shaggy head of curly red hair.

"Ever see them before?"

"Yeah," said Tim, getting out his tobacco to roll a cigarette. "Earlier today. While we were moving the press."

"I noticed them also. Ever see them before today?"

"Hard to say, but I don't think so. Why?"

"I'm paranoid by nature." Rebop grinned, then lifted her beer for a swallow. "I seek out new faces in town." She glanced at the two men to see if they were watching her. "I think they were watching us today."

"Really?"

"It's a hunch." Rebop motioned to Gino chatting up the two women. "That's why I'm only telling you. I want someone to compare notes with—without making any kind of scene around it. But after the bombing Saturday night, I wouldn't be surprised if the Feds were in town."

Tim's eyes hardened. It had been a long couple of days for him, but he had learned to trust Rebop's instincts.

"They'd put some undercover folks on the street for sure," said Rebop. "Those guys look ordinary enough, but I've been followed before. And I got this strange, uneasy feeling when I saw them this morning."

Tim sat back to light his smoke. "I didn't give them a second thought," he said exhaling. "But I'll keep an eye on them for sure now."

Rebop finished her beer then refilled Tim's glass but not her own. "The rest of this is for you and Gino. Thank you, Tim. Having that press means a lot to me. I can't wait to use it. You know I'll need some help."

"Oh, yeah. I'll get you up and running."

Rebop and Tim exchanged a power handshake, then she walked out of the tavern, touching Gino on the shoulder as she passed. Gino looked back to Tim. Tim lifted the pitcher, signaling that the evening had just begun.

Gino returned to the table to refill his glass as Dave Berman entered the tavern through the back door. After casing the joint in his usual paranoid way, he slid into the booth across from Tim. Gino stood beside the table.

Dave took another look around, then lowered his head to speak in confidence to Tim. Gino leaned in to listen. "Did you hear, Tim? Stoopid's condition has been downgraded. They moved him into intensive care. They're not sure how much longer he'll last."

Tim thumped the table hard with his fist. "No, damn it," he cursed through gritted teeth. "I haven't heard a thing. Been too fucking busy." Tim bowed his head, worried about his friend.

CHAPTER 18

Having been late to work two days in a row, Ray stayed at his place Tuesday night and deliberately got up early the next morning. He arrived at the house on Eighteenth Avenue before Spikes did. He went into the house and got a flashlight out of the tool box. He put on his gloves and crawled under the house to check the animal trap Spikes had placed beneath the house. When he saw that the trap was empty, he aimed the flashlight at the nook where they had seen the foxes. The nook appeared vacant, so he crept up closer to get a better look. The two baby foxes, neither much bigger than his hand, were curled up asleep in a hole dug out by their mother. One lifted its head when roused by the bright light.

Ray couldn't resist. He scooched up closer. The kits were so cute he wanted to show them to Adrienne. He picked one up, and with the baby in one hand and his flashlight in the other, crawled out from underneath the house on his elbows and knees. He put the kit in the tool box for safe keeping then went after the other one. By the time he was back underneath the house, he could hear the little one upstairs crying. He hurried as fast as his alligator shimmy allowed and gathered up the second kit. When he swung around to leave, the silhouette of the mother darkened the crawl space opening. She lifted her nose and growled.

Leading with the flashlight beam, Ray crawled ahead cautiously, flashing the light at the fox, hoping his size would scare it away. But he didn't seem so big lying flat on the ground—and the fox, with her baby screaming inside the house, was enraged. The animal stared at Ray from about fifteen feet away, showing its teeth and hissing. Stretched out on his stomach, Ray couldn't react quickly or defend himself very easily. He decided not to challenge the fox. He placed the baby in front of him, then slid sideways away from the kit so the mother could get it. Overhead, the baby in the toolbox continued to cry and squeal.

The mother fox crept forward and positioned herself between Ray and the kit, then turned on Ray, who had backed himself into a corner with nothing to defend himself except the flashlight. Upstairs the little one let go a long, low howl for its mother. Ray braced for the worst. Then he heard footsteps on the floor above, followed by a loud, "What the fuck is this fox doing in my tool box—besides pissing and shitting?"

Ray called out. "I need some help down here, Jack." The fox edged toward him, growling and showing her teeth. "I'm under the house. Hurry!"

The fox made a lunge at Ray, but a wave of the flashlight kept the animal at bay. Above, Spikes thundered out of the house and ran to the crawl space opening. Even without a flashlight he could see what was happening. "I should leave you there for being so stupid," he snarled.

"What if it's rabid?" whined Ray, unable to move forward or back.

"It ain't rabid any more than I am. Stare it down like Davey Crocket."

"Fuck that, Jack." The fox made another halting attack, and Ray swung wildly at her with the flashlight. "Use a stick or something to distract it. She's gonna bite me."

Spikes climbed to his feet and disappeared from sight.

"Jack, you can't leave me here," yelled Ray, while above the baby in the tool box let go with its own cry for help. The frustrated mother couldn't seem to figure out where the second kit was, and Ray feared she thought he had it. He flashed the light in the fox's eyes to keep it away, as Spikes appeared in the opening with his twenty-two.

"No way, Jack. No way."

Spikes just laughed. "Got a better idea? I ain't comin' in there after you." He got down on his stomach and leveled the rifle at the fox. "Slide as far to the left as you can."

"I can't go any farther left. Fuck! Don't shoot!"

Boom! Spikes shot the fox. It rolled over on its side, badly wounded, but not dead. It snarled and snapped in pain, making it impossible for Ray to crawl forward without risk. Spikes took another shot and killed it.

Ray squirmed from beneath the house with the other kit in his hand. "Thanks," he deadpanned, "I think I just stained my shorts."

Jack glared at the animal in Ray's hand. "And what the fuck you gonna do with that?"

Ray brushed the dirt off himself. "Give it to Adrienne."

Spikes held the rifle by his side and shook his head. "What a fool will do for love."

"Well, at least the foxes have been taken care of."

"If the male isn't someplace nearby."

A patrol car pulled up out front of the house. Two officers came across the yard to Spikes and Ray. One addressed them, staring straight at the rifle in Spikes' hand. "The neighbors reported hearing gunshots."

"We had a little fox problem," said Spikes.

Ray held up the kit. "The mom's under the house dead."

The officer nodded. "There's a fine for discharging a firearm inside the city limits." His partner pulled out a clipboard and began writing up the ticket. "It's a hundred dollars."

Spikes stared at the sky instead of cursing.

After the police were gone and Ray had dragged the fox carcass out from beneath the house, Spikes confided to him. "Sorry I was late today. Might have prevented any of this from happening. But I got lucky. I rented out the Madison house." It was his best property.

"Well, that's something, Jack. The deposit will cover the fine."

"Yeah, ain't that swell." He shook his head. "But I am looking forward to getting regular rent out of that place. That'll solve many a problem. Including paying you." Spikes jabbed Ray in the ribs with his forefinger then let go with a blustery laugh.

CHAPTER 19

Jack Spikes invited his friend Bob Yates to his girlfriend's house for dinner that night. Sheila Haines, once divorced, lived on three acres north of Eugene off Highway 99 with her twelve-year-old daughter Mary and her nine-year-old son Joey. She was a great cook and Spikes enjoyed having his bachelor friends over to get a taste of what he got every night. Spikes kept a room at one of his rentals, but he spent most nights at Sheila's place.

Spikes was in the backyard playing catch with Joey when Yates drove down the long, tree-lined driveway in his Oldsmobile Eighty-eight. A six-hundred-pound Hampshire pig was tied to a post beside a garage that was separate from the house. A little chicken coop projected off the west side of the garage. Spikes heard the car door slam and flipped the ball to Joey. As he came through the gate in the picket fence to greet Yates, a little Shetland collie slipped out of the yard and started barking.

Yates slapped his thigh and the dog ran up to him for a pat on the head. "Man, I can't say how much I've been looking forward to getting out here tonight. It's like a holiday for me. What's Sheila cooking?"

Spikes patted his friend on the shoulder. "Come on in. I'll let her tell you."

Spikes led the police officer up the backstairs, through a mudroom cluttered with rubber boots, overcoats, and raingear, into the kitchen. Sheila stood at the stove with an apron around her waist. She immediately greeted Yates with a hug. "Bob, it's been too long since you've been out here." Sheila was older than Spikes by five years. She was not a young beauty, but she had a certain solid feel about her. Her hair was bleached blond, and she kept in shape by running three miles each morning.

"He says he can't stand your cooking," chuckled Spikes, bringing up the rear and going straight to the refrigerator for a couple of cans of Blitz Weinhardt beer—Blitz to the locals.

"You know that's not true, Sheila. There isn't a better cook in Eugene."

"Lane County," said Sheila with a grin. "Get me a Blitz, too, honey."

Spikes gave her his and got another for himself.

Yates moved up close to the stove to get a peek at dinner.

"Don't touch that oven door," snapped Sheila. "I've got roast beef and Yorkshire pudding in there. Popping that door at the wrong time could cost you your life."

Yates jumped back as though he'd burned his fingers. "Yes, ma'am. I didn't touch a thing. But it sure smells good."

"Let's give Sheila some space." Spikes led Yates out to the living room and an over-stuffed chair covered in dog hair. Spikes fell onto a couch that was the same. The interior of the little bungalow from the 1930s was a bit dark because of all trees around it. The dark paneling and wall to wall maroon carpeting in the living room didn't help. But with a beer in hand no one gave a damn.

"Got some bad news for you, Bob," said Spikes. "But it's good news for me."

Yates tilted his can of beer back and took a long swallow. "Tell me whatever you want, but this beer is what I needed. Been a long day downtown."

"I got a renter for First and Madison."

"Shit, you mean I've got to move?" Yates had moved into Spikes' empty rental after losing his house to his wife. Spikes wasn't charging him, but it was also known to be a temporary situation.

"Could be worse. You got four free days out of it." Spikes grinned. "A nice-looking woman in a sharp suit and heels met me there this morning. She took it immediately. Wrote the check on the kitchen counter."

"She have a family? The place has three bedrooms."

"She didn't say. Must have some kids."

"She married?"

"Said she had a boyfriend. All I know is it's my best property and it can't be empty."

Yates nodded and took another long drink from his beer. "The Feds showed up Monday."

"The FBI?"

"Yep. Makes my skin crawl when those guys come around, but after the bombing, the Mayor demanded it. He's worried he's going to lose the Trials to the violence."

"Trials?"

"The Olympic Track and Field Trials. It would be big thing for Eugene, but they're a ways off."

"Don't know a thing about them. But I do know they ought to round up all those SDS drips, give them a haircut, and send them to Southeast Asia. Then maybe they'd have a better idea what they're protesting."

Although a vet, Yates had seen enough during his time in Vietnam to wonder about the purpose of the war. He wasn't against it, but he didn't argue for it—the way Spikes did. "I don't know, Jack. The only thing anyone learns over there is how to kill. And you know some of the vets have turned hard against the war. Those kinds of skills in a radical spell trouble to me."

Sheila came into the room with her beer. "You say FBI?"

"Yes, but you didn't hear it, Sheila. They're going low profile. Same goes for you, Jack. I shouldn't have said a word. Nor should I tell you I'm leading the investigation into the janitor's getting burned."

"Not the Feds?"

"That's what I thought, but Wilkerson says we have jurisdiction. We'll see how that works out." He finished his beer and went to the kitchen for another.

Joey stuck his head in from the mudroom and yelled through the kitchen. "When's dinner, Mom?" One of Joey's eyes drooped. His father had punched him in the face when he was five.

"Soon enough! Find your sister and both of you wash your hands." Sheila had lived in New Jersey. Three years earlier, she had gathered up her children and moved to Oregon to get as far away from her ex-husband as possible. She bought the house and started her own accounting business. She converted one of the bedrooms into an office, so she could work out of the house and have the farm animals, two dogs, and a cat.

"I heard you lost your house, Bob," said Sheila, sitting down next to Spikes on the sofa. She believed that Spikes would get rich with his property acquisitions and hoped to marry him. Spikes liked her because she was smart and knew he was too busy running a life on a shoestring to sign up for anything permanent—yet. Their relationship was in its second year, and it had been pretty good so far.

Yates shook his head sadly as he returned from the kitchen. "Yeah, last week I was out on the street with all my belongings in a storage locker. Now Jack's throwing me out. Can't go much lower than that."

Sheila laughed, but she had known something lower. She tipped her beer up, and without saying a word, drank to her new life. "What's Rhonda going to do with the house?"

"Move her boyfriend in with his two kids."

"She's a fast worker."

"At least you didn't have kids," said Spikes. "You got off easy just losing the house."

The kids and two dogs barreled into the kitchen from the back. "Wash your hands," Sheila called out before they could ask if dinner was ready. A buzzer went off in the kitchen. Sheila downed the rest of her beer and stood. "Find a spot at the table, boys and girls. It's time to eat."

CHAPTER 20

Ray rode his bicycle home from work that evening with the kits wrapped up in his t-shirt. Once in the house, he exchanged the t-shirt for a bath towel and placed them in a box on his bed. He hounded down two hotdogs wrapped in slices of bread and slathered with mustard, then showered and rolled a joint from a stash he kept under his bed. He smoked half the joint, carried the kits outside in the towel, nestled them into the basket of his bicycle, and was halfway across town before the marijuana hit him. He showed up at Blake College so stoned he forgot why he was there. The sound of the squealing kits brought it all back.

Dinner had already been eaten and cleaned up. Rain sat at the dining room table with Marsha, showing the younger woman how to make an astrological chart. Ray walked up to the table and opened the towel so they could see the kits. With their black eyes and little pointed ears, they could not have been cuter.

"How old are they?" asked Rain, petting one with her forefinger.

"I don't know. Two weeks maybe. Not much more. Found them under a house."

Adrienne came into the room from the kitchen. "What have you got, Ray?"

"Take a look."

"Oh, my!" She lifted one kit out of the towel. Curled up it wasn't much bigger than a baseball. "Where'd you find them?"

Eyes blood-shot, Ray beamed. "Under a house. The one we're moving."

"Where's the mom?" asked Adrienne, turning to Rain and Marsha.

"My boss shot her," blurted out Ray.

"Shot her?" Adrienne frowned. "Was that really necessary?"

"We had to get them out from underneath the house." Ray looked to the other women for help. "It was dangerous."

He got blank stares from all three women.

"I was trapped under the house. The mother was going after me."

"Because you were taking her babies?"

Ray hung his head. He looked up. "I thought you might like them."

"Not as much as their mother would. I can't believe you killed the mother. You could have moved them."

Ray now wished he hadn't smoked the joint. "You had to be there, Adrienne. I made the mistake of trying to get the babies, but once I'd blown that, we had to do something with the adult." He heard how lame he sounded as he said the words.

Adrienne stared at Ray, not sure what to say.

Rain spoke up. "This is the kind of awareness we want to teach here at Blake College. Not to get down on you, Ray, but there was a better way to get rid of those foxes."

Ray couldn't deny that. He grinned in spite himself. "The shit bucket's already been spilled. If you girls aren't about to expel me from school, we still need someone to take care of these kits."

Adrienne rolled her eyes. "You're suspended for three days, dang it, Ray." Then she nuzzled the kit up against her cheek.

"From sex?" gasped Ray.

Adrienne nodded soberly.

Rain chuckled. "Don't worry, Ray. She'll never last that long. Let's find a more permanent place for these little orphans."

Wednesday night was peanut night at Max's Tavern. The place filled up on Wednesdays like it did on Saturdays and stayed hopping until closing time at one. Almost everyone on the street stopped by at some point in the evening for the free peanuts and a beer.

The crowd flooded out the front door onto the sidewalk by the time Ray and Adrienne got there at nine. Four big Harleys were parked side by side on the sidewalk. Ray literally had to squeeze through the door, towing Adrienne behind. They snaked up to the bar, hip to hip in hippies and other denizens of the Eugene night life, not to mention the cluster of bikers in their colors packed into a booth at the back of the tavern.

The atmosphere was crazy. Adrienne and Ray thought of it as the wild west. And with all the mustaches, long sideburns, cowboy hats, and blue jeans it did have that look. But it also held the low vibe attached to hard drugs and gave Max's the authentic underworld feel that the other taverns near the college didn't have. On a night like this when the bikers were there in number and the peanuts shells were two-inches deep on the floor, it felt a little dangerous—like the jukies were having a ball. And of course, that was what made Wednesday night at Max's such a big thing. It was edgy with drunks, drugs, and liberated women.

Ray and Adrienne had already acknowledged that heavy drinking did little to enhance their love making—the third night of which lay ahead. But the thrill in the air and a street poet sitting beside them muttering doggerel kept them buying pitchers and sharing them with anyone who happened by.

About eleven, Adrienne nudged Ray and glanced to the entrance. Tim O'Malley stood in the doorway looking like a stork from outer space in his leather motorcycle helmet and red tennis shoes. Beside him was Gino, his long hair gassed back and wearing his yellow-tinted shooting glasses. They had just delivered the SDS flyers to Dave Berman and had decided they needed a few beers before crashing.

Tim and Gino sauntered into the bar, a psychedelic Laurel and Hardy. A few heads tipped in their direction; some hellos were muttered. Everyone knew Tim. Gino was just his pint-sized sidekick. They bellied up to the bar next to Ray. Tim put a stack of flyers on the bar and got out his tobacco and rolling papers.

"Remember him from the night we met," Adrienne said under her breath as though it were a secret. "He showed up on his motorcycle not long before the bombing."

Ray tapped Tim on the shoulder as he removed his leather headgear and replaced it with his cloth cap. "Can I look at that flyer?"

Tim bobbed his head as he rolled his smoke. Ray took one. It was a one-page screed against ROTC on campus. Ray and Adrienne quickly read it.

"Ask him if he wrote this."

By this time both Gino and Tim had thrown down a beer and were beginning a second at a slower pace. Ray leaned over to Tim. "Did you write this?" He drew his finger down the printed page.

"Naw," replied Tim. "I don't do no philosophizing. Just the printing."

"Mind if I keep this copy?"

"Not at all. They're here to pass out."

"Kind of wild stuff," tossed in Adrienne, leaning into the conversation.

Gino peeked around Tim's shoulder with a stoned grin. "Wild compared to what?" He lifted his shades to wink at her.

"Not as wild as that." Tim's eyes focused on the rear of the bar as five more bikers came in the back door, all wearing their colors and surly looks. The four bikers in the booth immediately stood up and blocked them from getting to the bar.

Gino came around Tim and leaned up close to Adrienne and Ray. "Gypsy Jokers and Free Souls. Watch out. Those guys are dangerous."

"They've got a little turf war going," added Tim. "Somebody got knifed last week, and there seems to be a need for a little biker justice."

Rough language spat back and forth between the rival gangs, rising in ferocity above the general din. One man pushed another in the chest. "Come on outside, you fucks," shouted another.

While everyone else was moving to the front, trying to get as far away from the bikers as possible, Tim glanced at the bartender, who held the bar phone in one hand, waiting for the right moment to call the cops. Tim nodded to the tender, then headed to the back.

Two of the bikers suddenly drew knives. The other bikers backed away, so the two men were faced off in a circle of onlookers. Tim strode right into the group of bikers. "Mike, you son-of-a-bitch, why you trying to ruin such a nice night? This is an evening for fun, not fighting." He touched the tin star on his vest. "Either find someplace else to fight or I'll have to give you all deputies' badges and teach you the law."

The bikers, including the two with knives, turned to see who had dared to interrupt them. Every one of them lit up with a smile. They all knew Tim. His 1938 Indian was the most admired motorcycle in Eugene, and Tim was the best gearhead outside of a racing shop that anyone knew. He had probably worked on every one of these guys' bikes at some time or another

One of the men holding a knife was Mike Rogers of the Gypsy Jokers. Big, bearded, and ugly, he looked like he could bite through barbed wire. He glared at tall, skinny Tim. "You're one crazy-ass fuck for coming back here, O'Malley. This ain't for you," he snarled. "It's between us." Then he grinned. "And what the fuck you talking about? Deputy badges, you silly shit."

Tim didn't blink. He stuck his hand into his pocket and withdrew the little matchbox of blotter acid. "Mr. Natural deputy badges." He used one finger to slide the matchbox open. "Any interest?" His eyes glowed like lanterns in the tavern shadows. "Took some myself this afternoon. Clear and clean as it gets."

The bikers looked around at each other. Most of them had gotten acid from Tim at some point in the last year. One by one they took a paper square from the box. They appraised each other again, then the whole group of them—Jokers and Free Souls—popped the acid into their mouths. Mike put away his knife and motioned to his buddies to sit down. The others made their way to the bar. Those watching returned to their booths. Tim rejoined Adrienne, Ray, and Gino. The bartender filled a pitcher of beer and put it on the bar in front of Tim. "Thanks for instituting the law."

Tim put a hand to the brim of his printer's hat and gave him a nod.

Ray couldn't believe it. "What did you say to those guys?"

"I told them I was Wyatt Earp. If they got any blood on the floor, I was going clean it up with their chin whiskers."

Ray looked at Adrienne. Gino burst into laughter, and Tim refilled everyone's glasses.

CHAPTER 21

The University of Oregon track team had come to prominence through twenty-two years of guidance from their coach Bill Bowerman. Bowerman had been a war hero, then a high school football coach in Medford, Oregon, and then was hired to be the track coach at Oregon in 1948. Bowerman advanced his own training scheme, particularly for distance runners, and gradually built Oregon into a national powerhouse, winning four national championships for the Fighting Ducks.

In the mid-sixties Bowerman and Phil Knight, once a runner for Bowerman, partnered in the shoe business, creating Blue Ribbon Sports, a company that distributed Japanese-made running shoes. While Knight did the majority of the groundwork, Bowerman, always an original thinker and largely responsible for America's love affair with jogging, experimented with designs. Like everyone else in Eugene, Bowerman and Knight hoped that getting the Olympic Trials would catapult Eugene—and Blue Ribbon Sports—into the spotlight.

Bill Bowerman and his wife Barbara lived on a large piece of wooded property situated on a hill a few miles north of the university. Their home overlooked the McKenzie River twisting through the south portion of the valley and the green pastures of neighboring farmers. Bowerman used the kitchen and the adjoining garage as a shoe lab. Having listened to hundreds of runners over his years as a coach, he knew they wanted lighter shoes and, more recently, an alternative to spiked running shoes. New synthetic running surfaces were becoming popular on tracks all around the world. The University of Oregon had installed a synthetic track at Hayward Field a year earlier. Spikes were not the best fit for the new surfaces, and runners were complaining. Bowerman wondered if a rubber-soled running shoe might not be the answer.

On Saturday morning, seven days after the bombing, Barbara cooked waffles for Bill and his youngest son Tom, who was visiting for the weekend. The conversation that morning centered on Bill's current political campaign. Always looking for new challenges, he was running as a Republican in a very close race for the State Representative in Oregon's Thirteenth District. While he and his son discussed election strategies, Bill became intrigued by the diamond-shaped pattern of the waffles on his plate. Abruptly changing the topic, he wondered aloud to his wife and son if this pattern might not make a good tread for the lightweight running shoes he'd been thinking about.

That afternoon he moved the waffle iron into the garage where he had been experimenting with several varieties of polyurethane resin. He took the pin out of the waffle iron hinge and poured black resin into the two halves. He allowed the rubber to vulcanize overnight. When he tried to remove the rubber the next morning, it was stuck so thoroughly to the waffle iron he couldn't get it out. After a few more experiments and some help from a local fabricator, he had enough polyurethane imprinted with the diamond-shaped tread by Tuesday to make a few prototypes.

Bowerman had been building shoes on his own for several years. He had the necessary sewing gear, glue, leather, and canvas in his garage— and the new rubber sole inspired him. He completed the first pair of shoes Wednesday night. Thursday morning he presented them to Phil Knight, who was forty years younger, and told him to give them a hard run on the track at Hayward Field. Phil called him that night. He told Bill the shoe was the lightest and most comfortable shoe he'd ever run in.

CHAPTER 22

Rebop Rodriguez might have an occasional beer, but she was not part of the Eugene drinking scene. She was a poet. Her public hangout was the Odyssey Coffee House at the north end of Willamette Street, across from the train station and squeezed in between Great Day in the Morning, a tiny organic café, and Eugene Stationary. She might show up at the Odyssey any time of the day—morning or night—get a cup of coffee and stay an hour to two, writing and reading, deliberately making herself available to women in the community. Rebop felt part of her job as publisher of a women's newsletter was to stay in touch with the women on the streets of Eugene where, in her mind, the movement had the most life.

Friday morning, Rebop sat at one of the tables at the back of the Odyssey, jotting words on a pad of lined paper and sipping coffee. The wall beside her contained a row of large windows that looked out onto the street and the train station. A long silver passenger train waited on the tracks for departure.

Every now and then Rebop would sit back and observe the people on the street or in the café. She watched a young woman with cropped brown hair come into the shop. Their eyes met. The other woman, Sue Hoffman, tipped her head to Rebop, got a cup of coffee, then joined her at the table.

Rebop was thirty-three years old. Sue was twenty-two. She was the treasurer and the only female member of the University of Oregon's chapter of the SDS. She wore blue jeans and a checked cotton blouse, not tucked in. No makeup. No jewelry.

Rebop got straight to the point. "I heard you guys had no connection to the incident at Campbell Hall."

Sue nodded. "What do you know about it?"

"Nothing. That's just it. No one does. And you're sure it's not someone in SDS, maybe someone leaning to the Weathermen?"

"We asked the same questions to each other a few nights back. We agreed that we need to make bold statements, but none of us have turned to violence. We aren't anarchist—yet."

Rebop stared at the train station for a moment then faced Sue. "I want to find out who did it, Sue. And so does Tim. The man caught in the fire was a friend of his. I'm asking everyone on the street. And so far, I've got nothing. You have contacts I don't. Keep your ears open."

"They already are. Dave is going nuts just like you are."

Rebop leaned up close to Sue. "I fear a provocateur."

Sue's brow creased.

"I've seen it before."

"I'm headed back to the office after this cup of coffee. I'll run that by Dave to see what he thinks."

"Tell him to beware. The bombing is sure to bring the Feds to town."

An hour later Rebop was still at her table. Rain Adams came in. They made immediate eye contact. Rain had as much respect in the community as a wild crafter as Rebop had as the editor of *Gorgons and Gargoyles*. Though both in their early thirties, they were elders in the community of the street. Rain got green tea and went to Rebop's table. Rebop stood to kiss her before they sat down. Briefly, a year back, they were lovers. Now they were sisters in arms.

Rebop asked her if she'd heard anything about the bombing of Campbell Hall. Rain's response was the same as Sue Hoffman's. "No one I know in the community has a clue. I wonder if someone did it to make the anti-war movement look bad."

Rebop nodded. "That's what's worrying me."

"God, I don't like this."

Rebop looked around and said softly, "The FBI is in town or soon will be."

"How do you know that?"

"A building was bombed. It's an act of terrorism. That's the FBI's jurisdiction. I would expect some undercover agents to be working their way into our community as we speak. Be on your toes."

"Wow, that's unsettling. Let me know if you learn something more."

Rebop took a tiny sip of coffee. "What's this I hear about your restarting Blake College?"

"Yeah." Rain beamed at the mention of it. "We took over Arthur's house and accepted a few students. It's really been great. Gloria's teaching yoga. A recent flame is teaching shamanism. Adrienne—I think you know Adrienne. She's teaching the students organic gardening. I'm doing wild crafting with them and astrology charts. You interested in coming over one evening to read some of your poetry?"

Rebop finally smiled. "Yes, that sounds good. I'd like to come over just to see what's happening."

"Come for dinner one night. I'll set up a time. You'll dig it."

CHAPTER 23

At that same time, in the basement of the university's Columbia Hall, in a tiny broom closet-like office, Sue Hoffman and Dave Berman, the two highest officers in the U of O Chapter of the SDS, huddled over a half-finished flyer announcing an anti ROTC demonstration the following week. A light knock sounded on the wooden door.

Sue looked at Dave. He shrugged. "Come on in."

The room was so small the door opened from the outside. Two men in dark suits and fedoras stood in the hallway. Todd Bascomb held out his wallet, showing his FBI badge. "Agent Bascomb." He turned to his partner. "Agent Franklin. We were hoping to talk to David Berman."

Dave glanced at Sue. She had already told him about Rebop's warning to be on the lookout for the FBI. *And Holy Shit, here they were!*

"Should I leave?" asked Sue.

"What's your name?

"Sue Hoffman."

"The treasurer?"

Sue nodded. She sat in the office's only chair. Dave stood.

"Why don't you stay. We have a few questions we'd like to ask—information from either of you would be welcome." Only one of the men could fit into the room. Behind Bascomb, Agent Franklin looked up and down the dingy basement hallway, casing the place.

Dave was smart and cocky. "Yeah, sure. If this is about the bombing of Campbell Hall, the SDS had nothing to do with it."

Bascomb was reading the poster on the desk. "You've got some pretty strong feelings about ROTC, Mr. Berman."

"But we aren't terrorists, Mr. Bascomb."

"Arsonists, maybe? Last spring? The ROTC offices? The SDS was part of that from what I've heard. That's why we're here now." Bascomb surveyed the pictures stuck at random on the minimum of wall space—

Che Guevara, Abby Hoffman, Jerry Garcia, a drawing of the American Flag with a swastika emblazoned on the blue background where the stars would be. "We plan to be in Eugene until we find who out did the bombing. You wouldn't happen to have any insights?" Bascomb's words were polite enough, but his tone and body language suggested something much different.

"You know, sir, if I did know something, I wouldn't tell you."

Bascomb frowned. "We're trying to be civil, Mr. Berman. We could go downtown."

"I'll tell you this," said Dave. "I don't know who did it. And nobody else does either. On the street, on the campus, we've quizzed everybody we know. Not a clue."

Bascomb looked directly at Sue. "How about you? You have anything more to add?"

"No, sir. I don't. Apologies for my wise-ass friend, but he's right. No one knows. This town might be crawling with communists, co-ops, and communes, but it's a close-knit community. You're looking for someone who's invisible from our point of view. Truly."

"Thank you, Miss Hoffman." Bascomb acknowledged her straightforwardness with his eyes. "You're likely to hear things we won't. Please let us know, and we'll all be the better for it." Halfway out the door, he stopped. "We'll talk again. We just wanted to introduce ourselves."

"Our pleasure," said Dave, dripping with sarcasm.

After the door closed, Sue jabbed Dave in the ribs. "You can be a real jerk." She frowned, then sat back in her chair. "What'd you think of that? Them coming here?"

"We should have expected it."

"Think they believed us?"

"I'm more afraid they're going to set us up. We're the perfect patsies."

"Would they use a provocateur?"

"It happens."

CHAPTER 24

The first weeks of Blake College focused on cooperative living—learning to cook together, keeping the two bathrooms clean, and plain old getting along. Marsha got it right away. Crow proved to be as solid as a rock. Tai did his part but was more interested in himself than the school. Van struggled with the free use of marijuana, and Janice tended to complain and act like an outsider amid the atmosphere of inclusion that Rain and Adrienne tried to foster. Tensions along these lines rose and fell as each person found their place. Gloria invariably served as a peacemaker and only her motherly influence allowed the school to get off the ground at all.

Ray stayed with Adrienne Friday night, so he would be available to help with the greenhouse that weekend. Saturday morning began with the squeal of the two foxes that slept in a box in Adrienne's bedroom. Adrienne got up and used a baby bottle to feed them. She sat on the side of the mattress and cradled them in one arm against her bare chest, allowing them to nuzzle into her breasts and suck at the bottle.

"It's like I'm breast feeding them," she said, turning to Ray as he roused from sleep. Both of them were now sleeping in the raw.

Ray woke up with an erection and squeezed up beside her, kissing her on the cheek. "When they're done, I'd like to do a little suckling myself."

"That looks like more than suckling to me, Mr. Happy."

Ray kissed down her neck.

"They are cute," said Adrienne, pretending to ignore him. "I'm glad you brought them to me."

Ray looked up. "Thank goodness. You weren't too happy about what happened to their mother." He leaned over and kissed her thigh.

"Wait, wait, wait," squealed Adrienne, giggling. "Let me put these guys in their box. We might crush them if we're not careful."

Crow, who had done the preliminary layout of the greenhouse and acquired quite a bit of used lumber, had already recruited Van and Marsha for the Saturday morning work crew. Ray used Adrienne's truck to get a chop-saw, skill saw, and an electric drill from Spikes for the weekend.

They began by building a wooden frame. Marsha had no experience with power tools, and Van was only comfortable using the drill and chop saw, which meant Crow and Ray did the real carpentry work and Van and Marsha acted as gophers. They completed the framing after working ten hours Saturday and eight on Sunday.

During the ensuing week, Crow and Van scoured the local junkyards and located ten sliding glass doors. The second weekend of work was dedicated to mounting the sliding doors on the greenhouse roof. Because of their weight and size, the glass doors were particularly difficult to get on top of the wooden structure. Crow leaned an extension ladder against the framing to make it easier. Marsha and Van would lay a glass door lengthwise on the ladder and slide it up to Ray and Crow, who would manhandle the glass door into place on the roof.

Even with the ladder this wasn't easy. Marsha and Van had to strain to lift the glass doors and slide them up the ladder. It was almost too much for slight-framed, five foot two Marsha, but she was determined to do her part without complaining. She held her own with the weight but pushing the glass door up the last foot of ladder put her on her tiptoes with the edge of the door at the ends of her outstretched fingers. They spent six hours, including the time it took Ray and Crow to secure the glass doors, getting seven of the ten sliding doors on the roof. The eighth was inches from Ray's and Crow's hands when Marsha lost her grip. The door slipped sideways across the ladder onto Van, forcing him to his knees and causing the ladder to slide away from him. Marsha was quick enough to catch the ladder, but even with her holding the ladder, Van could not move without losing hold of the glass door, precariously balanced on the edge of the ladder. Crow leapt off the building, ten feet to the ground, took hold of glass door with both hands, and lifted it off Van. Van rolled out of the way and stood up.

"Man, that could have been ugly." Crow laughed now that the danger was over. "We got lucky."

Marsha, however, was embarrassed and trying not to cry. She had dropped all the weight onto Van. He was fortunate to have escaped with only a long scratch on his right arm.

Crow pushed the glass door up the ladder by himself. Ray took hold of it, and with Crow joining him on the roof, levered it into place.

"Don't get down on yourself, darlin'," said Crow, when he was free of the slab of glass. "We're asking too much of you. We should have enlisted Tai for this part of the job."

"He's right," added Ray.

Marsha would have none of it. "No, I was trying to go too fast." She wiped the tears from her eyes. "I can do it. If Van still trusts me, I say we get the last two up there, so this part of the job is done. Nothing else will be this demanding."

"She's right," added Van. "Let's go. I trust her."

Crow and Ray looked at each other, both impressed by Marsha's determination and Van's willingness to continue despite narrowly avoiding a serious injury.

The last two glass doors went up without a hitch. By the time Ray and Crow had secured them to the roof, it was quitting time, and they all headed back to the house. Marsha walked beside Van.

"I'm sorry about earlier," she said softly. "I'm so thankful you weren't hurt."

Mild-mannered Van smiled at her. "I'm just glad we were able to get that done by ourselves." He looked over his shoulder. Crow and Ray were well behind them. "I'm not that fond of Tai. I greatly prefer working with you."

Marsha blushed. "Thanks for saying that, but are you really all right?"

"Yes, I'm fine."

CHAPTER 25

Gino's thing was antique bicycles. He rode a springer-front end, balloon tire classic from the 1950s, with a rocket shaped headlight that he had found at the Salvation Army As-is store and repainted to replicate the original. He didn't work fulltime with Tim. Not even close. He rarely got involved unless Tim was up against a deadline and needed to work through the night. Gino enjoyed working under pressure more than showing up every day at the same time to do the same thing. Aside from what little he earned from Tim, he added to his income by buying old bicycles, refurbishing them, and selling them on the street.

Living out of his panel truck had its inconveniences. Gino had no chest of drawers and no closet. When his guinea shirts or tuxedo pants got dirty, he would go to the Goodwill and find a new, used pair of pants and a shirt. He would change right there and leave his dirty clothes with the Goodwill. No one kept track, but at times it must have seemed as though the entire line of Goodwill tuxedo pants and guinea shirts were Gino's. He just dropped them off to get cleaned.

The street people of Eugene, of which Gino was a charter member, considered themselves artists—using their lifestyle as their central vehicle of expression. Gino fancied himself a street clown in the manner of Wavy Gravy. Occasionally wearing a red nose that squeaked when you squeezed it, he used his crazy sense of humor to disarm people with laughter. He lived a fulltime vaudeville act and never really got off the stage—if he could help it.

Gino had just acquired a clean set of clothing at the Goodwill and was biking through the Whitaker neighborhood on the north side of Eugene, when he noticed a new bicycle shop in one of the garages on Fourth Street. *Bikes: Good as New* was handwritten on a placard over the garage door. Used bicycles, minor repairs, and flat tire fixing, this was just the kind of place Gino loved to visit.

Gino saw Chris Mathers at the workbench, and not knowing that he was an FBI agent, rolled up the driveway. "Hey bro, can I look around?" Along with his black trousers and guinea shirt, he wore his usual attire— suspenders, porkpie hat, black slippers from China that looked like dancing shoes, and his shooting glasses with yellow lenses, that served as bicycle goggles.

"That's a nice one you've got there," said Mathers, eyeing Gino's bike. "You do the paint?"

Gino nodded proudly.

"Chris, is the name." He stuck out his hand.

"Gino." He exchanged the Black Power handshake without getting off his bike. "Got any old ones?"

"A few. Check'em out."

Gino climbed off his bike, set the kickstand, and followed Mathers into the garage. Four old frames without tires, fenders, or handle bars hung on the back wall.

"Yeah, this is the sort of stuff I'm interested in." He touched one of the frames. "Need any parts. I got just about anything you might want in a garage across town."

"Three-speed hubs?" Mathers had one unassembled on the workbench. "That's what my buddy and I are pushing to the college students. Cheap, used, three-speeds."

Gino edged up closer to one of the frames on the wall. "I'll give you three complete three-speed hubs for this one."

"Bring'em over. If they're in any shape at all, it's a deal."

"Right on." Gino looked around a bit longer, then hopped on his bicycle. "I'll be back in an hour."

When Gino returned, both Ball and Mathers were at the workbench. Mathers introduced Ball as Gino placed two of the three promised three-speed hubs on the work bench. Noting Ball's long ponytail, and thinking he had found like-minded freaks, he made an alternative offer. "I could only find two hubs, but I've got some acid."

This surprised the agents. They looked at each other. Mathers faced Gino. "Let's see what you've got."

Gino took a folded paper envelope out of his trouser pocket. Tim had given him sixteen hits to sell. At two bucks a hit, they would cover the paper and ink for the SDS printing job. Gino opened the envelope revealing two sheets of blotter and grinned. "Eight hits to a sheet. Two bucks each."

"Real LSD?"

Gino made a face. "Fuck, yes. From Owsley. I've taken several of these myself. Pure and clean as it gets."

Mathers knew LSD was illegal and that it was psycho-activating in some way, but he had never met anyone who had taken it and wasn't quite sure what to make of Gino—who presented a charming cockiness spun in with his goofy smiles and dumb jokes. "Okay. One hub is worth six bucks to me."

"Fair enough." Gino tore three of the tiny paper squares from one of the sheets. "That's three hits."

Mathers took the three squares from Gino and handed them to Ball to inspect. "How can I get more? A bunch more," asked Ball.

Gino thought nothing of this. "Not a problem. I'm on the street all the time. Usually on this bike. That's the best way to find me." He grinned.

"But where do you live?"

Gino laughed. "Anywhere I am." He lifted the bicycle frame he wanted off the wall, hung it on his right shoulder, and hopped on his bicycle. "See ya around." He pedaled off down the street.

Mathers and Ball looked at the three hits of acid for a long time, puzzling over the imprint of Mr. Natural. Ball found a baggie and put them away as evidence, along with a description of the contents and the source.

CHAPTER 26

Tim had spent Monday morning cleaning the plates for his letter press and was about to roll a joint when he heard two men approach the door to the shop, then knock.

"It's open," he called out, putting away his stash of weed.

The men knocked again. Tim crossed the shop to open the door. One of the men held out his badge. "FBI, son. Agent Bascomb. Tim O'Malley, is that correct?"

"That's the name my parents gave me."

"My partner Agent Franklin and I would like to talk to you." Both men wore dark suits and matching fedoras.

"Come on in," said Tim, who had expected a visit. "How can I help you?"

They came in cautiously, noting the various anti-war posters on the walls and the copies of the Weather Underground's *Prairie Fire* stacked in the corner. Bascomb took the lead. "We're here because of the bombing at the university. The police department gave us a list of the local activists. Your name was at the top of the list. Where were you the night Campbell Hall was bombed?"

Tim had been outspoken against the war for a long time. He had been arrested at protests in San Francisco, but not in Eugene. Always a cool customer, Tim took the offensive. "I was at Max's Tavern. Probably twenty people can vouch for me. But I'll tell you straight out, I had nothing to do with the bombing. And no one I know did either. The man burned in the fire was a friend of mine. I'd like to see you nab the bomber as much as anyone. Got any leads?"

Bascomb looked at Franklin, then back to Tim. "Just you and a couple others. What's this about?" He lifted an SDS flyer off the press.

Franklin retrieved a copy of *Prairie Fire*. "And this?" He wagged the paperback in Tim's face.

"It's about my job, boys. That's what I do. I print. I didn't complete high school and can barely read, so I have no idea what this stuff is about. I just do the job and don't worry about anything else."

"Then you ought to be more particular," said Bascomb.

"More than that," said Franklin, still waving the book around. "This is communist literature. This alone could get you in trouble."

"Well, I don't know why that would be. I think there's something in the Bills of Rights about free speech. Printing is protected by the same law. I'd really prefer helping you guys than trying to defend the politics of the people I print for. You talk to the SDS yet?" He knew they had.

"It's no matter of yours who we talk to, young man," said Bascomb, noticing a black and white photo on the wall showing Huey Newton holding a rifle. "You're playing with fire, O'Malley. Watch yourself."

"Hey, easy there, Mr. Agent. You're not hearing me. I had nothing to do with Campbell Hall. Neither did anyone else I know. Heck, if you need some help, I can mobilize a bunch of folks. And they're all angry about what happened. Both to my friend and the building. The people I know in Eugene are non-violent and don't want anyone screwing that up."

"That's not what this book says," countered Franklin.

"But those people aren't in Eugene. Like I said, I just do the printing. I'm a small business. I take what I can get. But you're missing the point, I can help you."

Bascomb exhaled out of frustration. "You come up with something, let us know." He gave Tim his card. "We have an office in town. Call me. Until then, just so you know, we'll be watching you."

Tim nodded. "Good. You'll discover I don't do much but print and ride my motorcycle. See that baby out by the house? It's a rare one."

"Wonderful," said Bascomb sarcastically. "Don't leave town."

"I've got no intention of leaving. I've got too much work to do."

"Good." Bascomb turned to Franklin and nodded at the door. The two men walked out.

Gino came into the shop shortly after the two men left. "Who were those guys?"

"The FBI," said Tim, lighting the joint he had just rolled.

"FBI?" Gino received the joint from Tim and took a toke. "What'd they want?" He passed the joint back to Tim.

"Me." Tim puffed on the joint and grinned.

August 8, 2019

Josh,

I have sent you my most recent novel. Despite the cover, it is not a horror story, but as you can see on the back, I call it Psy-Fy. It might qualify for light sci-fi, but I'm not sure it matters. In any case, it's set in Eugene and includes a political bent. I thought you might find it interesting.

I have read your newsletters and am impressed with both your energy and your writing. Excellent work. Although it really helps to get an agent and a solid publisher, as you are learning that can be a long haul. Judging by your effort, however, I'd say keep at it. You have the talent to make it work.

And yet, self-publishing is a way to get your work—in novel form—to your following while you continue to look at self-published novels. That has changed. In some ways, sending an agent a completed book is better than sending a synopsis and a resume. The completed book acts as its own marketing tool. It includes the cover artwork and the blurb on the back and a finished product. If the cover and blurb will sell the book off the shelf, then it might also sell it to an agent or publisher. I cannot say I have made this work. And I have tried. But in the meantime, I do have an audience. It grows slowly, and I do get some money out of the deal—but not much.

Anyway, just some thoughts. I'm sure you know what you're doing. However, if you begin to explore to self-publish, feel free to ask me more about it.

Best,

541-520-7236

"What'a ya talking about?" Gino took the joint back from Tim.

Tim exhaled a cloud of smoke. "They think I might have been the bomber."

"You didn't do it, did ya?" Gino took a toke.

"Fuck no, Gino. You know that!"

"Well," muffled Gino, holding the smoke in his lungs, "what'd ya say?"

"I told them I wanted to find the bomber as badly as they did. Even said I'd help them."

Gino exhaled laughing. "Help the FBI? That's a good one." He grinned. "I got a better one."

"Yeah."

"I found a couple guys who want to buy some of that acid. How much you got to spare?"

"At what price?"

"Two bucks a hit. That's what you said, right?"

"Yeah. How about forty hits? That leaves plenty for you and me. Sound good?"

"Yeah, yeah. And I've got some left over from what you gave me before."

"Good enough. We can use the money."

"To play pool and drink beer," chuckled Gino.

"Exactly," grinned Tim, now fully stoned.

CHAPTER 27

Monday afternoon, Sheila Haines turned her Jeep station wagon into the Edison Elementary School parking lot and found a place to park. She'd gotten a call three days earlier from one of the two student counselors. He'd asked her to come to his office to talk about Joey. The call had not surprised Sheila, but it had made her stomach sink. She worried a lot about Joey, and this call seemed to confirm her fears. She found the receptionist and was directed to Mr. Fairfield's office.

Mr. Fairfield stood from his desk as she entered and introduced himself as Nathan. He was probably ten years younger than Sheila and wore a white shirt with a striped tie. He offered her a seat. She was so anxious about what she might be told she was nauseous.

"Thank you for coming in, Mrs. Haines," said the counselor. "As I said on the phone, I'm worried about Joey—and so is his teacher."

"Well, I appreciate your calling me. I worry about Joey, too. Is he causing trouble in class?" This was not her real concern.

"No. It's his school work. A little bit more is expected from the third graders than we're seeing out of Joey. Children mature at different rates, but by age nine, he should be doing much better than he is. He's absolutely silent in class and shy to a fault."

This was what she was worried about.

"I've noticed he has an issue with his right eye," said the counselor. "Did he suffer a head injury?"

Sheila saw it all again. Her ex-husband Michael getting drunk one night and punching Joey in the face. There was a lot of blood. They lied about it in the emergency room. But it marked the end of the marriage for Sheila. Unfortunately, it was two years before she was free and another six months before she was in Oregon. She lied again. "It was a traffic accident four years ago. Joey's eye has drooped ever since."

The counselor nodded, not suspecting anything. "We're recommending special ed."

Sheila looked down at her hands, gripping and ungripping each other, as though trying to hold on to her emotions.

Sheila cried that night when she related this to Jack after the kids were asleep. Jack liked Joey because he was a tough little bugger and strong for his age, but he could also see the drooping eye and he knew how it had happened. He got the picture right away and was also shaken.

"He needs more than me, Jack," said Sheila after the tears had stopped. "He loves you. He idolizes you."

Jack lowered his eyes.

"Could you possibly commit to him?"

Jack's expression was almost entirely masked by his giant mustache. He had dark bushy eyebrows and dark brown eyes to add to his inscrutability. He knew she was asking him to marry her so that Joey would have a father. Unfortunately, Jack wasn't ready for marriage and he knew that as a fact. But he had a weak spot. For all his bluster and hard talk, he had a tiny, sentimental streak of unanswered fatherhood—because his father had been important to him and had died young. "Can we discuss this over the next couple of months? That's a big commitment, and there's plenty to talk about."

"You mean, you're not saying no?" Sheila nearly laughed and cried at the same time. She had asked him out of heart-felt desperation, fully knowing that Jack was not ready to get married.

The mixture of laughter and tears also struck Jack quite powerfully. He took her in his arms, also laughing now. "Well, then I guess we understand each other. That's a good start."

CHAPTER 28

Tuesday began slowly at Blake College. Gloria had been up since sunrise, but everyone else slept in past nine. Crow and Van were at the dining room table when Tai and Rain stumbled down from upstairs. It was nearly ten-thirty.

"Late morning for you guys," said Crow, sipping a second cup of coffee.

Rain, though looking a little tired, perked up. "We spent a long weekend out in Veneta at the Renaissance Faire. Didn't get back until late last night."

Van gave her a look. "Renaissance Faire?"

"It's like a giant Saturday Market. The folks who own the Odyssey put it together. It's the third time it's happened. But this one was much bigger than the previous ones. A hundred and fifty vendors—and I think they said twenty thousand people showed up. I had a booth out there and sold out midday Sunday. It was great. A little more money never hurts."

"It was basically a huge party—like a mini Woodstock," said Tai. "I think they plan to make it an annual event."

Marsha came into the kitchen through the back door. "A black car just came down the driveway."

Tai stood from the table to look out the front window. Two men in dark suits and fedoras were headed to the front porch. "Looks like the cops. I'm getting out of here."

Tai and Crow quickly slipped out the back door. A moment later, there was a knock on the door. Van watched Tai and Crow disappear into the backyard then answered the door.

"I'm Agent Bascomb." He showed Van his badge. "This is Agent Franklin." He motioned to the man beside him on the porch. "Is Arthur Kotke here? We'd like to talk to him."

"No, never heard of the man." Van's hair was slightly longer than when he'd arrived, but he still looked like the straightest guy in Eugene who wasn't in a uniform.

"According to the county records, an Arthur Kotke owns this house," said Bascomb. "Anyone else here?"

"Rain will know more than I do. I'll get her."

The two agents looked at each other. "Rain?"

She came to the front door. "My name is Rain Adams. How can I help you?" The calm in her voice made an immediate impression.

Bascomb showed her his badge. "We're looking for Arthur Kotke."

"He left Eugene five months ago."

"What about Blake College? Didn't Kotke run a school here?"

Van was standing behind her listening. He knew bits and pieces of the school's history but nothing about Arthur Kotke.

"He's on sabbatical," lied Rain, who could lie better than anyone because she always seemed so sincere. "I run the school now. What do you need from Arthur?"

"We want to ask him some questions. Where is he now?"

"He's kind of a free spirit. He doesn't stay in touch. Did he do something wrong?"

Bascomb looked at his partner. "There was a bomb detonated at the university three weeks ago. It's a federal offense. We're in Eugene to find out who did it. The authorities at the university told us that Mr. Kotke taught a history of revolution class five years ago and that he had left the university to start this experimental school. He's someone we want to talk to."

Because of Rebop's heads up, none of this surprised Rain. She thought of herself as a revolutionary and felt that Blake College and the anti-war movement were extensions of her activist philosophy. "I don't know what else to tell you, sir. He's been gone, like I said, five months. I doubt he would know anything about the bombing." Rain smiled pleasantly, as though it were as easy as that.

And it was. The two agents believed Rain and felt that Kotke was not really a person of interest. "Thank you for your time, Miss Rain," said Bascomb, a little confused. He hesitated a moment then returned to the sedan with Agent Franklin.

Minutes later, Crow and Tai came in the back door for a briefing. Rain was sitting at the living room table with Van.

"What was that about?" queried Tai.

"It was the FBI," said Van.

"The FBI?" echoed Crow.

Rain nodded. "Looking for Arthur Kotke. In connection with the bombing. Kind of strange."

"They were here looking for the bomber?" said Tai. "Wow, that's heavy."

"Arthur's the guy who officially owns this place?" asked Crow.

"Yeah. He's been gone for months."

"So, he couldn't have done it," said Tai.

"That's what I told them."

"But who did?" asked Crow.

Rain shook her head. "I'm pretty well connected to the political left in this town, and as far as I can tell, no one has a clue. But where were you guys?"

Tai looked at Crow, then to Rain. "With my little stash of exotic drugs, I thought it was best if I wasn't here."

Rain shrugged as though this were nothing.

Crow looked down at the floor. "I don't have an ID. Things could have gotten sticky."

Rain left it at that. Crow didn't have an ID, and it wasn't any of her business to know why.

CHAPTER 29

Spikes had never lifted a house off its foundation on his own. He had helped others a couple of times, but lifting the house on Eighteenth Avenue would be pretty much trial and error until the moving company came in and put the thing on wheels. The task was to lift the entire house twenty-four inches off the foundation and then structurally reinforce it so that it could make the trip across town.

Now that the foxes were gone—except for the sharp smell of their urine—Spikes and Ray pulled away all the skirting to address the dry rot. The house was forty years old, and a lot of the two-by-fours at the level of the foundation needed to be replaced. They also discovered one large, active wasp nest and piles and piles of rodent shit.

Spikes and Ray spent the rest of the morning preparing places for the twenty-four jacks they would use to lift the house. They lay on their sides beneath the house, scratching at the ground with the blade of a shovel to make a level spot for each jack. They were both filthy when they crawled out from beneath the house for a lunch break.

"I've gotta go by the Madison house," said Spikes, as he brushed the dirt from the legs of his jeans. "The renter called about a plugged drain. I'll buy you a burger at MacDonald's on the way across town. We'll fix the drain and then come back here. Figured you might like a break from working beneath the house." Spikes grinned somewhere behind his big moustache.

Ray hadn't complained but digging in a crawl space was about as bad as it got. "That's a lot better than leaving me here alone."

"Shit, didn't even think of that. It'll only take one of us to fix the drain." He laughed in his loud way as Ray's face sagged. "Just kidding, Ray. Let's get some food."

A burger, fries, and a coke provided the impetus for the second half of the day. Ray and Spikes pulled up to the two-story house where Yates had been staying. Twenty-five hundred square feet of living space on a quarter-acre lot at Madison and First, the house was Spikes' most valuable property. He had recently repainted it inside and out and re-carpeted the downstairs because the previous renter's cat—pets were not allowed—had so thoroughly marked it.

Only a week had passed since the new renter had moved in. Getting a repair call from a house that should be functioning perfectly had a bad feel to it. Spikes approached the front door slowly. He looked back at Ray standing out on the sidewalk then knocked. A large bearded man in the blue jean vest of a Gypsy Joker opened the door.

"What'd ya want?" the man asked with no effort at civility.

"I'm Jack Spikes, the landlord. I got a call this morning about a plumbing problem. I'd like to take care of it." Spikes could see a Harley Davidson motorcycle parked in the center of the living room on a canvas tarp. Two other bikers sat on the floor beside it with a six pack of beer. They appeared to be taking the bike apart. "Is Karen here?"

"No, she's at work." The man came out onto the porch and looked around as though he expected someone else. He stared at Ray for an extended moment. Ray recognized the man as Mike the biker he'd seen in Max's Tavern two weeks earlier.

"Who's that guy?" the biker asked.

"My helper," said Spikes, not happy about the inquisition nor the Harley on the new carpeting.

"Alright, come on in. It's the toilet in the downstairs bathroom."

Spikes turned to Ray with an exasperated look and followed the huge biker into the house. The bathroom that Spikes had cleaned a week earlier stunk of shit and urine. Wet towels lay on the floor and draped over the side of the tub. The toilet was filled to the brim with brown fluid and wads of toilet paper.

Spikes looked at Mike. "You try a plunger?"

"Karen doesn't have one."

Spikes nodded. "I've got one in the truck."

Spikes thudded out of the house. When he reached Ray, his face had turned purple with rage. "Take the plunger in there and unplug the toilet."

"That's all it is?"

Spikes wanted to scream. "Just do it." He got in the cab and waited for Ray to return. Ray came out of the house ten minutes later and threw the plunger in the back of the truck. When he climbed into the cab, Spikes turned on him. "There's a place in the tool box for the plunger—not haphazardly thrown in the back."

"Not that plunger. After what I just cleaned out, I think we need a new one. That was disgusting. Going beneath the house on Eighteenth is going to be a step up."

Spikes was angry enough to snap back at Ray, but he'd made him do the dirty work, and he let it go. He started the truck and pulled away from the curb. Two blocks from the house, Spikes screamed, "Mother fuck," out the window at the top of his lungs. Then to Ray with an underlying seethe. "That woman has a Gypsy fucking Joker for a boyfriend. Nothing could be worse. I don't believe it. Three fucking grown men in that house, and they called me to use a plumber's helper! Jesus Christ." He shook his fist in exasperation. "And did you see that!" He pounded on the steering wheel. "A motorcycle in the living room! On my new rug! Fuck!"

Ray understood the frustration. Bikers as renters were like an infestation of giant rats. "What can you do?"

Spikes glared at him. "As long as they pay the rent on time, I'll swallow it. But once they're overdue, I'll be finding a way to get them out."

Good luck, Ray thought to himself.

No one could deny the influence of the drug culture on life in Eugene. As in many cities of the 1970s, two drug worlds existed. One world, essentially the counterculture, preferred soft drugs—marijuana, hashish, mushrooms, peyote, and other hallucinogens. The other world, bikers and other low-lifes, liked hard drugs—meth, heroin, cocaine, and all variety of prescription narcotics. If one dared to generalize, it appeared one world was intent on trying to expand its consciousness, while the other was trying to eliminate it. Of course, there was overlap. That's where the hippie world met the biker world, more often than not to exchange money for drugs in the alleys behind the bars and taverns of Eugene or the neighboring city of Springfield. Beer served as the universal solvent, and on a good night bikers and hippies and rednecks fired them down standing side by side at a bar. On a bad night, fights broke out.

The Gypsy Jokers motorcycle club dominated the western Oregon outlaw biker scene. Eugene was not special to them in any way except the Merry Prankster LSD connection. But the recent emergence of an anti-war splinter group among the Jokers added a new complexity to the crossover of bikers and peace freaks. Most of the bikers were hugely patriotic and supported the war, but a good portion of them had been to Vietnam and now stood united against it. Mike Rogers was a vet and the leader of this growing splinter group. This was the issue behind the biker standoff in Max's two weeks earlier. Many of the local bikers, especially the rival gang the Free Souls, were angered by Mike's effort to bring anti war politics into the Oregon motorcycle community—and it made Mike a target.

CHAPTER 30

Three weeks after the FBI arrived, it became clear that the five people at the top of its list of suspects were Rebop Rodriguez, Tim O'Malley, Dave Berman, Sue Hoffman, and Arthur Kotke. As far as anyone knew, Arthur had left Eugene five months earlier, but the other four were highly visible leaders in the counterculture community. They were either interviewed or watched or both. Rebop asked the other three to meet her at Max's Tavern, warning them to be wary of being followed.

They gathered in a booth at the back of Max's Tuesday night. Dave, Sue, and Tim split a pitcher of beer. Rebop drank coffee. She opened the conversation. "Has anyone got a lead on the bomber? We need to know who did it."

"I've got nothing," said Tim, rolling a smoke. "But all I've done is ask folks. Been too busy to do any real detective work. Dave, Sue, you seen or heard anything?"

Sue shook her head no.

"Same for me," said Dave, "and I've really quizzed the folks I know. Any word on Stoopid, Tim?"

"Still in intensive care. Hanging on by a thread. Just thinking about it makes me angry."

"Could it have been a provocateur?" asked Sue.

Tim lit his smoke and exhaled. "That's what I'm beginning to think. Someone's trying to fuck with us."

"All too possible," said Dave. 'What's this about being followed, Rebop? Is this something you've experienced?"

"That's the other reason I asked you to come here. There are two men in Eugene that Tim and I have had our eyes on. After three weeks of watching them, I've concluded," she glanced at Tim, "and so has Tim, that they're undercover FBI agents."

"Wow! That's creepy," said Sue.

"No kidding," said Rebop, "that's why you needed to know."

"How do you know their FBI?" asked Dave.

"We don't know for sure, but the Feds are definitely in Eugene," said Rebop. "And they're likely to have brought some of their people to work undercover."

Tim bobbed his head in agreement.

"I've managed to take a couple photos of these guys." Rebop withdrew two Polaroids from her jacket and put them on the table.

Dave and Sue took turns looking at the photos. They both said they had seen the two men in town.

"Could they be the provocateurs?" asked Dave.

"It's possible," said Tim. "Maybe that's something we need to explore."

Rebop nodded.

"This is bad." Dave, now in enhanced paranoid mode, scanned the tavern. "I don't much like being watched."

"Yeah, this scares me," said Sue.

"It's scares all of us," said Rebop. "I'm thinking it's time to tell the entire community who they are and to watch out."

"We could get *The Augur* to put those photos on the cover of the next issue. That would do it," said Sue. "Maybe they'd leave."

"No," said Tim, taking a swallow of beer. "I think we should find a way to get the information out without letting them know we're on to them. That way we can use them instead of them using us."

The others didn't seem to understand.

"I've been thinking about this a while." Tim took a pull from his smoke and exhaled. "I say we assemble an army of look-alikes."

"What do you mean?" asked Rebop.

"We get a bunch of tall thin guys and get them to dress like me. And we do the same with Sue and Dave. Rebop, you'll be a harder match than the others. But we can give it a try. We send our look-alikes out onto the street, and from a distance the Feds won't be able to tell them apart. We'll lead them around in circles."

"Just to fuck with them?"

"Yeah, like Jerry Rubin and the Yippies," laughed Tim. "Make them look like fools. It's better than throwing firebombs."

"Maybe that's a way to get into their heads," added Sue. "Maybe even get an insight into this provocateur thing."

Tim bobbed his head. "Exactly."

Contrary to what the two agents believed, they had not successfully infiltrated the Eugene counterculture. Within days of the meeting in Max's, the entire street community knew who they were and began to act as one, taking every opportunity to send the agents on one wild goose chase after another. This evolved into a kind of sport for some folks on the street, Tim particularly. He knew he was one of their primary targets and that they were following him on a regular basis. He took them anywhere he pleased just for the fun of it. The only problem with the plan was that Gino, who had traded acid to the agents for a bicycle frame, was one of the last people on the street to discover who the agents were.

CHAPTER 31

Not surprisingly, the first issue to arise at Blake College—in the age of "free sex"—was sex. Some of it was the open nudity. Adrienne, Rain, and Tai seemed to believe modesty was below them. They weren't exhibitionists, but they didn't always close the door when they showered or cover themselves with a towel on the way back to their rooms. Gloria and Crow paid it no mind. Ray, who was there four or five nights a week, tried to ignore it, and Van and Marsha found it intrusive and felt an undercurrent of peer pressure, real or imagined, to do the same. For Janice, however, it was a challenge. She wanted to overcome her own self-consciousness for being slightly plump. Uncomfortable situations arose regularly in the first month of school, but in Rain's opinion, this was all part of the education provided by Blake College, learning to accept the human body.

One night, after midnight, Ray and Adrienne, sleeping side by side, were awakened by the sound of Rain and Tai making love on the other side of the bedroom wall. Rain tended to outbursts of pleasure at climactic moments, and Tai made his own ecstatic grunts and groans. At first, Adrienne and Ray just looked at each other and giggled as they listened to the neighboring couple frantically humping. But it went on and on, ten minutes steady.

"Wow, how can they do that?" whispered Adrienne after the sounds had finally faded into silence. "We never last that long."

Though Adrienne was not being critical, Ray heard it that way. Nothing else was said and they fell asleep.

A few days later, on an unusually warm and sunny October afternoon, Ray, off work a bit early, rode his bike to Blake College. When he didn't find Adrienne in the house, he ventured into the backyard. He found her in the garden in her usual sunny day attire. Joining her in the garden, however, was Tai, also wearing nothing but rubber boots and gloves. Ray observed this from afar without saying anything, then walked away unnoticed.

That night, when Adrienne and Ray slipped into bed, Ray lay there with his hands behind his head, staring at the ceiling. Adrienne snuggled up to him, but Ray didn't snuggle back. Adrienne pushed herself up on one elbow. "What are you thinking about?"

"Nothing."

"I know you better than that, Ray. What is it?"

Ray took a deep breath then let it out dramatically. "You know when you work out there in the garden?"

"Yeah."

"I think you should at least wear shorts or something."

Adrienne sat up. "Really?"

"Yeah. There are older men living here, and you're squatting there for all to see. It's a bad idea." That he didn't like Tai and his pretense about sacred drugs only added to his jealousy.

Adrienne's first impulse was to get mad, then she remembered she'd been out in the garden with Tai that day. She didn't know Ray had seen them, but her intuition was screaming that he had. It was nothing to her. They were out there working. Nothing more. Yes, Tai whispered to her that she had the nicest ass in the house. So what? Every woman there knew Tai made those kinds of comments. Yeah, she had looked at his penis a couple times. It was hard not to. Big deal. Human anatomy. She liked Ray for being Ray, not for his body parts. He was a hard worker just like she was. "Nudity is nothing, Ray. We're all trying to get beyond that." She slid up close to him.

"I want you to wear shorts when you're out there from now on."

Again, Adrienne did not like this, but she told herself relationships involve compromise. "When Crow or Tai are out there, okay. Fine." She got up on one elbow. "But otherwise, I'll do what I want. It feels good to be naked."

If he'd only admit it, Ray loved Adrienne for this part of her, her rebelliousness and need for freedom. But attachment can change things, and he had been badly steamed seeing her naked with Tai. "Fair enough," he muttered, then rolled over and kissed her. "Forgive me for bringing this up. I love you."

One thing Adrienne had made a point of during the short time she had known Ray was never to tell him she loved him. That was just a quirk with her. He'd said it to her several times, always very seriously, but she had never responded with the same. On this night, she changed that. "I love you, too, Ray."

Of course, Ray didn't miss this. And it immediately made him feel better.

Janice had a different take. She had been drawn to the lifestyle of the street and aspired to be hip and cool like Adrienne and Rain. She wanted to stroll down the hall naked as though it were nothing. It was something new and daring to her. Yes, she wore her short shorts and her tight T-shirts, but nudity was something else, and she wanted the kind of confidence in her body that she saw in the others.

The first time she ventured naked from the bathroom was a big deal. She planned it so that innocent Van would be the first to see her. She knew Van was downstairs and would soon be returning to his bedroom. After her morning shower, she hovered naked in the bathroom doorway, waiting for Van to come upstairs, and appraised herself in the mirror. Being a platinum-blond, she had almost no body hair except a dash of blond above her vagina. She knew she had fabulous tits for her age. She turned sideways to the mirror. They stood straight out with nipples shaped like pink Hersey's kisses, but her rear was round and well pronounced—and she wasn't sure if it was fat or sexy.

When she heard Van at the top of the stairs, she grabbed her towel, and holding it in one hand by her side, strolled right past Van. Van did his best not to look directly at her, but he did turn around as she passed—at the same time Janice looked over her shoulder to see if he would.

Nothing could have pleased her more except what happened two days later. She performed the same premeditated naked parade for Tai. She'd had sex with three men in her life. A couple of times with a boy in high school, once against her will with her older brother when she was thirteen, and a few times recently in Gino's panel truck. But she wanted handsome Tai as a conquest and had decided to go after him. One parade was all it took. Tai told her she had the nicest body in the house. She slipped into the shower with him two days later, beginning a secret affair.

Rain knew what kind of man Tai was—smart, good looking, nice body, very hip, big ego. She had known other men like Tai, but she had confidence in herself and felt she could deal with him. She had other male friends and could flirt just as Tai did, but she didn't sleep around like she suspected he might.

Rain went into town after lunch one day for grocery shopping. She took Tai's van. When she returned at three that afternoon, she walked in on Tai and Janice going at it doggie-style in her bed.

"Don't stop for me," she said as though it were nothing. She got what she wanted, and on leaving said, "Next time, Tai, not in my bed." There was no anger in voice. It was just a reasonable request.

But when Rain got downstairs, she started crying. That night, lying in bed, she confronted Tai. "She's a girl, Tai. Just a baby with a big round bottom. How could you do that?"

"You've seen her, Rain. She's been spending more time naked in the hallway than all the rest of us put together." He smiled. "Don't blame me. She knows what she wants. She sought me out. Plus she's got great tits."

"Fuck you," snapped Rain uncharacteristically. "She's barely god damn seventeen! Find another bedroom if it's tits you're after." Lithe Rain had little more than nipples for breasts.

Tai got the message loud and clear. He grabbed his pillow and took to sleeping in a corner of the basement that he curtained off into a tent-like room.

A couple of nights later, Gloria and Van made spinach lasagna with a big salad and two loafs of fresh-baked, whole wheat bread. Everyone, not counting Ray who wasn't expected and Janice who was, had been served. The chowing down was well underway when Janice came through the front door after hitching a ride from downtown to get there.

She said nothing and sat down at the table in a huff. She tore a big piece of bread from the loaf and reached past Adrienne to get the butter. Being on time was not imperative at Blake College. A certain amount of leeway was granted on just about everything—except work details, but Rain commented anyway. "Glad you could make it, Janice."

Janice knew what Rain had said to Tai about her. She looked directly at the older woman. "Why's that? I thought you might be pleased if I didn't show at all."

Tai was the only one who understood what was behind the tension. "Be cool, ladies."

Adrienne glanced around the table. "What's going on?" Everyone knew Tai had moved into the basement and now the reason was becoming obvious.

"She's just jealous," snapped Janice.

"Fuck you, you little slit. Why would I be jealous of you?"

Janice smiled sweetly. "You tell me." She was dying to let everyone know that she had stolen Tai from Queen Bee Rain.

Rain puffed up with anger. Before she could say anything, Gloria interceded. "Okay. What's this about? We're all at the table. Let's get it out in the open. That's part of why we're here. Learning to talk about our differences."

"Ain't no differences anymore," said Janice.

"What's that mean, Janice?" asked Gloria. "What's going on?"

Rain didn't want to talk about it. She'd been hurt and wasn't used to it.

Janice beamed. "Rain's up tight because she doesn't think I'm old enough to fuck on my own."

Tai looked down at his plate. Rain found her voice. "An adult man cannot have sex in Oregon with a girl under eighteen. It's called statutory rape."

"It wasn't rape, Rain. I wanted it. Besides, I thought this was Blake College. Ordinary rules don't apply," she grinned ugly.

"Fuck you."

"No, I fucked Tai," Janice snapped back.

"Wait, wait," said Gloria, holding up her hands. "If we're going to live together, we have to be civil, even if there's good reason not to be. How old are you, Janice? Your application says seventeen. Is that right?"

"What difference does it make? I'm my own woman. I can put my pussy anywhere I want."

Rain was seething. "I want this girl out of here, now. She's too immature for what we're trying to do."

"And *she's* too jealous."

"Cork it, Janice," said Crow, sitting to her left. "We've got a problem to work out." Crow, who was part Black African and part Seminole Indian, had attained a high level of respect in the group and his word meant something to everyone—even Janice. "We're here trying to do this free thing, and it sounds like someone got a little too free."

After a long, uneasy silence, Gloria asked, "Rain, what kind of commitment has Tai given to you?"

Rain looked at the ceiling. "None. It's my fault. He can do whatever he wants."

Janice started to speak. Crow put his hand on her shoulder. "Only if it's constructive, little lady. We need to learn how to talk this out. Insults and name calling don't help."

"Tai and I have a thing going. And my age doesn't matter. I'm in love with him."

"And what's your commitment to Janice, Tai?" asked Gloria.

Tai didn't want to be there. "None," he said angrily. "It was my mistake. She's not eighteen. I'm the adult. I should have told her it was wrong."

Janice burst into tears.

"What?" Rain shook her head. "Now she's the one that's hurt."

"Eat me, bitch," spat Janice, who suddenly stood from the table and ran upstairs to her room. Gloria looked around at everyone, then got up and went after her.

Gloria found Janice lying on her bed—a mattress on the floor—with her face in the pillow, sobbing. She knelt beside Janice. "Can we talk?"

Janice turned her head and glared up at Gloria with eyes of fire, then buried her head again.

"I understand, Janice. It's your body and you want to own it. But you can't just go around fucking as you please. There's something more to it. I can sum it up in two sentences."

Janice turned her head to look at Gloria. She'd never heard her say *fucking* before.

"First, there's a state law that prohibits men from having sex with women under eighteen—unless they're married. It's called statutory rape. Tai could be imprisoned for it.

"Second, the act of intercourse has the clear potential for creating another human being. When you have sex, you must do it with full responsibility for the outcome and know that your partner has committed to the same."

The heat in Janice's eyes began to recede. Gloria was leveling with her in a very real way.

"The way you've been acting since you arrived at the school does not reflect a mature woman. You've got an attitude and a lot of anger. Let's work on changing that."

Janice sat up. She knew Gloria was right.

Gloria nodded slowly acknowledging the connection. "I think you're a beautiful young woman, smarter than most believe. And you've come here to get away from your family. Probably for a good reason. As the oldest woman in this house that we share, I believe it's my duty to give you all of myself that I possibly can. I mean that."

Janice compressed her lips, holding on to her emotions.

"I've noticed that you've been influenced by the other women in the house. Rain and Adrienne are very immodest. There's an appealing confidence in that. You've been experimenting with this."

Janice gave her a sheepish look.

"Yes, everyone has noticed." Gloria smiled easily.

Janice looked down at her hands.

"You needed to do that. But engaging with Tai. That's different. Maybe you learned something. Who knows? But he's not the sort to commit to anyone at this point in his life. I think Rain just learned that." Gloria leaned in close and hugged Janice. Janice hugged her back. "I think we all need to get beyond this," she whispered over Janice's shoulder. "Tai is not for you."

After Gloria and Janice had left the table, nothing was said for quite a while. Rain was clearly upset, and Tai was sitting in a pile of his own making. No one was too happy. Van was the first one to speak up. "The day I arrived I happened upon Adrienne in the backyard, gardening without clothes on. My experience is not so great, and, if you'll excuse me for saying this Adrienne, you are very pretty and I was aroused."

Van was not a big talker, and everyone was surprised that he should suddenly open up in this way.

"I have never lived with people other than my family," he continued. "And I have really enjoyed this experience. It's been good for me, but I wish there were a little more modesty, not for your sake, but for mine—and Marsha's. And when you're having sex, at least close the door and be aware that anyone upstairs can hear you."

Both Rain and Adrienne glanced at each other, realizing there was more than one way to think about nudity, especially in a school setting.

Marsha followed. "I don't know about Van, but I admire you all for being so open and free. I have nothing against it, but it almost feels like a rite of passage here—and I'm not there yet."

Again, the truth of what she was saying sank it. Step by step, they were all learning what it meant to live together.

CHAPTER 32

The second issue to come up at Blake College, again not surprisingly, was drug use. Tai was the leading culprit. Every evening after the meal he would pull a joint from his pocket, light it, and passed it around. Because it could stimulate conservation, it became a regular routine, even though Gloria and Van did not partake—Gloria because she didn't want the smoke in her lungs, Van because he knew it was illegal and wanted to obey the law.

There was an unwritten rule in the house against hard drugs of any kind—speed, heroin, or cocaine. But pot was everywhere in Eugene and Tai explored hallucinogens in his shamanism class as part of the curriculum at Blake College. One weekday morning after a night of rain in mid-October, Tai had everyone—except Ray who was at work—pile into his van. Rain then directed them out to a cow pasture west of Eugene where the popular liberty cap mushrooms grew. They contained psilocybin and were a relatively mild hallucinogen. Tai felt they were a good introduction to the psychedelic high, and that the experience of locating them was part of the teaching.

"I know people who have found artifacts from the Kalapuya Indians in this field," said Rain, as they spilled out of the van at the edge of the field. "They think it might have been a ceremonial site. So, while you're looking for mushrooms, keep an eye out for pieces of broken pottery or obsidian arrowheads. It adds to the fun."

With Tai experienced at identifying the proper fungi, they had little trouble collecting a good number of the little 'shrooms. It was the first time for Marsha and Janice; they ate five. Adrienne, Crow, and Rain had all done them before—they had ten each. Gloria and Van didn't eat any, and Tai ate twenty. No one found any artifacts.

Afterward, Tai suggested that Van drive them all forty miles farther west to the Oregon coast to watch the sun set. When they got to the ocean, Crow and Gloria drew a giant flying saucer in the sand. Rain, Adrienne, and Marsha lay on their backs and made snow angels in the sand that looked to be flying around the saucer. Janice added a parade of little spacemen.

After watching the sun set in brilliant oranges and somber purples, Tai built a huge bonfire. They sat around the fire until it burned out. They didn't get back to Eugene until four in the morning. Instead of going to bed, they stayed up and made buckwheat pancakes from buckwheat they'd wild crafted on an earlier field trip with Rain.

Later in the day, Van found Marsha laying out the mushroom harvest on drying screens in the greenhouse.

"What did you think of the mushrooms, Marsha?"

"I enjoyed them. Not so strong like Tai said. But I definitely felt them. I almost took my clothes off on the beach." She laughed at her admission. "I couldn't have been too high. I decided against it." She laughed again.

"I wish you had."

Marsha blushed, then grinned. "Then you would have had to!"

Van chuckled. "No, I wasn't eating mushrooms."

Marsha filled one screen and got a second. "I liked the way it made me think. Like everything was connected. That was the most profound thought I had during the entire trip."

They stood side by side, between them a clear plastic bag of the root beer colored mushrooms. Van took a handful from the bag and began laying them on the screen with Marsha.

"I liked the sunset best," said Marsha. "Silly as it might sound, I think that was the most beautiful sunset I've ever seen."

"Maybe they all look like that on the Oregon coast."

"Each one different but each the most beautiful."

They both laughed.

Neither of them said anything for some time while they continued to sort through the fungi, looking for worms and picking out blades of grass. Out of the blue Marsha turned to Van. "I feel more comfortable with you, Van, than any boy I've ever met."

Now Van blushed and lowered his eyes. "I feel the same way about you." They already knew they liked each other, but they hadn't said it aloud. "Maybe it's this crazy school."

"No," Marsha said seriously. "I think it's us." And she kissed him on the cheek.

Tai was determined to get Van to try pot and maybe later some mushrooms. Every evening when he produced a joint of his latest exotic herb, he would prod Van into trying at least one hit. This had gone on nearly every night since Van arrived.

One night when the joint reached Van, Tai repeated his standard barb. "Come on, Van, be a man, take a toke."

Joint in hand, Van spoke firmly, "I don't appreciate the pressure you've put on me to smoke this stuff, Tai. Be a man. What does that have to do with smoking pot?"

Everyone at the table knew Van was right. Ray, who was there that night, couldn't hide his smirk.

Tai shook his head and shrugged. "Just jivin' you, man. Lighten up. Of course, it has no relationship to being a man."

Van passed the joint to Adrienne. "If Blake College is the free school you all profess it to be, then much like the nudity issue, I should be free to do as I like in the same spirit that you do. There is a freedom to choose not to do things as well as a freedom to choose to do things. I've been at Blake almost two months now, and I've really enjoyed my time here. For the most part this experiment in education has been just what you've said it would be." He looked to Rain and Adrienne. "But this steady push to get me stoned is not in the true spirit of the school."

Crow applauded softly at Van's honesty. Gloria nodded in agreement.

Tai just grinned stoned-stupid and said, "My apologies." He took the joint from Adrienne and dramatically took a big hit.

When the joint came to Van the second time around, he did an about face and took a hit. He exhaled a cloud of smoke then coughed. No one said anything, and he passed it to Adrienne. Van only took that one hit, and as often happened on the first time with marijuana, he confessed to Marsha later that he hadn't felt anything.

The following night, he took three hits. He got very silly and spoke more than he had at any other gathering. After nightfall, he walked down to the river with Marsha.

"I appreciate your courage in front of the others," Marsha said, as they sat on the bank, watching the Willamette flow by in the moonlight. "You've said things that I was thinking but was afraid to bring up."

Van smiled. "That's nice of you to say." He and Marsha were arguably the two most intellectually gifted people in the house. Marsha had been a merit scholar. Van had come close to a perfect score on the SAT tests.

Van gave her a kiss on the cheek. She kissed him on the mouth. They embraced, then made out for an hour, never removing their clothes. When they walked back to the house, they held hands. Their innocence seemed entirely out of place in the atmosphere of freedom at Blake College.

CHAPTER 33

The counterculture had fixed on co-ops as an answer to what was considered the aggressive, and to some immoral, methods of capitalism. The idea that workers should own their business, share equally in the work, and share equally in the profits rang true to the young people who had decided to turn on, tune in, and drop out. There was a better world awaitin' and it wasn't in the sky. It was right here on Earth!

The attachment to co-ops came out of San Francisco and drifted up the Interstate to Eugene and Portland and Seattle. In Eugene, it began with food buying clubs. If the idea was to live simply with less, that meant less money, and while spending money on food was unavoidable, getting better deals on that food by buying in bulk as part of a group could cut food bills dramatically. The larger the group the cheaper the food. This logic spawned a new entity in Eugene, the neighborhood food co-op.

In one neighborhood south of the university, a young couple, Pat Riley and his wife Laurel, decided to turn their house into a cooperative grocery to serve their neighborhood. They lived on the second floor, the store was on the first floor, and storage was in the basement. Pat worked fulltime as co-op manager and took only enough pay to make ends meet. All the other members, including Laurel, were required to volunteer at least two hours a week for the right to shop at the grocery, which at first only stocked bulk dry goods. Gradually, due to Pat's energy and initiative, the store diversified beyond dry goods into local organic fruits and vegetables, various cooking oils, juices, honey, herbs, and just about any food item that could be bought in bulk regionally and stored without too much extra effort.

Barrels of dry goods were lined up against one wall on the first floor. Two sets of scales were on an adjacent counter. A member would come in with his or her own container or bag, weigh it, then fill it with whatever was needed. After subtracting the weight of the container, they could pay for the product in cash or take a debit on their account. Another wall contained bins of vegetables and fruit. Four refrigerators in the kitchen served as cold storage, and the basement was reserved for surplus dry goods.

The co-op not only saved money for its members, but because the members often worked and shopped together, it also fostered closer relationships in the neighborhood. This was the stuff of real community. Over time, similar co-ops sprang up in many of the neighborhoods in Eugene. Gradually these individual co-ops began working with each other to create what became the most enduring network in the alternative community of Eugene—organic food distribution.

The risk of using illegal drugs was one bond among those in the counterculture, but many of the back-to-nature hippies didn't really care about drugs. They cared about good clean food, simple living, and in many cases, Christian ethics. Pat Riley fell into this later group. He was a long-hair dedicated to the concept of neighborhood unity because of his Christian ideals. He wasn't one to quote from the Bible or mention his beliefs at all, but he went out of his way to help the other co-ops get up and running because it was the right thing to do. Much like Tim O'Malley, but without the drugs, Pat focused his energy on making the alternative approach to life work in Eugene.

On a rainy morning, a week after his meeting at Max's with Dave, Rebop, and Sue, Tim parked his Indian motorcycle at the curb in front of the Southeast Eugene Neighborhood Co-op. Pat Riley was unloading boxes of fresh produce into the display bins when Tim walked in dripping from the rain. Pat immediately smiled. Tim and Pat were friends, not close because of Tim's wild side, but certainly both comrades in the quest for an alternative world.

"What brings you in here, Mr. O'Malley?" Pat was tall and lanky like Tim and prone to dry humor. "If you're trying to drum up some printing business, you've come to the wrong place."

Tim grinned at his friend. "No printing today. Just need a little favor." Tim had a large, brown paper bag in his hand.

"What's that? Deliver weed? No thanks, O'Malley, I've got work to do."

"I think you owe me one, Pat."

Pat looked up. "Doubtful. But alright. Out with it. What do I have to say no to?"

"We've got a little who-haw brewing downtown."

"Who-haw?"

"The FBI has two undercover agents in town, trying to find out who bombed Campbell Hall. They've been following me around for a month. They seem to think I had something to do with it."

"Did you?"

"Damn, Patrick, no! I'm just a printer, not an arsonist. More importantly, nobody I know in this community knows a thing about it. Not the SDS. Not the people in the street. No one. But the FBI thinks it's us freaks—and is pointing at me."

"So, what's this favor you're asking? Does it involve a federal offense?"

Tim grinned. "Not if dressing like someone else is a crime."

"What?"

Tim lifted the bag. "I want you to wear these clothes a couple of days a week."

Pat took the bag and looked in. He frowned, then lifted out a black vest, a pair of black Carhartt's, a pair of red converse high tops, and last—Pat dangled it above the bag—an antique leather motorcycle helmet. "Are you shitting me"—shit was the one four-letter word Pat would use—"you want me to dress like you?" Pat retrieved a dime-store sheriff's badge from the bottom of the bag. "Really?"

"You might look good for once."

Pat looked down at the stained grocer's apron he wore over his khaki chinos and laughed. "So I'll be a decoy?" His eyes rose to the heavens—with the full intimation of what that might mean.

"Just to put the Feds off track." Tim bobbed his head. "And you won't be the only one. I've got enough leather headgear for two others."

Pat was conservative in his person but not in his politics. He was hip in the downdest way. He was solidly anti-war and anti-capitalism and felt there was nothing better than getting free of the system—with special emphasis on getting free of the chemical laden, industrial food system. "When do you want me to do this?"

"Any time you feel like it. Go anywhere you would normally go."

"Is there any chance I might get shot?"

Tim grinned. "Looking like me is a risk, yes—but the red shoes will protect you."

"You mean, if they shoot me in the foot." Pat laughed. "Fine, Tim. I'll do this, but you owe me big time."

"No," Tim said, "with this, we'll be even."

"Get out of here, O'Malley."

CHAPTER 34

Two men were setting posts for livestock fencing at the back of a small valley west of Eugene. The fall rain had begun in a big way. The men had been at it for six hours now, and it had been raining off and on for a week. One of the men, Maynard Smith, was at the wheel of a tractor. The other, Maynard's hired hand Thomas, stood at the top of a slight but steep hill where they wanted to drill the next posthole. Attached to the back of the tractor was a drilling rig that could cut through the wet ground as though it were tub margarine. Maynard had to maneuver the tractor in reverse up the grade to set the drill. It was a short climb, no more than twenty yards, but it was muddy and slick, and he'd failed at it once already.

Maynard gave the John Deere a little gas and went at it from thirty yards away, trying to hit the hill with some momentum. As soon as he reached the grade, the tires began to rip and tear at the sod. The green and yellow tractor bucked and slid this way and that, throwing chunks of grass and mud all over Thomas, who was trying to direct Maynard into position. With a lot of effort and even more spent diesel, Maynard inched to the brink of the hill. The tractor held a few moments, then slid slowly back down the grade.

After another attempt with the same result, Maynard let the tractor come to rest at the bottom of the slope. He cut the growling motor. It answered with a backfire and a puff of smoke. Thomas slipped down the grade and tramped over to the tractor. Maynard climbed out of the rig and stood next to his hired hand. Both were wearing full suits of olive green raingear and black rubber boots with red neoprene soles. Both were soaked inside and out. For several minutes, neither of them said a word.

Of the two, Thomas, his hood cinched tight around his face and spattered from head to toe with field muck, looked the worse. With a black Oregon State Beavers ball cap pulled down tight on his head, Maynard just looked fiercely determined. His silence was a building one. Thomas attempted a few words of solace, "At least it ain't cold like it could be, Maynard."

Maynard wiped his face with a soaking wet, red paisley handkerchief and stared hard at the other man, saying nothing because he didn't want to curse. He had lived on this farm since he was fifteen, when his family left the dust bowl forty years ago. His baby sister died during the move, his mother sixteen years later. He and his father hung on to homestead eight hundred acres out of the raw Oregon wilderness. Only in the last few years did Maynard feel that the job was near complete. It could seem so bitterly ironic at times like these when it rained for days on end. The old place in Kansas had fallen victim to dust storms. His father, who died eight years back, had decided on this part of the country because of the certainty of rain.

Maynard couldn't really complain though. With several hundred sheep, a sizable herd of dairy cows, a big hen house, and an organic dairy that his daughter and her husband ran, Maynard's job was primarily maintenance. But it wasn't easy. He worked a lot harder than most and got less for it.

The sternness of the life made him tough, stubborn, and religious in the way a lot of farmers are. He believed in cold hard honesty and faith in the land. His satisfaction came from day-to-day progress on the farm. It was a simple, good life, and most of his problems were like the one before him now.

"Maybe we got a chance here," Maynard said after a few minutes of silence. Sometimes it seemed that he spoke as little as possible. "Take the end of the tow line up there and wrap it good around that fat Doug fir."

Pretty soon Maynard had put his scheme together. It was something he'd done before. A winch on the back of the tractor powered the drill and was fitted with a reel of metal cable and a hook. Thomas anchored the cable to the fir tree, and Maynard used the winch in conjunction with the tractor engine to get the vehicle up the slope.

It took some doing, but Maynard got the tractor to the top of the hill. Thomas secured it with the cable and freed up the winch to use the drill. The first time they tried lowering the drill, the tractor bucked left, then right, broke the cable loose and slid down the hill half-sideways. They were at it again immediately. The second time the drill bit into the wet ground. A minute later, the hole was done. They unhitched the cable, and Maynard let the tractor slide down the hill. Hard or easy, this was the way everything was done on the farm—one muddy step at a time.

Because Maynard wanted these fences to last, he was using some big posts he'd cut from the forest and prepared with creosote. When the posts were wet—like today—it took both men to lift one and drop it into place. Maynard struggled, slipping and sliding, back up the grade to help with the post.

By the time Maynard reached the hole, Thomas was watching it fill with water. He waited for Maynard to appreciate this. "You know, Maynard, this rain holds up much longer, we'll be wastin' our time with these posts."

Maynard didn't say anything. After working in this climate all his life, he hated to stop because of the rain. He'd invariably go at it until it sucked him in up to the armpits, then he'd pull himself out with a come along and spend the next couple of days in the barn working on machinery. He looked down the line of forest that separated his eight hundred acres from the five thousand owned by his not-so-friendly neighbor Walt Arnold, a lumber magnate, who farmed Christmas trees on the side. Some two hundred more posts needed to be set. Maynard sensed that Thomas wanted to take a break, at least until the rain let up. But Maynard had no intention of stopping now. Another week or so and they'd be done for the winter. Every day they delayed, it was only that much more likely to rain the next. He took his position on the post and Thomas did the same. They strained to lift it, then dropped it into the hole, forcing the water out with a thick sucking sound. Nothing else was said about the weather.

After the post was packed with gravel and set snugly in place, the two men slipped down the hill to the tractor, prepared to move on to the next posthole. Before Maynard climbed onto the tractor, Thomas spoke up, "Hate to say it, Maynard, but I saw a bunch of kids in that field by the bog yesterday."

Maynard's eyes narrowed with a distant anger then fixed on the hired hand's face. Thomas nodded his head to the understood question. Maynard stared off into the shifting curtains of rain. "God damn mushrooms." Maynard did not like to use the Lord's name in vain, but with this news he did.

CHAPTER 35

On the same day Maynard Smith was drilling postholes, Gino brought Patrick Ball and Chris Mathers up to the print shop to buy acid from Tim. Gino didn't knock; he just opened the door, and the two FBI agents followed him into the shop. "Hey, man, got that acid?"

Tim was crawling around on the floor next to one of his presses, looking for a lit joint he'd dropped. He climbed to his feet with the thing pinched between his fingers and took a hit. He handed it to Gino then realized who was with him.

Gino passed the roach to Ball. He took a tiny puff, then passed it to Mathers, who did the same, and returned it to Tim, who was none too happy with Gino and trying to hide it.

"Well," asked Gino, "you got the LSD? These guys have the cash."

Ball took four folded twenties out of his flannel shirt's breast pocket. "Right here."

"Too bad, guys." Tim took a hit off the joint and handed it to Gino. "I don't have it. Someone else beat you to it."

"Fuck, Tim," muttered Gino. "I told you I had it sold."

Tim shrugged. "Bird in the hand's worth two in the bush."

"What?" Gino shook his head stunned that Tim had done this. "Can we get some more?"

"Not that I know of. It was just a freak that I had it."

Gino didn't get it. He took a hit from the diminishing joint and offered it to Ball, who intentionally dropped it on the floor during the pass off. "Too small to hold."

Gino picked it off the floor. "Not for me." He took another hit and smudged it out on the layout table.

"So, you've got nothing?" asked Ball.

"That's what I got. Sorry, boys. Hate to disappoint you."

Ball looked at Mathers. "Apparently we're in the wrong place. Let's get going."

Gino went out with them to apologize for not being able to complete the deal. When he returned to the print shop, he could see it in Tim's eyes.

"What?" screeched Gino. "What?"

"Those guys gone?"

"Yeah, they just rode off on their ten-speeds."

"They're undercover agents for the FBI."

Gino's eyes went big. "Says who?"

"Me. They've been on my tail for a month. I can't believe you didn't know."

"I've been trading bike parts with those guys for weeks. Why didn't you tell me?"

Tim realized it might have been his error, not Gino's. "I thought I did."

"I don't think so." Gino shook his head. "Shit, those guys led me on."

"That could have been ugly. I've got two ounces of weed in here also. Damn, that was close."

"I don't like being tricked. Maybe I got one more deal to make with those freaks."

"Stay away from them, Gino. They've got nothing we want." Tim thought a moment. "You know where they live?"

"Shit, yes, I've been over there a couple times."

"Got an address?"

"I don't know the street number, but they've got a bike repair place on Fourth Street in the Whit. Between Hayes and Garfield. You can't miss it. Why?"

"I don't know. Just a thought. Might like to turn the tables a bit—do a little spying on them."

CHAPTER 36

Spikes had two large jobs to do while also managing his ten rental properties. One was lifting the house on Eighteenth Avenue off its foundation; the other was building a foundation on the lot where the house would be placed. With the arrival of the rain, Ray and Spikes had spent the week at Eighteenth Avenue because most of the work was either inside the house or underneath it.

One of Spikes' renters, Henry Pozlowski came to the job midweek to help. Henry was a graduate student in the history department at the U of O. He had worked three summers as a plumber's assistant in upstate New York where he grew up. Now he lived in one of Spikes' rentals with his wife and baby daughter. He did odd plumbing jobs for Spikes in exchange for rent. He was there to disconnect the plumbing so Spikes could begin the process of lifting the house.

Henry turned off the water at the street, removed the two toilets and the hot water heater, then shimmied beneath the house to disconnect the water line and the waste water drain. Spikes and Ray followed him through the crawl space. The water line was easy enough. Henry took a hacksaw to the galvanized pipe and ten minutes later he disconnected it, threaded the open end, and capped it. The six-inch, cast iron waste drain was a different story. It came out of the ground near the center of the house. The pipe had a collar with an inside diameter that was slightly greater than the exterior diameter of the drain coming from the house. Forty years earlier, the builder had melted lead into the collar to secure the connection. The only way to free the drain from the sewer line was to cut the cast iron pipe or melt that lead and pull the pipes apart. Henry opted for using a propane torch to melt the lead.

Lying on their sides, Spikes and Ray used two, eight-foot, two-by-fours to lever the drain upward, while Henry, also lying on his side, heated the coupling with the torch. Because of the shortage of head space, it was difficult to see if the lead were melting, so Ray and Spikes applied steady upward pressure, knowing that at some point the two pieces of pipe would separate. It took some time.

After a lot of cursing and twice setting the flooring on fire—which Henry put out with a spray bottle he had been smart enough to bring with him under the house—Spikes and Ray finally felt the pipe give. They made one hard push and the pipes separated, draining ten inches of heated water from the six-inch pipe into Henry's face and dousing the torch. Fortunately, it wasn't hot enough to scald him, but he screamed as though it were. "Spikes, you mother fucker, you didn't say that drain still had water in it!"

"At least it didn't have a turd in it." Spikes roared with laughter.

They took a brief break to let Henry get cleaned up and to eat an early lunch. They sat on tool boxes inside the house and delved into their lunch bags. Halfway into the meal, Spikes addressed his plumber, "You're the most educated man I know, Henry. What can you tell me about learning disabilities?"

Henry cocked his head in thought. "Not a lot, Jack, but my niece back east has been diagnosed with a reading disorder. I think they're saying she's dyslexic."

"What the hell does that mean?"

"I'm no expert, but I believe it means she sees words backwards. They used to call it word blindness. It takes her hours to read a single page. My sister is worried she won't be able to keep up in school."

"How old is she?"

"Eleven. And they just figured this out after she barely passed third and fourth grades."

"What do they do for her?"

"Special classes."

"Does that cost extra?"

"If my sister hired a tutor that would cost extra, but the public schools almost always have a class for slow learners."

Slow learners. The words hurt as Spikes thought about Joey.

"Why do you ask?"

"Got a friend with a child who's having trouble in school," said Spikes. "I was just looking for insights."

Ray had seen enough at Sheila's to know it was Joey.

"Well, there's more than one kind of learning disability. It can be physical, like my niece, or emotional. It's a tough thing to deal with."

"I figured." Spikes finished his sandwich with one big bite and stood up. "Let's get back to it."

Henry stayed on the job the rest of the day to help Spikes and Ray finish placing the jacks beneath the house. To save money, Spikes had rounded up a mixed collection of twenty-four jacks—some for houses, some for cars, some hydraulic, some screw. The three men wedged two jacks beneath each of twelve, twelve-foot, four-inch by eight-inch wooden beams, situated at right angles to the floor joists, so that raising the jacks would lift the beams, and with them the entire house. This was way too many moving pieces—jacks and beams—for an efficient job, but everything Spikes did was about using what he already owned or what he could get for free. Something-for-nothing Jack's central business principle was based on money flow—*don't spend a nickel you don't have to.*

Once everything was in place, the three of them crawled around under the house, giving each jack a turn or a pump. The three men scurried around like chipmunks from one jack to the next, steadily lifting the house in half-inch increments. To keep the upward movement as even as possible, Henry used a make-shift hydraulic system—water-filled coffee cans connected by rubber tubing—to monitor and level the lift. The first day went very slowly. They lifted the house twelve of the needed twenty-four inches, then blocked it with railroad ties and called it a day.

Ray and Spikes came back early the next day to finish the job. Though they only had two people to man the jacks, they had the routine down from the day before. It was a lot of work scrambling around beneath the house, but they had completed the lift by the end of the day.

CHAPTER 37

Two days later, Tai drove his van out to the mushroom field that Rain had shown everyone as part of his class. He went alone with the specific intention of collecting as many of the mushrooms as he could and selling them in Eugene. He had recently purchased two pounds of marijuana to sell and wanted to add some variety. He drove his van a mile past the field and parked on the side of the road, then walked back to the field. He climbed over the barbed-wire fence and settled into the slow, methodical work of combing the pasture for the little liberty cap mushrooms.

Maynard Smith, who owned the field, had spent the first half of the day away from his house, setting those same fence posts. He and Thomas had been doing this for six days straight. The rain had let up and they'd made good progress. The job might be done in a couple of days if the weather held.

Maynard was feeling quite satisfied as he drove his pickup back to his house for lunch. Thomas had gone into town to eat and pick up supplies. Maynard smiled to himself as he drove. The farm was nearly ready for winter.

As he approached his driveway from the west, he noticed the brightly painted van parked on the side of the road. He slowed his pickup as he continued down the road, past the field where Thomas had spotted the mushroom pickers the previous week. The muscles in his jaw gradually tightened as he scanned the pasture. A man was in the field, on his hands and knees, picking things from the ground and putting them into a plastic bag.

"God damned mushrooms," Maynard cursed through his teeth. But he didn't stop to interfere with the long-haired man in the field. He was so angry he was afraid what he might do. Instead he mumbled to himself as he motored up the long gravel driveway to his house, completely forgetting to stop at the mail box on the way.

Maynard was hot when he entered the house. "Damn it, Ann, we got another hippie out in that field." The door bounced on its hinges behind his slam. "I've been pretty god damn lenient up to now—but this time," he gritted his teeth and angrily pondered the various measures he might take. "I don't know. Maybe I'll call the state police."

Out in the dining room, seated at the table, was the silent half of this conversation, Ann, Maynard's wife of twenty-eight years. There was nothing anyone could say when Maynard was wound up like this. That he was cursing was the giveaway. He wasn't a regular at the local church, but without much show, he tried to live by the Ten Commandments. It was only at times like these when his usually bridled temper broke that he'd begin to curse.

His lunch sat on a plate across the table from Ann. "Come on in here, Maynard. Have something to eat."

Maynard didn't seem to hear her. He paced back and forth across the living room, entirely distracted by the thought of the picker in his field. Finally, he came to a stop before the big picture window that overlooked the field. Though it was some distance off, he could still see the picker as he popped in and out of sight. He muttered another curse then went into the dining room.

Lunch passed in a seething silence. Afterward, when Maynard headed back down the driveway to meet Thomas, he noticed that the van was gone and so was the picker. He immediately relaxed. By the end of the day it had slipped to the back of his mind.

CHAPTER 38

That week four officials from the United States Olympic Committee flew into Eugene's Mahlon Sweet Airport from Seattle. These men were not the selection committee, but they were doing a preliminary round of visits to cull out some of the potential sites. Those that survived the cut would be reviewed again once the selection committee was formed.

The officials were greeted at the airport by U of O President Robert Clark and Mayor Les Anderson. They took a limousine tour of Eugene in the pouring rain, ending at Hayward Field, where they were met by Bill Bowerman and several of his track stars, including Steve Prefontaine, his prize long distance runner from Coos Bay, Oregon. Everyone was wearing rain gear.

After walking around the track facility and inspecting the new synthetic surface of the track itself, the Mayor, Clark, and Bowerman took the four men out to dinner to plead their case, that began by assuring the officials that it didn't rain in Eugene in June—which was not entirely true.

At the end of the meal, one of the committee members asked about the recent bombing and the "atmosphere of resistance" that existed in Eugene.

"It's something that's on the campus of every major university and college in the United States, and I'm sure the protests will continue as long as the war does," said President Clark. "The bombing in September got a lot of publicity because one of our janitors got caught in the fire. We don't believe that was intentional."

"But the bombing was," said one official. "We couldn't have something like that at the trials. It would be a disaster."

"The athletes would be in jeopardy," said a second official.

"I think the bombing was very much an anomaly here in Oregon," said Bowerman. He was a decorated veteran from World War II. The

135

man was respected for his coaching ability, his ingenuity, and his heroic patriotism. "I don't think there's anything to worry about."

"We've got the FBI in town right now," said the Mayor with more confidence than he had. "I fully expect them to track down whatever bad element was responsible before the year is out."

Clark and Bowerman both agreed.

"What we have here," continued the Mayor, deliberately changing the subject, "is one of the most beautiful locations on the west coast. It won't be as hot as LA or as clogged with traffic as any of the other big cities. The focus will be on the event, not the scene surrounding it, meaning less distraction for the athletes. I don't see how you could ask for more."

"I think the Mayor's right about that," said Bowerman, the man at the table commanding the most attention, and a possible candidate for the selection committee. "This setting makes everything easier for the athlete to compete. They can stay in the university dorms and walk to the track. They won't even need a car to go out to dinner or get anything else they might need."

"Is there enough lodging for those who come to watch the Trials?" asked a third official. "That's something we haven't addressed."

"We would expect twenty to thirty thousand at the least," said another official.

"There's plenty of lodging," said the Mayor. "We've had crowds of more than forty thousand here for football games. And if more rooms are needed, I suspect local residents would make rooms in their homes available."

"And we'll certainly have extra space in the dorms during the summer session at the university," added Clark. "The only thing we need is your vote of confidence."

The four officials looked around the table. One man nodded in agreement. The other three maintained poker faces. Afterward they were taken to a hotel adjacent to the university for the night. The Mayor had arranged for them to be driven to the coast the next day. It was a fifty-mile trip through the Coastal Mountain Range and an excellent way to show off the surrounding countryside.

It would be at least two months before they would know if Eugene had made the cut.

CHAPTER 39

While Blake College and its members steadily stumbled down the bumpy path to intellectual freedom, the school's funds were tight, especially when it came to building projects—like the kiln that wasn't even a pipe dream without some cash. Crow, who proved to be remarkably worldly, suggested they make large batches of granola both to eat at the school and to be sold at the natural food stores and co-ops in Eugene. The idea won unanimous support. Crow took the lead, salvaging an old industrial-grade oven and rewiring it. Rain made a recipe, and working in two-person shifts, they made granola in fifty-pound batches. Crow managed the operation, and under his guidance they began to make money. Not a lot, but enough to cover many of their expenses and minimize the amount the school needed from the students and faculty. Four times a week, Crow would run his crews through the procedure—toasting trays of rolled oats, spraying honey water on almonds and cashews and toasting them, then mixing raisins, along with the nuts, into the oats, and finally sealing it all up in five-gallon plastic buckets. On Saturdays Van and Marsha used Tai's van to make deliveries.

In a relatively short time, the second-generation, experimental college gained a reputation on the streets of Eugene. At the end of October, they had an open house to educate the community about the school. About seventy-five young people showed up, some from the street and some from the U of O. Many of them brought beer. The open house became a party with lots of drinking and pot smoking. Around midnight, someone put the Grateful Dead on the record player and turned up the volume to its maximum.

An hour later, a patrol car cruised by the house. On the second pass, they pulled into the driveway. Bob Yates and his partner Eldon Taylor, in navy blue uniforms with holsters and black brimmed caps, sauntered up to the front door in a light rain. After knocking, not nearly loud enough to be heard over the music, they walked unnoticed into a crowd of dancing youths. The place reeked of marijuana. Everyone they saw held a can of beer regardless of age. Janice did the frug stark naked in the center of the living room. And Crow, who had seen the patrol car pull up, was one of a handful who had quickly slipped out the back door to hide in the heavy brush along the river.

Yates nodded to his deputy. Eldon pushed through the dancers and lifted the needle off the vinyl. Somebody screamed, "Who cut the music?" Then a frantic echo, "It's the cops! It's the cops!" ignited a wave of paranoia throughout the house. Janice continued to dance to the music in her head until Adrienne and Ray came into the room and got her attention.

"Where's the owner of this house?" called out Yates.

Ray recognized Yates and quickly slipped upstairs so he wouldn't be seen. Rain stepped forward as Adrienne dropped a dress over Janice's head and pulled it down past her hips. "It's a school," said Rain. "We run it cooperatively."

"What about," Yates glanced down at his note pad, "Arthur Kotke? Isn't he the owner?"

Adrienne stepped up. "He moved out and left me in charge. My name is Adrienne Stephens. This is Rain Adams. We've run the school to pay the mortgage and utilities for Arthur."

Yates turned to his partner, then the stoned partiers gawking at them. "Do all of these people live here?"

Van, neat and clean, the only person at the party—besides the cops—without beads, stepped out of nowhere. "No, just eight of us."

"We're having an open house," said Rain.

"To show people how a cooperative works," followed Gloria, coming into the room from the kitchen. "We opened the doors to recruit students."

"Yeah, looks like the cream of the crop," muttered Eldon.

"That's Deputy Taylor. My name is Yates. There's good reason to believe underage drinking is going on here." He looked straight at Janice. "And the place stinks of marijuana. Both are illegal."

Rain had not been drinking or smoking marijuana. "Yes, you're right, officer," she said with stunning candor. "I had already decided that the party needed to come an end." All the young people stood back and said nothing, as taken in by Rain's composure as the officers were. Meanwhile, Tai was in the basement gathering up his stash of drugs.

"What about this young woman?" Yates nodded at Janice. "She's clearly not twenty-one, appears inebriated, and was naked when we came in."

Janice started to interrupt, but Marsha came up from behind and whispered, "Not a word, Janice."

"She's my niece," lied Rain. "She's here visiting. It's my fault that she had anything to drink. If I'd seen her naked, I would have spanked her like an eight-year-old and sent her to her room. Thankfully she's not in public. But she's in my house, under my supervision, and if anyone is to be charged with negligence, it should be me."

Again, the officers felt Rain's remarkable poise and appreciated her admission. Clearly, she was intelligent and responsible. The two men looked at each other. "You could be in a lot of trouble with what's going on here, Miss Adams," said Yates. "Do this for me. Clear everyone out of the house immediately. And be sure to give this young lady proper guidance from now on. I'm only issuing you a ticket for disturbing the peace. It's a hundred dollar fine. Plead guilty, and you can pay it at the courthouse without a trial—and they'll reduce it to fifty." He opened his pad and began filling out the ticket.

"Thank you for understanding, Officer Yates."

Behind Rain, Adrienne and Van began directing people to the doors. Down in the basement, Tai squeezed out one of the basement's casement windows with a black plastic garbage bag and ran down to the river to hide in the brush. He didn't know Crow was already there until the patrol car drove away and they both returned to the house to see what had happened.

Everyone was seated around the dining room table when Tai and Crow entered. Rain summed it up. "That was close. We might believe we're trying to push the boundaries of freedom, but underage drinking isn't part of it." She looked at Janice who had laid her head on the table. Knowing Rain had stepped in on her behalf, Janice lifted her hand and gave her a peace sign.

Van looked at Tai and Crow. "Where were you guys?"

"I have a criminal record," said Crow. "I was dead meat being here with what was going on. My apologies, but now you know. I've got baggage of my own."

Tai held up his black plastic trash bag. "I had too much booty here to get caught." When no one said anything to support him, he added,

"Be thankful I got this shit out of here. If things had gone differently, we'd all have been busted."

"Maybe we should talk about that, Tai," said Ray, coming down from upstairs. "If we get busted, who do the drugs belong to? The collective? Or you?"

Tai didn't like the question but knew there was only one answer. "Me. Full ownership."

There was more to this than came out. Yes, Tai had his stash of exotic herb and mushrooms, but he also had two pounds of commercial weed and a small personal stash of cocaine. Only Janice, the other co-op member with the dark shadow, knew this. The open use of marijuana was common behavior at Blake College. No one was going to deny that. But cocaine was a no-no, and there had been no agreement about dealing drugs from the house. Several of the school members would have come unglued if they had found out.

That night, after the party, Marsha and Van slipped out the back door and went into the greenhouse with a blanket. Two weeks had passed since their first kiss. It was the first time for them both. In a way the progression was inevitable. After the night was over, they called it the most educational experience they'd had at Blake College to date.

CHAPTER 40

Mid-morning two days later, one of Tim's housemates, Jeannie, a young woman from Texas who worked downtown as a waitress, left a message for him on the kitchen table. Tim's friend Prairie had called from the hospital. Stoopid had been moved out of intensive care and was available for visitors. It was great news, and Tim rode his balloon tire bike to Sacred Heart immediately upon reading the message.

He paged Prairie as soon as he got there. She escorted Tim to Stoopid's room. There were two beds; one was empty. The bandages were off Stoopid's face and head, but the burns had left him badly scarred and with very little hair on his head. He sat up and twisted his face into something resembling a smile.

"Damn, Stoopid," said Tim, moving up close to the bed, "that's some haircut."

Stoopid sort of laughed, prompting some gurgling in his lungs and a cough. He was out of intensive care, but still far from being released. "Thanks for coming by, Tim," he said, fluid sounds behind every word.

"They wouldn't let me visit you until today. Gino and I stopped by about a month ago, but you were sealed up in the burn unit. Do you remember us coming by?"

"I think that got lost in the blur of pain killers."

Prairie touched Tim on the shoulder. "I've got to go."

"Hey, thanks for calling me." Tim faced Stoopid. "How do you feel?"

"Awful, Tim. Most of my body looks like my face. And all those cigarettes I've smoked are fucking with my lungs. Ever get that springer front end?"

"No, with all the excitement, it slipped my mind."

"It should still be there. It's a nice one. Be sure to get it."

"I'm more worried about you." Tim smiled, then turned serious. "What do you remember from that night? Did you see anything?"

Stoopid, clearly still in pain, lifted his head in thought. "Only the explosion, then riding in the ambulance."

"Did you see anyone prior to that? Someone wandering around the building that wasn't supposed to be there? I'm hoping to track down the jerk who did this to you."

"I got nothing, Tim. And the cops don't either. They came by earlier today."

"Sure would like to find the guy. A little payback might be in order." He nodded his head for emphasis.

"I just want to get out of here."

"Any idea when that will be? It's about time for another newsletter."

"That would be nice, but there's no set date. It seems I took in a lot of smoke. You can hear it in my voice."

"You'll be out soon enough. Just hang in there."

"Not much choice." Stoopid's smile was a tortured one.

"Well, I got some stuff to do. But I'll be by whenever I get the chance. Might even bring that dipshit Gino with me next time."

Stoopid tried to laugh, but it came out as a wet cough.

"Easy old boy. There's some good times yet to come."

Stoopid struggled with his breath and only nodded in response.

"Next time, comrade."

Stoopid gave Tim a mock salute as a good-bye.

Afterward, Tim rode to the Odyssey Coffee Shop. He saw Rebop at a table when he entered. He got some coffee and joined her. While Tim rolled a cigarette, he saw Mathers ride by on his bicycle.

"Damn," he exclaimed. "I just saw one of those FBI fucks on a ten-speed. I wonder if he's been tailing me?"

Rebop took a sip of coffee. "I assume it's happening all the time."

Tim pointed. "There goes the other guy."

"It makes me crazy," said Rebop. "I can't wait until we're rid of those assholes."

"I still haven't learned anything more about the bombing. And man, that seems impossible after all this time." Tim shook his head in frustration. "How about you?"

"Same thing. Nothing. I thought something was sure to shake out after we let everyone know who those guys were."

"I did too. On a more positive note, I saw Stoopid today. He's been moved out of intensive care. Still not out of the woods, but it's something. I quizzed him a bit about the bombing. He wasn't much help." Tim suddenly sat up to watch one of the agents ride by, then looked around the coffee shop. "Is there a phone in here?"

"Behind the counter. Who are you going to call?"

"A few folks. I'm sick of those FBI agents following us around. I think it's about time to put my plan into action."

"Plan?"

Tim grinned. "The look-alikes."

Rebop shook her head, thinking it was a crazy idea.

Tim went up to the counter and asked the cashier if he could use the phone. The cashier was a longhair who had worked at the coffee shop for more than a year. He knew Tim and showed him the phone. Tim called Pat at the Southeast Neighborhood Co-op. He told him to change into the clothes he had given him and that he would be at the co-op shortly. He also called his friend Horace at the Downtown Bicycle Shop and his friend Earl who worked the bar at Lucky's, Tim's pool hall of choice.

Tim returned to the table to finish his coffee. Both Rebop and Tim saw Mathers ride by again. Tim threw down the last of his coffee, gave Rebop a wry smile, and strode out of the coffee shop. He hopped on his bicycle and headed southeast across Eugene. He didn't notice anyone following him, but he continued to Pat's co-op anyway. Upon arriving, he went inside.

Pat was standing at the counter in the same attire Tim had on— except for the headgear. "You sure I've got to wear these red shoes, Tim?"

"Oh, yeah. They stand out."

"Yeah, like clown shoes," muttered Pat. "What's going on?"

Tim was staring out the window. "I was being followed. I thought this might be a good time to try a little game of misdirection."

"Can you see anyone now?"

"No, but let's proceed as though one of them's out there. They ride ten-speeds. You have someone to mind the store for a few?"

"Yeah, Laurel upstairs. What do you want me to do?"

"I'll go out the back and take your bicycle. You go out the front and take mine. Go to Horace's bike shop and then come back here. Change out of the clothes and continue with your day. Easy, right?"

"What if I see someone following me?"

"Pay no mind. And if they come in here asking for me just play dumb." Tim grinned. "Shouldn't be too hard."

"Very funny."

Tim bought an apple and went out the back door.

Within minutes, Pat put on the leather headgear and left through the front door. Mathers was waiting a block away and saw Pat leave. Thinking Pat was Tim, he took off after him on his bicycle. Pat noticed the man on the ten-speed right away, and instead of going straight to the bike shop took a long meandering route.

Meanwhile, Agent Ball, who had been on the backside of the building, saw Tim leave. He waited until Tim was down the road before taking off after him, thinking that Mathers would do the same. Tim saw the man riding some distance behind him and slowed down to let him get closer. When he could see that it was one of the agents, Tim headed to the pool hall at a leisurely pace.

When Pat got to the bike shop, Horace, also a tall, thin man, was attired just as he was. They did the same thing Tim and Pat had done. Horace went out the front door, and Pat went out the back. Both rode off in opposite directions—Pat back to his store and Horace down the street to get some lunch.

Earl was at the bar in full Tim-attire when Tim strolled into Lucky's. Both men grinned, but neither said a word. Earl had a backup bartender already in place. He went out the front door and Tim went out the back.

Now Mathers was following Horace and Ball was following Earl, each thinking his partner had lost track of Tim—when in fact they both had.

Tim's plan involved more than messing with the undercover agents. He wanted to do a little investigating of his own. While the two agents were riding around chasing his look-alikes, he took off on his bike to the Whitaker neighborhood. He went straight to Fourth Street and immediately saw the placard out front of their garage: *Bikes: Good as New.*

Tim rode by the house twice, casing the joint. He stashed Pat's bicycle a block away, then hiked down the alley to approach the house from the rear. The back door was locked, so he went around to the less obvious windows, looking for one that wasn't latched. The bathroom window had been left partly open. It was behind a thick laurel bush and was hard to see and hard to get to. Tim squeezed through the laurel and hoisted himself onto the window ledge, then slid in headfirst, nearly stepping into the open toilet as he swung around to get his footing.

He quickly sized up the place room by room. One room was clearly an office, and he methodically pawed through the paperwork on the desk and then in the drawers. That the two men worked for the FBI became clear immediately. He found files on himself, Rebop, Dave, and Sue and went through them page by page, looking for any clues they might have found or any hint that the agents might have done the bombing themselves. There were none of either.

Meanwhile, Earl and Horace returned to their jobs after thirty minutes and changed their clothing. Ball, who had tailed Earl, ventured into Lucky's to look around. It was a big place with twenty professional pool tables, three racks of pool sticks, a long old-fashioned bar, and a glass display case showing off a large collection of cigars, pipes, and tobacco, but no Tim O'Malley.

Mathers did much the same at the bike shop, also finding no trace of Tim. Figuring they'd lost their man, both agents headed back to their house, wondering what their partner might have discovered.

Tim was still in the office when he heard someone come in the front door. He quickly straightened out the desk and, with no other choice, hid in the closet.

Someone came upstairs and into the office. Tim slid deeper into the closet that was mostly empty. He heard the shuffling of paper and a drawer open and close, then someone else coming into the house downstairs.

"That you, Patrick," called out Mathers.

"Yeah, I lost the guy," he said, coming up the stairs. "How about you?" Ball entered the room.

"I lost him, too. I have no idea what happened. Think there could be two of those guys in Eugene?"

Tim stifled a laugh.

"Fuck, I don't know. This town is so full of hippies I can't tell them apart."

"Yeah, all I know is these people are nuts. To tell you the truth, I don't think any of these folks we're following did it."

"I hear you. Not quite like the people we're usually chasing."

"Well, somebody bombed that building," said Ball. "And we haven't a clue who it was. You ready for lunch?"

"Yeah, let me finish with these notes and I'll be right down."

Tim heard Ball leave the room and clomp down the stairs to the kitchen. He held still, listening to Mathers scratching notes with a pencil. After a few minutes, he heard a drawer open and close, then Mathers leave the room and tromp down the stairs.

Tim had two choices. Stay in the closet and wait for them to leave the house or take a chance and try to slip out the front door while they were in the kitchen. He decided on the latter. He gently turned the closet door knob and pushed the door open. As he stepped out of the closet, the floorboards creaked the way they always do in old houses. He untied his shoes and pulled them off. Holding them in one hand, he tiptoed out of the room to the landing.

Tim could hear the two men in the kitchen, opening and closing the refrigerator, clattering silverware, making something to eat. He knew the layout of the first floor from his initial walk through. The front door was across the living room from the stairway. The kitchen was on the opposite side of the room with an open entryway. To get from the stairs to the front door meant being in plain sight for three or four seconds.

Tim crept down the stairs that offered their own assortment of creaking sounds. At the foot of the stairs, he peeked around the corner. He could see Mathers standing at the counter with a loaf of bread and Ball seated at a table, facing the living room. It was too big a risk to make a break for the front door. Tim retraced his steps and went back to the office, knowing he needed to distract the two agents somehow. The office's lone window overlooked a small backyard and patio. Tim gently opened the window. It had no screen. He looked around the office hoping to see something he could toss out the window to create a distraction. Everything he saw was too obviously from the office and would give away that he'd been there. He reached into his pocket and retrieved two quarters and a nickel. He used his shirt to clean his fingerprints off one of the quarters and tossed it out the window, hoping to hit the tin trash can at the edge of the alley, but he missed. He tried with the second quarter and missed again. Only the nickel was left. It was smaller and harder to throw than a quarter. He wiped it off with his shirt, then leaned out the window as far as he could and pitched the nickel underhand at the trash can—again he missed. *Damn*!

Tim glanced around the room looking for something else to throw—nothing. He dug into his pockets—all empty. Then he remembered the sheriff's badge pinned to his vest. As a last resort, he removed the tin star from his vest, wiped it clean, and again leaning far out the window, flipped it with his wrist—like a frisbee—at the trash can. It sailed out over the patio in a big curve and landed right on top of the can with a clear bing and bounced off. Almost immediately, he heard Ball say, "What was that?"

Shoeless, Tim quickly went down the stairs and peeked around the edge of the staircase into the kitchen. Being undercover agents, both men were curious about what had made the sound. Ball stood up and went out the kitchen door onto the porch. Mathers went to the window to watch. Tim took three long strides and was out the front door, but inadvertently let the screen door bang behind him.

Mathers heard the screen door. With Ball outside, he went to the front door to see if someone were there. He stood on the porch looking around, but no one was in sight. He opened and closed the screen to recreate the sound, then returned to the kitchen, scratching his head, as Ball came back inside.

"Nothing out there. Must have been something that fell from a tree." He laughed. "But I did find this dime-store sheriff's badge out there in the alley." He pinned it on his shirt. "How's that look?"

Mathers shook his head. "Stupid."

The look-alike plan had been a rousing success in terms of silly fun, but Tim's detective work hadn't helped as much as he had hoped. Ball and Mathers were definitely FBI. That was important to verify. But it was clear from their notes and their conversation that they were legitimately looking for the bomber and had not done it themselves. If there had been a provocateur, it wasn't anyone associated with the FBI. In terms of new information—Tim was still at square one.

CHAPTER 41

"Check 'em out," said Tai, reaching into the side pocket of his jean jacket to retrieve a clear plastic baggie. "Fresh ones like these go for fifty bucks a hundred."

A hip young couple from the university sat across from him in a booth at the back of Max's Tavern. The man wore a flannel shirt and blue jeans. The woman had jeans on as well, with a white peasant blouse.

Tai turned the baggie upside-down. A glistening heap of fresh psilocybin mushrooms, none larger than the tip of his forefinger, piled up on the table like root beer colored gum drops. They could have been gold nuggets for the way the young couple's eyes widened. They had never tried or even seen "magic" mushrooms before. Both of them selected one from the pile and inspected it beneath the booth's dim yellow wall light. The little brown mushrooms were translucent like gelatin, with a tiny transparent nipple on top.

"The hallucinogenic mushroom is sacred in many cultures," said Tai, pulling absently at one of his dreadlocks. He'd been nibbling on the mushrooms all day and was quite stoned. "I like to think of them as the fruit of the Tree of Knowledge," he pronounced with drama. "You know, the knowledge of good and evil." He raised a single eyebrow.

The young woman was cute and blond, probably from California. She held a mushroom daintily by its thin stem. She had no idea what Tai was talking about.

He glowered red-eyed at her like a being from another planet. "It's a true psychedelic high. Like LSD. But it's organic."

The girl sniffed the mushroom and made a face. "Smells like dirt." She dropped the musky fungus back into the pile as though it might have been a live scorpion.

"How many do you take to get high?" asked the young man, all business, paying no mind to Tai's banter.

"Fresh like this, five will work. Ten is better. Twenty—who knows?" Tai grinned at the woman. "I have to laugh whenever I do this. It's not like selling speed or cocaine. They're just drugs." He lowered his voice. "These little babies have been eaten as a way to see God for as long as man has been on the planet. They're the real thing. Soma. Mescalito. Magic," he hissed in a whisper, then laughed—a little too loudly.

The girl didn't like it. "Then maybe you shouldn't be selling them. Maybe it's bad karma."

"You mean, like I should be giving them away?" Tai chuckled. "I don't think so."

The young man wasn't listening to any of this. "How much for all of these?"

Tai scooped up half the mushrooms and let them fall through his fingers like Thompson raisins. "This is sixty 'shrooms. How about thirty bucks?"

The young man looked at his girlfriend. She shrugged. "I'll take'em," said the man. He pulled out his wallet and found a twenty and a ten as Tai put the mushrooms back in the plastic bag.

"Where do you find these things?" asked the young woman, while the exchange of money was made.

"It's a secret." Tai winked at her. "Told only to very close friends."

The young man gave Tai a look. "We better get going." He stood up. The woman did the same.

"Happy trails," Tai glimmered as the couple wandered off with their score. He had five hundred more to sell. Halloween was the next day, and the mushrooms were going like hotcakes. He'd go back to the field as soon as he could.

CHAPTER 42

Two days after Bill Bowerman learned that he had lost his bid for state representative by less than a thousand votes, he stood with Phil Knight at the edge of the running track at Hayward Field. The state-of-the-art track was just one of the reasons many in Eugene felt the Olympic Trials should be held there.

Bowerman and Knight were timing two runners circling them on the track and periodically glancing at their stopwatches. One of the runners was Steve Prefontaine. The other was the Mayor's son, Jon Anderson. Jon ran cross country for Cornell, but he had graduated in June. He came back to Eugene to train with Bowerman for the ten thousand-meter, hoping to gain a spot on the 1972 Olympic team. Jon was a long shot, but he was also a Eugene boy and getting him into the Trials, especially if they were held in Eugene, would be victory enough for both the runner and his coach.

The runners were grinning when they pulled up to the clicks of the stopwatches. "Love these shoes, Coach," said Prefontaine. "How was the time?"

Bowerman suppressed a smile. "Two seconds off your best, and better than that for you, Jon."

Jon was beaming now. "They're so light. I think you've hit on something, Coach. How many pairs you got?"

Bowerman looked at Knight, then tipped his head. "Four right now. You guys are wearing half my stock." His smile was of satisfaction. He knew his shoe was a breakthrough, especially for the new track surfaces.

"Now all we have to do is get the Trials," said Knight, "and when a couple runners win events wearing our shoes, we'll be selling them all over the United States."

"And the rest of the world," added Bowerman.

That night Jon Anderson had dinner with his parents in the house he had grown up in. After Jon told his father and mother about the shoes, he confessed to them how much he wanted to run the ten thousand in the Trials.

"Got any chance to make the team?"

"Extreme long shot, Dad. But right now, I just want to run in the Trials. Any word from the committee?"

"No, it hasn't even been formed yet," said his father, "but the violence at the university has me worried."

"Truly?"

"We want to pitch Eugene as an All-American city. A beautiful setting, working class people, and a Mecca for runners. This anti-war stuff goes entirely against the image we're trying to create."

"But it's happening at all the universities. It's the times."

"The protest argument falls apart as soon as they start resorting to violence and vandalism. Trashing the ROTC building last spring and the bombing this fall, that's more than anti-war—that's terrorism."

Jon had his own opinion on the war. He'd attended several demonstrations at Cornell and had heard the whole array of speakers. His feelings were much different than his father's. He decided to change the subject. "You still thinking of making a run at governor in seventy-four?"

His father smiled at the thought, then frowned. "If we get the Trials, I've got a chance. It will be the biggest thing for Oregon since Terry Baker. Bigger. But if we don't, I'll be lucky to get out of the primary."

"When will you hear about the Trials?" asked Maureen.

"The decision won't be until next fall. They want someplace with a climate like Munich's. Seattle, Berkeley, Eugene, a bunch of other cities are in the running."

"If you're worried about activism," said Jon, "Berkeley hasn't a chance."

"Maybe we don't either."

"Boy, would I love to run in front of a hometown crowd. It would probably cut minutes off my time. I might even make the team."

His father actually smiled. "Wouldn't that be the capper! We get the Trials and you make the team."

"Wouldn't that be great," said Jon, laughing.

"By the way, when you saw Bill today, did he mention the election? He had to be disappointed, especially with the tally so close."

Jon nodded. "He didn't talk too much about it to me, but I heard him tell Phil he was asking for a recount."

"Really? It's rare for that to change the outcome."

"I'm sure he knows that, but he's also not a good loser."

CHAPTER 43

It hadn't rained in a week, so Spikes told Ray to meet him at Twelfth and Jefferson to work on the landing spot for the house on Eighteenth. Ray got there early riding his bicycle. Spikes showed up towing a Bobcat on a rental trailer. He climbed out of the cab with a big grin half-hidden beneath his mustache. "What do you think?" He motioned to the front loader. "We've got some digging to do. And there isn't anything more fun than playing around with one of these little buggers."

"Never used one," said Ray, moving up close to the trailer to inspect the compact white tractor on four large tires. The one-seat cab was surrounded by an elaborate cage of roll bars and steel mesh. A shovel was mounted on two long arms that levered off the rear of the vehicle. "Do I get to run this thing?"

"Hell no." Spikes stalked around the trailer admiring his toy. "I gotta get some thrills out of this ugly business." Then he laughed at the expression on Ray's face. "I've got the damn thing for two days. You'll get your chance."

"There's a lot of levers. How's it work?"

"Watch." Spikes released the winches and chains that secured the Bobcat to the trailer. He and Ray dropped the ramp into place, then Spikes climbed into the cab like a five-year-old on a twenty-five-cent spaceship ride. He turned a key to start it, fiddled with the levers, lifted the shovel off the surface of the trailer, and backed the beast down the ramp into the street. The back wheels turned instead of the front wheels, meaning it could do a donut on a dime. Spikes roared with laughter as he ran the thing in circles before driving it up over the curb onto his property.

The first day with the Bobcat, Spikes dug out a rectangular trench for the foundation footings, measured to match the house at Eighteenth Avenue. They would build forms in the trenches and fill them with concrete. Three courses of cinder blocks on top of the footings would complete the foundation. It would take them two weeks if they got the weather.

On the second day with the Bobcat, Spikes wanted to get started on the sewer service. That meant digging down to the existing sewer line, then digging a ditch from the sewer line to the foundation. Spikes gave Ray the key to the Bobcat to begin the task. The locate people had told Spikes where to dig, but they had not said anything about the depth. After an hour of digging, Ray was six feet down with no sign of the line. The rental trailer had been unhitched the previous day, so Spikes drove to a nearby market and called the utility company to see if they knew anything about the depth. They told him it could be as deep as twelve feet. After he hung up, he screamed, "FUCK," as loud as he could.

He roared back to the job in his pickup, bounced up over the curb, and came to a stop beside the big hole. "It could be twelve feet down," he exclaimed jumping form the cab. "Let me take over."

By the time Spikes reached the sewer line, ground water was ten inches deep in the hole. It was so muddy Spikes struggled for traction. When he tried to back out, the sides of the hole gave way, making it impossible to get out. "MOTHERFUCK!" he screamed. "WHY THE HELL WAS THIS LINE SO FUCKING DEEP?"

Spikes slipped out of the driver's seat and climbed on top of the cage to get out of the hole. "How the hell are we going to get this thing out of here?" He surveyed the situation. "We could extend the hole back ten feet, so it won't be so steep. But damn, we can't turn the bastard around."

Ray, wary of Spikes' anger, made his own appraisal. "What if we laid sheets of plywood on the backside of the hole. Maybe you could get enough of the back tires onto the plywood to get the thing out of the mud and up out of the hole."

Spikes frowned as he thought about Ray's idea. He had five new sheets of plywood for the house at Eighteenth Avenue in his pickup. He scratched his chin, then said, "Why not? Getting this bugger out of the hole is a higher priority than clean plywood. Let's give it a try."

It didn't take them long to throw the plywood into the hole. They both got down in the mud and jammed one of the sheets up under the back tires of the Bobcat. Despite all their effort, they couldn't get the tires more than a few of inches onto the plywood. Spikes climbed into the Bobcat, turned it on, and spun the tires on the plywood to the edge of combustion—not the plywood, Spikes' brain.

Again, he exited the cab with a stream of vulgarities and curses thrown at whomever watched from above—scaring the hell out of Ray. Spikes scratched his head, looked around, and then spit on the ground. "Get in the pickup, Ray. We'll attach a chain to the Bobcat. When I try to back that thing out, you pull with the truck. Maybe between the pickup and plywood we can get that bitch out."

They put all the pieces together. The pickup was positioned at the edge of the hole with a chain attached to the Bobcat. On the word *go*, Spikes applied gas to the Bobcat and Ray to the pickup. Rather than pull the Bobcat out, they came within a foot of pulling the pickup into the pit. At that point, Spikes threw up his hands in frustration. He and Ray, both covered in mud, drove to the corner store six blocks away. Spikes called the rental outfit from a phone booth and requested they bring their biggest tractor to the site to rescue the Bobcat—on his dime. The guy at the rental store knew Spikes. Ray could hear him laughing through the phone. They'd be there in an hour. Spikes bought a six pack of Blitz, and he and Ray headed back to the site to drink in the cab of the pickup while they waited for the tractor.

They had each downed a beer when Spikes pointed out the windshield to a woman walking down Jefferson toward Twelfth. "Who's that?"

Ray squinted out the filthy windshield. It was Rebop Rodriguez, striding down the street in jeans that looked as though they'd been painted on her. He had seen her a couple times on the street and vaguely knew who she was.

"Wow, I think that's a hooker," continued Spikes. "Legs clear up to her ass. And that green hair! Holy shit! In broad daylight!"

"No, she's a poet. She runs some kind of women's newspaper."

Rebop walked right past them. Both Ray and Spikes just stared at her from inside the pickup. Spikes couldn't resist. "That's quite an ass!" he called out after she had passed.

Rebop turned around and gave him the finger, then continued on her way.

Spikes turned to Ray and grinned. "I think I'm in love."

"I hear she's a lesbian."

Spikes' face went blank. "Really? What's her name?"

"Something weird. I think it's Bebop or something like that."

"No, it's Rebop." Spikes opened another beer and handed it to Ray, then opened one for himself. "I've heard about her. There's a painting of her in one of the bathroom stalls at the Alibi Club."

"That redneck tavern in Springfield?"

"That's the one. And who are you calling a redneck?"

"You know what I mean."

Spikes laughed. "I do, but I wouldn't go in there saying that—and I'm a card-carrying redneck."

CHAPTER 44

Tim was stacking flyers he'd printed for the dairy farmer John Walters, when John, who was married to Maynard Smith's daughter, came into the print shop to pick them up. John, like Tim, was a tall man, and looked somewhat stately in a straw cowboy hat, a plain yellow button-down shirt, and neat, relatively new blue jeans.

"Hey, John, perfect timing. I just finished the flyers." Tim had smoked a joint prior to John's arrival and the shop smelled of pot.

John, somewhat stoic in presentation, could not have missed it and did not approve. But he knew how much Tim did for everyone in the alternative community—organic farmers included—and didn't mention the marijuana. "I try to be on time, Tim. Just like milking the cows, timing's important." He took a folded check from his wallet and handed it to Tim. "Fifty dollars, right?"

"That's right. A deal at half the price."

"What do you mean?"

Tim laughed. "Just a dumb joke, John. How are things at the market?"

John still didn't get it. "That's what these flyers are about. Saturday Market closed last week, but a handful of us are putting together a couple of weekends indoors at the fairgrounds in December to see what we can do with winter crops and dairy products. It's a long shot, but a bunch of the farms have things to sell."

"Will this include the crafts people?"

John picked up one of the flyers to look it over. He spoke without looking up. "No, we're doing this ourselves."

"Wouldn't you both do better working together? Especially with Christmas coming."

John was intent on the flyer and didn't reply.

"You'd save money," said Tim. "And the crafts people would attract customers for you, and you for them. That's got to be good, right?"

John laid the flyer on top of the stack. "Personally, I'm not too impressed with what they sell. Seems like a lot of junk to me."

Tim laughed gently. "Pretty harsh there, John. Those people are just like you, trying to make it on their own initiative. I know a lot of folks who would want to buy handcrafted Christmas gifts this time of year."

"That's probably right, but I don't think of them as the same as us." John eyeballed the roach lying on the table beside the stack of flyers, subtly suggesting what he wasn't going to say.

Tim tilted his head in thought. "I think we're all in this together, John, whether we smoke pot or get high on biodynamic broccoli. Linda has put a lot of energy into making that downtown spot work. Give her some credit. I'm thinking everything works better when people help each other." Tim had a way of presenting common sense with a lot of common sense.

John picked up the stack of flyers. "Of course, Tim. But it's more than that. There's not enough space downtown."

"But if they can get the park blocks, like I know they're trying to do, there'd be plenty of space. Hell, do your holiday thing at the fairgrounds, but get on board with the park blocks. That's the future for everyone."

John hesitated, then said what he really felt. "I don't like working with those hippies. We want our own thing."

"Well, you work with me, and to tell you the truth, I figure all of you farmers are hippies too—going back to the land and all that."

"I'm not a hippie," said John.

"Where you from, John?"

"Connecticut. Went to school in Wisconsin."

"Look in the mirror," chuckled Tim. "You've got a straw cowboy hat on, a big mustache, and hair longer than mine. You look like a Dead Head to me."

John finally let out a little laugh. He shook his head. "Well, I don't know. I'll talk to the other farmers, but they think the same way I do."

"I don't think Rain does. Her booth's in there with the farmers, right?"

"She's a hippie."

"And a farmer."

"Wild crafting is not exactly tilling the land."

"It's easier on the planet."

John rolled his eyes, knowing Tim was right. "What's it to you, anyway?"

Tim started to tap the tin star on his chest, but it wasn't there. He grinned big, then dug into a drawer that contained several more of the sheriff's badges and pinned one on his chest—*then* he tapped the star with his index finger. "I'm the sheriff in this here town," he said with a fake drawl. "I like to see people gittin' along."

John shook his head. "How fucking stoned are you right now, Sheriff?"

Tim lifted the roach from the table. "Not quite stoned enough." He lit the roach and took a toke. He extended it to John.

John shook his head. "None of that crap for me. I'm outta here, you fucking freak."

Tim grinned. He knew he'd broken through to John when he'd cursed in jest.

Later that evening, Tim met Gino for a couple of games of pool at Lucky's, then moved down the street to Max's to finish off the night with a couple of beers. Gino and Tim were hoisting them at the bar when Prairie came in wearing her scrubs. Tim saw it in her face immediately.

Prairie embraced him. "Stoopid died about an hour ago."

"I thought he was getting better," said Tim over her shoulder, fighting his emotions. It had been ten days since he'd visited his friend.

"He got pneumonia." Prairie released him. "It was always a risk."

Tim hung his head. Gino put a hand on his shoulder. "Shit, man, that makes finding the bomber all the more important."

Tim lifted his head. Tears were in his eyes. "God damn, yes." He shook his head. "But where do we go from here? We've got nothing. Fuck!"

Prairie got a beer, but no one said anything for a long time. Tim, his eyes now firm and fixed, broke the silence. "We have to come up with some money to cremate Stoopid. I know that's what he wanted."

Gino took off his hat. "Might as well start now." He moved down the bar and made his pitch. Before the evening was over, he had collected eighty-four dollars. Four went to another pitcher of beer.

Across town, the Mayor got a call from Wilkerson with the same message. "Fuck, why'd he have to die? It just puts a bigger stain on this city. God damn! God damn!"

CHAPTER 45

John Walters powered his three-quarter-ton GMC up Maynard Smith's driveway the following evening. Joyce, John's wife and Maynard's daughter, sat beside him. John pulled up beside Maynard's beige Dodge, and they climbed from the cab somewhat hesitantly. They were coming over for dinner, but unbeknownst to Maynard or Ann, the couple had an agenda to work through during the meal. They had plotted it out, step by step, what each of them would say during the meal and in what order, hoping to get the best possible reaction from Joyce's parents.

John and Joyce lived a half mile down the road from Maynard. They came over for dinner a lot. Tonight was nothing special, except that there would be no meat dishes. John and Joyce were vegetarians and tried to eat entirely organic food. They also didn't drink. Ann didn't either, but Maynard always cracked a beer at the end of the work day. He threw down the last of his Blitz when he heard John's truck door slam. Ann pulled her veggie lasagna out of the oven as they came through the front door. A big salad was already on the table, and Joyce had brought a loaf of fresh-baked rye bread. Both couples had worked all day, and they sat down at the table ready to eat. John and Joyce would only stay for dinner. They had evening chores to do before going to bed. Running a dairy farm demanded a twenty-hour day out of both of them.

"How's sales?" asked Maynard before he'd taken a bite.

John's mouth was full. "About the same," answered Joyce.

"Thin," said John. He was the one who had convinced Joyce to make the dairy organic. Maynard had not liked the idea. Finding markets was a problem for organic products. They could be touted as chemically clean, but they were also more expensive and had less demand.

"Any clarity on the downtown market?" asked Ann. It had really helped sales in the last year.

"We'd like to get the park blocks downtown," said John. "The market manager made a presentation to the City Council last week. It didn't seem to impress them very much. So, I don't know what we're doing beyond our two weekends at the fairgrounds next month."

Maynard focused on the lasagna to keep from saying, *I told you so.*

John was thirty-two. Joyce was twenty-six. Three years back John had come to Oregon in the first wave of back-to-the-land hippies. After getting a Masters in Biology at the University of Wisconsin and five years of teaching high school biology in the same state, he packed his things into a Volkswagen bus and headed west, intent on getting a farm and going organic—because he was tired of books and wanted to get his hands dirty. He drove straight to the Willamette Valley and used his savings to lease ten acres and buy a tractor. He met Joyce at the Methodist Church his first summer in Eugene. Six months later they were married. John was suddenly in a family with eight hundred acres of pasture land. Nothing could have been better.

"I recently read a book by a professor at Stanford about world population," said Joyce, tall, lithe, fair-haired, and pretty in the unadorned, homespun way of a farm girl. "He contends uncontrolled population growth is one of the greatest threats to the future of the planet."

Her mother looked up from eating.

John glanced at Maynard whose eyes were on his plate. The two men had never quite seen eye to eye. "I read the book also," said John. "Because of the demographics, population continues to increase for several years after the birth rate reaches replacement—two children per couple. The author compares it to stopping a freighter at sea. Even after the engines stop, the freighter continues to go forward for quite some time."

Maynard looked up at his son-in-law. One thing that John had brought to the family was an awareness for the environment. Joyce had never considered it until she'd met John. Now with their organic dairy, she had become more vocal than John.

Ann passed the basket of bread to John. "That's an interesting comparison. What's it mean?"

"That you have to plan ahead," said Joyce.

"What about you and John," asked Ann, "any babies on the horizon?"

Maynard continued to work on his lasagna, but he was listening intently.

Joyce glanced at John. The conversation was progressing faster than they had intended. John's eyes acknowledged that they might as well get to it.

"Well, Mom, that's something that's on our minds."

Maynard looked up. "More hands are always helpful on a farm." Ann and Maynard had a second child, a son born two years after Joyce. He died inexplicably in his crib at five months old.

"Especially with a hundred head of dairy cows," said John. "We're learning that, for sure."

"Are you trying to get pregnant?" asked Ann, daring a smile.

"Now Ann, that's their business," said Maynard, though he was as interested as his wife.

"No, it's fine, Dad. This is actually something John and I wanted to talk about tonight."

"Oh, really," said Ann, looking to Maynard, then back to her daughter.

"We've decided to adopt," said John.

Two mouths fell open. "Because of the world's population?" asked Ann.

"Yes," said Joyce. "Rather than adding people, we'd like to raise a child who's already been born."

"That's what you want to do, Joyce, truly? Wouldn't you at least like to have one of your own before adopting?"

"That's not the plan right now, Mom."

"Whose idea was this?" asked Maynard, looking straight at John.

"It was mine," said Joyce. "John fought me on this, but it's what I think is right." She glanced at John. "And I want to make sure I have your support."

Maynard got up from the table, walked into the living room, and began to pace. Tears began to accumulate in Ann's eyes.

"It's all right, Mom," said Joyce. "We knew this would be difficult for you. But I had to bring it up. I want you both to think about it a while, then we'll talk again in a month or so."

"Is your mind made up, Joyce?" asked Ann.

"Yes."

Maynard came back into the dining room. "I don't like it. The population problems are in Africa and India and China, not here in

Oregon. Barely two million people live in this state—and you're concerned about too many babies? That kind idealism is only for fools and kooks. I don't like it."

"I didn't think you would," said Joyce.

Ann didn't eat another bite of food. Maynard didn't even bother to sit down. He left the room muttering, "This is the stupidest thing I've ever heard in my life."

CHAPTER 46

Of all the lesbians in the city, only Rebop commanded the respect of working-class men like Spikes. They might laugh at the other women with their cropped hair and motorcycle boots, but Rebop, even with all her masculine aura, was sexually alluring in the most baffling way to these same men, and it frightened them. In one bar in Springfield, the city across the Willamette River from Eugene, a stall in the men's bathroom was dedicated to Rebop. The owner of the Alibi Club encouraged all types of graffiti related to Rebop to be scratched on the walls of what was known as the "Rebop Room." If men build memorials to individuals out of respect and honor, then this toilet stall was a shrine generated out of fear, jealousy, and petty wickedness in tribute to the imposing presence of Rebop Rodriguez in the redneck world. The things that she could do, according to the scribbling on the stall walls, could only have been inspired by the most penetrating and soul-searching horror in the men that imagined them.

Rebop had heard rumors about this bathroom stall and had always wanted to see if it really existed. Late one afternoon when she was at the Odyssey, Ball and Mathers arrived on their bicycles and came in—totally unaware that they stood out like bozos wherever they went. They ordered coffee and sat down like ordinary patrons, though everyone there knew who they were. Rebop caught their glance a couple of times. Although Tim had told her about his visit to their house and that he did not believe they were provocateurs, she still considered them a nuisance and decided to see if they were following her.

She finished her cup of coffee and walked out. Like the agents, she was riding a bicycle. She got on her bike and headed east across town to Springfield. The trip was about six miles, over a bridge and about two miles of open bicycle path. She rode slowly along the bike path to see if the agents had taken her bait. She glanced over her shoulder and saw

164

that they were about hundred yards behind her.

Rebop pedaled into downtown Springfield to the Alibi Club. Happy hour had just begun and the funky little tavern was about half full when she walked in. The hubbub of the drinkers suddenly stilled. Amid smirks and a growing buzz of tittering laugher, all eyes followed her as she sat at the far end of the bar and ordered a beer.

Tiny Rogers, the owner of the tavern and father of Mike Rogers the biker, was there that afternoon, and he, more than anyone else, found Rebop's arrival the most fascinating. He sat in a booth not far from the bar with his cousin, Walt Arnold, Maynard Smith's neighbor and one of the three or four most powerful lumber barons in Oregon.

Tiny, a very fat man, three hundred pounds or more, leaned over the table and whispered to his cousin. "You've got to admit, that's some woman." He winked. "For a lesbian."

Walt, a stocky man in his mid-fifties, nodded. "I'd say she's got some nerve to come in here."

Tiny barely heard the words. He just stared at Rebop, absolutely tickled pink she should be there, while similar conversations took place at almost every table in the joint.

Shortly after she got her beer, Mathers and Ball parked their ten-speeds out front and walked in, figuring it was a leftist hangout like the Odyssey.

Rebop's arrival created a stir, but the two long-hairs generated something entirely different in the bar filled with patriotic construction workers, loggers, and aging alcoholics. While no one had the courage to confront Rebop straight on, hippies were an open target.

"I wonder if these boys know where they are," said one patron loud enough for the FBI agents to hear.

"Must be foreigners," smirked someone else.

"Or war protesters," said a big logger in the booth directly across from them. "Must be lost or something."

Rebop hid her grin. Tim might want to lead the agents on wild goose chases, but she had a more dangerous game to play. She knew she could handle the rednecks, but she wasn't so sure these pretend hippies could.

Ball and Mathers sat at the opposite end of bar from Rebop and ordered beers. She could see their faces in the mirror and they could see hers.

After a few minutes, the logger in the booth advanced to the bar and addressed Ball and Mathers. "I'd like to buy a couple beers for you—uh, boys." He grinned big and drunk. "Just to welcome you to the Alibi Club." He winked at the bartender, which Ball and Mathers—and Rebop—saw in the mirror.

Even carrying concealed weapons, Mathers and Ball understood they were in the wrong place and should leave. Ball faced the logger who had a huge, overgrown brown beard. "Thanks, mister. The beer we have is all we need." He threw down what remained in his glass and started to stand.

The logger put his hand on Ball's shoulder to keep him in his seat. "That's not very friendly. I think you ought to stay." He grinned. "At least until they put the music on. We don't get to dance too often in this little dive." Besides Rebop, no other women were present.

Throughout the bar, the attention had turned from Rebop to the logger and the FBI agents. With every exchange, the laughter in the bar got louder and uglier. The bartender placed two beers before Ball and Mathers. Neither of them took a drink. If there were going to be a confrontation, they didn't want any more alcohol in their system than they already had.

The logger shook his head. "I don't much like it when my hospitality gets ignored." He turned to the eager faces peering out of the booths on the opposite wall. "That ain't very friendly. Is it?"

A chorus of *noes* sang out.

Ball looked at Mathers. It was either reveal who they were or make a hasty retreat. With Rebop there, their cover was too important. There was a third choice. Mathers smiled at the logger, then reached into his jacket to his shoulder holster. He withdrew the revolver without anyone seeing it, except the logger, and pressed it into the man's ribs. "I appreciate the beer, my friend," he said. "But I believe it's time for us to go."

The logger's eyes went big. Ball and Mathers stood up and walked out to a vicious series of insults about their masculinity.

The logger turned to the angry crowd. "Hate to waste good beer on communists." He threw down one beer then the other.

When the excitement had calmed down, Rebop watched Tiny stand up and walk to the men's room. She finished what remained of her beer, then slid off her stool, and headed to the restrooms. With everyone watching, she entered the men's room, not the women's.

Tiny was so intent on pissing he didn't notice her enter. She ducked behind him to peer into the hallowed stall. Along with the graffiti that adorned almost every inch of the stall interior, a full-body portrait of Rebop had been painted on the inside of the door, showing her sprawled on a tiger skin rug with her tongue out and legs spread. A thick penis lay between her legs. It was pushed off to one side, revealing a vagina where the scrotum would be. Beneath the picture was a caption, "...and if I can't find some young thing to ride, I just tuck this beaut into the tunnel of love and rock back and forth until it gets hard and pokes out my ass."

Rebop closed the stall and stepped up to the urinal next to the owner. He immediately froze and pressed his three-hundred-pound body into the urinal. Rebop unzipped her black jeans, and with unusual deftness, began to relieve herself while standing.

Tiny was so intimidated by Rebop's presence that his stream of urine stopped. Rebop stared at him until he dared to look at her. "Whoever painted that portrait of me over there did a fine job, but he forgot one thing."

The owner, who felt terribly stupid standing there pretending to pee, answered out of embarrassment. "How's that?"

"I've got balls." Rebop backed off, zipped up her pants with an exaggerated hitch, and went to the sink to wash her hands. Tiny remained pressed into the urinal until she exited.

Rebop strode calm and collected to her seat at the bar. No one could believe it when she ordered another round. No one spoke, and no one went into the men's room until she finished her beer and walked out.

At that point, Tiny came slinking out of the men's room to tell his story to the aghast crowd. "The portrait's inaccurate," he said. "She has one, but it's bigger and includes the rest of the family jewels."

The myth could only grow.

CHAPTER 47

Tai made his third trip to the mushroom field the week after Halloween. He parked his van off the road, not as close to the pasture as he had before, and walked back to the field. Standing alongside the fence, Tai took a quick look up and down the highway, then slipped between the strands of barbwire.

Tai didn't want to be seen by anybody, not the owner of the field or others passing on Route 45, whether it was the state police or other mushroom seekers. The presence of one picker in a field could lead to others pulling off the road to join in the hunt. Tai wanted to avoid this, for his own precaution and profit. He moved to the back of the field and began his methodical combing harvest. He wore a green fleece jacket and black jeans so he wasn't easily spotted. He kept low and alert, moving from one patch of tall marsh grass to another with his eyes on the ground. For the next two hours, he crept slowly across the back edge of the field and stilled at the sound of any approaching vehicle.

The liberty cap mushroom was very small and hard to detect in the grass. An inexperienced hunter could pass through a field in full bloom without seeing a single 'shroom. Experienced pickers try to map the growing pattern unique to each field. The underground root system, the mycelium or tree of the mushroom, would generally extend throughout the entire pasture, and from one day to the next, depending on how wet it was, either higher or lower areas of the field would produce the most fruit.

Tai had his own theory. He always ate the first five or so mushrooms he found. He felt that with their high his eyes became attuned to the colors of the field. The tiny mushrooms stood out and were easier to find. It was also easier to get into the role of being invisible when he was stoned. He stuck to this procedure today and ate seven mushrooms right away.

A little after noon, Tai recognized the drone of an approaching pickup long before he saw it. He ducked behind a tall clump of marsh grass and was well out of sight when the old Dodge stopped at the mailbox labeled M. Smith, then turned into the driveway. Once the truck began to ascend the hill, Tai returned to his picking.

When Maynard reached the top of the driveway, he cut the Dodge's engine and climbed from the cab. He started toward the house, then turned and gazed out over the valley. All the land as far as he could see was his or his daughter's. He'd made it his life to wrest it from the surrounding press of the wild. Every day he held it, its value went up. At three thousand dollars an acre, he was almost three times a millionaire. This amounted to the wages for all the hours of labor in his life. At an hourly rate, it didn't amount to all that much, but the farm was his and his family's—and that was what mattered.

Maynard turned his gaze to the lowest, wettest part of the valley, where the mushrooms grew. It was about two acres of thick marsh and about three of very wet, partially submerged pasture. This five-acre parcel of land held more than a mushroom history for Maynard. It spoke to the difference between his father's way of thinking and his own.

Forty years ago, when they were first laying out the farm, his father found quite a few Native American artifacts on this low-lying piece. "Something very special happened here several hundred years ago," he told fifteen-year-old Maynard. His father came to believe that it had been a sacred site or burial ground for the Kalapuya tribe that had lived on this land long before he had claimed it. Out of deference to this ceremonial site, he decided to leave this little parcel, out of all their eight hundred acres, alone. He never felled a tree, never tried to till.

Maynard didn't try to convince his father otherwise, but he was not of the same mind. Maynard thought of this piece of unused land as a blemish, a symbol of superstition and irrationality. Less than a year after his father's death, Maynard cleared the five acres and tilled it. As it turned out, about half the parcel was too low to use. It flooded every year and proved to be a perpetual swamp. The rest made for good pasture part of the year but was too wet the rest of the year. That the mushrooms should bloom in this pasture only added to the peculiar feelings Maynard had about it.

Despite his decided turn to cold rationality and simple faith, he was often visited by strange thoughts about this low-lying pasture. More than once he'd dreamed about it. In one such dream, a silver blimp hovered over the field, sprinkling mushroom spores into the grass like an airborne Johnny Appleseed. On another occasion, he imagined that the mushrooms were the sprouted eyes of the Kalapuya buried there. Images of painted Indians, dancing naked, holding mysterious mushroom rites, confiding in the world of spirits, haunted him off and on through the years like a deep racial memory. It made him superstitious in a way he didn't like, and against all his better judgment, he often wondered if something weren't amiss in his beautiful valley.

Maynard had fought the elements all his life. No task had been so hard it couldn't be done. He'd used his brain. He'd used his brawn. Only to the Will of God and the Fire of the Glory did he bow. But there's a wrinkle in every mind out there, and in the case of Maynard Smith, his wrinkle was this piece of land.

This little wrinkle was also part of the reason he'd never called the police or interfered directly with the pickers—aside from posting the field with no trespassing signs. He'd even overdone that one year, putting up so many signs he'd all but marked the field as the one with the proper fungus. He didn't quite understand it, but something about that marsh and the time of year and the mushrooms made him thoughtful in a way he usually wasn't.

Gazing down at this piece of land from above, Maynard chanced to spot the mushroom picker moving slowly across the far west edge of the pasture. His heart rate began to climb. He clenched his jaw. His eyes darted to the shotgun in his pickup's gunrack. He struggled mightily not to get it out.

Tai suddenly sensed that he was being watched. He peeked up from his crouch to see the farmer standing by his truck, looking down on him from the hill. Tai stopped moving, but kept his eyes on the man, waiting to see what the man was going to do. Tai imagined for a moment that he, at this impossible distance—two hundred yards or more, had caught the eyes of the man above and that a communication had passed from the farmer to him. The overriding message was disdain. The farmer knew exactly what he was doing. Picking the magic mushrooms and selling them. Tai went from feeling invisible to feeling naked. He felt so guilty for being there that he considered going up to the house to ask the farmer for permission to pick the mushrooms. But he was too high for that now. Besides, the man was turning away and heading into the house. Tai decided it would be wise to leave before the man drove back down the driveway. He picked ten more mushrooms, then began to work his way out of the field.

Ann heard the front door open and close. She was in the kitchen making lunch. She stepped away from the counter so she could see into the living room.

"Hi, Honey," Maynard said, shedding his work jacket.

"Did you see that young man down there in the field?" Ann asked warily.

"Don't remind me." He shook his head in frustration as he entered deeper into the house.

Ann came into the dining room with a plate in each hand. A glass of organic milk from Joyce's dairy was already at Maynard's place. "I wonder what it is about those mushrooms that makes the kids come out here like they do?"

Maynard didn't answer Ann's question, mostly because he didn't want to use profanities. He turned to look out the living room window. He couldn't see the picker. Even though Maynard was certain the man must still be there, it was easier to take when the picker was out of sight and stayed out of sight. He could seem fairly harmless out there alone. But when there were five or ten of them, Maynard was likely to blow his stack and shoot them all. No fences could last a season of thoughtless mushroom pickers—and it only took one to get that started.

Maynard drifted into the dining room and sat down, entirely forgetting that his wife had asked him a question.

When Ann placed a plate in front of him, she asked again, "Why would anyone want to eat something that grew in a field of cow manure? That's what gets me. I mean, that's stooping pretty low to get high." She smiled at her own words. "How could it be worth it, Maynard?"

Maynard looked down mercifully at the sandwich on his plate. He decided again not to use profanity. He knew if he began to speak on this subject, which of late had also been nagging him, he'd never get to his lunch. So he calmed himself and said, "Haven't a clue, Ann." Then he whispered a word of thanks to the Lord, prayed that Joyce would change her mind about adoption, and bit into his meatloaf sandwich.

Ann sat down across from him. "Could it be like drinking alcohol? And getting drunk?"

"Got me." Maynard chewed a second mouthful of sandwich.

"This does puzzle me, Maynard," she said with mock exasperation. "Joyce told me it's like smoking pot or taking tablets of LSD. Could that be? Could we be growing LSD right out there in our cow pasture?" What she'd asked quieted her for a moment.

Maynard looked up from his sandwich. He gazed at his wife, then took another bite, nearly finishing off the first half of the sandwich. When he'd fully chewed that mouthful and washed it down with a swallow of milk, he responded. "You know, Ann, you might have answered your own question."

"How's that, Maynard?"

Maynard realized his anger was gone. He even felt a smile trying to twist his old face out of its perpetual emotionless mask. "Those mushrooms are probably just like LSD."

Ann thought a minute. "What's LSD like?"

CHAPTER 48

Tim followed through on what he believed Stoopid would want in a funeral. He used the money collected at Max's and rounded up another hundred dollars to have Stoopid's remains cremated. He brought the ashes to the print shop and put them in an empty Tops tobacco can. Stoopid, like Tim, smoked cigarettes, and they had always joked about them, referring to them as coffin nails. In Stoopid's case, the smoking had its impact on his lungs, but it was the smoke he took in during the fire that sealed his fate.

Tim used a half-page from one of Stoopid's newsletters to roll a full ounce of marijuana into a foot-long cigar, as thick around as a broom handle. As he held it up admiring his work, Dave and Gino entered the print shop. They knew Tim had planned the ceremony for that day. Gino, like Tim, had known Stoopid since his time in San Francisco, and Dave felt a strong connection to Stoopid because he had been fighting the scourge of capitalism longer than anyone Dave had ever met.

Tim showed them the ashes, then placed the can on a shelf with a copy of Stoopid's favorite book, Smedley Butler's *War is a Racket,* and Stoopid's canvas satchel, still filled with copies of his last newsletter. Below on the floor in cardboard boxes was Tim's collection of his friend's work, newsletters going back to before Tim was born.

Tim removed his printer's cap. Gino did the same with his hat. Dave wore no hat but slipped his headband off as a gesture of unity.

With the three of them standing in a circle, Tim bowed his head and repeated the dedication line from the Weather Underground's handbook, *Prairie Fire*—a quote from Chairman Mao: "It only takes a single spark to start a prairie fire."

Gino and Dave said, "Amen."

Tim then struck a match and lit the foot-long joint. Without a word, they passed it around until they couldn't stand. Tim unfolded three lawn chairs, and they finished the joint sitting down.

Red-eyed, stoned on their asses, they sat together for thirty minutes lost in space. Tim was the first one to break the spell. "Now we have to figure out who killed him."

"But we don't know shit," said Dave.

"And judging from my little caper at the agents' house, they don't either."

"And you're sure they didn't do it just to fuck with us?" asked Dave.

"I heard them talking, and it didn't seem to fit."

Another long silence ensued, again broken by Tim. "Who haven't we talked to? I mean, who else in Eugene that we know, could possibly have done it—and us not know about it?"

Dave shrugged. "I've talked to everyone I know."

Gino, who was walking around the shop looking at the photos on the wall, turned to face them. "You try, Dick Danger?"

"No," said Tim, sitting up.

"Dick Danger? Who's that?"

"He's a guy we know," said Tim. "The head honcho out at the Lorane commune. He's as radical as they get—a pot grower, been in prison twice, and has a fascination with guns. Doesn't come into town very often. I haven't seen him in months, but man, if he didn't do it, he might know who did. Good idea, Gino."

Gino grinned wide and crazy. "Always do my best thinking when my brain stops."

CHAPTER 49

Midweek Marsha's mother, Mimi Lee, called and said she was coming to visit Marsha and see the school. She was flying in from Seattle Friday afternoon. Marsha had finally met a boy and all of a sudden her mother was coming! What could be worse? "Van," she whined after talking to her mother, "through some deep telepathic connection between mothers and daughters, I think she knew the moment I lost my virginity. Damn!"

Prior to Mimi's arrival, Marsha sat down with everyone and asked for help. "She's only going to be here Friday night and Saturday. She flies out early Sunday morning." She looked at Tai and Crow. "She's not exactly hip. It would be good if you could minimize the pot smoking, so my mother doesn't see it."

Crow and Tai said no problem.

"And it would be nice if everyone wore clothes when my mom's around. Is that possible?"

Again everyone agreed to her request.

"Also, for now, I'm not planning to tell my mother about Van and me." She lifted her hands as a sign helplessness. "If she guesses," Marsha squinched up her face and looked at Van, "which she might, I'll open up and tell her. Just try to play along with me, okay?"

And of course, everyone said that was completely fine.

Marsha had one other request. No one had made any attempt to decorate the downstairs of the house. The furniture was sparse and secondhand, which was fine—the open space was nice, but what was on the walls was either unframed photographs cut from magazines or posters from rock concerts or really anything that could be taped into an open space. Marsha wanted to upgrade the wall art.

During the first two months of school, Rain had been teaching Marsha how to dry and press wildflowers and also how to make colorful astrology charts. The day prior to her mother's visit, Marsha and Rain went to the Goodwill and bought ten used picture frames at fifty cents each. On returning to the school, they used the frames to mount seven of their dried flowers and three of their astrology charts. They removed the haphazard array of things on the wall and replaced it with their artwork. These quite lovely additions changed the feel of the downstairs significantly, and really pleased Rain, who felt the dried flowers reinforced the message of nature and the environment that the school sought to promote. They also served to display the work that was ongoing at the school.

Mimi arrived at the Eugene airport late in the afternoon on Friday. She rented a car and drove to her hotel. After she had checked in and freshened up, she drove to the school. Marsha had been waiting anxiously all day for her mother's arrival. Determined to ease her into the ambiance of Blake College, she came out of the house as soon as she saw the rental car roll down the driveway.

"My what a lovely house," said Mimi, after hugging her daughter and kissing her on the cheek. "Is this part of the school?"

"This is the school, Mother. There are only four students."

Mimi was second-generation Chinese and not quite fifty. She wore an expensive conservative suit and high heels and looked stunning with perfect makeup and styled hair. Marsha had not told her much about the school on the phone or by letter, which was what inspired Mimi's trip to Eugene. "Four students? I knew this was a small school, but I didn't understand how small. Are you learning anything?"

"Absolutely. I can't imagine going to school anywhere else. Let's walk the grounds, and then we'll go inside to meet the other students and the faculty. We'll all eat together tonight. I'll be making dinner with one of the faculty."

"You're making dinner?"

"We take turns. Learning to cook is part of the curriculum."

Marsha showed her mother the garden and the green house and the location where they hoped to one day build a kiln. Mimi was expecting something much different—more school-like, but she was a gardener herself and was impressed by the quality of the vegetables in the greenhouse and the greens in the garden. When they went into the house, Mimi was immediately drawn to Marsha's and Rain's artwork, particularly the pressed flowers.

Marsha made the meal with Adrienne. After everyone had found a place at the table, they served eggplant parmesan with homemade French bread and a salad from the garden. The school members had on their best clothes. Janice wore her print dress for the first time since she'd arrived. It looked great on her. Ray was there as usual for the weekend dinner. Van sat across the table and down from Marsha, so their connection would not be any more obvious than necessary.

Mimi was a reserved woman and smart like her daughter. She watched everyone throughout the meal but didn't say much. The usually animated Blake College conversations were limited to the faculty introductions and Gloria's description of yoga and meditation.

After the meal, Crow got out his guitar, and they sat on the floor in the living room—Mimi sat on the couch—and sang folk songs, something they did a couple of times a week.

On Saturday, Marsha and her mother drove to the coast, spent some time walking on the beach and visiting gift shops, then returned to Eugene. Instead of eating at the school, Mimi took Marsha out for dinner.

After the meal, Marsha and her mother had their final talk of the visit over tea. "I really enjoyed seeing the school, Marsha," said her mother. "It's not what your father and I imagined when we sent you off to college, but it does look fun. The gardening and yoga impressed me, and I'd love for you to show me how you pressed those flowers."

Marsha could feel it coming.

"I don't know what to think of the man with his hair all knotted up, but I guess hair is only hair."

Marsha nodded and took a sip from her cup of tea.

"I liked the boy, Van. He seemed quite nice."

Marsha brightened. "Yes, he is nice. He's become my best friend at the school."

"I noticed he was watching you. Be careful. You're living in very close quarters." The implication was obvious.

Marsha nodded. "We do well together, Mother—all of us. And it's a good experience for an only child to live with a lot of people. I really like it here."

"Well, I can see that. But I don't think you should stay another year. This school is child's play for you. There's no math and science. No college-level classes. Your father and I talked about this before I came. We want you to apply to Stanford again. This is fine for a year off, but you need to go to a real college."

"I thought you might say that, Mother. And I get it, but I'd prefer if you left that decision to me. And I won't know about next year until I've completed this one."

"But you need to apply now if you want to get into a good school. If I'm not mistaken, applications are due in February. Would you at least do that? Apply." She reached into her purse and withdrew a manila envelope. "I took the liberty of writing to Stanford for the material." She smiled in a motherly way and handed the envelope to Marsha.

Marsha opened the envelope and looked inside. She had lived a protected life and had never disobeyed her parents. That she came to Blake was more an oversight on her parents' part than Marsha doing what she wanted. But now that she'd broken the parental tie, living away from home for the first time, her life felt more like her own. She pulled the material from the envelope and read the cover letter. "The application is due February fifteenth. That gives me three months. I'll make a decision by then."

Mimi caught the edge in her daughter's voice. She sat back. "Well, you'll be home for Christmas. If you haven't sent it in by then, you and I and your father can sit down and talk about it." Her tone suggested the decision had already been made.

Marsha answered with a non-committal, "Yeah." She felt like telling her mother she was no longer a virgin and was taking birth control—but she didn't.

CHAPTER 50

The forecast was for several more days without rain. Spikes decided to use the dry weather to build the forms for the new foundation. Ray arrived at Twelfth and Jefferson early. He was sitting on the curb beside his bicycle when Spikes drove up. Ray could see the steam coming out of Jack's ears as soon as he leaned out the window of his pickup.

"Hop in," growled Spikes. "We've got a rental problem to solve before doing anything over here."

Spikes didn't say another word as he drove across town to the house at First and Madison. The renter, Karen, had called late the night before. The electricity had gone out in the kitchen and laundry room. Spikes told her to check the fuse box to see if any of the fuses had blown. She called him back in the morning to say she couldn't tell if a fuse had blown. Spikes knew it wasn't always obvious, but the woman's biker boyfriend should have been sharp enough to figure it out. He wasn't too happy about this second visit to the house.

Ray followed Spikes up to the front porch. Karen met him at the door. She was about to go to work. It was obvious why Spikes had rented to her. She was a good-looking woman when dressed up in a suit and high heels. From the doorway Spikes could see that the motorcycle in the living room was now entirely in pieces, spread out on a drop cloth on the floor. Mike Rogers and another biker sat in the center of it all, cleaning the parts with solvent soaked rags and drinking beer. It was eight-thirty in the morning. Mike caught Spikes' glance from across the room. Spikes acknowledged the man with the slightest nod.

Spikes tried the light switches in the kitchen and the laundry room. The power was clearly off. Spikes, Ray, and Karen went down to the basement to look at the electrical panel. Spikes had rewired the panel when he first acquired the house. He knew exactly which fuse protected the circuit in the kitchen. He had labeled it, but it was clear when he pointed this out to Karen, she had not made that connection. Spikes was polite. He unscrewed the fuse and inspected it beneath the single naked light bulb that lit the basement.

"Yep," he said, relieved that it wasn't some other problem. "This fuse is blown." Spikes returned to the electrical panel. Three replacement fuses were on top of the box. One of them was the same amperage as the one that had blown. He showed this to Karen. "I left these here in case something like this happened." He demonstrated how to screw the new fuse in. "Next time, you can do it yourself." He smiled the entire time. When they went upstairs, Karen tried the lights and they worked perfectly.

As Karen led Ray and Spikes to the door, Mike, still sitting on the floor, called out to Spikes. "Karen says you're a vet."

"Yeah," said Spikes, steamed that the motorcycle freak hadn't replaced the fuse himself.

"Same as me," said the heavyset man.

Spikes acknowledged this with a nod then pulled open the door.

"We've got a little group forming," continued Mike before Spikes could leave. "Vets against the war. Any interest?" He grinned as though he already knew where Spikes stood on the war.

Spikes stopped halfway out the door, gave a fiery look to Ray, then turned to the biker. "No, thanks," he said, gritting his teeth to prevent him from unleashing a stream of vulgarities. He quickly stepped out onto the porch and pulled the door shut behind him.

"God damn," he cursed, as he and Ray climbed into the pickup. "Vets against the war. Fuck! What about vets for the war? Did you see those dicks in there? Jesus Christ! Think maybe one of them ace mechanics might have figured out how to change a fuse? FUCK VETS AGAINST THE WAR."

Spikes fumed all the way to Twelfth and Jefferson and for the rest of the day, a non-stop diatribe against bikers and hippies.

CHAPTER 51

The property around Blake College was extensive. Most of it was in the back, a two-acre strip along the Willamette, where the river was wide and deep and took a lazy turn to the south. Adrienne had claimed about six thousand square feet of the property for her garden. Deer were prevalent along the river, so she and Ray fenced it off with four-foot by eight-foot cattle panels, two panels high. They added a chicken coop to one corner of the enclosure and bought six hens and a rooster. Adrienne wanted the eggs as well as the manure. It all worked pretty well except that the chickens got out every now and then. It wasn't much of a problem because of the space. The birds could wander for a long time without leaving the property, although every now and then one would find its way into the house, which invariably led to a lot of chicken shit to clean up and a potentially lethal confrontation with Lena the cat, the baby foxes—or Adrienne's dog.

Moxie hated the rooster from day one. He caught it before a week had passed, but Ray was right there and saved the bird. On a positive note, the rooster never crowed again. The four in the morning wake-up call was even too much for Gloria the early riser.

With the building of the greenhouse, the integration of the chickens into the garden, the granola business, and all the lessons learned about co-educational living, Blake College was actually doing what it set out to do. A school for hands-on learning, built upon a foundation of self-reliance and cooperative living. No one was getting rich. Applications didn't fill the mailbox, but the bills were getting paid, and the entire group was getting better at what they were trying to do—both as students and as instructors.

Three weeks into November, just as their success was becoming apparent, and it was clear that the tiny experimental school was in fact doing something good for all involved, Gloria announced at a Friday dinner that she had been diagnosed with pancreatic cancer. She would not last through the end of the school year. She was fifty-eight.

Gloria did not have health insurance or a savings or even a family to turn to. The Blake College co-op rose to the occasion. After an outpouring of emotion and support, they decided that Gloria should remain at the school to teach and to address the cancer through her own regime of natural herbs and alternative medicine. The fun and spontaneity at the school took a hit, but the camaraderie heightened.

The morning following her announcement, during her yoga class, which for the first time had full attendance—and included Ray, Gloria told the group that she was expanding the purpose of the class.

"Throughout these classes," Gloria began, "I have emphasized technique in both the poses and the breathing exercises and have deliberately said very little about the spiritual aspects of the yogic tradition."

Gloria's first classes had been held outside when the weather was nice, but with the onset of the winter rain, they had moved all the furniture, except the sofa, out of the living room to create an indoor workout room and yoga space. Now they all sat cross-legged on mats facing Gloria. To their left was a bank of three windows, looking out on the front yard and two lovely old oak trees with long sprawling, moss covered branches.

"Because of the state of my health, I want to add the study of *The Tibetan Book of the Dead* to the class." One by one, Gloria made eye contact with the others. "If you will indulge me, this will allow me to prepare for my lasts days. This means we will explore the Tibetan concepts of dying and the afterlife—plus all the relevant metaphysics that go with these ideas. I didn't do this at the start of the class in September because it includes notions linked to mysticism and spiritualism—but I am going to die in the foreseeable future and, not surprisingly, my interest in spiritualism is increasing. I'd like to include it in my teachings."

Within the group, Tai and Rain were already deeply involved in the occult. As seekers they had studied metaphysics and all the new age philosophies that had percolated out of the counterculture—from astrology and the I Ching to telekinesis, astral travel, and extraterrestrial contact. Gloria had not mentioned metaphysics at any time before, but she had long been a spiritualist as part of her own yogic practice. Crow had spent some time on an Indian reservation in North Dakota. He had seen too much in the Native American belief system to deny the spirit world and had no problem accepting the unexplained.

The others were all much younger. They'd had their fair dose of hippie mysticism, but Adrienne and Ray were into the land, and the only invisible things they talked about were the microorganisms in the compost and the soil. Van and Marsha had come from advanced high school programs and had a predilection for science. They needed proof to believe in anything more than the doctrines of chemistry and physics. Janice was a leaf in the wind. She believed whatever last tickled her fancy.

"No one needs to take part who doesn't want to," continued Gloria. "But I truly believe there's immeasurable value for all of you to accompany me on this path, especially if we can do it as a committed group. I will ask you to read several esoteric texts and to learn and practice Buddhist and Native American chants and recitations." Again, she made eye contact with each of them. "What do you say? Is this asking too much?"

Rain spoke first. "Not at all. I would be honored to join you."

"Absolutely," said Tai and Crow.

"Absolutely," echoed Janice.

The others looked at each other. They had only the vaguest idea of what would be involved and shrugged almost as one. "We're with you, Gloria. All of us. Take us on your journey," concluded Adrienne with nods from Van, Marsha, and Ray.

Thus Blake College took on its most serious educational effort yet. They would delve the meaning of death and dying by accompanying one of their own through the process.

Every day afterward, the entire school—Janice more often than not and Ray when his job allowed—met in the morning for the regular yoga regime and meditation. After meditation, they practiced a variety of chants, recited Tibetan prayers from *The Book of the Dead*, and talked about the afterlife as described by a variety of cultures. Gloria was determined to face death with her eyes wide open. Death, as she repeated to everyone, including herself, should be experienced as an ecstatic act. "Conjoining with the clear light" was how she put it. There was "an art to it."

Gloria added European metaphysics to her interpretation of the Tibetan death rituals. In both traditions, the other side, as she called it, was not unlike a Freudian dreamscape, a kind of psycho-spiritual soup.

"If the ancient texts are correct, the soul must spend some amount of time after death on the lowest spiritual plane before ascending to the higher realms," she told the class one morning after forty-five minutes of yoga and a brief period of silence. "Spiritualists call it the astral plane. Catholics would liken it to purgatory. To all believers, it's the spirit world, a waystation for wandering souls, prior to conjoining with the clear light."

"And the dead experience this consciously?" asked Van, perhaps the most skeptical in the group.

"Yes, death is not an absence of sensation. It's an excess of sensation, and so real that the greatest difficulty for the recently dead is to realize that they are dead. In fact, for the uninitiated, the experience of the astral plane is so confusing and frightening it can become a hell in itself. It contains the fluidity of a dream, no sense of duration, and complete discontinuity from ordinary space. That's what the breathing exercises, recitations, and chants are for—teaching you how to still your mind amid the turmoil of the astral plane.

"Yogin masters can bring about a trance using the meditations and chants we've practiced. They can leave their body and spend time on the astral plane, much like a dry run for the experience of death, and then return to the material world. I have achieved such a trance only a few times in my life, and I hope to open such a possibility to all of you in my few remaining months."

"Several Native American tribes use peyote to help them attain that kind of head space," said Tai. "I experienced it last year on the rez in Chinle."

Gloria nodded. "And you did this as a group?"

"Yes, with more than twenty others. But only after many hours of chanting did we leave our bodies. It was the most profound experience in my entire life—even more profound than my time at Millbrook."

Gloria smiled at the thought of it. "It's my goal for us to achieve that same kind of resonance in our group before my final day."

CHAPTER 52

Mike Rogers sat on the living room floor in Spikes' house at Madison and First, staring at the motorcycle parts strewn around him. It was three in the afternoon. He had been struggling for five days to put his 1956 Harley KHK back together. He had been haunted for the last week by dreams of his time in Vietnam and had used drugs to self-medicate the related depression. He was so fucked up on heroin now he couldn't tell if he was putting the bike together or taking it apart. He sat frozen in place with no clue what to do next.

When he finally gathered enough focus to move, he decided to try snorting a little meth to help his concentration. He found his way into the kitchen and lined it up on the counter. Two long snorts and he was back in the living room stumbling over the parts on the floor. A volume of the Encyclopedia Britannica—that he'd stolen from the library—lay open on the couch. He picked it up and read through the encyclopedia's description of a Molotov cocktail. He tore the page out and dropped the book back on the couch. It bounced on the seat cushion and fell on the floor.

By now it was dark outside. Karen would be home from work in an hour. He wandered into the kitchen and cracked a can of Blitz. He finished it off in four long swallows. He reached beneath the kitchen sink to retrieve a nearly empty bottle of Jack Daniels. He unscrewed the top, tilted the bottle over his head, and drained it. He went out to the garage and filled the empty whiskey bottle with gasoline, then jammed an old rag in the top to cork it. He stuck the bottle and a can of yellow spray paint in the saddle bag of his other Harley, a 1967 Sportster.

Mike rode the Sportster to the Alibi Club, where he could drink for free. He parked behind the building and came in through the back door. His father wasn't there, but the manager, Toad—a short, stocky ex-biker with a wide, flat head—was behind the bar. Twelve other patrons sat at tables or at the bar, regulars so regular and alcoholically picturesque one might wonder if Norman Rockwell had painted them into place. Mike removed his leathers and went behind the bar. He gave Toad a Nazi salute, then drew himself a pitcher from the tap.

Photographs of famous athletes from the University of Oregon were the central motif in the dark, narrow tavern. An Oregon football helmet, much like that of the Green Bay Packers, and a signed football were in a glass case beside the front door. A mahogany bar ran down one side of the tavern, matching booths down the other. At the back were a few tables and the restrooms. If Mike stayed there long enough, he figured some of the other Jokers would stop by looking for free beer. He took a table in the back and settled in for the evening.

Two hours and two pitchers later, Mike was still alone at the table. He went into the fabled restroom and took a piss, then stretched out two lines of meth on top of the soap dispenser and sucked them up with a rolled up twenty. He strode wildly back to his table, threw down the last of his beer, pulled on his leathers, and left the place using the back door.

He fired up his Sportster and headed back to Eugene. When he reached the University of Oregon, he turned left on Agate Street and parked his bike across from Hayward Field. He looked around to see if anyone was watching, then took the gasoline-filled whiskey bottle and the can of spray paint out of the saddle bag. He jammed them under his leather jacket, and sticking to the shadows, crossed the campus to the main administration building Johnson Hall. It was dark and cold; no one was in sight. He quickly used the spray paint to scrawl *Fuck ROTC* on the side of the brick building, then applied a Bic lighter to the rag stuffed in the bottle. The saturated rag burst into flame so suddenly Mike nearly dropped it. He took two longs strides and threw the bottle through a window, then hightailed it back across campus to his bike. A quick kick of the starter and he was off to the Alibi Club.

Halfway there, as he passed through a little industrial strip between Eugene and Springfield known as Glenwood, four motorcycles pulled out of a side street and powered up behind him. One glance in his rearview mirror and Mike knew they were Free Souls. He immediately turned right onto Highway 99 instead of going across the bridge into Springfield. The dismantled KHK was his ride, but the Sportster was faster, and if given half a chance, he'd shake these buttholes.

He managed to stay ahead of them for a while, but they broke into two groups—two following him and two veering off on another road, figuring he was taking the back way to the Alibi Club. Sensing they had guessed his destination and were going to cut him off, Mike took the ramp off Highway 99 onto Interstate Five, then took the next exit onto Thirtieth Street in south Eugene. One biker managed to stay close and was gaining on him. Mike felt a sharp sting in his left side, lost control of his bike, and slid sideways across Thirtieth Street into the curb. One biker then a second sped by him shouting, "Go to hell, you commie!"

Mike had taken a bullet in the side. He managed to lift his bike up and get it going. Fighting the pain and losing concentration, he wound his way back to Madison and First. Karen found him lying on the garage floor, conscious, but bleeding badly.

Karen sat him up, then helped him out of his leather jacket. Blood covered his chest and back. The bullet had passed through him, leaving a large hole through the excess flesh above his waist. Karen stripped his shirt off and led him to the bathroom. She cleaned him up, wrapped a towel around his midsection, then strapped in on with duct tape.

"Thanks, baby," he gritted through his teeth. "There's some heroin upstairs. Get me a fix. This hurts like hell."

Karen loved Mike. She saw what he went through with the terrors left over from the war. He had turned her against the war, and she had done her share of demonstrating at the university during the last year. She was pretty woman, who leaned to the sleazy side—hanging out with the Jokers didn't do much for anyone's reputation. She got the smack from a drawer in their bedroom and quickly fixed Mike, then snorted some meth for herself.

"We gotta get outta here," said Mike after the initial rush of heroin. "Those fucks are out to get me. We need a place to hide."

CHAPTER 53

The forms for the foundation at Twelfth and Jefferson were complete, and the forecast showed three consecutive days of dry weather, so Spikes had ordered a delivery of concrete. Henry Pozlowski joined Ray and Spikes for the pour. Spikes had helped with many concrete jobs, but this was the first time he was in charge of a job this big. The work was hard and took all day, as Ray, Spikes, and Henry used hoes and shovels to make sure the forms filled properly. Spikes was on edge the entire time, then was ecstatic when it all went off without a hitch.

Henry went home to his family, and Spikes took Ray out to Sheila's house for dinner to celebrate. He stopped at the corner grocery store, called Sheila to tell her he was bringing Ray, and bought two six-packs of Blitz. They each had one down by the time they turned into Sheila's driveway, where they were greeted by barking dogs, clucking chickens, a grunting hog, and two amped up kids.

Sheila liked having guests and knew Ray from several other occasions when he'd been over for dinner. She also knew how worried Spikes had been about the pour and was as happy for his success as he was. She had a chicken roasting in the oven when Spikes and Ray tromped through the mudroom into the kitchen. Sheila pulled a beer off the open six-pack and joined Ray and Spikes in the living room for a toast to the new foundation.

No sooner had she sat down than Mary and Joey came into the house with the dogs trailing behind. Joey sprinted across the living room and jumped into Spikes' arms. Jack caught him in his hands and turned the boy over on his stomach on the floor. He tickled Joey until the boy rolled away, practically in tears from giggling. Then Sheila got the kids to start cranking the ice cream maker so that dessert would be ready after the meal.

Several beers later, Sheila served the chicken, roasted with carrot slices and potato wedges. Asparagus and whole wheat dinner rolls filled out the meal. The kids refused to eat the asparagus, and Spikes would only eat one spear. But the rest of the meal was devoured. The homemade strawberry ice cream was almost too much to ask. Afterward, Ray went out to the living room with a cup of tea, while Sheila cleaned up the kitchen and Spikes escorted Mary and Joey upstairs to do their homework.

When Spikes came down to take Ray back into town, he stopped suddenly and stared out the living room window. "Someone's coming down the driveway."

Headlights flashed across the living room as soon as he said it. Sheila came into the room. "I'm not expecting anyone. Who could it be?"

"I'm going out there." Spikes pulled on his work boots and went out the front door. He recognized the car as soon as he saw it. It was his renter Karen's Chevy. She got out on the driver's side and walked up to Spikes as he came out to the driveway.

"Oh, I'm so glad it's you," she gasped. "All I had was the address where I send the rent check." Her usually perfect hair was disheveled, and she wore jeans and a half-buttoned flannel shirt with her bra visible beneath.

"Is there a problem at the house?" asked Spikes, wondering what would bring her out to Shelia's.

"No, it's my boyfriend," she said, turning to the car. "He's hurt bad." She opened the car door. Mike lay across the back seat. Even in the poor light the excess of blood was obvious.

He struggled to lift his head. "We didn't know where else to go."

"So, you came here?"

"You're a vet, bro."

"Yeah," said Karen. "I need to redo the bandages and thought you might help. He's bad off."

"Why not White Bird? It's a free clinic."

"It's a bullet wound. Mike doesn't trust them. And you've surely seen some bullet wounds."

Sheila came out onto the porch. "What's going on, Jack?"

Karen answered. "We just need a place to..."

"Hide out." Spikes looked over his shoulder. "Get back in the house, Sheila. I got this."

Sheila didn't move.

"Get in the house," roared Spikes. He turned to Karen. "You've got a gang of bikers after you, don't you?"

Shaking with fear, Karen nodded. Sheila disappeared into the house.

"I want you both gone. I got a wife and kids. I don't want any of that gang shit here."

Mike barked from the back seat. "Fuck you, asshole. We're also giving you notice. We've moved out of your place. We want the rent deposit before we go anywhere."

Sheila came out of the house with a shotgun. She stomped down the porch stairs and leveled it at the car from her hip. "This is my place. I want you out of here." She looked mad enough to shoot. "It's thirty days' notice for moving out, and there ain't no rent deposit until the place gets inspected." She motioned with the shotgun at Karen. "Get in the car."

Karen slid into the driver's seat despite a string of vicious threats from Mike. "Thought you might be a decent man," he screamed as Karen started the car. "Especially for another vet. Fuckhead!"

Karen hit the gas, sending the car twisting and turning in reverse down the long driveway out to the highway.

Spikes looked at Sheila standing beside him. "You sure look sexy with that gun at your hip."

Sheila shook her head. "Don't even go there."

Spikes laughed out loud. "That was quite an entrance. You were impressive."

"All I needed to hear was *gang of bikers*. Was he really a vet?"

"What difference does it make? He's a jerk no matter what. His presence here put us all in jeopardy. And might yet."

"I don't want you leaving," said Sheila. "Let Ray drive your truck into town. He can come get you in the morning."

CHAPTER 54

Ray drove into town in Spikes' pickup. He went straight to Blake College. He had been spending almost every night with Adrienne, and their relationship had evolved into something more than their time in bed.

He got there a few minutes after eleven o'clock. Adrienne was in the living room with Moxie lying at her feet and the two foxes curled up in her lap. They were old enough now to follow her around like Moxie did. Ray and Adrienne walked down to the river with Moxie and the little kits not far behind. Ray told Adrienne about the biker and why he was driving Jack's pickup.

"I'm glad you didn't get involved," said Adrienne, looking into Ray's eyes. "I sure would hate to see you get hurt." She touched him on the cheek before looking off at the river then back at Ray. "Would you be at all interested in joining the co-op and helping out at Blake College on a regular basis? You and I could share the bedroom, and you wouldn't have to pay rent somewhere else."

Ray had fallen head over heels for Adrienne. Still stinging from Laura, he was worried he liked Adrienne more than she liked him, and this request surprised him. "I would love to." He leaned into her and kissed her on the cheek. "I would still need to work for Jack, and I'll have to give him notice of some sort. But I can think of nothing better than living here with you."

CHAPTER 55

After Mike and Karen left Sheila's, they pulled off the road into an abandoned gasoline station at the junction of Highway 99 and Route 45, so Karen could give Mike a fix. The heroin habit Mike had picked up in Southeast Asia was the main reason he hated the war. He knew too many GIs who had come back to the states hooked on H.

Mike was from Eugene, and though an outcast in general, he did know people in the area. Before getting drafted, he had worked two summers at his uncle Walt Arnold's Christmas tree farm. Now, bleeding badly and wary of going to the hospital, he told Karen to head west on 45. He directed Karen to his uncle's property, then up a logging road to a little cabin at the edge of the Christmas tree farm. Mike had lived there one summer when he worked for his uncle. The cabin was no longer used, and the water had been shut off. But it was safe, had a wood stove, and provided sanctuary from the Free Souls while Mike struggled with the hole in his side.

CHAPTER 56

Spikes called the Eugene Police Department the next morning while he was waiting for Ray to come get him. He asked for Yates.

"What's going on, Jack?"

"Hear anything about a shooting last night?"

"No, you read the paper?"

"Not yet. Why?"

"Someone threw a firebomb in the window of Johnson Hall."

"Shit. More anti-war fucks?"

"Judging from the graffiti, the same ones who bombed Campbell Hall. No one got hurt, and there wasn't much damage. But it just adds to the tension around here. You should have heard the Mayor this morning. Jesus, he's on edge. What about this shooting?"

"One of the Gypsy Jokers lives in that house at First and Madison."

"You threw me out for him?"

"His girlfriend tricked me, but that's not the point. The guy came out to Sheila's last night looking for help. He was bleeding badly from a gunshot. Some kind of biker clash. I was wondering if you'd heard anything?"

"Why'd he go to Sheila's?"

Spikes growled. "He's a vet. Thought I might have sympathy. I told him I wanted nothing to do with him. Now I'm afraid he might retaliate."

"Wonderful. I'll check if anything came in last night that could be related. You okay?"

"I can handle myself, but I don't like the idea of that jerk knowing where Sheila and the kids live."

"How can I help?"

"Just be on the lookout and tell me what you find out. I'm hoping the other gang chased him out of town."

"That's some wishful thinking."

"I spent the night sitting on Sheila's porch with a shotgun on my lap. That's where I'm at. Find a place to live?"

"Yeah, I got a shitty little apartment out West Thirteenth. It'll do." Yates paused and looked around the office to see if anyone was listening. "I think I'm in love, Jack."

Spikes laughed for the first time all day. "Yeah, who's the lucky girl?"

"A couple of weeks back I broke up a party at a big Victorian on the river. It was mostly college students and hippies. Pot smoking and underage drinking. All the fun stuff. The woman who seemed to be in charge said her name was—of all things—Rain." He chuckled.

"Yeah, you mean a hippie girl."

"Hippie or not, this woman was both beautiful and remarkably—I don't know—remarkably composed. She felt so different than Rhonda, I had to wonder—what would she be like if I really got to know her?"

"Good luck on that one, Bob, you're nuts."

"Hey, I saw her once. Now I can't get her out of my mind. I sure would like to talk to her again. She was something else."

"Talk to her? Right, you horny dickhead. Just let me know when you run down these bikers. And get to work on that firebombing."

"Fuck you. That's the FBI's problem."

Spikes was sitting on the porch with his shotgun when Ray arrived. Ray got out of the truck. "Hear anything more after I left?"

Spikes came off the porch with the shotgun. "Not a word. I even talked to Yates to see if the police department had any information on an incident involving bikers. Get in the truck. We're going to the Madison Street house." Spikes climbed in on the driver's side and put the shotgun in the rack below his twenty-two.

"What's the gun for?"

"Protection. I've got to check that house. I'm not sure what I'll find—but it can't be good. We turned that asshole down last night. Those fucks thrive on revenge. The house could be trashed or burned to the ground for all I know. I just hope the guy left town or died."

They reached Madison and First in twenty minutes. Spikes drove around the block twice as a precaution. The house appeared empty. Karen's car was not there. He pulled into the driveway. They both got out of the truck. Spikes left the shotgun in the rack. He approached the front door with Ray trailing behind. They could see into the living room from the porch. The motorcycle parts were still spread out on the floor, but there was no sign of Karen or Mike or anyone else. Spikes rang the doorbell to be certain. No one came to the door. He rang several more times then let himself in. He told Ray to wait in the living room and to give him a holler if anyone drove up.

Spikes stalked through the house, upstairs and down. After about ten minutes, he rejoined Ray in the living room. "All their clothes are gone. The kitchen is empty of food. No overt damage, except a lot of blood in the bathroom. Thankfully, it seems they've left."

"But the furniture is still here."

"All that furniture is crap or stuff that was already in the house. They don't care about that. They've got someone after them. They're on the run."

Ray picked up a piston from the floor. "What about all these motorcycle parts?"

Spikes glanced around the room. "That's a little more worrisome. The guy's a biker. He'll risk his life to get this bike—even if it's in parts. And if the Free Souls know it's here, they'll steal it. Fuck! Mike will be back sure as shit—wanting these parts and the rent deposit." He shook his head. "What a deal! I won't be able to rent this place until we work something out. Fuck, more money down the drain!"

Ray saw a page torn from an encyclopedia lying on the floor. He picked it up. On one side was the description of moles and their living habits. Adrienne was having trouble with moles in the garden; he stuffed the page into his pocket. "What are you going to do, Jack?"

"Change all the locks. If they want this stuff, they'll either have to break in or call me. If they call, I'll meet them here and provide protection for the house, while they get those bike parts and whatever portion of the deposit I decide to give them."

"You worried?"

"Yeah. I figure it's fifty-fifty they break in. I knew I was in trouble as soon as I saw those lowriders. Shit. Let's go. We've got to check the concrete we poured yesterday. Then we'll get back to preparing the house for the move."

On the way across town, Ray opened up to Spikes. "I'm moving out of the rental, Jack."

Spikes didn't divert his eyes from the road. "Got another place?"

"I'm moving in with Adrienne. She shares a big house with a bunch of other folks. It's as cheap as your rental and," he glanced out the side window, "Adrienne and I have gotten too close not to live together."

Spikes liked Ray in his rental because he knew he was responsible. He didn't want him to move out, but it wasn't his business if Ray found something better. "When are you moving?"

Ray looked down at his feet. "Thirty days or whatever works for you. I haven't spent a night there in weeks. I'm basically out already."

Spikes nodded. "I'll tell you what. Find someone to take your place and you can skip the thirty days."

"You don't need to do that."

"But I am. Go for it."

"Thanks, Jack."

"When do I get to meet this girl?"

"How about this afternoon?" Ray beamed. "I'm meeting her at Max's at five. Let's head over there at four-thirty. I'll buy you a beer and she'll be there before we're done."

"Oh, boy. My favorite place. Hippies and college students."

Spikes and Ray grabbed a booth when they got to Max's that afternoon. Ray bought a large pitcher, and Spikes got a cigar, which he promptly lit. About halfway through their first glass, and submerged in a dense cloud of cigar smoke, Ray saw Adrienne's pickup pull up across the street fifteen minutes before he expected her. He didn't say anything, but Spikes couldn't help commenting on the truck. "There's a beaut. Too bad the owner doesn't take better care of it. It's a classic."

Ray contained a grin as Jack watched Adrienne climb from the truck and slam the door. She was wearing her favorite pants, a pair of vertically striped, hip hugging bell-bottoms, and a blue jean jacket. The pants flared at her knees but were skin tight on her thighs and haunches. The wide belt sat about two inches below her navel.

Not yet connecting her to Ray, Spikes eyed her with a deep intensity as she crossed the street and swayed through the door. The cigar fell from his mouth when Ray stood up and introduced her. "Adrienne, this is my boss Jack Spikes."

Spikes stood awkwardly, stubbed the cigar out in an ashtray, and offered her his hand.

"Jack, this is Adrienne."

"Pleased to meet you, Jack." Adrienne shook his hand and smiled, nearly knocking Spikes back into his seat. She removed her jacket and hung it at the end of the booth. She wore a tight, navy-blue, long-sleeved crew neck jersey.

"Looks like I'll need a glass," she said, glancing at the pitcher. Ray started to get it, but she waved her hand and went to the bar.

Spikes watched her walk away, then turned to Ray. "Jesus, dude, I'm not big on bell-bottoms, but boy, she sure makes them look good. Congratulations, Ray."

"Congratulations?"

"Yeah, you got lucky. She's a knockout."

Ray was still shaking his head when Adrienne slid into the booth beside him and poured herself a beer.

"I love your truck, Adrienne," said Spikes, very captured by her. "What year?"

"Nineteen Fifty-four. I'd like to fix it up. But right now, I'm still scraping the cash together to pay for gas."

"My dad had a fifty-six, brand new. I always wanted one myself."

"I got that one for a hundred dollars."

"Did it run?"

"Not a first, but I got it going."

"Yourself?"

Her smile lit up the booth. "I know a mechanic or two. I got some help."

Duly impressed, and staring too much, Spikes only stayed long enough to finish his glass of beer. "It was nice to meet you, Adrienne. But I gotta get going. I hear you two are moving in together. There must be some serious stuff to talk about."

"Ha-ha," muttered Ray. Adrienne laughed.

Jack looked around at the tavern's clientele that slowly increasing in anticipation of happy hour. "Besides, these hippies are making me nervous. I need to go home." Eyes flashing, he grinned at Adrienne through his mustache, barely able to keep himself from flirting with her. "Thanksgiving's in a few days. Maybe both of you should come over to my girlfriend's place. She's a great cook."

"That would be nice, Jack," said Adrienne, "but we've already got a feast planned at the house."

"Fair enough. You should come out for dinner another time." He stood up, jabbed Ray in the shoulder, and walked away.

"I like Jack," said Adrienne. "He's pretty funny."

"I do too, but he wasn't joking about the hippies. He's a vet and believes in the war and the flag."

Adrienne made a face. "Well, I still liked him."

CHAPTER 57

On Tuesday, two days before Thanksgiving, Tim and Gino took hits of acid to begin the day. Around noon they decided to ride their bicycles to the University to check out the damage to Johnson Hall, figuring being high would make them more perceptive.

Tim had not inspected Campbell Hall after it was bombed, but when he learned that Stoopid had been caught in the fire, he had gotten a copy of the Register-Guard to read what was in the paper. The front page carried a color photo of the damaged building, which included the spray-painted door, emblazoned with the *Fuck ROTC* slogan in bright yellow paint. That same slogan was the first thing Gino and Tim saw as they coasted to a stop outside the yellow plastic ribbon that cordoned off the west side of Johnson Hall. Then they saw the sheet of plywood that covered the window broken by the firebomb. Very little other damage had been done to the building. The sprinkler system had stopped the fire from spreading beyond the office where the firebomb landed. They climbed off their bicycles and walked up close to the red brick building where the bomber had signed his work.

Tim had saved the Register-Guard from the earlier bombing as a reminder of what had happened to his friend. He had the front page folded up in his pocket. He showed it to Gino. "What'd ya think? It looks like the same style of writing to me."

"Yep, and same color paint, as best I can tell from the photo. I'd say whoever blew up Campbell Hall, also did this."

Tim nodded. "And killed Stoopid."

They began to walk around the site, looking for anything the authorities might have missed. They were quite high, and their approach was to follow their eyes—which they now imagined were like spotlights, allowing them to focus on the detail of anything they saw. Tim noticed a few footprints within the yellow ribbon. No matter how he gazed at them, they were too muddy and smushed up to reveal anything about the shoes other than that they were large and most likely worn by a man. Gino wandered far from the building, sidetracked first by a co-ed crossing the campus and then a quarter lying on the sidewalk. Well away from Tim, he knelt to stare at a remarkably large slug.

"Hey, Gino," called Tim, "you're getting off course. Come back this way."

"Amazing designs on these banana slugs."

"Right. Come back this way."

Gino stood, took two steps toward Tim, then suddenly stopped to stare at something in the grass ahead of him. Gino pointed his finger at whatever he saw and followed his finger about ten yards to a spot in the grass and knelt.

"What is it?"

"I saw a dot of red in the grass. Here it is." He pointed to a piece of red plastic mostly buried in the wet grass and mud.

Tim came over to Gino, trying to get him back to the crime scene. He stared down at the grass as Gino used a pocket knife to dig the piece of plastic out of the mud.

"Hey, this is cool." He stood to show Tim the small plastic cylinder. It had a slot cut into the side and a tiny, hollow stem at one end. He handed it to Tim. "This must be something."

Tim rolled it over in his palm for a minute or so. "No doubt about that, Gino. It's definitely something."

"It's certainly not nothing."

Tim held it up between his fingers. "Right again. It' certainly not nothing." They looked at each other and burst into laughter.

Gino suddenly became serious. "It's a spray paint nozzle." Gino used a lot of spray paint for refurbishing old bicycles. "But not like any I've ever seen."

"Yeah, I think you're right. This must be a new design."

Gino pointed to the yellow paint around the pinhole opening. "Same as on the building."

Tim bobbed his head. "I'll bet it fell off the spray can when the guy ran off. Good eyes, Gino. The FBI even missed it. How the hell did you see it?"

Gino grinned and touched the side of his head. "X-ray vision."

"That would mean you could see through things."

"Yeah, that too."

As they got on their bicycles and made one last appraisal of the scene before leaving, Gino stared at the spray-painted slogan. "You know, I recognize that yellow. I've seen it somewhere else. I can't make the connection now, but something tells me that's important."

"Looks like safety yellow to me. Pretty common for spray paint."

"Maybe, but there's something about it. I think I've seen it before. It'll come to me."

Tim laughed. "You mean when you're appropriately stoned." *As if they weren't already!*

"Exactly. Once I stop thinking about it. Isn't that the way it always happens?"

"Yeah, when half your brain cells are gone or you're eighty years old."

"Eat me, asshole."

They pedaled off certain they had found an important clue.

CHAPTER 58

The firebombing of Johnson Hall had caused another major tremor in the life of Eugene's Mayor Les Anderson. Les and his wife Maureen had initially planned to host a big Thanksgiving dinner with several close friends, but the firebombing of Johnson Hall had so infuriated the Mayor that he canceled, saying he and Maureen had come down with the flu. Maureen cooked a small turkey, and dinner included only their son Jon and their daughter Tina, a sophomore at UCLA, who had come home for the holiday. Not even turkey, stuffing, and mashed potatoes, however, could lift Les' spirits. The family sat at the table chowing down, while Les, always a big eater, picked at his plate.

"Dad," said Tina, a petite blond, "it's Thanksgiving. Can you at least let go of this stuff for a couple of days—while I'm home?" She smiled wide and bright. "We're here to celebrate the things we're thankful for, and our family's been blessed with everything we could possibly want from comfort and food to good educations."

"I'm sorry, Tina. You're entirely right, but I can't shake this thing. Getting the Trials would make my mayorship special, remembered and important."

"And give you a shot at a governorship," slipped in Jon.

"Don't remind me."

"Come on, Les," said Maureen, "I want to hear thanks coming from your end of the table."

Les grimaced. "I'm thankful for Bill Bowerman. He's sure to get on the selection committee."

Tina shook her head. "Not good enough, Dad."

Les finally broke. "No, it's not, I'm sorry. I'm thankful for my family. All of you have put up with the crazy politics and politicking that goes with what I do. I couldn't ask for a better wife, son, or daughter. Especially if Jon makes the Olympic team."

Everyone laughed at this but Jon, for whom this was as serious an issue as the Trials were to his father. "Well, I'm thankful for Bill Bowerman, too," said the distance runner. "He's given me a chance to achieve something I never thought I could." He grinned. "And I'm thankful for the new shoes he's making. They've shaved thirty seconds off my time for the ten thousand."

"Wonderful, Jon," said Tina, shaking her head. "But your thanks seems a little self-centered."

"Not really, the only way I make the team is if the Trials are held here in Eugene—that's as much for Dad as me. I'll need the hometown crowd to get me over the finish line."

"Here, here," said Les. "What about you, Maureen?"

His wife smiled, clearly thankful to be with her family. "I'm thankful I don't really have the flu."

CHAPTER 59

John and Joyce Walters scurried around their small kitchen, gathering up the things they were taking to Joyce's parents' house for Thanksgiving dinner. Ann was cooking a turkey for Maynard and herself, but John and Joyce were bringing tempeh, which Joyce had marinated in teriyaki sauce and cooked in her oven. She also made a pumpkin pie. John made mashed potatoes and creamed string beans and onions.

As they packed their portion of the meal into two cardboard boxes, John brought up the question of adoption. "Are you sure you wouldn't like to have a child of our own before adopting?"

Joyce looked up from the box she was filling. "Yes, I am sure, John. Are you changing your mind? I thought this was settled long ago."

"It's what your mother said when we first told your parents. It stuck in my head, and then the other day your father pressed me on it. He can't believe I don't want a son from my own blood line—and with the loss of your brother..."

"John, this is not about my father or his needs. It's about us doing what is right. We talked about all of this before. We must be entirely united in our decision. My parents are not happy with the idea, and if they think we're hesitating, they'll fight harder against it."

"That's why I brought this up now. It's really between us and not them."

"And you're getting cold feet?"

"No. I just wanted to air my concerns before we get over there." John picked up his box and headed to the truck.

"This conversation isn't over, John." She grabbed the other box and followed him out the door.

"So," said Joyce, sliding in on the passenger's side of their pickup, "are we together on this or not?"

John put the key in the ignition and stared out the windshield.

"Well," continued Joyce, clearly irritated, "we know it will be hard. Adoption can be difficult, and then the child can be also. We are either locked in on this or…what?"

John turned to her. "I'm locked in on it, Joyce. I am, but that doesn't mean I don't think about it. It's difficult. If my father were alive, he'd say the same thing your dad did. I'm trying to be honest, not combative."

"I could never have guessed."

"Come on, Joyce. I am human."

"And I'm not?"

"Joyce."

She crossed her arms and looked out the side window. John started the truck. Five minutes later they were chugging up Maynard's driveway. When the couple entered the house, Joyce and John were all smiles.

Maynard greeted them with, "I can't believe anyone would eat tofu on Thanksgiving instead of turkey."

Joyce hugged her father and kissed him on the cheek. "Get used to it, Dad. The times are a changin'."

CHAPTER 60

Tai knew that the season for liberty cap mushrooms was nearly over. Although he had been seen the last time he was picking, he decided the Monday after Thanksgiving to make one more trip out to the field, knowing a good day could bring in a five-hundred-dollar payday.

He made every effort not to be seen. He wore a recently purchased set of fatigues in camouflage print and drove out route 45 with Rain's bicycle in his van. He parked the van on a side road two miles from the field, then rode the bike to the field and stashed it in the weeds before climbing over the barbwire fence. Determined to get every mushroom, he started at the back of the field, ate the first ten he found, and worked his way back to the fence.

Maynard didn't see the VW van as he returned to his house for lunch that afternoon, nor did he see the bicycle in the weeds. After stopping at the mailbox, he took a long look at the field, then motored up the driveway, entirely unaware of Tai's presence.

After lunch Maynard lingered in his chair long after Ann had cleared the table. He was idly looking out the window at the pasture. He didn't see the picker, nor did he even think he was there. He wasn't in a state of agitation, and he allowed himself to ponder the field he would usually rather forget. He thought a long time about something that should have been obvious all along. Finally, he got up from the table and ambled out of the house to his pickup. Before he got into the cab, he stopped and gazed down at the field.

For his entire life Maynard had seen God through nature. He imagined that changes in the weather directly and indirectly reflected God's various moods. God was always in communication with him in this way. He didn't think of himself as special in this. It was just that living as he did in his own valley, his own corner of the universe, everything that happened, good or bad, wet or dry, seemed to be a reflection of God's feelings toward Maynard Smith, even Joyce's decision to adopt. Thanksgiving had been difficult. The issue had come up again, resulting in a long argument. But today, with the sun shining so benevolently for a change and his decision about the field made, he was not nearly as angry as he had been at the dinner table.

During the past summer, he had complained to his neighbor Walt Arnold about the pickers and had asked him if they ever came onto his property. Though Walt and Maynard had quite different attitudes about the land, and didn't really talk much, Walt told him that the secret was not to pasture the field. "Don't let your cattle graze in the field and let the grass grow long," he said. "Without the fresh manure, the mushroom population will diminish, and the long grass will make those that do come up harder to find." During lunch Maynard had decided to follow his neighbor's advice. He wouldn't pasture the field. He would abide by what seemed to be the wishes of both his father and the Man upstairs.

Maynard climbed into his pickup and motored slowly down the gravel driveway. When Maynard reached the bottom of the driveway, he came to a full stop. He looked out into the pasture, still not seeing the picker, though half-imagining he would.

In this rare empathetic moment, Maynard recalled the question Ann had asked about the mushroom high. He found himself wondering if the picker would eat the mushrooms while he picked them. Or did he eat them alone at night or at parties with other mushroom pickers? Or what? L-S-D. L-S-D. These three letters ran through his mind. He repeated them aloud, "L-S-D." What was it anyway? He remembered seeing something about it in the newspapers. A hallucinogenic drug. That's what they called it. Technology's answer to God. Religion in a tablet. An ugly idea, he thought. Turn on, tune in, drop out. What did that mean? It was too foreign to him to understand. A farmer's life was tuning in. Tuning into the land, not some kind of dream world in a tablet.

He turned right out of the driveway and pulled the truck up to the south edge of the pasture. He got out and let himself into the field through the cattle gate. His curiosity had finally gotten the better of him. He was going to find one of the little buggers.

The moment Tai heard the truck door slam at the top of the hill, he had stilled himself behind a clump of tall marsh grass. Completely hidden, he watched the truck roll down the hill. He was certain he hadn't been seen, but his heart began to race when he saw M. Smith pull up alongside the gate, climb out of his truck, and enter the field. In the suit of camouflage and stoned on mushrooms, Tai didn't think it was the best time to get up and introduce himself. He committed himself to invisibility and lay out on his belly in the cold, wet grass.

There weren't many mushrooms that day, and it took Maynard quite a while to find one. Walking at random in the pasture, head down, stooping every now and then to inspect the ground, he recalled his dreams that portrayed the mushrooms as the sprouted eyes of the Kalapuya. Suddenly two of them, like eyeballs on thin white stems, were peering up at him from the grass. Although many types of mushrooms grew in the valley, something told Maynard these were the ones. He knelt and delicately plucked one of them. Thinking of it as a sprouted eye, he held it up in the sunlight.

From Tai's perspective, not fifteen yards away, the scene was stunning in its immediacy. His senses were tuned to the utmost, and his mind was in that transient state that tends to highlight the symbolic in everything. In wide splaying angles of light, the farmer had walked between Tai and the sun, gone to a knee, and picked a mushroom. Tai couldn't believe it. It looked as though the man were going to eat one.

From across the short distance, Tai could hear the farmer speaking in a soft, low voice—*praying*. The trees, the clouds, the sky, the wide open were fraught. The farmer's words, directed to some invisible entity, seemed to walk one by one, suspended in dilating time, across Tai's mind.

"Sometimes, Lord, I think us farmers are the only ones who have any idea who you are anymore. I wake up each morning about the same time as you, then start dealing with the problems of existence as soon as I can get a cup of coffee down and a seat on the throne. I believe you and I see eye to eye most of the time, and I sure try my darndest to be straight with you when we don't.

"We all have personal struggles. That's what life is about, if you ask me. And yeah, I'm having a little trouble with my daughter, but my struggle, year in and year out, is mostly with you. Fighting your seasons, your weather, your whim. It's my farm against your nature. Be sure I've pounded many a stake in your name.

"But I know for sure, the clearest, cleanest vision of life comes from your garden. And no one is closer to that than the plain old diggin-in-the-dirt farmer. I know I can be pretty dang slow sometimes, but let's just say I think I've finally heard the message you've been trying to tell me for some time now. Pardon the mule in me, but Dad was right. This piece of land was not meant to be cultivated for some reason a lot bigger than me or this farm, and it has something to do with these mushrooms." He looked at the one in his hand and slowly shook his head. "I can't say I understand, but it ain't for me to understand everything."

Something in the elements had sprung in Maynard. He had never spoken spontaneously aloud to his god. It felt a little strange to him as he pondered the mushroom in his hand, but it also felt good. "Lord, I'm giving you back this land."

When Maynard caught up with the words that had tumbled from his mouth, he bowed his head. And as he did so, out of the corner of his eye, he caught the movement of the lowly mushroom picker eavesdropping in the grass. His emotions were so filled with premonition, he held his composure and pretended not to have seen through the veil of camouflage.

Maynard had no idea that he would pray when he entered the field. He'd meant what he said, and he'd spoken more emotionally than he knew he could—a simple man humbled before his god. It embarrassed him that this sentimental outpouring had occurred before a stranger. Then he was ashamed for being embarrassed for speaking openly to his god. But he was still angry as hell about the invasion of privacy and property. Only Maynard's sense of humor prevented what could have been a very ugly scene.

"While I'm here, Lord," Maynard continued as though he'd seen nothing, "I'd like you to pass something along to that fella who does your mushroom picking."

Tai was already poised on every word, but when the farmer mentioned "mushroom picking," his ears glowed red. From any other perspective, it was manifest absurdity. The one man on his knee was whispering to a man prone in the wet grass fifty feet away. A scream could not have made the farmer's message any clearer.

"Now, I'm not one to cast judgment on another man's life," said Maynard, "and I know deep down that picker is just another pawn, like me, in your larger munificence. Maybe he's just someone you had to invent to get your message across to me, I don't know. But could you, please, ask him something for me, next time you see him?"

Maynard took a covert glance at the camouflaged picker, noticing the man's strange, knotted fingers of hair. "Ask him what in hell's name he's doing with these magic mushrooms? Because as far as I'm concerned, they're mine, and I don't want to be part of a drug operation. And then tell him, if I ever catch him out here again, I'll shoot his camouflaged-ass so full of rock salt he'll think he ate Mexican for a week. So help me, God. Amen." With that, Maynard stood, tossed the mushroom into the air, and walked back to his pickup.

When the farmer's truck was long out of sight, Tai stood up and hiked out of the field, both embarrassed—because he knew he had been seen—and impressed by the farmer's words. He would not come back to this field to pick mushrooms because he now understood that they were sacred—as he'd always believed—and were not to be sold. He would keep the mushrooms he'd picked, but he would either consume them himself or give them away.

CHAPTER 61

It had been almost two weeks since Stoopid's funeral. Tim had been busy and had yet to make the trip out to the Lorane commune to talk to Dick Danger. The firebombing at Johnson Hall had gotten the city talking again, and Tim couldn't put it off any longer. He pushed aside all his printing jobs, and worried that he might be followed, got up one morning before sunrise and fired up the Indian in the dark. At pitch-black, oh-dark-thirty he sped out of town, checking his rearview the entire way. Twenty miles out of town on Lorane Highway, shortly after the sun had peeked up in the east, he took one last glance in his mirrors, then turned up an old logging road. It was seven in the morning and, as Tim knew, the commune came to life at sunrise.

Another five miles up the road through thick forest, he came to a gate. He got off the bike and opened the gate, then pushed his bike through. As he closed the gate, he noticed someone peering out at him from within the forest. The Lorane commune was not a place to enter without caution. It was the oldest commune in the area and grew the best weed in the region. With Dick Danger running the show, it was staked out with gun-carrying sentries—some men, some women—from where Tim turned off the highway all the way to the main house. Tim didn't go there often, but he had been part of the commune for six months during his first year in Eugene, and a few of the folks he'd known were still there.

He threw a leg over the Indian and was about to give it a kick, when a long-haired man of Tim's age came out of the woods carrying a rifle. It wasn't someone Tim recognized. Instead of starting the bike, he just stood there straddling the thing.

"This is private property. What ya doin' out here?" said the man.

"Come to visit Dick," said Tim. "He's an old friend."

"Who are you?"

"Tim O'Malley. Lived out here a while back."

The man continued to size him up. "Leave the bike. I'll walk you up to the house. We'll let Dick decide if you should be here or not." Tim did not want to leave his bike, but he knew how the place was run.

As they walked up the dirt road to the house—his armed escort in the rear, Tim noted the tree houses and little handmade huts scattered deep into the woods where some of the forty or so commune members lived. Along the way, six or seven hippies and two barking dogs filtered out of the woods to check out the visitor, of which they had few. Had it not been the summer, half the people would have been naked. But it was late November, wet and cold, and those he saw wore anything from handmade leather clothing to fancy dresses from the Goodwill store in Eugene. All of them, men or women, had extremely long hair, mostly tangled and uncombed, and were generally unkempt. A few hundred yards up the road, Tim spotted the tumble-down, unpainted house. The porch sagged on the right side where a post had been replaced with a bark covered piece of timber. Rusty cars, tires, and all sorts of junk surrounded the house. The place looked more like a homestead in Appalachia than a hip hangout. It hadn't looked like this when Tim lived there. The original commune had been organized in 1965 and maintained by some of the sharpest folks Tim had ever met—and that was its reputation. What Tim saw now was the flip side of the hippie culture he believed in. These folks had simply turned into pot smoking hillbillies instead of investing their time and effort into an alternative way of living.

While the onlookers stood back like wide-eyed children, a tall, gaunt man with a thick brown beard and gray-streaked hair pulled back in a long braid came out of the house. A joint poked out of his mouth and a holstered Colt 45 hung on his hip. "What the fuck. Looks like Eugene's answer to Ben Franklin has come to visit," said the man, stepping down off the porch. He appeared to be in his mid-forties, with a rugged face and deep horizontal lines creasing his forehead.

"Hey, Dick," said Tim with a glance over his shoulder at his escort. "Wanted to see what kind of weed you got out here. October harvest must be ready by now."

Dick greeted Tim with a power handshake, then handed him the joint. "Try this. It's pretty much the best of what we have."

Tim took a long pull off the joint and returned it to Dick.

"Come on in. Got some coffee on."

Tim followed the man into the slightly off-kilter house, that had been build fifty or sixty years earlier by loggers. A wood stove sat off to one side of the main room. A long-haired, blond woman with a full-length skirt on, but no top, sat in a rocking chair beside the stove, nursing two babies from long, milk-filled breasts. She smiled when she saw Tim. "Wow, Tim O'Malley. Excuse me for not getting up. Coffee?" She pointed to a cup on the floor.

"Howdy, Tulip." Tim had known her—in the Biblical sense—back when he lived there. "No need for formality. Good to see you." He went over and kissed her on the forehead, then poured himself a cup of coffee from a pot on the wood stove.

"These are Dick's," she said proudly, presenting the twin infants sucking at her nipples.

"Yeah," said Dick, passing the joint to Tim, "these gals all figure they got a hold on me if I help them produce a kid or two." He grinned. "Shows how little they know me."

Two musty stuffed chairs and a small table on a filthy throw rug filled out the small room. Tim took one chair. Dick took the other and sat down with a cup of coffee. Dick had come to the commune a year after Tim left. He'd taken over and turned the place into a marijuana plantation that brought in a lot of money. Now, he was lord of the manor, twenty years older than anybody else, and well caught up in himself, the money, and all the young women. Tim thought he was a jerk, but still wanted to quiz him.

"Decent weed," said Tim, returning the joint to Dick.

"Gal in the kitchen's making some pancakes. We slather them in maple syrup and weed butter." He took a deep toke. "Makes for quite a breakfast."

Tim received the joint back from Dick. "What's a pound of this go for?"

"To you. Five hundred up front."

Tim nodded. "How about a quarter for one-forty?"

"Hate to break up the pounds, but I think we can work that out—if you got cash."

Tim got out his wallet. He pulled out seven twenties and handed them across to Dick.

Dick called to the woman in the kitchen. "Heather, weigh out four ounces."

Heather, a very young woman, wearing a long flannel nightgown, came out of the kitchen with two plates of pancakes, covered in syrup and butter. "Try these." She gave a plate and fork to both men.

Tim took a few bites, then looked up from his plate. "You hear about those bombings at the university?"

Dick shook his head. "Don't get the paper. No TV. We do our best to stay uniformed." He grinned with his mouth full.

"Didn't hear anything about the dynamite blast in Campbell Hall? Two months back. A man got killed."

Dick eyed Tim hard. "Maybe I did, maybe I didn't. What's it matter?"

"FBI's in town. They think I did it. I'm a little curious. No one in town knows a thing. I figured you folks were just crazy enough to do it."

"Is that why you're out here? Checkin' up on me?" Dick liked his power and got edgy as soon as anyone began to question him.

"Partly, that and the weed. And these pancakes." He glanced over at Tulip and smiled, then took a sip of coffee.

"Well, I didn't do it. And no one else out here did either. Hope that doesn't ruin your day."

"No, I think it's the pancakes that are going to be the problem." He tipped his head. "Should make for an interesting ride back to Eugene."

"Don't give'm more than an hour." Dick's laugh had no humor. "You won't be able start that bike of yours."

"I think I can handle it. Know anyone around here who might have done it?"

"Done what?"

"The bombing?"

"One track mind, bro. Why the intensity?"

"The man killed by the bomb was a friend of mine. I got his ashes in the print shop. This one's personal."

"And what the fuck would you have done if I'd said it was me?" His tone was antagonistic.

Tim tapped the star on his chest. "Have to take you in, big boy."

Dick frowned, but Tulip laughed.

Tim withdrew the red plastic nozzle from his pocket. "Ever see one of these before?" He held it out in his hand.

"Fuck, no. What is it?"

"It's from a can of spray paint. Gino found it at Johnson Hall after the firebombing."

"Good luck, Sherlock."

Heather came out of the kitchen with Tim's bag of weed. "A quarter pound," she said, presenting it to him.

"Many thanks. Pancakes are great."

Heather looked at Dick and then Tim. "You going back into town? Mind if I hitch a ride?"

"I'm on a motorcycle. You'll have to ride on the back."

Dick handed Heather his plate. "What'd ya need to go into town for?"

"There's a band I want to see tonight."

Tim could feel the tension. The commune was not what it had been. Dick Danger, gun on his hip, was just that—dangerous.

"Fuck it, I don't care. Go for it." Dick stood up and left the room.

"How soon you leaving? Is it Tim?"

"Yeah. I'm nearly done with the pancakes and I got the weed. Anytime you want."

"I'll be ready as soon as I put on some jeans."

Dick came back into the room, lighting another joint. He handed it to Tim. "You know, if you're playing detective, O'Malley, follow the dynamite. The best way to get it without leaving a trail would be stealing it from a road construction crew or one of the big logging operations. That's how I'd do."

"Hadn't thought of that. But that makes sense. I guess I got a little sleuthing to do." Tim took one last toke for the road, then returned the joint to Dick.

"And don't lay a finger on that girl." Dick winked. "She's only fifteen."

Tim and Heather walked down the dirt road to his bike. As they walked, Heather glanced over her shoulder twice as she spoke to him in a whisper. "Thanks for the lift, Tim. I got to get out of here."

"You're not coming back?"

"No way. Too heavy. Dick's gotten weird with all the money coming in from the pot sales."

"I can see that."

"By the way, Dick knew all about those bombings. He keeps track of that stuff."

Tim nodded. "Think he had anything to do with them?"

"He's crazy enough to do it, but he's so caught up in himself, politics mean nothing to him anymore."

"Yeah."

"I've been here since July, and I don't think he's left the commune once."

"That pretty much verifies what I was thinking. Thanks for the honesty."

They climbed on the bike and flew into town. Tim dropped Heather at the People's Café, then returned to the print shop. The trip to the commune had been a dead end, but Dick's dynamite angle was something to think about. Who did he know who might have the nerve to steal explosives off a construction site?

CHAPTER 62

During her tenure at Blake College, Gloria had often spent her free time at the back of the property, sitting on the riverbank in the lotus position, watching the rippling waters of the Willamette. Ten days after she announced her illness, Tai obtained a huge teepee from friends of his in the Rainbow family. Tai and Crow set it up on the back of the property within sight of the river, then furnished it with woven blankets, animal pelts, and Native American totems. The morning after it was ready, they led Gloria down to the river to show her the teepee. She broke down in tears she was so pleased. The teepee would become her sanctuary. She would spend several hours each day sitting out front of the teepee, or sometimes within, looking at the river.

One cold, rainy morning in early December, when Gloria sat in the teepee alone, wrapped in blankets, watching the gray day unfold on the river, Janice peeked into the teepee.

"May I join you?"

Gloria had grown close to Janice, when no one else really could. She smiled and welcomed the younger woman in. Janice wrapped herself in a blanket and sat quietly beside Gloria for quite a while, watching the river mist disperse.

"I have a problem," said Janice, breaking the silence, glancing at Gloria before looking down at her lap.

Gloria seemed to already know. Her tired eyes saddened. "Tai?"

Janice knew she had let Gloria down. "I don't know."

Gloria put her hand on Janice's.

"What should I do?" the younger woman asked.

"How long has it been?"

"Eight weeks or so."

Gloria let out a sigh. "It's something you must work out for yourself."

"I wish I could trade this new life to preserve yours."

"Thankfully that's not a thing we can do."

"Why do you say that?"

Gloria almost chuckled. "We'd end up with too many grandmothers."

Janice pushed aside the blanket and hugged Gloria. "I don't want you to go. You're the only person I know who wouldn't scream at me for being pregnant. I know, I know," she repeated over the woman's shoulder as she hugged her, "you told me how important it was to be responsible. And I haven't been." She was crying now.

"Any idea who the father is?"

Janice let go of Gloria and sat back. "One of three. How stupid can a girl be?"

"It happened to me."

Janice was stunned by the admission. "How old were you?"

"About the same as you. I told no one and had the child aborted." Gloria looked up at the peak of the teepee. "Haven't thought about that in a long time, and now it makes me sad. I never did have a child of my own."

"Do you think I should keep mine?"

"With what I'm feeling now, and my time running out, I do. Yes, I do. But you won't have anyone to help you. Not even me."

"Maybe the others in the co-op."

Gloria shook her head slowly. "That might be too much to ask."

"I could confront Tai and tell him it's his."

"We all know who Tai is. He has his good side, but he'll deny it and try to skate on you."

"Maybe he would help pay for an abortion."

Gloria reached out for Janice and embraced her. "Maybe nothing would be better for you than becoming a mother—if you could do it right."

Janice looked into Gloria's eyes. "Do you think I really could? Without a father?"

Gloria nodded. "Any woman can if she really wants to."

CHAPTER 63

Walt Arnold was one of the richest men in Lane County. He spent between sixty and seventy hours a week in his office in downtown Eugene, but the rest of his time was either at his palatial home in the Coastal Range west of Eugene or at his cousin's tavern in Springfield. A small portion of his five thousand acres was set aside to grow Christmas trees, but the rest was dense forest—and in the center of that forest was his home—a luxurious log cabin with a six-car garage. He loved his privacy and he loved the woods. He would walk for hours in the forest around his house to relax and forget about the high-tension lumber deals he made one after another all day long every day. He thrived on the trading and bidding and strategy of his business, but he ended each working day with two stiff martinis, and depending on the weather and his mood, a long walk.

Walt was one of the few local business men who did not want the Olympic Trials to come to Eugene. He didn't want national recognition for the northwest United States. Oregon was perfect the way it was. Somewhere out west where no one ever went. Recognition would only bring more people to the area. More people would bring environmentalists and that would lead to bad press. There would be increased criticism of the lumber industry and the swaths of clear-cut forest throughout western Oregon, parts of Washington, and Northern California—and clear cuts were already being frowned upon by the Nixon administration. No, Eugene didn't need the Olympic Trials; Walt Arnold was completely happy getting rich out of the light of day.

Halfway through his first Martini, the phone rang. His wife Lucy answered it. "It's for you, Walt," she called from the kitchen.

The phone was on the table beside his La-Z-Boy. He picked up the receiver. "This is Walt."

"Walt, it's Billy. Got a little issue out here at the tree farm." Billy managed the Christmas tree operation.

"Disease in the trees?"

"No. Your nephew and his girlfriend are holed up in the cabin. I saw their car parked up there this evening. I'm not sure how long they've been there, but they turned the water on and are using the fireplace. You want me to tell them to get out?"

Walt took a deep breath. He knew Mike was a heroin addict and he knew he was against the war. "No, leave him alone. He's got enough problems to deal with."

"You sure? The guy makes me nervous. Him and his biker friends."

"No, leave him be. If he's still there in a week, I'll go talk to him. Thanks for letting me know."

"Sure, boss. No problem."

CHAPTER 64

After her talk with Gloria, Janice decided to confront the man she most suspected was the father of her child. Late one afternoon, she noticed Gino's bicycle parked out front of Lucky's and went into the establishment that catered to men and had only one bathroom—for men. Janice stalked into the smoky pool hall with a rare sense of purpose, drawing looks from the men leaning on their pool sticks or hunkered over a pool table.

She saw Gino right away. He was playing pool with Tim in the back corner. Gino grinned as he saw her coming. He had slept with her several times in the last ten weeks, and he liked her because she was so young and seemed to value her freedom over a relationship.

"Nice to see you, baby," said Gino, as she came up to the table. He put an arm around her and kissed her on the cheek. "What brings you to a dive like this?"

Tim, who was lining up a long shot, looked up. He'd never been formally introduced to Janice, but her youth and figure were hard to miss. He refocused on his shot.

"Gino, we need to talk," said Janice, glancing around the pool hall, diverting the stares of those watching her.

"I'm in the middle of a game right now, baby. How about later? I can meet you anywhere you want."

"No, now—in private."

Her tone was not one Gino recognized. "Sure, Janice. Let's go outside." Gino told Tim he'd be right back, then he escorted the tightly packaged blond that everyone was watching out the side door into the alley.

"What do you need?"

"A dad."

"What?"

"I'm pregnant, Gino. It's yours."

Gino stepped back. "Whoa. We only did it a few times. Why me?"

"Cause you're the only one." It was a lie.

Gino looked around nervously. He was not good at being serious. "You want to get rid of it? I could scrape up some money, I guess."

"No, I want to keep it."

"Really?"

"The baby will need a father."

Gino did a spin. "I don't think so, Janice. I'm not the family type. That's got to be obvious."

"Then why didn't you use a condom?"

"Well, uh, all the girls I know use birth control. It's their body. They're in charge of that."

Janice might have outweighed Gino by five pounds. She punched him in the stomach, hard, bending Gino over with groan.

"Why'd you do that?"

"Because I need some help. And you're the one."

"Okay. Okay. Let me think about this. Maybe you should see a counselor."

"Will you come with me?"

"Wow, that's asking a lot."

Janice puffed up as though she were about to punch him again.

"Alright. Let's see a counselor. That's a good idea. You set it up. And let me know when it is."

"You are a jerk, Gino. You do know that?"

"Oh, yeah," he said, trying to be cute. "Just find me when you've got a time and a place."

He started to walk away from her. Janice grabbed his arm. "Don't blow me off, Gino."

"Oh, I won't. Don't worry about that."

"Yeah, sure."

CHAPTER 65

Six days after learning of his nephew's arrival, Walt Arnold drove out to the Christmas tree farm on a rainy evening. He parked his Land Rover beside Karen's late model Chevy. The curtains on the cabin windows were drawn, and a thread of smoke was coming out of the chimney. He drew his jacket up around his neck, gave a tug to his ballcap with his company's name, Pacific West Lumber, emblazoned above the bill, and slipped out of the Land Rover.

Walt saw the curtains move as he approached the cabin. He knocked on the door. When there was no response, he knocked again. He was an impetuous and strong-willed man, who got what he wanted when he wanted it. He was about to walk in when Karen opened the door.

Walt entered the cold, one-room cabin without a word to this woman he had never met. Two candles on a table in the center of the cabin and a smoldering fire made with wet wood provided the only light. Mike lay on the bed with a wide strip of cloth wrapped around his torso. An open bottle of whiskey stood on the floor beside the bed. He forced a grin as he recognized his uncle.

"Uncle Walt, how nice of you to come visit." Karen stood off in one corner, looking frightened and uneasy.

"We need to talk." He glanced at Karen.

Mike winced as he struggled to a seated position. "Karen, go out and sit in the car. We've got some family business to take care of."

Karen, already wrapped in a blanket for warmth, was only too happy to leave, even if it meant sitting outside in her car. After she was gone, the two men heard her car start up. Walt looked around. "Think she's leaving?"

"Who cares?" muttered Mike.

"I do," said Walt with force. He went to the window and lifted the curtain. He could see Karen wrapped in her blanket, sitting in the passenger seat. She had started the car to get the heater going.

Mike grimaced a weak smile. "Did you bring some money?"

Walt looked down at the bottle on the floor, then the used syringe on the table. "We had a deal. You were supposed to leave town, permanently. Why are you still here?"

"I want more money."

"You don't look to be in any shape to ask for anything."

"I took a bullet because of what I did for you. I need some help. And I don't believe you can turn me down." Mike grinned more drunk than loaded.

Walt frowned at the suggestion. He withdrew his wallet from the breast pocket of his jacket. He opened it up and thumbed through his cash. He pulled out five twenties and a fifty. "Here, this will get you another fix and enough gas to get to California." He dropped the money onto the bed. "Be gone by tomorrow."

Mike continued to grin. "That ain't near enough, Unk. I need a couple grand to get out of state. Be here tomorrow with the bread and I'll be gone the next day. Deal done."

The money was nothing to Walt. He was rich beyond his ability to spend it. But he was a powerful man who didn't like being fucked with—especially by his punk nephew. He didn't say anything as he thought through his choices.

"Well, Unk, what do you say?" Mike's pain showed in his face. "This is your loyal nephew asking for a little well-deserved help."

Walt reached down to the bed to gather up the money. He turned away from Mike without a word and walked out the door.

Mike screamed at him. "Be back tomorrow with the money or else."

Walt approached the passenger's side of Karen's Chevy. He tapped on the window. She rolled it down halfway. Walt could feel the heat rush from the car. He handed the fifty to Karen. "Get some dry wood." He glanced toward the cabin. "And tell Mike, it's a busy time of year. I'll get back to him when I can."

CHAPTER 66

Janice stayed at Blake College over the holidays, but Van and Marsha went home for Christmas. They left the same day and agreed to come back in a week out of concern for Gloria's health.

Tai drove them to the airport at six a.m. They sat together on the flight to Seattle. Marsha's father met her at the airport. Van went on to Cleveland where he caught a bus to Youngstown. His parents—Tom, who worked as a manager for Coronado Steel, and Rita, who worked part-time in the nearby middle school—met him at the bus station at eleven-fifteen that night.

Van had barely talked to his parents since leaving home. The ride from the bus station to the house was less than ten minutes. Little was said. His hair was longer. His mother asked about that.

Youngstown with its steel factories and tall brick smoke stacks was dirty and depressing in the winter. The street lamps illuminated gray snow, two-feet deep, plowed from the street and frozen into ice. The trees between the houses stood out like leafless scarecrows against a dim sky of reflected light. Van missed Oregon's perpetual green before he even walked in the door of his family's small house on the south side of town.

Van knew he had changed in the few months he had been in Oregon. He had always been a quiet, unassuming son with a good mind for math and science. He had never caused any trouble at home, and willingly shared the chores with his sixteen-year-old brother, Jimmy, and his twin twelve-year-old sisters, Carol and Connie. On the surface, he was still that young man, but he had changed.

The first three days at home Van dodged and weaved around the questions his parents asked about school. He had always been open and honest, but now he found himself describing Blake in ways that pushed the limits of the truth. His description of Adrienne's organic gardening class made it sound like traditional biology. Tai's class on shamanism became a survey of world religions, and Gloria's yoga class was experiential philosophy.

Van shared a bedroom with his brother. They had slept in the same bunkbed for ten years. His third night home, in the wee hours of the night, Jimmy, in the lower bunk, started asking the questions no one else would.

"What are the girls like?"

Jimmy, like Van when he was in high school, had yet to have a girlfriend.

Van told his brother about meeting Adrienne his first day at the school. Jimmy hung on every word and still couldn't believe it.

"It's true. And Adrienne's a very pretty woman."

"Is Eugene just really loose?"

"Yeah, it's not like Youngstown at all. Lots more hippies and people smoking pot."

"Have you tried it?"

Van lied to his brother. "No."

"Have you met any girls?"

Van couldn't help himself. "I have a girlfriend. Don't say anything to Mom and Dad. It'll get too weird."

"I know that," sneered Jimmy. "It's your business. But really, you have a girlfriend? Do you have a picture of her?"

"Yes, really, and no pictures."

"What's she like?"

 "She's Chinese."

"Chinese? That's weird."

"No, it's not, you jerk."

"Kind of weird. What's her name?"

"Marsha."

"That doesn't sound Chinese."

"She's an American—with Chinese heritage. She's just like you and me, but she's a girl."

"Have you, uh, seen her naked?"

When Van hesitated with an answer, Jimmy got excited. "Have you done it? What's it like?"

Van felt obligated to tell his younger brother the things that no one had told him—and wished someone had. Little by little over the next two nights, he recounted the whole story, with some details about his first encounter with Marsha that "are strictly between you and me—against penalty of death!"

The family sat around the table for a chuck roast dinner on Christmas Eve. Thomas sat at the head of the table, Rita opposite him at the other end. The twins sat on one side of the table, the boys on the other.

Toward the end of the meal, Rita asked Van why the school only had a week off for Christmas.

"I'm not sure, Mom. It's just the way they do it."

"Well, it seems a shame you'll be leaving three days after Christmas—and not even be here for New Years. I just don't see what the hurry is."

"I know," said Connie with a big grin. "He wants to go back to see his girlfriend."

Van wanted to disappear. Below the table he grabbed his brother's thigh and squeezed.

"I didn't say anything," blurted out Jimmy.

"What's going on? Girlfriend?" asked Van's father.

"She's Chinese," giggled Carol.

Van was furious. He glared at his sisters with a heat that said *don't say another word—either of you!!!*

"What's this?" asked his mother.

"We heard them talking through the wall," tittered Connie and Carol. "Everything!"

"Is that true, Van?" continued his mother. "You have a Chinese girlfriend at school."

Van swore to himself he would never come home again. "Yes," he answered just above a whisper, wondering what other horrible secrets his sisters might reveal once he'd gone back to school.

"Is that why you're going back so soon?"

Not soon enough ran through Van's mind. "No," he admitted, finally giving in. "One of the teachers has cancer." He aimed another hot glare at his sisters. "She's going to die. I want to be back before that happens. She's the yoga teacher and she's really nice."

Even Jimmy didn't know this, and it shut everyone up for several minutes. No one took a bite or lifted a fork.

"Is that your girlfriend?" asked his mother.

"No. This woman is older than you, Mom."

"How old is this Chinese girl?"

Van exhaled. He couldn't believe this conversation was happening. "She's the same age as I am. I just met her. It's nothing. She's a good friend who happens to be a girl."

Below the table Jimmy jabbed his thigh.

The next four days couldn't pass fast enough for Van.

CHAPTER 67

The Oregon winters were not particularly cold. December was a continuation of the rain, not the arrival of snow. Some nights Gloria would sleep in the teepee. On occasion, as she got weaker, which was happening more quickly than expected, Crow would join her to make sure she was all right. At times he would lay beside her and hold her or sometimes he would play his guitar.

Gloria decided to spend Christmas Eve in the tent. Crow stayed in the tent with her through the night. Christmas morning, when it was still dark, they went down to the river bank to watch the sunrise, which could be so spectacular if the sky were clear, as it was on this morning. Crow put a piece of black plastic on the wet ground and over that a blanket for them to sit on. They positioned themselves looking east and waited for the break of day.

Just as the sun appeared, a bright orange ball peeking over the hills to the east, Crow broke a long period of silence. "I've known plenty of white folks in my time, Gloria. Some of the white men I worked with became friends, and some of the white women I've known I slept with. But you are the first close white friend I've ever had—maybe the friend I'm the most comfortable with regardless of color."

Gloria smiled. "I've known very few black men or women, Crow. Very few. None I would call close friends. Most of my best friends have been women. But I feel differently about you. You are special. I can't imagine a finer man to spend my last days with." She touched him on the cheek. "I've grown to love you as friend." She sighed. They had enjoyed physical intimacy a few times. "I wish I had been thirty years younger when I met you."

Crow smiled and nodded. He dabbed a tear out of her eye. She leaned against him, and he put his arm around her. "Gloria, if you recall, I told everyone that I have a record."

She looked up at his face as he spoke.

"No one here has asked about it. No one. That's more respect than I usually get, but it's not a secret I want to keep from you. It might be late in this friendship," he said wistfully, "but your openness demands greater openness from me." He bowed his head to kiss her on the forehead. "I went to prison for killing a man."

Gloria's eyes widened.

"It was a car accident. I hit a man on the street one night. I'd had a drink or two and didn't see him—until I hit him. I spent ten years in prison in Illinois for manslaughter. Followed by five years of probation."

"But you served your time."

"I did, but I blew off my parole officer my second year out and left the state. It was a mistake. I've made a few."

"Could you be arrested for that and be taken back to Illinois?"

"Yes. And maybe serve another year or two, I'm not sure. But now I'm on the lam and have been for too long to change."

Gloria reached up and placed the palm of her hand on the side of his face. "I'm glad you told me. I'm sorry about what happened, but it makes me feel closer to you. You know I'm dying. And I know you broke parole."

Crow laughed. "Doesn't quite seem even."

"But breaking parole crushed a certain part of your life."

"I can't get a real job or a driver's license or have a bank account. Everything is part-time or pickup. Cash only. And being black only makes it harder."

Gloria stroked his beard. "I'm sorry."

Crow nodded slowly. "What's next, Gloria? You've studied Tibetan philosophy and metaphysics. What follows death?"

Gloria sat up and took a breath. The sun sat two diameters above the hills in the east. The sky had turned from steel blue to a pale mauve. "The same thing I've spoken about in class—non-materiality. A conjoining with the Creator's consciousness. No more self, no more Gloria. Just everything as one."

"But isn't there an individual soul?"

"That's one belief. I imagine a universal soul. Something we all share and that inspires each life."

"Are you ready for no more Gloria?"

She nodded. "I hope to be."

Crow looked down at his lap, then up into Gloria's eyes reflecting the sunrise. "What about someone like me, who accidentally killed an innocent person? Where does that put me?"

Gloria smiled. "What makes you think I would know?"

"Because to me, it feels like you do know."

"Okay," she said, taking hold of his hand. "I think we all go to the same place regardless of the way we've lived our lives."

"No purgatory, no hell?"

"Only in that you must be prepared to accept your karma—that is, face your demons and move on."

"And you're ready for that."

"I believe so."

CHAPTER 68

Spikes bought Joey a new baseball glove for Christmas. After opening the presents, he took Joey to the elementary school to throw the ball on the baseball diamond behind the school, where Joey played little league in the summer. The field was wet and muddy, and it was cold, but Joey was in heaven. A new mitt! What could be better than that!

Despite the difficulties at school, Joey was remarkably agile and athletic. Jack had seen that right away, and when he had time to throw a baseball or a football or bounce a basketball with Joey, he pushed him like a coach, and the kid ate it up.

They played a game that began with one player standing two steps away from the other. Each time the ball was thrown and caught, both players took a step backward. Meaning each throw was longer than the previous. This continued until a throw was dropped or thrown wild. Then the players would start over—two steps apart. Jack and Joey were good at this game. More often than not they were throwing the ball from rightfield to leftfield—a massive throw for Joey at nine—before the ball hit the ground. They had played this game for more than a year on this same field and knew exactly how long their longest caught throw had been. This made for even more fun. No matter what day they came to the field, they were always trying to break the "world record," as Jack referred to it.

On this day, Jack threw one from the rightfield foul line to Joey standing in leftcenter. Joey had it in his glove, but he couldn't hold on. He came running back to Jack to start the game again. "If this glove was broken in, Jack, I would have caught it. I know I would have."

"Give it some time. You know it takes a while to break in a glove. That's why I gave it to you for Christmas. It will be perfect when the season starts in the spring."

"Yeah! You're right."

When they stood up close to each other for the first toss of the new round, Joey held the ball and looked up at Jack. "Am I dumb?"

Jack was caught off guard. "Well, no, you're not dumb. Why do you say that?"

Joey compressed his lips, making his slumping left eye close. "They put me in a class with the kids that wear thick glasses or are in wheelchairs. None of them even play baseball. I think it's the class for dumb kids."

Jack felt his chest swell up and his emotions rise. He knelt so that he was looking eye to eye with the boy. "First of all, you're not dumb. Second, the other children in your class aren't either." Jack's voice began to crack.

"Is it because of my eye?"

Jack had no idea what to tell Joey about the special ed class. He didn't want to lie, but he couldn't tell the truth either. "No, no. I'm sure it was because there were too many kids in the other class."

Joey knew it was more than that. "So, they took out all the ones that were different?"

Jack was stuck. He gave up the words and reached out and hugged the boy. When he let go, he grinned big and ugly. "Forget all that stuff." He looked at his watch. "We've still got enough time to go for the world record one more time."

Joey grinned and tossed him the ball.

CHAPTER 69

Maynard and Ann Smith drove over to Joyce's and John's house for Christmas dinner. John had gotten a live tree from Walt Arnold's tree farm, placed it in a big pot, and decorated it for the holidays. He would plant it beside the house after the new year. Joyce roasted sweet potatoes, carrots, and turnips to go with spinach gnocchi as the main course. Ann brought the salad and an apple pie for dessert. Maynard threw a pack of hotdogs and some hotdog buns in a brown paper bag to make sure they had at least one meat dish. The family food issues were a constant. Ann played them down; Maynard could barely make it through a meal without a remark.

After the meal, Joyce made herbal tea for John, Ann, and herself. Maynard had coffee laced with brandy, then Ann brought out the pie and vanilla ice cream to complete the meal.

One bite into her dessert, Joyce said what she had planned to say at exactly this moment in the evening. "John and I have found an obstetrician in town who's going to help us find a child. His name is Thomas Rosenberg."

The conversation that had started two months earlier had progressed to the point that Ann had accepted Joyce's and John's decision, but Maynard had dug in his heels. He frowned at Joyce's announcement, but didn't say anything.

"Well, that's an important step," said Ann. "You're looking for a newborn, and who would have better access to newborns than a doctor who delivers babies."

"He also performs abortions, Mom." Joyce glanced at her father. Abortion had been made legal in Oregon the previous year. Both of her parents thought abortion was immoral.

"That puts him high on my list," muttered Maynard, knowing his opinion on the subject would not change his daughter's mind.

"Well, Dad, we'll be saving the life of a child who might otherwise be aborted. That's a good thing. At least admit that."

"What color will the baby be?"

Ann stopped chewing her mouthful of pie to hear the answer to her husband's question.

"We won't know until there's a child," said John.

"We've requested a closed adoption, Dad. The parents won't know who we are, and we won't know anything about them—except that the doctor will review their medical records and tell us anything we need to know."

Maynard had intended his question to be incendiary, but Joyce's answer was, in his mind, even more outrageous than his question. "You've got to be kidding?"

"No, that's the way we want it."

"What if it's a black child?" asked Ann.

"It makes no difference. The child will be ours."

Maynard nearly blew a mouthful of pie across the table. "I'd just as soon have a grandchild from outer space."

"Easy, Maynard," said John. "The child will be local. Someone that lives in the valley. He or she will almost certainly be Caucasian."

Maynard wiped his mouth with his napkin. "God damn better be!"

"Then you've accepted that we're going to do this?" asked Joyce.

Maynard's eyes bulged in their sockets. "I didn't say that."

"But it was implied, Dad."

Maynard loved Joyce more than anything in the world. Even more than Ann or his farm. But the discussion of adoption had cut him to the quick. He bit onto the words he was thinking and instead said, "It's your life, Joyce. I just want you and John to be happy. I'm only afraid you'll have regrets."

Joyce smiled. "If that's the case, then I'll pop one out on my own."

John grinned. "Well, you might need a little help."

Ann stifled a chuckle.

Maynard shook his head. "No talk of sex at the table." He frowned then burst into laughter. Everyone else joined in.

When the laughter settled, Joyce got up and went over to her father. She kissed him on the forehead. "I love you, Dad."

Maynard blushed. "I love you, too. Merry Christmas."

CHAPTER 70

A few days after Christmas, early in the morning before the co-op was open, Pat Riley slashed the top of a fifty-pound bag of brown rice with a razor knife, then hunkered over a barrel to empty the bag into it. Laurel came down from the upstairs where she and Pat lived. The register and bulk bins were in what had once been their living room. Pat straightened up to face her, holding the empty rice bag in his right hand.

"I'm not sure I like your arithmetic, Pat." Laurel was short while Pat was tall. She held out the account book for the co-op. Pat had been doing the books until a couple of weeks ago. Now Laurel was. "It looks like you've been dipping into our personal account to keep things balanced. Am I reading that right?"

Pat looked at his feet. "This place doesn't always account for itself."

"Because you take so little profit from the goods we sell."

Pat put his left hand on his neck. "Well, yeah. That was the idea."

"But we've also given up half of our house to do this. I know it's right. But you're going at it like a masochist. You have to call a meeting of the membership and show them these numbers."

"And then what?"

"Tell them we can make this work, but not at our expense. It just can't be." Laurel wasn't usually like this, but she was upset. "You've got to be honest with them or this whole co-op concept becomes a lie."

Pat took a deep breath. "Okay. Let's go through the numbers together and determine exactly where the line is drawn. Then I'll present it to the membership when we meet at the end of the month."

Laurel closed the book and came up close to Pat. She touched him on the face and looked into his eyes from about a foot below. "You've got a problem with trying to be too good."

"Beats the hell out of marrying a wife beater," replied Pat with a grin. He bent over to kiss her, but she was gone before his lips hit their target.

CHAPTER 71

It had been three months since Stoopid was burned in the explosion at Campbell Hall. Tim hadn't given up on finding the bomber, but he still had no idea who it was. The only clue he had was the nozzle Gino found at Johnson Hall. He sat in the print shop on New Year's Eve morning, smoking a joint and staring at the nozzle as though expecting it to tell him something. Gino came into the shop, nursing a cup of coffee. "I thought I smelled herb."

Tim extended the joint to Gino, who felt there was no better way to start the day than with a cup of coffee and a smoke. He took a deep hit then noticed the nozzle sitting on the layout table. His eyes lit up as he exhaled. "I know where that came from."

"The nozzle?" Tim reached for the joint.

Gino nodded as he took another hit before giving the joint to Tim. "Brooks Auto Parts in Glenwood."

"Yeah?"

"I was in there two days ago looking for motor oil and remembered they had a new line of Rust-oleum in spray cans—safety yellow, orange, and red. I checked them out. They all had that nozzle."

Tim put a hand to his chin, thinking. "I'm not sure what that tells us."

"Hey, man, I haven't seen that paint anywhere else. And I've looked. Who shops at Brooks? Only serious gearheads and bikers."

"But anyone could stop in there and get that paint. Besides, there aren't many anti-war gearheads other than me."

Gino shrugged. "What about the Gypsy Jokers?"

"Hmmm. You know, Gino, I've quizzed everyone I know who's against the war, except those guys. It just didn't seem to fit. Maybe it's time to track them down."

Three days later, Tim decided to find Mike Rogers. In a way, Mike was like Dick Danger—trouble waiting to happen. He recalled how Dick had gotten edgy with all the questions. The same could happen with Mike or any of the Jokers if he got too inquisitive. To get into their heads, he'd have to catch them drunk. He could go to the Alibi Club. Mike Rogers would likely be there, but that was his father's tavern and basically Mike's home away from home. Tim wanted to catch him without the homefield advantage he'd given Dick Danger. There was a biker hangout in west Eugene where he might find Mike or some of the other Jokers—a cowboy bar called the Ten-gallon Hat.

Late that night, Tim rode the Indian out to "The Hat," as it was called, to see who was out there. The giant neon ten-gallon hat and its accompanying dancing neon cowboy boots stood out against the night sky from two blocks away. Tim didn't see any motorcycles when he rolled into the parking lot, but he went in anyway. The place was loud and smoke filled, with décor that looked like something you might see in Cheyenne, Wyoming. Mounted steer horns, spurs, fancy cowboy boots, and lariats decorated the walls. The deep voice of Conway Twitty serenaded the patrons from a vintage jukebox—boom, boom, boom. Tim stood up to the bar, figuring he'd stay for one beer, hoping to run into some Jokers in a way that would appear totally accidental.

When the bartender delivered a Blitz, he removed his leather helmet and replaced it with his black cloth cap. He took a sip, and with Merle Haggard singing "Oakie from Muskogee" in the background, pulled out his tobacco pouch to roll a cigarette. An older man in a cowboy hat watched from two seats down. The man turned to him and drunkenly asked, "That ain't marijuana, is it?"

Tim looked up. "No, just tobacco. I like to roll my own."

A hefty man wearing cowboy boots and a big silver buckle, barely visible beneath his protruding belly, stepped up to the bar between Tim and the other man. He sized Tim up with an ugly look. "Who the fuck is this? Ichabod Crane."

Tim focused on rolling his cigarette and didn't look up. The man ordered a shot of whiskey and threw it down, then watched Tim finish up the cigarette, put it his mouth, draw it out, and light it. "The way you put that cigarette in your mouth makes me think you might be a dick smoker."

Tim ignored the comment.

The man slid down the bar closer to Tim, smelling heavily of alcohol. "You a faggot?"

This got the man in the hat laughing, but Tim knew this wasn't going anywhere good. "You got the wrong man," said Tim. "Just here for a beer."

"Just here for a queer?" the man mocked, edging up to Tim, pushing his shoulder against him.

"Back off, man," said Tim, moving down the bar a few feet.

"Hey, I think we got a faggot here," said the man, loud and obnoxious.

This drew another cowboy to the bar. "Yeah, I noticed them red shoes. I sure would like a pair. I wonder how hard it'd be to get them off this fairy's feet."

Tim was not a fighter, but also not one to back down. And yet, this was the wrong place for him to get too brave. He threw down what remained of his beer and turned away from the bar, headed to the door.

"Not so fast, fucker," said another man, blocking his way. "I think my friend's interested in them shoes. Right, Frank."

As Tim was trying to decide if he should take the shoes off or throw a punch, the door opened from the outside and three big, tattoo ugly Free Souls came in, wearing chains and leather.

"That's right," said the man with the silver belt buckle. "Ichabod ain't leaving with them red shoes."

The Free Souls were wired or drunk or both, but not so fucked up to miss what they'd walked into. The largest of three bikers stepped in between Tim and two men harassing him.

"Ichabod, my ass." He had about four teeth and arms as big around as his neck. "This is my friend, Tim O'Malley. He's a peace abidin' hippie. If you're lookin' for a fight," he turned to his friends, "I know where you can find one."

The other Jokers laughed and moved up on either side of Tim, making sure everyone in the building knew where they stood.

"Come on, Tim, you're with us. These dicks have shot their wad. I believe we owe you a beer."

Tim tipped his head, trying to recover his charm. "No, I believe it's me buying the beer tonight, boys." He looked at the man with the silver belt buckle. "Wanna join me and my faggot friends?"

The man and his friend backed off and returned to their table. The man in the cowboy hat at the bar turned away and stared into the shelves of bottled liquor. Tim and the three bikers found a table and sat down.

Tim had hoped to run into the Gypsy Jokers, maybe even Mike Rogers, but the excitement of the moment had broken through several layers of psycho-necessity, so the Free Souls would have to do. They took to Tim like their long, lost buddy, making sure everyone knew he was a special dude, while also reveling in their dramatic entrance. It was the perfect time for Tim to get some information without having to force it. He drank until closing with the Free Souls, whose names he didn't even know and had to figure out from their conservation. But it was easy, they were flying high on something, and Tim could drain the oceans of beer and maintain focus.

According to what he learned that night, the Free Souls biggest beef with the Jokers was the issue of the war. Tim already knew this. When Tim edged into the question of protests against the war, the Free Souls told him that the Jokers' big deal for the year was to ride to Washington, D.C. to join the Vet's Against the War march in July. When he asked about the bombings, they told him that of all the Jokers only Mike Rogers was capable of "that kind of crap." They didn't know of anything he'd done specifically, but they thought he was so over-the-top in his stand against the war, they wanted to kill him and had tried six weeks ago. Two of the men at the table were among the four who had chased Mike that night in November. They described the motorcycle chase in detail, with one saying he'd fired the shot that hit Mike.

Tim took all of this at face value. He knew Mike was crazy enough to do it, but nothing he heard suggested he had. When he rolled out of the parking lot that night, he didn't feel any closer to solving the mystery, but he still wanted to talk to Mike—and knew he was damn lucky to be wearing shoes!

CHAPTER 72

After the new year, Gloria began to fast. The teepee transformed into a hospice. Under any other circumstances this would have been impossible for Gloria. She had no money, no family support. But the group of Blake College instructors and students universally believed that helping Gloria leave the world would be as educational and meaningful an experience as any the school could offer.

Gloria spent her time either walking the river bank or in the teepee falling in and out of sleep. Individuals might stop by during the day, but the group of them made a point of sitting with her for some part of every evening. Sometimes they meditated in silence, sometimes they chanted, sometimes they prayed, sometimes they intoned Tibetan recitations, sometimes they simply conversed as they would around the dining room table, smoking pot and sipping tea.

Gloria had some very specific ideas about her last hours of life. She had discussed these ideas several times with Rain over the last month, but now that she had begun to fast, she wanted to make sure everyone knew what to expect when the time came. They all sat cross-legged in a circle around Gloria's pallet in the teepee. Gloria was thin as a stick and struggled to stay warm even on this relatively mild January evening. Rain saw her shaking and put a third wool blanket over her shoulders.

"During these last few days of fasting, I've made a breakthrough," said Gloria. "I've been going into a trance every time I meditate. I had gone into a trance only a few times before in my life, but now it comes easily. I'm spending large parts of each day outside of my body. I hover in the ethers like a kite tethered to my failing body. It's as though I'm living in a parallel world filled with spirits. I've been there so much recently I can feel them around us now."

Gloria drew the blankets tighter around her shoulders. "I think there's an opportunity here—with my death—for the rest of you to witness the realm of spirits as I do now." She spoke slowly and with effort, but with total mental clarity. "If all of you can achieve the trance state—as a group—much as Tai did in the Navajo sweat lodge, it might be possible to have a very special experience.

"According to the Tibetan teachings, which we've been studying for almost two months now, when my heart stops, I will enter a state called the swoon. It can last a few minutes or stretch out a few days."

Rain reminded everyone that the swoon ended when the spirit left the body.

Gloria nodded. "So, with this in mind, at the moment I stop breathing, I want everyone to begin the simple *om* chant, the most powerful of all the chants we've practiced, and to continue that chant—if possible—until the swoon ends."

"How will we know when that happens?" asked Janice.

"The experienced Tibetan priest would feel it, but it's possible," continued Gloria, "given the closeness of this group, and the weeks of group meditation, and the dedication I've seen in everyone's eyes, that all of you could attain such an elevated state through chanting that you might feel or even see my spirit leave my body."

"See it? Is that really possible?"

"I'm not sure, Van. It's something I've only heard about, but never witnessed. Maybe it won't happen, but it would change the lives of everyone present if it did."

"No doubt," said Crow

"One thing that's important to remember through all of this is that birth and death—the bookends of every life—share a commonality and a balance. Some texts say the soul or spirit enters a new life at the moment of insemination. I believe it's at the moment of the infant's first breath, the first intake of prana, when there is a tiny opening in the fabric of our reality—one might call it a portal to the astral plane—that allows a spirit to enter the new being and inspire its life."

"Physicists might call that a worm hole," said Tai, "connecting this side of life to the other side."

Van nudged Marsha beside him and rolled his eyes, but Gloria nodded and continued. "At the end of the swoon, we have the opposite. A portal, or worm hole if you like, opens to allow the spirit to return to the astral plane and begin its journey." A shiver of pain caused Gloria to close her eyes then open them. "I've asked Rain to supervise the last hours of my life and the chanting. I feel sure that you will come together for this, and that the experience will be worth the effort and dedication."

"I can't see how it won't be," said Crow.

"It will be sad," added Rain, "but it will be beautiful."

"And that's the best way to think about it," concluded Gloria, who now lay back in her bed, exhausted from talking. "Sad but beautiful."

CHAPTER 73

When Les Anderson entered his office the first week of the New Year, he saw a letter on his desk. As he got closer, he saw the five over-lapping Olympic rings in the upper left-hand corner of the envelope. He quickly tore open the envelope and unfolded the letter inside. The first paragraph told him what he wanted to know:

> The United States Olympic Committee is pleased to announce that Eugene, Oregon, Seattle, Washington, Los Angeles, California, Bakersfield, California, and Des Moines, Iowa are the finalists for the 1972 Olympic Trials. The members of the selection committee will be announced in July. Their decision will be due in October. The committee will make one visit to each city as part of the process. You will receive a letter informing you of the date of that visit as soon as the committee is formed.

The mayor had hoped for something more conclusive, but Eugene had made the cut despite the firebombing of Johnson Hall and the janitor's death. That was good news. He read deeper into the letter:

> The unrest in Eugene is a concern. We understand the most recent incident was minor, but it is still disturbing. We hope that two things occur prior to the committee's visit—that those responsible for the bombings are apprehended and that there are no more acts of violence on the University of Oregon campus.

This was the Mayor's greatest fear—more violence. He needed to prove that Eugene was safe and sane before the committee came to

244

Eugene. He hit the zero button on his intercom. "Sally, put in a call to Bill Bowerman."

When the light flashed on his phone, the Mayor picked it up. "Bill, we haven't spoken in too long. My condolences on the election."

"Yeah, the recount got me about eight more votes. So it goes. Maybe it's just as well. I've got plenty on my plate already."

"Maybe more."

"What do you mean?"

"I got a letter from the Olympic Committee today. It's down to five locations—Eugene is one of them."

"And I've learned that I'm being considered to lead the selection committee."

"Wouldn't that be nice."

"Even if I'm not picked to lead the group, I'm certain to be part of it."

"Fantastic. Then our only real concern is campus violence. They referred to the incident at Johnson Hall in the letter. It can't happen again."

"Any word from the FBI?"

"No, I'm calling them as soon as I hang up. I want to make sure they know how important this stuff is to Eugene."

"Good. Let me know what they say."

"Of course."

When Anderson hung up, he punched the intercom again. "Sally, get Todd Bascomb on the line."

Soon afterward the light on line one began to flash. "Todd, I'm glad I caught you. I'm just curious. You've been in Eugene three months now. What's the latest on the bombings?"

"Our suspects remain the same, but we have nothing else. Either the entire anti-war community is working against us or they had nothing to do with it. Our undercover agents have completely integrated into Eugene street life. If there's something out there, they'll find it."

"That's it? After three months?"

"This can be a slow process, Mayor. The only evidence at Campbell Hall was the slogan sprayed on the door."

"Any finger prints inside the building?"

"Nothing viable. We found some remnants of the firebomb at Johnson Hall, but that's not much either—pieces of glass from a broken whiskey bottle. Bear with us. We won't quit until we've got something."

"Of course. Thanks for the update." Anderson punched line one to end the conversation, then cursed. He punched zero. "Sally, get Wilkerson on the line."

Moments later line one was blinking again.

"What's going on, Mayor?"

"Have you come up with anything on Campbell Hall, Hugh? I'm getting antsy. What's the latest?"

"We never had much to go on, Mayor. Trying to connect the death to the bombing is tough. There's no real motive. As far as we can tell, it was happenstance that the janitor was there. Have you called Bascomb? The FBI must have more than we do. They're working on the Johnson Hall bombing as well."

"I just spoke to Bascomb. His story is the same as yours."

"You know, Mayor, we might not find anything."

"That won't work. Find someone—if only to make it look like we've eliminated the problem."

CHAPTER 74

After seven days of taking only water with a slice of lemon and a dash of bicarbonate of soda, and sleeping most of the time, Gloria experienced two extremely difficult days, then, on a Sunday, an abrupt decline. Rain gathered everyone in the teepee that evening. They formed a circle around Gloria's pallet. As the students and instructors scooted up close, Gloria's eyelids lifted slightly. Clearly in pain, she acknowledged that the moment they had prepared for was near. Rain propped her up with pillows, while Crow and Tai lit a ring of candles around the outside of the circle.

"Gloria's passing is at hand," said Rain, when everyone had settled in. "We all knew this day would come." She glanced at Gloria and glimmered a weak smile.

"As Gloria has told us," she continued, "after the physical death of the body, the spirit will linger in the corpse for as long as three days before departing. For those with especially pure spirits," Rain again made eye contact with Gloria, "the spirit leaves more quickly, and the spirit may depart in less than the time it takes to eat a meal. For the highest bodhisattva, the spirit's departure is immediate."

In the days since Gloria's decline, Rain had become the understood leader at the school. No one doubted her personal strength or her commitment to the counterculture. Much like Tai, she had been captured by the vision quests of the times. Tai had traveled the world seeking psycho-tropic drugs and sacred herbs. Rain's path, like Gloria's, had led to meditation, yoga, and new age spiritualism. With the addition of her wild crafting and astrological studies, she felt as though she were perfectly centered—in tune with the stars, the Earth, and herself. This was the source of her confidence and remarkable demeanor. Regarding death, Rain, like Gloria, did not believe in any single tradition. She felt there were threads of truth in each doctrine, and she would weave them all together for the ceremony of Gloria's passing.

"For the most part," Rain continued, "deaths are witnessed by a few family members or a close friend or two. As you know, Gloria wants to bring something more to her passing and has asked all of us to be here." Rain glanced at Gloria. "Any parting words?"

"Thank you for being here…all of you…your support means everything to me." She was short of breath and speaking was difficult. She smiled weakly. "For some of you…this process might be harder on you…than on me. If it helps…try to imagine that I am not dying…so much as returning to my beginning. This is not a sad moment…it is a profound moment…as profound as one's birth." She winced in pain, then gathered her strength. "Bless you all."

Rain smiled at her dear friend, then addressed the others. "Please join hands." The circle alternated gender—Tai, Janice, Van, Marsha, Ray, Adrienne, Crow, Rain and back to Tai. Moxie was squeezed in between Adrienne and Ray. The two little foxes were in Adrienne's lap, and Lena the cat was curled in a ball beside Rain.

"The ceremony we are about to begin deserves a few words of warning." Rain paused and looked at each person in the circle. "We are opening ourselves to the spirit world much as one would in a séance. Should any or all of us achieve the astral realm, which only Gloria and Tai among us have experienced, don't be frightened by what you see. Understand that spirits are nonmaterial entities, and like visions in a dream, they can do you no physical harm. By opening ourselves in this way, however, we also open ourselves to lost spirits—which might try to enter one of us as a way back to the physical realm. To avoid this, we will begin with a prayer for protection from vagrant spirits." She closed her eyes.

"Oh, great spirit that is in all things, we humbly dare to bask in your radiance for the moment of Gloria's passing. Please know our motives are only the purest and allow the unity of this circle to shield us from the incursion of vagrant spirits when we open ourselves to the astral realm. Amen."

Rain opened her eyes. "During the ceremony, do not let go of your neighbor's hand. Our unity is our greatest protection from some lost soul looking for a home."

Marsha and Van exchanged a glance. They understood the solemnity of the moment. Their friend Gloria was about to die. But they did not believe in ghosts or immortal souls and had voiced skepticism to each other about the existence of an astral plane and *all this other stuff.* They were happy to participate but to them it seemed like theater.

A mason jar sat on the ground beside Rain. She lifted it for everyone to see. It contained a gloppy mixture of brown fluid and undissolved organic material. "Tai blended a special elixir for the evening. What did you say, Tai, a light stimulant? To reproduce what he experienced in Arizona."

Tai grinned. "Crow donated three peyote buttons. I added two handfuls of dried liberty cap mushrooms, a little powdered jimson weed, and a lot of fresh squeezed orange juice. It's not so strong to send you tripping—just a buzz to heighten the sense of mystery."

"What if I decide to skip Tai's elixir?" asked Van, who had now smoked marijuana four times.

Rain opened the jar. "Just take a little sip, Van. For the ritual of it. It's like wine at communion. It won't get you high, but taking a sip adds meaning and connection to the ceremony." She took more than a sip, frowned at the taste, and passed it to Tai.

"You'll barely feel it." Tai took a long swallow and passed it to Janice. She took a swallow and handed it to Van. He took the slightest taste—it was very bitter—then a gulp, and passed it on.

When the jar returned to Rain, she placed it on the ground beside her. Gloria appeared to be asleep and no longer listening to them. "Let's begin by closing our eyes," said Rain. "Seek quiet in your mind."

All of them closed their eyes. A quarter hour later, as though Rain had called for it, they opened their eyes and looked around at each other. The period of mediation had thickened the mood. The candlelight wavered behind them on the teepee canvas.

Gloria muttered, a barely audible, "It's so cold."

Rain pulled another blanket up around Gloria's shoulders and used a white handkerchief to wipe a thread of drool from her mouth, then kissed her on the forehead. "We're all here," she whispered, then turned to the others. "Anyone that's getting stiff. Take a moment to stand and stretch. I think we're very close." Behind her Gloria's breathing had become labored and raspy.

Everyone stood, including Rain. Marsha left the tent to squat in the grass and relieve herself. The others raised their arms above their heads, twisted and stretched. A jug of water was passed around. When Marsha reentered, a chicken slipped into the tent. Moxie growled and the bird disappeared into the shadows. Again, they formed a circle sitting cross-legged around the pallet. Crow took out his guitar to play the Joni Mitchell song, *Both Sides Now*. The meaning of the moment seemed to expand with each note as Crow picked out the melody of Gloria's favorite song.

Tai filled a pipe with some of his best herb and passed it around. No one refused. The marijuana high added another layer of extra-reality to the gathering. Gloria's pallet seemed to float in the halo of flickering candles.

Gloria suddenly uttered an urgent chirp. Crow put his guitar aside. Gloria gasped several times, fighting for air. Rain used a handkerchief to wipe a milky residue from the corners of her mouth. Gloria gasped again and shuttered. She thrashed her head from side to side, clearly in pain, then suddenly froze in place with her eyes wide open. She exhausted a faint mew—and expired. Rain leaned over and used two trembling fingers to close Gloria's eyes. Janice began to cry quietly. The others bowed their heads in respect and anguish.

Rain rose to her haunches and placed her hands on Gloria's throat. She used her forefingers to compress the carotid arteries on both sides of her neck. Rain spoke with difficulty. "This will force the spirit to exit from the top of Gloria's head." Again, this was something they had talked about many times before, but the morbidity of manipulating a corpse unsettled Van, Marsha, Janice, and Ray, who all turned away, struggling with their emotions.

After ten minutes, tears rolling down her cheeks, Rain removed her hands from Gloria's neck. With Tai's help, she turned Gloria on her side and covered her face with a white silk scarf. Rain and Tai returned to their spots in the circle and everyone clasped hands. Rain looked around the circle. "Please, everyone, gather yourselves as best you can. I know this is difficult. Work with me." Her voice trembled. "Gloria's swoon has begun. We will stay here until her spirit frees itself from her body, whether it takes an hour or a day."

For a second time, she passed the jar around the circle. When it reached Van, he hesitated. "I think I'm starting to feel this stuff. It seems pretty strong."

"Go with it, Van," said Rain.

Van took a second swallow and passed it on.

When the jar returned to Rain, she whispered, "Close your eyes. Still yourselves." She gave everyone a few minutes to center. "Now, everyone, a simple *om*—Gloria's favorite chant—all together." Rain began. One by one they joined in, trying to match her tone.

After preparing for this moment for two months, they were as closely tuned as a team of synchronized swimmers. Almost immediately the teepee's canvas shroud began to resonate softly with their chanting. Some unmeasured period of time passed as they hummed along like a Gregorian choir. Gradually, as the chanting eased them into an altered state, the tent grew warm and their minds began to fill with images, so alive and dynamic they couldn't tell if their eyes were open or closed. Dim amorphous wisps and diaphanous floating things swarmed around them, buoyed on a tangled blanket of voices in a myriad of languages and rhythms. Layered in, over, and around them were the primordial forests that once covered western Oregon. The river bed beside them twisted and turned through its thousands of years of change, at times flooding, at times running dry. They saw the building of their Victorian house and its one hundred years of aging, spun together with a billion years of untold futures. This was the astral realm—all time at once. And in the center of it all hovered Gloria's corpse, suspended in the flimsy present.

After an hour of steady chanting or was it two or three, a fine, luminous white mist flickered at the top of Gloria's head, then threaded itself upward like cigarette smoke until it separated from the crown of her head. It passed in and around them like an airy serpent, pausing at moments, it seemed, to take a last look at Janice, then Adrienne, and one by one the others—before dispersing and vanishing, leaving a pale blue mist in its absence. The mist began to rotate slowly around them, gradually increasing in speed and condensing, forming a swirling blue vortex above Gloria's body. No one moved or spoke as they focused on the spinning blue cloud. It brightened, then spun out nebula arms of light that reached out to each of them and disappeared into the pupils of their eyes like worms down a hole.

The fluid space around them abruptly stilled into three-dimensions, and the tangled voices fell silent. They found themselves, eyes open, staring at each other, unsure of what they'd seen, but knowing they had all seen it—because of the looks on their faces.

After a long, suspending silence, their grief transformed to wonder, Adrienne breathed it out in a long hush, "What was that?"

"It had to be Gloria's spirit," whispered Rain. "We saw it leave her body just as she said we would."

"And it entered us through our eyes. Did you see that!" said Tai in disbelief. "It was absolutely beautiful. I don't know what it means, but it was stunning."

Crow shook his head. "It doesn't fit. A pure spirit doesn't stay around to enter its friends. It leaves."

"And if Gloria wasn't pure, I don't know who would be," muttered Adrienne.

"Perhaps she entered us because she needed to," said Rain.

"Maybe there was something she still needed to do," added Tai, "and could only accomplish through all of us."

"And with Gloria," said Marsha, "I'd be happy to help her."

Crow wasn't buying it. "It doesn't feel right to me. Her spirit was meant for release not unfinished business here on Earth."

"But no one really knows that," said Rain softly. "All of us have baggage that none of the others know about."

Crow's eyes met Rain's.

"All I know," said Ray, looking around with wide, bright eyes, "is that was the strangest thing I've ever seen in my life, and that I'm high as a kite from that potion. I feel like I'm in a damn movie." He giggled at his own words.

"Maybe it was the drugs." Van stood up. "I didn't like it."

Marsha looked up at him. "I don't think it was something to like or dislike, Van. It simply was."

Rain was staring across the circle. "Janice, are you all right?"

Janice had the most blank face in a tent full of blank faces. Her usually spitting mad attitude was gone. "We just saw evidence of God," she hushed in a whisper.

"We did," added Tai. "We saw proof of the infinite spirit. That's more outrageous than seeing a UFO!"

Then they were quiet again. Silenced by the idea that they had, in fact, seen beyond the veil of life and peeked into the world of spirits. Suddenly the chicken that had been hiding in the teepee squawked— scaring everyone—then skittered out of the tent with a yapping Moxie on its tail.

CHAPTER 75

After Rain and Adrienne wrapped Gloria's body in a sheet, the entire group slipped out the teepee's oval opening. The light of the rising sun was just visible in the east. They had passed the entire night in the teepee without realizing it. Marsha and Van walked down to the river hand in hand. The others drifted back to the house. Everyone was stunned to silence by both sadness and what they had experienced.

Adrienne and Ray went to the chicken coop to get some eggs for breakfast. Adrienne, always a positive young woman, who thrived on hard work, had been shown something beyond her imagination. It shook her up. Before she reached beneath a hen for an egg, she hugged Ray for a long time, not crying or making any sounds, just seeking comfort by holding onto him.

Ray was no less shocked, but he thought it was the drugs and was far more concerned about Adrienne's reaction than any greater meaning the event held for him. She was always solid as a rock; he'd never seen her so needy.

When Adrienne released him, there were tears of grief and fear in her eyes. She held him by the hips and looked up into his face. "What did we just see?"

Ray touched her cheek to comfort her. He loved her and wanted to marry her. "Beats me. I'm writing it off to Tai's brew. Jesus, I'm still buzzing from that stuff."

Adrienne couldn't brush it off. "It was more than that, Ray. We all saw it. People don't share the same hallucination. That blue vortex must have been Gloria's spirit. I mean...what else could it have been?"

Ray hugged her this time. "And if it was her spirit, isn't that a good thing? Shouldn't we be encouraged to know we've got souls and all that?"

"That's what I'm struggling to grasp. That there is more!" She squeezed him tight. "And if Gloria did somehow enter us, and that's how it appeared, it's got to be good, right? Gloria was nothing but the best." She tried to smile through her sadness and confusion.

"Yes, Adrienne. Yes. And let's try to honor her by grabbing a few of these eggs and cooking up breakfast for everyone. I'm hungry."

"I'm not sure I can eat."

"Come on, girl." He leaned over her and kissed her on the forehead.

"Yeah, yeah," she muttered. "Focus on the eggs."

After a long period of introspection on the river bank, watching the reflection of the sunrise on the water, Marsha and Van had their own version of the same conversation, but they were more scientific in their analysis.

"What did you see, Marsha?" asked Van. "Describe it as accurately as you can."

Marsha took a while to answer. Like the others, she was still struggling with the reality of Gloria's passing. She was also very high from Tai's strange brew, and the colors spreading out on the river were too stunning to turn away from. She spoke looking straight ahead. "A luminous mist rose up out of Gloria's head, dispersed, then coalesced into a spinning ball, hovered, and then separated into threads and entered our eyes."

"That's what I saw, but I'd add that the luminous mist and the spinning ball were different colors."

"That's right. There was a change from luminous white to luminous blue."

"How do you interpret that?" asked Van.

"I don't know."

"Could they have been separate entities?"

"I'm not sure I can make that distinction. Can you?"

"No, not really. It was all too weird. But there was a change of some sort."

Marsha leaned up close to Van. "Very Van-like thinking," she whispered, then kissed him on the cheek. "Whatever it was, I've never seen anything like it." She shook her head. "I'm just afraid this is going to turn me new age." Then she laughed in spite of herself.

"Yeah, I've always thought I was an atheist. Now I'll be forced to believe."

"Did you feel the effect of Tai's potion?" asked Marsha, vibrating with the stuff.

"Oh, my gosh, yes, and I still do. That was no mild high. It was interesting but a little frightening. I wish I hadn't taken it."

"Really?"

"Yeah, I don't know what part it played in what we saw." Van looked out at the river. "It's hard to tell what was real and what was hallucination."

"Kind of exciting though, wasn't it?"

"More than that."

They both stared out at the sky and the surface of the river.

"Sure is a beautiful morning down here," said Van.

"After last night, I'm wondering if all of this," Marsha opened her arms, hands outstretched, signifying everything they could see, "isn't simply the reflection of—dare I say it—God."

"Jeez, Marsha, you have gone new age."

This got a chuckle out of them both. Van took Marsha's hand and led her back to the house. "I'll be curious to hear what the others say."

As soon as Rain got to the house, she called the doctor who first diagnosed Gloria and asked him to come to the house to write a death certificate. The body would remain in the teepee for three more days, as requested by Gloria, then would be cremated at the Eugene Mortuary. The ashes would be brought back to the house and taken to the back of the property to be sprinkled in a circle around the teepee.

CHAPTER 76

Walt Arnold met Bluto Harris for a drink at the Vet's Club at four that afternoon. Walt and Bluto were two of the richest men in Lane County and often met to complain about local politics and brag to each other about how rich they were. Two sips into his bourbon on the rocks, Walt targeted Washington, D.C. "To think I voted for Nixon," he sneered. "And now he's turned into a damned environmentalist."

Bluto laughed. "It's his Secretary of the Interior."

"Fucking Hickel is pushing for timber harvest limits in Oregon. I wish those folks in Washington would mind their own business."

"Just a few more regulations, Walt. Shouldn't be such a big deal."

"A few more regulations. I'm sick of it. They've already hit me twice this year. First with restrictions on clear cutting and then Nixon took away the tax credit for replanting. I'll be damned if I'll bother to replant this year at all."

"Life's a bitch then you die," laughed Bluto. "You seem to be doing all right."

"Says you." Walt took a sip from his drink. "In my opinion, the politicians in Washington should leave Oregon to the Oregonians. Hickel has no idea how we log out here, and he should keep his nose out of it."

"I understand that well enough, Walt, but I kind of like the attention. Eugene is primed for a period of strong economic growth. That's the basis of every decision I make. I see a doubling of the population in twenty years or less—and that means double the profit."

"For you, perhaps, but not for me. I like it here just the way it is."

"Sorry, Walt. That's a losing proposition. Things change and the key is keeping up with the changes."

"Yeah, and with all the extra people, they're going to want more regulations. The tree huggers will make it illegal to cut down trees entirely, and then McCall will push through his stupid bottle bill. It's all a bad joke. To Hell with them. If I own the property, I'll harvest it any way I please."

"So, if I buy a piece of land to develop, I should be able to build whatever I want on it."

"Of course."

"No, there have to be limits. What if some asshole wanted to build a twenty-story building in downtown Eugene. Suddenly we've got skyscrapers. Even I don't want that. Some regulations are necessary. Hell, if we get the Olympic Trials, none of this will matter. Eugene will suddenly be on the map—and that means more money all around."

"Olympic Trials, my ass. I hope we don't get them. I don't want the attention."

"Walt, you're a Neanderthal," laughed Bluto, loud enough to be heard throughout the lounge. "I've got everything riding on those Trials."

Walt shook his head. "I knew you were a dick."

Bluto laughed again. "I spoke to the Mayor Friday. He got a letter from the Olympics people. They've narrowed the location to five cities—Eugene is one of them."

"LA's where they were before. That's a better venue than here."

"With all the traffic and pollution? No, Eugene's perfect. The only concern is this anti-war stuff. According to Les, one more of these bombings, and they'll toss us off the list."

Walt nodded slowly. "What a shame. Maybe I should become an arsonist."

"Same as tearing down the forests."

"Eat me."

CHAPTER 77

Dinner that night at Blake College was the first time everyone had gotten together since Gloria's death. The mood was respectfully somber. They lit a candle for Gloria. Very little was said while they ate dal—brown rice and lentils—Gloria's favorite meal—with a large salad of mixed greens.

Tai produced a joint at the end of the meal, took a hit, and passed it to Adrienne beside him. "I'm just too unsettled from last night to get stoned," she said, passing the joint to Ray.

Ray and Crow took a hit, but no one else was interested. Instead of prompting conversation as usually happened, the meal ended on a flat note, with everyone going off to different parts of the house.

The next day was much the same. Chores were done but little else. That night the meal passed again in silence. When the plates were cleared, however, Rain opened up. "I don't know about the rest of you," she looked at the faces around the table, "but I had the strangest feeling last night. I woke up about two in the morning, and it felt as though someone else were in my head, looking out of my eyes—like maybe it was Gloria. I know we talked about her spirit entering us, but I don't know," she said, shaking her head. "Did anyone else get that feeling or is it just my imagination getting the better of me?"

"I get that feeling all the time," said Tai, lighting a joint. "But for me, I think it's from taking too much LSD."

This caused a chuckle, but Crow was serious. "I had a similar feeling this morning when I woke up. It felt like someone else was in the room. I thought of Gloria also, but it was unclear what I was feeling. Very strange."

"After the other night!" laughed Ray. "What's strange anymore?"

"If I focus on it," said Janice. "I think I can feel something too, but it's nothing I can really grasp. It's got to be Gloria. What else could it be?"

Marsha glanced at Van, then everyone around the table. "I hate to say it, but I feel something, too. I hadn't noticed it until Rain mentioned it just now. It's subtle—behind my thoughts—like your conscience or a song you can't get out of your head."

"I don't feel anything," said Adrienne, more upset than the others, "but now you've got me thinking about it. I don't like this conversation."

Ray put his arm around her shoulder. "Let's not go overboard. The more we talk about it, the more we'll think about it. Then we'll convince ourselves of something that's not really happening. I can't say I feel any different than I did last week."

"But it's got to be Gloria," said Janice. "We all saw it. Her spirit was right in the center of teepee. And then it just streamed right into our eyes! What else could it be?"

"I'm inclined to agree with Janice." Tai passed the joint to Crow. "But we don't know anything for sure. Maybe we'll all wake up tomorrow and it will be gone—no more than the aftermath of a very profound moment."

"Or some very strong drugs," said Van.

A long silence held.

"I brought it up," said Rain, "but I'm with Ray. We should stop talking about it. As I understand metaphysics, once the spirit is free of the body, it can hang around for a few days or longer—even years. That's what a ghost is—a lost soul trying to find its way beyond the astral plane. Maybe that's what's happening. Gloria wants to stay with us a little longer, and we're feeling it."

"But isn't the mortuary coming in two days to take Gloria's body?" asked Marsha. "How does that impact the spirit?"

"It shouldn't matter," said Rain. "The spirit doesn't have to stay with the body. It tends to go where it's most comfortable or hang around those it loved. That must be what's happening. Gloria is sharing herself with us until she moves on."

Adrienne held hands with Ray under the table. "God, I hope that's what it is."

"And if she has unfinished business and needs to stay," added Janice. "I can deal with that."

CHAPTER 78

Ray got up before sunrise Wednesday morning and headed to Eighteenth Avenue on his bicycle. The day had finally arrived. They were moving the house. No one was more excited or anxious about the four-hour excursion across Eugene than Jack Spikes. Ray met him at the house at four-thirty. It was still dark out and thank goodness it wasn't raining.

The house movers had arrived at four. They had placed four twelve by twelve, thirty-foot wooden beams beneath the house the day before. The first thing they did Wednesday morning was place their massive jacks beneath the beams and lift the house high enough to roll an over-sized gurney underneath. The gurney was then hitched to a semi-truck to haul the house across town.

The journey began at five-thirty, long before anyone but newspaper boys were on the streets. Spikes straddled the peak of the house and rode point, lifting the telephone lines so the house could pass beneath. Once they got rolling, Spikes eased up and began to hoot and holler from the top of the house, like Paul Bunyan riding Babe the blue ox.

The route across town had been worked out with the city three weeks in advance. Barricades had been put in place the day before to prevent parking on both sides of the relevant streets. The traffic lights were run manually by policemen, so that the house never had to stop until it got to Twelfth and Jefferson. The entire process was hugely thrilling and came off without a hitch. Even Ray, badly distracted by worries about Adrienne and what they'd witnessed two days earlier, managed to forget about these other issues and become absorbed in the massive move.

Afterward, Spikes invited Ray and Yates over to Sheila's for a celebratory dinner. Ray told Adrienne he didn't need to go, but she urged him to go have fun while she was working through her emotions. The phone rang in the middle of the meal.

Sheila went into the kitchen to answer it. "Hey, Bob, it's for you."

Yates looked at Spikes. "Who would call me here?"

"It's Rhonda," said Sheila, coming back into the dining room.

Yates cursed, then apologized to the kids. He spent ten minutes on the phone before returning to the table.

He shook his head as he sat down, clearly steaming.

Spikes found it humorous. "What'd she want?"

Yates grimaced. "Apparently I didn't get everything out of the basement that was mine. She wants it all gone by the weekend." He looked up at the ceiling.

"What did you leave?" asked Sheila.

"Just junk. A bunch of paint, some fishing equipment I never use, and four old tires. I can't believe she couldn't get her boyfriend to take care of it. He could have the fishing stuff as I far as I'm concerned."

The phone rang again. Sheila started to get up, but Yates stopped her. "If I know Rhonda, it's her again—with another request."

Yates answered the phone, but it wasn't Rhonda. "It's a woman, Jack. You know a Karen. Says she's one of your renters."

Sheila waved her hand. "Call her back, Jack."

"No way. That place is still unrented. I've got to talk to that woman—now."

The first call was bad enough, but the second call completely ruined the celebration. Karen wanted to exchange her key for the rent deposit and get some things she'd left behind. Spikes told her to meet him at the house the next day at ten. They'd walk through the house and determine how much of the deposit he would return. Karen verified that Mike would be with her to get the motorcycle parts. The looming confrontation was all Spikes talked about the rest of the night. He didn't like having to deal with bikers and wanted to be prepared for anything.

"Look at this," he said, after the children had gone upstairs to do their homework. He used a piece of paper and a pencil to draw an overhead view of the house and the adjacent streets. "I'll be on the front porch with the shotgun on my lap. Ray will be here in the pickup." He drew a rectangle for the pickup. "He'll have the twenty-two, held below window level."

He turned to Yates. "I want you two blocks away." He drew a rectangle for Yates' car. "In uniform and wearing your revolver."

Yates shook his head slowly. "Don't you think you're going overboard, Jack? You're just returning a rent deposit."

Spikes ignored his friend's comment. "If things go as expected, I'll walk through the house with them, return half the deposit, and stay there at the house until Mike has gathered up the parts to his motorcycle. Should be easy."

"Do I get paid double for carrying a gun?" asked Ray.

"Only if you use it," said Spikes, serious as could be.

"No," said Yates. "His gun won't be loaded. He'll just look ready to use it."

Sheila passed a basket of rolls to Ray. "Jack, this seems like too much. Do you really think there could be a problem?"

"I have no clue. Those bikers are trouble waiting to happen. And Mike is a loose cannon who wasn't too happy about my response to him the night he was shot. As far as I know, he's got a grudge going. He might show up with his anti-war biker friends and really set me off. I'm trying to avoid trouble by being prepared for it. Are all of you with me? Ten o'clock tomorrow morning."

"I'll be there," said Yates. "But not in uniform and in my own car."

Ray nodded. "I can be there."

"Good. And I'll get Pozlowski to show up."

Yates gave Ray a ride home at the end of the evening. "What do you think, Ray? Will there be a problem tomorrow?"

"Boy, I don't know. The guy seems dangerous to me."

"I think Jack's overreacting. I say we follow his plan and be very pleased when it turns out he didn't need us."

"I hope you're right. I'm not that excited about having a gun in my lap."

"I'm not that excited about this either. If something stupid happens, it could be my job."

"Thanks for saying no bullets in the twenty-two. I don't want to shoot anybody."

"Good. Hey, you're not living in Spikes' rental any more. Where am I taking you?"

Ray directed him to Blake College. Yates recognized the place immediately. "You live here?"

"Not officially until two weeks ago, but I've been sleeping here with my girlfriend Adrienne almost every night since September."

Yates nodded. "I broke up a party here earlier in the fall. You might have been there."

"I don't think so," he lied.

"What's that woman Rain like?"

"About as nice as they get. Very smart."

"And attractive."

"Absolutely."

"She have a boyfriend?"

Ray tipped his head, thinking this was an odd question from Yates. "Not right now—that I know of. She seems to be pretty independent."

"What's she do for a living?"

"Wild crafting."

"What's that?"

"She collects herbs and plants in the forest. Then sells them at Saturday Market." Ray climbed out of the car.

"Seems like a hard way to go," said Yates from across the seat.

"She's pretty sharp. She makes it work." Ray closed the car door and went inside.

Back at Sheila's house, Jack and Sheila were putting the kids to bed. Jack spent some extra time with Joey.

"I heard you talking about guns, Jack," said the nine-year-old. "Why do you need guns?"

"Oh, we probably don't. I was just talking. One of my renters is moving out. It's not always an easy process."

"Will it be dangerous? I don't want you to get hurt."

Jack smiled. "It will be fine. And don't worry about me. I'm too ornery to get hurt."

"What's ornery mean?"

Jack laughed. He did like the kid even if he'd been placed in special ed. "Ornery means," he grabbed the boy by the ribs and started tickling him, "tough and mean."

When Jack came out of the bedroom, Sheila was in the hallway. She took Jack's hand and led him downstairs to the living room. They sat down on the couch.

"You know how good you are for that boy, don't you?"

Jack nodded.

"He's having a hard time with the special ed class. He keeps asking me why he's not with the other children."

"Yeah, I can see it's thrown him off."

"But not around you."

"So it seems." Jack bowed his head.

"Any further thought about what I asked you? We haven't talked since then."

"I haven't really had the chance, Sheila. I've had too many other things on my mind."

"I wish I did." Sheila looked down at her hands. "But now that you've moved the house, shouldn't things get a little easier, less tense?"

Jack gave her a noncommittal tip of his head.

Sheila knew Jack wasn't the sort to push into anything, but she was worried about her son and couldn't help herself. "Think about it, please. Maybe we revisit this in a week or so?"

"Sure."

Sure was not a *yes*, but Sheila kissed him anyway.

CHAPTER 79

Later that night, after everyone had gone to bed at Blake College, Adrienne let out a scream that awakened the entire household. Everyone but Tai, who slept in the basement, raced to Adrienne's room and clustered in the doorway. The overhead light, a single naked bulb, was on, and Ray, wrapped in blankets, held Adrienne in his arms, trying to comfort her. "She had a bad dream."

Adrienne shook her head. "It wasn't a dream at all. It was that feeling Crow described—like someone you can't see is in the room—or sharing my eyes or something. I feel it now. And it sure doesn't feel like Gloria."

Tai stumbled up the stairs and down the hall into the group. "What's going on?"

"Adrienne had a nightmare," said Van.

"It wasn't a nightmare!" snapped Adrienne.

"You could be right, Adrienne. It might not be Gloria." Rain took a deep breath. "I've been reading up on this all night. It might be a vagrant spirit. Something drawn to our ceremony that took advantage of the opening it provided and entered us to escape its astral wandering."

"Jesus Christ, Rain," muttered Ray, who like Van had major doubts about all of it. "You've got to be making this up."

"It's real, Ray," said Adrienne. "I feel it now."

"And I'm not making it up."

"But it could still be Gloria, right, Rain?" posited Janice, clearly unsettled.

"I hope so. But who knows? What we did Sunday night was like opening Pandora's box—it could be anything."

"But we were holding hands," said Adrienne. "Wasn't that supposed to protect us?"

"That's what I thought." Rain bowed her head. "But I'm not sure I really know anymore. Are you all right?"

Adrienne shrugged. "I'm not sure."

Ray gave her a forlorn look.

"Okay, everyone go back to bed," concluded Rain. "We have to be ready early tomorrow when the mortuary comes to take Gloria."

Rain stopped by Crow's room—Gloria's old room—on the way back to her bedroom. Crow was sitting on the bed. A single candle burned on the milk crate that acted as a bedside table. "Are you all right, Crow?" He had been very quiet since Gloria's death. Only Rain knew how close they had become.

Crow looked up at her. His eyes were brown and deep and sad. "I miss her. She was the best thing here for me. She was an uncommonly good woman."

Rain nodded

"Whatever's in us," Crow continued, "it's not Gloria. I'm not sure I know what a vagrant spirit is, but I feel something. Maybe acknowledging it makes it stronger, but it's not Gloria. I'm sure of that."

Rain stared down at the worn wooden floor.

"Don't blame yourself, Rain. Maybe what we saw was worth it."

She shook her head. "It was certainly profound."

"You know, Rain, when I told everyone I had a record, no one asked me what I'd done. That impressed me. It was trust without question from a group of white folks."

Rain smiled weakly.

"I killed a man in a car accident many years ago. I served time for manslaughter."

Rain lifted her head.

"I've always believed that man's spirit followed me around, but I never saw anything like what we saw Sunday night."

"I hope it wasn't all a big mistake."

"Wasn't the ceremony Gloria's idea?"

"I was a part of it."

"What happened, Rain, whatever it was—good or bad—needs no blame."

Rain nodded slowly. "I appreciate your saying that. But as far as I'm concerned, I was responsible. Now I'll have to find a way to resolve it."

CHAPTER 80

No one slept in. Hardly anyone even went to sleep after Adrienne's scream. By six-forty-five everyone had gathered around the dining room table with tea, coffee, and/or a bowl of the school's granola. Moxie and Lena joined them. Everyone but Ray and Van said they felt as if something were in their heads. It faded to the background when one was engaged in something, but during idle moments, particularly upon going to bed or simply daydreaming, a vague presence seemed to hover behind their thoughts.

Rain tried to circle the wagons. "Either Gloria is still with us or we've been possessed by a vagrant spirit."

"Or you're all imagining it," deadpanned Ray.

"All possibilities are open until we have an answer," said Crow.

"If it's Gloria," continued Rain, "she'll go away on her own. If it's a vagrant spirit, we'll have to confront it somehow—and that might mean repeating the ceremony in the teepee."

"With Gloria's body there?" asked Janice.

"No, the mortuary people will be here in an hour. I want to go to the library and see what more I can find out about this stuff—and what we can do about it."

Ray frowned. "You mean like having an exorcism?"

"If it's not Gloria, yes, that's what I'm thinking."

Ray shook his head and looked up at the ceiling. "This is getting dumber and dumber."

The mortuary hearse came at eight on the dot. Ray, Crow, Tai, and Rain carried the stretcher to the hearse. The others followed. No tears were shed as the hearse drove away. Returning to the tent had turned them inward.

A dark, somber mood settled in at the school. Everyone went about their business without a word. Rain went to the library. Adrienne and Ray decided to clean out the teepee and wash the blankets.

Adrienne had changed, and Ray was concerned. Well into the job of cleaning, while they shook out the largest of the wool blankets, he asked her how she was.

"Horrible," she said, exhaling with exasperation. "Something feels wrong inside my head, and I don't know what it is. I feel it in my eyes. Like I'm wearing the wrong prescription glasses or something."

Ray hugged her. He wanted the strong, confident Adrienne back. "Give it some time, Adrienne. This spiritual stuff just doesn't seem quite right to me. I think it's a hangover from the drugs. That was strong stuff."

"I don't know what it is, Ray." Adrienne laid her head on his chest. "But when Rain brought up the idea of another séance this morning, I wanted nothing to do with it."

Ray held Adrienne a long time before releasing her. "I'm supposed to meet Jack in town." The confrontation with the biker and his girlfriend was scheduled for ten. It was well past nine. "It's important. Will you be all right if I'm gone for a few hours?"

"Yes, there's plenty to do here."

"I'll be back for dinner, if not sooner."

Marsha and Van were in their bedroom, standing on either side of their bed—a queen-sized mattress on the floor. They both bent down at the same time to straighten the covers—and bumped their heads. They laughed, and then nearly did the same thing again, reaching for a book Van had left on the floor. They looked at each other.

"You know what?" They both said it at once and stared at each other open-mouthed.

"You first," they both said over top of each other, then burst into laughter.

Van pointed at Marsha.

"We're reading each other's thoughts." She pointed at him.

"That's what I was going to say."

"Maybe that's what love does?" Marsha grinned. "Our brains have synchronized."

"Or it's that thing in our minds?" joked Van, who was still as skeptical as Ray.

Marsha shook her head. "I don't think so." She smiled slyly. "Not with what's running through my mind right now!"

Van grinned. They both simultaneously undressed and shared the most intimate and fulfilling sex they'd had yet.

Afterward, while they lay side by side in the bed, Van sat up. "You know, I hate to say it, but damn, I think I'm feeling it."

"It's subtle, Van."

"Yeah, so subtle I can't tell if I'm imagining it or not. It's weird, but I still think it's from the drugs."

"Or maybe the entire experience."

"Or the power of suggestion."

CHAPTER 81

Spikes' pickup was parked on Madison Street half a block from the house when Ray arrived on his bicycle. Spikes wasn't in the cab, so he put his bike in the back of the truck and went over to the house. As Ray reached the yard, he noticed Yates' black Oldsmobile parked a block and a half farther down Madison to the north. The headlights flashed on and off. Ray lifted a hand in acknowledgment. In the other direction, Henry Pozlowski was across First Street in his blue International Travelall. Ray found Spikes inside stalking through the house with his shotgun gripped in his left hand.

"How long before you expect them, Jack?"

He looked at his watch. "Ten minutes. Go get in the truck. Take the twenty-two off the gunrack. Just sit tight. I'll be on the front porch."

Ray sensed how tense Spikes was. He had no idea what to expect but knew a crazy biker was involved. As he went out the door, Spikes called to him. "By the way, there are bullets in the rifle. No sense having one in your hand if ain't loaded."

Ray hesitated then continued out to the truck. He slid in behind the wheel, took the gun off the rack, and laid it across his lap. Jack never even asked if he'd fired a rifle before. He had. Hunting with his father. Five minutes passed. He stared out the windshield anticipating the arrival of Mike Rogers and his girlfriend.

As the tension built, Ray became increasingly aware of his own thoughts. Up to this point, Rain's idea that something had gotten into their heads had not rung true to him. But now, for the first time, it impressed him that someone was sitting beside him—watching what he was doing. He thought about Adrienne and her waking up in the middle of the night. She had really been scared, and it surprised him that such a rough and tumble girl like Adrienne was that upset. He didn't want to believe the feeling was real. It had to be a leftover from the drugs; it had to be.

He felt a vibration in the pickup. The ballpoint pen on the dashboard rattled against the windshield. He heard them before he saw them. Ten Gypsy Jokers motored down First Street in formation on their Harleys, half of them with ape hangers and extended front forks. Mike and Karen followed in Karen's Chevy sedan.

Ray sat up straight in the seat and watched the bikers turn onto Madison. One by one they pulled their bikes up to the curb in front of Spikes' rental and cut their engines. Karen parked in the driveway. Ray could see Yates watching from his car. Henry appeared to be reading the newspaper.

Spikes stood up from his seat on the porch, gun in hand. Mike, wearing his colors, and Karen, in blue jeans and a sweatshirt, got out of the car and walked up to the porch. "Howdy, Jack. Nice of you to bring your shotgun. You know we're only here to get my bike and our rent deposit." The other bikers sat back on their bikes and watched.

"That why you brought all your friends?"

"Of late, I don't go anywhere without them." Mike grinned. "There's another bike club in town that doesn't like me too much. Besides, I've got to put that bike together before I can take it anywhere. I might need some help."

"No, that's not going to happen. You can box it up and find somewhere else to assemble it."

"I didn't bring any boxes, Jack, and my ribs are still a little sore. I might need three or four days. You can take it out of the rent deposit. Should be no problem, right?"

"And suppose the Free Souls show up and destroy my house. Start gathering up the parts. I'll find some boxes."

Mention of the Free Souls got the other bikers talking. Mike turned to them, then back to Spikes. "No, Jack. I'm gonna ride that bike out of here."

One of the bikers pulled his bike back on its kickstand, slipped off the seat, and walked into the conversation. Another vet, he sported an artificial arm and a severe burn scar on the left side of his face. His black leather cap was pulled down low on left, so the bill nearly tipped into his eye. "Just give him a chance to assemble his bike and all of us will be gone, Mr. Landlord. Otherwise." The biker grinned through speed darkened teeth. "Who knows? Maybe we'll all stay another month."

Yates got out of his car and began walking down the street. Ray saw him coming in the rearview mirror and lifted the barrel of the twenty-two so that it rested on the edge of the open window.

"Karen said she was moving out more than a month ago," said Spikes. "I've already started cleaning the place and have an ad in the paper to rent it. I'm losing money as we speak. I'm not leaving until that bike is gone—and it better be today."

At this point, Yates reached the confab. "I'm a police officer, gentlemen." He flashed his badge in a way that revealed the shoulder holster beneath his jacket. Many of the bikers recognized him. "Is there a problem here?" He glanced across the street to the barrel of the twenty-two aimed at the array of bikers. Then to Henry who had brought his antique Winchester.

The bikers looked around assessing the situation. The biker with the artificial arm laughed. "Not quite the manpower of the Free Souls." Three of the bikers, one wearing a German-style helmet, revealed handguns of their own. Another sported a sawed-off shotgun in a leather holster attached to his bike. "You boys sure this is something you want to get into? For a couple days' rent?"

With eyes darting this way and that, and the tension building, the velvet purr of a perfectly tuned motorcycle made everyone—many thinking Free Souls—look to the north end of Madison.

Tim O'Malley, wearing his leather motorcycle helmet and goggles, motored down the street on his Indian. He came to a stop alongside the string of motorcycles. He grinned as though stoned way beyond any ordinary sense. "I thought I heard you guys coming into town. What's the occasion?"

While no one else dared to move, Tim climbed off his motorcycle. He took two steps toward the other bikes, as though he wanted to check them out, and lifted his goggles up to his forehead—then noticed Spikes' shotgun—and the bikers' array of weapons.

"You know, boys," Tim grinned, now also recognizing Yates as a police officer, "I think I'm at the wrong tea party. Unless this little get together is about motorcycles, you don't really need me."

The bikers couldn't help chuckling at Tim's entrance. They knew he was nuts and also remarkably capable. Spikes, who had seen Tim in town on his Indian but had never spoken to him, called out, "Can you put a Harley together in four hours?"

Tim tipped his head in thought. "Maybe six. But if you've got that shotgun pointed at me, I might be able to trim that down to five."

Yates tried to hide his grin. Ray, watching from the pickup, had seen Tim in a similar situation before and couldn't believe it was happening again.

"With Mike helping," said Spikes, "you might get that down to four."

"This some kind of contest?" asked Tim. "Is there a cash prize or something like that?"

This made Spikes laugh. "No contest. Just a Harley in my house that's in parts. I want it assembled and gone."

Mike looked at Tim. "Tim, you got some time? I spent four weeks taking my KHK apart and cleaning it up. It's inside ready to assemble. I could use a hand. Especially someone with your knowhow."

Tim didn't know the details, but he got the idea pretty quickly. He had seen Spikes before. He knew he was a Eugene slum lord, and it was clear Mike needed to get out of his house. He also knew Mike was prone to getting evicted and having trouble with landlords. "Let's take a look at it, Mike. You know me, nothing I like better than rebuilding motorcycles."

"What do you say, Jack? We'll be out of here before dark."

"Tell your friends to go home. Officer Yates will stay here with me and so will my other friends." He glanced at Henry and Ray. "We'll provide protection while you get the bike put together."

Mike looked around, then shrugged his shoulders. "That works for me. Guys, thanks for the backup. I think we got this handled. I'll find you when my bike hits the street."

And that was how it ended.

When it came time to assemble the motorcycle, Tim did most of the work, but he also found himself thinking about that spray paint nozzle and the firebomb at Johnson Hall. He might know all the outlaw bikers, but that didn't mean they were trusted friends. He always approached them like sticks of dynamite—they were fine until something lit their fuse. Mike was no different.

As they put the bike together, they drank two beers, but Mike was otherwise sober and didn't seem nearly as crazy as the Free Souls portrayed him. With Spikes and his policeman friend wandering in and out, Tim had to walk a thin line between working on the bike and quizzing Mike about his anti-war activities. Tim asked him about the

Jokers' trip to Washington, D.C in July. This got Mike going, but there was no suggestion of anything close to violence. When Tim mentioned the bombings, Mike said he only knew what he'd read in the paper. Then he asked Mike where he got his motorcycle parts. Without any hesitation, he said, "Brooks, same as you." This wasn't exactly incriminating, but it left the door open.

Near the end of the job, Tim went into the garage to toss out two empty cans of oil. He dropped them in a trash can that Spikes had filled with crap he'd cleaned out of the house. He was about to walk away when he noticed an aerosol can stuffed in with the garbage. He lifted it out of the other junk and saw that it was a can of Rust-oleum—missing its nozzle. Without the cap, it was unclear what color it was. He dug deeper into the trash but found no cap, so he put the can aside to take with him when he left.

Tim had Mike's KHK on the road in five hours and left the place with no clear hit on Mike, other than the can of spray paint he'd stuck in the Indian's saddlebag. Spikes gave Karen half her deposit. Neither she nor Mike complained. They'd be high on heroin before the day was over.

When Tim got back to the print shop, he retrieved the nozzle from the shelf with Stoopid's ashes and stuck it in the can of spray paint. The pressure was too low to get anything out of it. He shook it up, heated it a little with a lighter, tilted it this way and that with his finger on the nozzle, and got it to sputter out a couple of drops of paint—safety yellow. It wasn't exactly a smoking gun, but pretty damn close. And easily the best lead he had. He'd have another talk with Mike before it was all over.

CHAPTER 82

The day after the confrontation at First and Madison, Bob Yates saw that a death certificate had recently been filed. The doctor's report said the body had been in a teepee. He recognized the address and immediately thought of Rain. If a first impression meant anything, he imagined Rain to be the antithesis of the woman he had just divorced after seven years of marriage and a year of separation. He decided to use the death as a reason to return to the old Victorian and talk to Rain a second time. On this occasion he went alone.

When the squad car drove up, Crow went out the back door. Tai, who had consolidated his drugs since the last visit, grabbed his stash and slipped out the basement window as he had before.

Yates knocked on the front door. Adrienne answered it. He remembered her from the night of the party. "I'm Officer Yates of the Eugene Police Department. You might recall my coming here one night in the fall."

Adrienne was not her usual self. Ray had told her in bed that morning he had also sensed something in his head, which further unsettled her. Seeing Yates at the door didn't help. It took her a moment to respond. "Yes, sir, I do remember that."

"I heard someone died here on the weekend. I wanted to pass along my condolences."

"You know, officer, Rain's the one to talk to. She made all the arrangements with the doctor and the mortuary." Adrienne let him into the house and pointed out the dining room window. "She's out back. In the teepee. You can see it from here."

Yates, thinking Adrienne might be stoned, nodded politely and headed out through the kitchen. Crow and Tai saw him coming and sank deeper into the brush along the river.

Rain's day of reading at the library had convinced her a second séance was the best way to address the uneasiness that gripped the school. She was in the teepee preparing for the ceremony when Yates stuck his head in the oval opening. "Rain Adams, do you have a moment?" He saw that his voice startled her.

"Well, yes, officer." She stepped out of the teepee. The sun highlighted the blush in her skin and the red in her hair.

"I saw the coroner's report. Gloria Freeman died out here Sunday night. The report said something about cancer and starving to death. I just wanted to make sure everything was all right."

Again, this caught always composed Rain off guard. "We're fine. Gloria fasted the last ten days of her life."

"She fasted to death?"

"Not quite, the cancer was very far advanced. It was her way to prepare for the inevitable. Is there something wrong?"

Yates was captivated by Rain's face and the radiance in her eyes. "No, the doctor's report supports what you've said. With the starving and all, I was worried you might not have enough to eat out here."

Rain almost laughed. Her smile heightened her beauty. "We've got tons of food, officer. We make granola to sell in town. We have a greenhouse and a huge garden that we maintain through the winter. We probably eat better than anyone else in Eugene."

"You told me about your co-op. I just wasn't sure what that meant." He tipped his cap. "Sorry to bother you, and of course, my condolences. I remember meeting Gloria briefly. I'm sure her death was a great loss to the school."

"Very much. We all loved her."

Yates headed back to his cruiser, taking the long way around the house. He saw Janice come down the driveway and enter the house. She looked as though she'd put on some weight.

Rain returned to the house to verify that Yates had left. Crow and Tai entered the house shortly after she did.

"What was that about?" asked Tai.

Rain shook her head. "I'm not sure. He was worried we didn't have enough to eat."

CHAPTER 83

Shortly before noon, Sheila picked Jack up at Twelfth and Jefferson. Jack told Ray he was taking Sheila out for lunch. "I'll be back in an hour or so. There's more than enough work here to keep you busy. Take thirty minutes for lunch."

Ray went to get his lunch bag, and Spikes climbed into Sheila's Jeep wagon. "Now where's this we're going?"

Sheila put the car in drive and angled out into the street. "The medical center on River Road. I took Joey out there a few days ago. A Doctor Keller—I told you about this—gave Joey some tests and talked to him. I also told him why Joey's eye drooped."

Jack watched his property vanish behind them. "And now he's going to give us his evaluation?"

"Right, and I know you're busy, but I really wanted you to come with me. I know, I know," she lifted one hand off the steering wheel, "you haven't made any commitment yet. But you're still thinking about it…right?"

Jack's nod was unconvincing.

The conference was devasting.

"Joey is emotionally disturbed," said Doctor Keller, an older man, bald on the top, a fringe of white on the sides. He spoke slowly and with feeling. "The incident with your ex-husband did more than what we can see."

Sheila and Jack sat side by side across from the doctor.

"He's showing all the signs of attention deficit disorder. It's not something we know a lot about. Most of the accepted treatments recommend medication."

Jack leaned forward. "Medication? What do you mean?"

"We have four or five different drugs—psychostimulants—that can give Joey a little more focus."

Jack gaped at the doctor. "You mean speed?"

"Ritalin isn't really speed. But, yes, that's one way to think about it."

"Is this attention deficit thing something new?" asked Sheila.

"Well, I imagine it's been around a long time, but it's only recently that we've put a name on it."

Jack and Sheila looked at each other.

"The medication will allow him to move out of special ed and get back on track at school."

The doctor wrote them a prescription. They walked out of the building in shock.

"We're not putting him on fucking medication," snarled Jack the moment they were in Sheila's car.

Sheila was on the verge of tears. "Then what do we do? We can't leave him in special ed."

"I don't care what class he's in!" shouted Jack. "We're not giving Joey speed. I don't like it. I don't like it at all. Next thing you know he'll be a fucking meth-head biker."

CHAPTER 84

That afternoon, Tim met Gino at Lucky's for a few games of pool. They smoked a joint in the alley then ambled in as though they owned the place. Earl called out from behind the bar. "We're charging hippies double. Pay upfront, gents."

Gino gave him the finger. Tim led the way to the bar and asked Earl for a pitcher. "I'm sure you meant half-price, not double." He laid the full price for a pitcher and a rack of balls on the bar.

"For you maybe, but that little wiseass you're with pays triple." Earl placed a rack of balls on the bar and took half of Tim's money. "You've got table four."

Tim had his own stick. Gino took one from a rack on the wall. As Tim stood beside table four chalking the tip of his cue and Gino leaned over the table racking the balls, John Walters and Linda Sheedy came into the pool hall arguing.

"Fuck," muttered Tim. "There's goes our pool game."

Gino looked up. "What do you mean?" Then he saw John and Linda heading straight for them. Gino went over to the table where Tim had put two glasses and the pitcher of beer. He filled both glasses, then chugged half of his.

"We thought we might find you here," said John.

"We already tried the print shop and the Odyssey," said Linda. "Max's was next."

"I gotta find a better place to hide," said Tim with a wry grin. "Let me guess, space problems?"

"Yeah," said Gino, lining up the cue ball to break. "Outer space."

"The only one in outer space is you," said Linda, then turning to Tim. "The City Council turned us down on the park blocks. The farmers want to split off."

John Walters pursed his lips. "We've got twice the number of farmers we had last season. Without the park blocks, we need a place of our own."

"So, you came here to ruin my pool game and vent." Tim looked over at the pool table. Gino had broken, but none of the balls had gone in. Tim edged up to the pool table, sighting his shot as he spoke. "Where do they want you to go? Back to Tenth and Oak?"

"That's the worst of it," said Linda. "The businesses at Tenth and Oak don't want us there anymore."

"They don't like hippies," said John straight-faced. "One of the city councilors suggested the fairgrounds' parking lot."

"Plenty of space, but it's not downtown. We'd get half the business." Linda shook her head. "And they want to charge us."

Tim pulled back his pool stick and struck the cue ball. The five ball shot into the corner pocket. He stood up and moved around the table. "You have a backup?"

"No," said Linda. "We were so sure we'd get the park blocks we never thought about it. Now we're stuck with nothing."

Tim stroked the ball again. This time knocking the three into the side pocket. He straightened up and moved around the table like a cat on the prowl. "So, John, what's your plan—if you go it alone?"

"I'm not sure. We want to be downtown."

"Why didn't the City Council go for it?" asked Tim, sighting down the length of the table, targeting the one on the rail.

"Like the businesses, they don't like our scene," said Linda

"Too counterculture for the image of the city," added John.

Tim hit the cue ball with side English. The ball hit the outside edge of the one. It hugged the rail right into the corner pocket.

"Fuck you, Tim," snarked Gino. "When do I get a shot?"

Tim reached for his glass of beer and took a long swallow. "What's the thing the City Council is always talking about? The most important thing?"

John and Linda looked at each other. Gino muttered, "Money."

"Exactly. The economy is the biggest issue. You need an angle that they can understand. All this organic food and handcrafts is Greek to them. Talk dollars and cents."

"Like how much money we bring in each weekend?" asked John.

Tim zeroed in on the seven and a side rail bank. "And how many people you draw into downtown on a Saturday." He hit it just right. Boom into the side pocket!

"Muthafuck," snapped Gino. "You run the table. You buy the beer."

Tim looked up from the table. "I think you've got that backwards, bro."

Linda had begun to pace. "Do you think we should go back and ask for the park blocks again?"

"Damn straight," said Tim, standing and facing her. "Tell them you represent one hundred small businesses. And that each one has the potential to incubate another. Tell them people, who would otherwise be unemployed, are taking the initiative to make it on their own. They might look like hippies, but they're really budding capitalists," Tim grinned, "adding to the local economy—and because they also pay taxes—adding to the state coffers. Tell them you are exactly the financial stimulus Eugene has been looking for."

Linda and John looked at each other again: *Tim's pitch just might work.*

"Could you write that down, Tim?"

"No need," said Linda. "I've got it. And I like it. Thank you, Tim. Maybe this won't work, but it's worth a try."

"And don't be afraid to pass around sign-up sheets," said Tim. "Bring in a few thousand signatures from your customers. Just saying they're regular clients. That might help."

"We can do that," said John. "We have customers who swear they won't eat anything other than what our farmers grow."

Tim leaned over the table. The eleven ball sat in front of the far corner pocket. The cue ball streaked across the table, hit the cushions on either side of the eleven, grazing it as it did so. The ball dropped into the pocket.

"This sure is fun," mumbled Gino, refilling his glass.

"But you don't need to worry about the beer," said John. "I'm setting you up." He put a hand on Gino's shoulder. "Thank your partner. He's tough to beat."

"Any insights into the bombing, Tim?" asked Linda. "I know you've been more than casually interested."

Tim shook his head, thinking again of Stoopid—and the can of spray paint he'd found at First and Madison. "Nothing worth mentioning."

Linda and John apologized for interfering with the game, and John laid a five spot on the bar as they walked out.

CHAPTER 85

Janice and Crow had dinner duty Friday night. Crow had caught an eighteen-pound winter steelhead off the river bank. He grilled part of it outside and smoked the rest. Janice made the standard super salad and a rice pilaf of her own invention. Aside from her relationship with Gloria, learning to cook was one of the best things she'd gotten out of Blake College. The school's garden was the first she'd ever participated in. She nurtured a bed of herbs, and the mushrooms in the pilaf had been wildcrafted with Rain.

Despite the lovely meal, a pall hung over the household. The idea that something was in their heads was foremost on everyone's mind, but no one mentioned it, as though they each knew what the others were thinking and there was no need for further elaboration. Crow said a short prayer for Gloria. Then they ate in near silence. Tai and Ray complimented the salmon, and Rain, who was doing her best to remake her relationship with prickly Janice, complimented the rice dish. But that was it.

As was the usual practice, they stayed at the table after the dishes were cleared. For the first time since he'd arrived, Tai did not light a joint after the meal. Everyone noticed this, but again no one said a word. Even the dog and cat seemed perturbed by the mood in the house. Moxie lay in a corner, seemingly asleep, but if closely watched, one eye opened from time to time to appraise the situation. Lena sat bolt upright on the sideboard. Her eyes wide and yellow, at a level slightly above the heads of those at the table.

Rain broke the spell. "Something unexpected happened to us the night Gloria died." A chicken that no one knew was in the house tottered into the dining room and promptly leapt onto the window sill beside the table. Usually someone would have thrown it outside immediately, but such was the atmosphere in the dining room, no one even commented on the chicken's presence.

"I think we were sorely amiss in what we were doing," continued Rain. "None of us, neither Gloria, Tai, nor I, had the experience to open us or anyone else to the spirit world." Rain paused to glance around the table. It was clear they were all on the same page.

"Because I feel responsible for what happened, I did some reading yesterday. Although I haven't given up on the idea that it could be Gloria who's with us," she glanced around the room as though she might see Gloria's spirit floating across the ceiling, "it seems more likely that we were possessed by a vagrant spirit—and in a very common way—ignoring the dangers of opening ourselves to the spirit world without a proper guide. Unfortunately, I found nothing in my reading about the possession of eight people at once." She looked at both Ray and Van who had admitted earlier in the day to sensing what they initially had not. "As a group, though, we have one thing going for us. By talking about it, maybe we can figure out who or what it is. What it wants and how to get rid of it."

"And if it's real," added Van.

"Real meaning what?" demanded Tai.

"We have no proof of anything, Tai. Did we simply convince ourselves of something or is what we're feeling real?"

"A fair question," said Rain. "Does anyone still think it could be Gloria?"

"I do," said Janice, as did Tai. Marsha wasn't sure.

"I only sense an undefined presence," said Rain. "It doesn't seem to be influencing my actions. I just have the feeling of being hyperconscious—of myself and all my actions. Does anyone have any more insight than that?"

Ray had transformed from skeptic to full believer. Part of it was the change he'd witnessed in Adrienne, and part of it was the hyperawareness he'd experienced while waiting for the bikers in Jack's pickup. That feeling of something shadowing his thoughts had persisted and had put him on edge. "I don't know what it is, but I don't want something in my head, watching everything I do." He closed and opened his eyes. "It's fucked up. I don't like it." His anger was directed at Rain.

Crow sat across the table from Ray. He leaned forward. "Can you feel anything more than that, Ray? Male or Female? Young or old?"

"No. It's just there, lurking like some kind of voyeur—but instead of outside the window, it's in my head."

"I have no grasp of it at all—none," said Van. "I sense no gender, no age. It's so subtle I still wonder if it's not a leftover from the drugs or simply proof of the power of suggestion."

"I can't describe it either," said Marsha. "It's like trying to catch your own shadow."

"It could be an animal spirit," said Crow. "That's common in Native American traditions. The spirit world is not limited to humans."

Moxie lifted his head.

"Nor to this planet," added Tai.

Everyone looked at him. Lena the cat twitched her tail.

Crow agreed. "The Native American traditions call them star people—spirits from beyond our world."

Ray was having none of it. He got up from the table and glared at the others. "This is bullshit. Star people? Fuck all of you and this stupid mysticism." He stomped through the kitchen and out the back door. Adrienne got up to chase him down.

"I'm not too comfortable with the idea of ghosts or any of this other stuff either," said Van. 'But if I have to go there, I wonder if this presence—whatever it is—might not be something good." Van looked around the table. "What if it's actually empowering us? Marsha and I have talked about this."

"What do you mean?" asked Tai.

"Try this," said Van. "I'm thinking of a number between one and a hundred. Write it down."

No one questioned the request. Pens and paper were always on the table. They all reached for a slip of paper and scratched down a number.

"Fold them and give them to me." Van collected them on the table in front of him, then said, "The number was three."

Janice gasped. When Van opened the five slips of paper, the number three was written on three of them, thirty-three was on another, and forty-three was on the last one.

"We've got a little Vulcan mind meld going on here. That's kind of cool," said Tai with a chuckle. But no one else laughed.

Adrienne came in the back door with Ray, who looked none too happy.

"What number, Ray?" blurted out Tai.

"Three."

Another layer of dread passed over the group.

"What'd I say?" Ray looked at Adrienne. "What'd I say?"

Crow stood up and pointed. "Look at the animals!"

Moxie was sitting up staring at them. Lena had been attentive all evening, and the chicken on the window sill twitched its head from side to side, as though following the conversation. At that moment, the two foxes wandered into the room. Adrienne gathered them into her arms. "How'd you guys get out of your box?"

"All of them—the cat, the dog, the chicken, and the foxes—were in the tent when Gloria died," said Rain. "It might be in them, too!"

"No way," muttered Ray. "No way it's in the animals. No way. Stop this crazy stuff. It's ridiculous. You're making it worse."

Marsha spoke up. "Van and I discovered this psychic sympathy earlier. At first we thought it was because we had become such good friends." She looked at Van with a smile. "But it's obvious now that it's something more. Our minds have become connected in some way."

"Because we all took Tai's stupid concoction," snapped Ray.

"That's what I thought," said Van. "But after my little experiment, I'm not so sure anymore."

"It's more than the drugs," said Crow. "Something is in us and seems to join our minds in some way."

Ray stalked away from the table. "Bullshit. Ghosts. Star people. This stuff is just plain stupid." He shouted the word *stupid*, then pounded on the sides of his head until Adrienne grabbed his hands and held him.

Rain was as stumped as anyone. "I came to the table tonight to propose that we return to the teepee and recreate the ceremony we had Sunday night. Maybe if we could attain that transcendent state again, the entity would identify itself or leave us or even be Gloria. But I'm hesitant to try for fear of making things worse."

"There must be some way to exorcise this thing—whatever it is," said Marsha.

"Maybe we need a Catholic priest," said Adrienne.

"That would be worse than a vagrant spirit," said Crow. "I say we try it again."

"It's got to be Gloria," said Janice. "Let's find out."

"Absolutely," said Tai. "I think we have to confront this thing head on. It ain't going nowhere, and we need to know what it is."

"Shut up, Tai," spat Ray. "For all we know we'll go down there and get doubly infected. I won't take part." He gripped Adrienne's hand in his.

"Doubly infected?" queried Crow. "What does that mean?"

"Some other damned thing getting in our heads."

Crow sat back and looked at the others. "I guess that's possible, but I think we need to try it."

"Fat fucking chance," said Ray defiantly. "I won't do it. And neither will Adrienne. If we run this place by consensus, you've got two nays right off the bat."

"No, Ray," said Adrienne. "I've changed my mind. I want to do it. I need to find out who or what it is."

"If it's real," emphasized Van.

"If it's real," repeated Rain, "and if it is, is it Gloria."

CHAPTER 86

They went down to the teepee with the agreement that there would be no psychedelic elixir or marijuana. It was a clear, cold night. A nearly full moon sat low in the east and was reflected on the surface of the river. Rain stared at the moon for a long time, then ducked into the teepee with the others following her. She lit a candle in the middle of the teepee, while Van, Marsha, Janice, Adrienne, and a reluctant Ray sat down to form a circle. Crow and Tai lit ten more candles situated around the circle, then sat down so that everyone was seated in the same order as during the original ceremony. The two foxes sat in Adrienne's lap, Moxie squeezed in between Adrienne and Ray, Lena curled up in Rain's lap, and then, just as they were settling in, the chicken clucked into the tent and stood attentive at the edge of the circle.

"There you have it," said Tai, staring at the chicken. "I thought it was just a coincidence when the chicken showed up in the dining room. But fuck no! Something got inside every living thing in the teepee."

Van pointed to a spider web spun across the tent poles at the peak of the teepee. "Even that spider?"

Tai laughed. "Yep, probably even that spider."

Rain focused the group with a long period of silence. When she felt the time was right, she began to *om*. The others fell in with her. They had practiced this together for so long they hit Rain's note like an octet of oboists. The trance came on more easily and more powerfully than it had before. Although they chanted with their eyes closed, it seemed that their eyes were open, staring into a timeless dreamworld of incomprehensible voices and silky vapors. All of a sudden, vivid blue rays of light projected from their eyes, the animals' as well—and, though no one noticed, from the spider's above—and met in the center of their circle, forming a luminous blue vortex spinning in the air before them.

Viewing down the rays of light, they could see into the vortex as though looking into a crystal ball, and it seemed that they—all of them— were traveling through space, sailing out into the stars, past spinning planets and their orbiting moons. They veered off toward a planet, dropped down into its atmosphere, and glided over its surface like a flock of birds. Several hundred pale blue, manta-like creatures flew with them, as they swooped through luxurious mountain valleys filled with long grasses and palm-like trees of bright yellows and greens or sailed high above sprawling desert plains, dotted here and there with large pyramidal mounds and small lakes. Overhead, two bright tangerine suns stood out against an aquamarine sky. It was breath-taking and beautiful.

Then, just as suddenly as this stunning and heart-stopping journey had begun, they were seated in the circle, staring at the blue globe spinning in the air before them. A manta-like creature, like the ones they had flown with, hovered inside, fluttering its wide, flat body like a fish in a fishbowl. Scores of tentacles, like those of a jellyfish, dangled from beneath the creature, and three protruding eyes sat on stems on top of its smooth manta-body. The eyes turned independently, rotating three hundred and sixty degrees, looking out at those looking in.

The abrupt change and the peculiar creature caused several of the chanters to lose rhythm. The trance dissolved, and the blue vortex broke up and reentered their eyes, leaving them staring at each other in much the same way they had after the first ceremony. Ray immediately got up and left the teepee. Adrienne chased after him, trailed by Moxie and the two foxes.

No one had the nerve to describe what they had just seen. Even Tai was wide-eyed and speechless. After many minutes of silence, Crow spoke up. "That wasn't Gloria," he said soberly. "I'm not sure what we just saw or where we went, but because of the way the blue light came out of our eyes, I'm guessing that creature is what we've felt inside our heads—and it's clearly not from this planet."

Janice began to cry quietly. Rain went over to her and tried to comfort her. "I wish it had been Gloria, Janice."

Janice looked up at her with searing anger in her eyes. "Damn you, Rain! What was that thing?" she exhorted with tears running down her cheeks. "You got us into this mess! Now get us out!"

They were all frightened by what they had seen. Rather than stay in the teepee, they returned to the house. Adrienne sat alone at the dining room table when they walked in.

"Is Ray all right?" asked Marsha.

"I don't know." Adrienne fought back tears. "He's up in the room, upset and angry—and scared."

"But we're all upset and angry and scared," spat Janice.

"And we've got to get beyond that," said Crow, the last to enter the room.

"But how?" demanded Janice.

No one had an answer.

"Well, at least, we know how our thoughts are linked," said Van, as stunned as anyone.

"Yeah, but did you see that thing?" said Tai. "Like Crow said, that was not something from Earth."

"It showed us where it came from," said Marsha. "That was pretty amazing."

"But what does it want from us? And why us?" asked Adrienne.

"I'm guessing it found us by chance," said Rain. "We opened ourselves up, and it took advantage. Now we have to find a way to get rid of it."

"And who fucking knows how to do that?" slammed Janice.

Everyone looked at Rain. "I certainly don't."

"Maybe we can find someone who does," said Marsha.

"Fat fucking chance. Who knows how to exorcise aliens?" sneered Tai. "And where do we go to find them—Mars?"

"Who's going to believe us, anyway?" said Van. "I'm not even sure I believe it myself—and I saw it."

"Okay, okay," said Crow. "Besides linking us in some unusual way and taking us on a trip to its home, has anyone felt, at any time, that it was directing their thoughts or actions?"

"It's just there," snapped Janice. "That's enough."

"But has anyone done anything they didn't really want to do?" continued Crow. "I mean, it's there, yes, but it's an astral entity with no material presence—and seemingly no physical impact."

"Yet," said Van.

"Yeah," said Tai. "Maybe we'll wake up tomorrow and it will be sitting at this table."

Adrienne found Ray lying on the bed in their bedroom. He sat up when she came into the room. "I've got to get out of this nut house. This place is driving me crazy."

"No one is liking this, Ray," said Adrienne, sitting down beside him. "Everyone's as scared and worried as you are."

"But why bring it on? I didn't want to go out there and dive back into that black hole. Tai and Rain, they're fucking freaks. I just don't need this stuff."

"Come on, Ray. That thing we saw unnerves me just as much as it does you. But I don't want to leave."

"I can't get it out of my mind, Adrienne. My brain's been infected by that fucking blue thing—whatever it is." Ray lay back down and stared at the ceiling, his hands behind his head.

Adrienne stretched out beside him. She touched his face and stroked his cheek. Ray didn't move. Adrienne leaned over and kissed him on the forehead. "Don't block me out, Ray. I love you. Support me on this, and I'll support you. We can get through it."

Ray continued to stare at the ceiling. Determined to get his attention, Adrienne slid her right hand down to his belt buckle and undid his pants. Ray pushed her hand away. Instead of leaving him be, she scrunched up close to him, pulled his shirt up, and gently kissed his belly. Ray continued to glare at the ceiling as she steadily worked her way down to her target. But it wasn't arousing Ray the way any hint of oral sex always had. Still she took him in her mouth, trying to get his mind off the thing that was bothering everyone.

After a minute of licking his penis, she sat up. "Damn," she said, trying to be funny, "kind of hard to suck a wet noodle."

Ray sat up abruptly. "Then leave it alone." He pushed her away.

"Ray?"

"Fuck all of this. That damn thing has stolen my brain. Crazy thoughts are running like freight trains through my head. I can't even get it up." He turned away from Adrienne and rolled over on his stomach, nearly in tears.

Adrienne tried to stroke his back, but again he pushed her away, snapping at her, "Leave me alone!"

"Fuck you, Ray. I'm trying to help."

"Well, give it up. You're making things worse."

"Maybe I should give you up!" Adrienne got up and stomped out of the room, now just as pissed off as Ray was.

CHAPTER 87

One by one, shortly after dawn Saturday morning, the school members began showing up at the dining room table with either tea or coffee and maybe a bowl of granola. Adrienne came down from upstairs looking for Ray. Everyone else—even Janice—was at the table. No one had seen him.

"Wow, I wonder where he went. When he wasn't in the room, I figured he was down here."

"Maybe he's out in the henhouse collecting eggs," said Crow.

"Yeah, that's probably it." Adrienne made a cup of coffee and joined the others.

"How are you doing, Adrienne?" asked Rain.

"Not good. Ray was very upset last night. I ended up sleeping on the couch." She shook her head thinking of her failed attempt to arouse him. "Neither of us is doing too well."

"Who could be?" said Janice.

Six somber faces told the story.

"So, what are we going to do?" demanded Janice.

"Until we come up with something, I say we just go about our regular duties," said Rain. "The only way to get it off your mind is to do something that engages you."

"I have the feeling that it's there in my head," said Van, "but other than that it has no real impact on me."

"Maybe it's harmless," said Tai. "It's been several days and nothing bad has happened. I didn't sleep much last night, but that's the worst of it."

"Fuck! You guys are nuts," said Janice. "We have some damn alien entity in our heads, and you want to ignore it? I can't."

Rain finally broke. "Then tell us what you want to do, Janice."

"I think we should go to the FBI. Maybe they have some secret files on these things."

Tai laughed. Janice gave him the finger. But Adrienne was having none of it. She got up from the table and looked out the window toward the garden. "Where the heck is Ray?"

"He'll be here," said Marsha. "Maybe he needed some alone time. Maybe he's down by the river."

"I'm going out to look for him." Adrienne headed to the kitchen. The screen door banged as she left the house.

Marsha called after her. "I'll come with you." Then she was out the back door.

"So, what's next?" asked Tai.

"I want to repeat the séance," said Crow. "I think we've got to confront that thing. That's the only way we can learn anything."

"Maybe you're right, Crow," said Rain. "But having someone more experienced than I am would be wise."

Crow shook his head. "I don't think we want to include anyone else. We know too little about what has happened to risk adding others. Besides, we've already seen that this thing connects us in some unusual way. I think we are best on our own."

Adrienne's scream came from the greenhouse. They saw her run across the backyard pulling at her hair. Marsha staggered after her, flailing her arms and crying.

Crow ran straight to the greenhouse. Tai got there right after Crow. Ray hung from a rope tied to the rafters. Rain had already guessed it and chased after Adrienne. Van caught Marsha in his arms. Janice stood beside them as Marsha blubbered, "Ray killed himself."

Rain found Adrienne laying half in, half out of the cab of her truck, sobbing. When Rain touched her shoulder, she turned on her viciously, shouting angrily, "What's going on, Rain? What's going on?"

Rain tried to get her to sit up, but Adrienne pushed her away, hammering at the car seat with her fists. Janice burst out of the house. Rain caught her in her arms before she could get to the pickup. "Ray is dead," Janice repeated over and over. "Ray is dead!"

"I know."

Janice looked into Rain's eyes. "What's going to happen to my baby?"

Rain didn't know Janice was pregnant, but she'd seen the changes in her body and could have guessed. She hugged the younger woman. "Oh, Janice, I don't know. I don't know."

Van came out onto the porch. "Everyone get inside. We need to talk."

Rain didn't argue. She and Janice managed to get Adrienne out of her truck and into the house. She cried the entire time.

The others were already seated at the dining room table.

"We have to call the police," said Tai, as the women sat down. Adrienne put her head on the table sobbing. Rain was beside her with an arm over her shoulder.

"Tai and I were about to take him down," said Crow, "then we realized it would be a mistake to move him until the police have seen the body."

Rain nodded. "I'll call Officer Yates. He's been remarkably fair to us."

"I can't be here," said Crow. "As soon as you call, I'm leaving."

They all knew about his record, but only Rain knew he'd killed a man.

"Will you come back?" asked Marsha, whose eyes were red from crying.

"How could I not? We still have this other thing to deal with."

"What about you, Tai?" asked Rain. "You leaving too?"

"No, I'll stay, but I need to get all the drugs out of the house and off the property. No telling how John Law will react to Ray's death."

"What are we going to say?" asked Van. "They're sure to ask us if Ray was upset or depressed or something?"

Adrienne raised her head. "Yeah, what are we going say?" she demanded angrily. "That we've been possessed by an alien—and Ray couldn't handle it. Well, I can't either! It's not harmless. Something terrible just happened. And maybe I'll be next! Should I tell them that?"

An abrupt silence followed while Adrienne seethed.

Rain took a deep breath. "If nothing else, we have to stay together on this."

"With this thing in our heads that should be easy enough," deadpanned Tai.

"Maybe we can use that to our advantage," said Van. "If the police talk to us separately, we'll all be on the same page."

"Which will be what?" asked Rain, trying to get the group to focus.

Tai leaned back in his seat, edgy and anxious. "Yeah, what's our story?"

"Ray and I split up. It's the only thing they'll believe. If we start talking about spirits and aliens and magic mushrooms, they'll put us all away."

"Will you be able to talk to the police, Adrienne?" asked Rain.

Adrienne started crying again. "I don't know. I don't even know who I am anymore."

CHAPTER 88

Rain called the Eugene Police Department and asked for Yates. He wasn't immediately available, but he called her back as soon as he got her message. Yates was excited to get the call from Rain until she told him about Ray's suicide. That he knew Ray made it worse.

Yates arrived at the house fifteen minutes later with his partner Eldon Taylor. An ambulance followed them down the driveway. Rain took them to the greenhouse. Yates shook his head at the ugliness of it all. Eldon took photos with a Polaroid, then the medics cut down the body to take it back to the police morgue.

Yates asked Rain to gather everyone inside. A few minutes later, everyone but Crow was seated with the two policemen at the dining room table. They started by taking everyone's name and checking their driver's licenses. Marsha's, Van's, Rain's, and Adrienne's IDs were in order. Tai had a passport that said he was Steve Latarski and a driver's license that said he was Tai Sky.

"Why two names, Mr. Latarski?"

"I changed my name."

"As an alias?"

"No, I wanted a name that was more like me."

The two officers glanced at each other.

"Haven't I seen you hanging around downtown, Steve?" asked Yates. The implication of drug dealing lurked behind the words.

"No, must have been some other longhair."

"Not with hair wound up in rattails," muttered Eldon. He had also seen Tai downtown and had suspicions of his own.

Janice was last. She had no driver's license or ID of any kind.

"Last time we were here, Miss Adams," said Yates, "you told us Janice was your niece. Are you still looking after her?"

"Yes," she looked down at her hands.

Yates didn't press it.

"What can you tell me about the deceased?"

Adrienne spoke up. "He was my boyfriend. We shared a room in the house—until a couple of days ago—when we broke up. I told him to leave yesterday afternoon. I thought he had until I discovered him this morning." Despite the lie, she couldn't stop the tears.

"You found him?"

Adrienne nodded.

"I was with her," said Marsha.

"Did you touch the body?"

Adrienne shook her head.

"None of us did," said Marsha. "We knew you'd want to see him as we found him."

"Did he do drugs, Adrienne?" continued Yates.

Adrienne looked at him through bleary eyes. "He smoked pot sometimes. Nothing else."

"Had he been smoking last night or this morning?"

Adrienne shrugged in despair. "I don't know."

Yates thought a moment then addressed the group. "This is the second death to occur out here in the last six days. There's nothing to suggest foul play. But I have to wonder about drugs. I'd like to search the house. You can let me. Or I can get a warrant."

Rain looked around. "Go ahead search the house." They'd already scoured the place of half-smoked roaches and pipes, and Crow had taken his few possessions with him. Yates told Eldon to start upstairs.

"We'll have to do an autopsy on Ray." Yates looked at Adrienne. "If what you say is true, there should be no problem. Perhaps some paperwork to fill-out. We'll contact his parents, unless, Adrienne, you want to do that."

She shook her head. "Go ahead. I never met them. They might not know my name."

Because of Rain, Yates was not as pushy as he might have been. He had no real suspicions—other than the possibility of drug use. "Will you keep the school open?"

"It's where we live," replied Rain, who had already sensed Yates' interest in her. "We'll focus on the co-op and keeping the bills paid. It might be a while before we return to having classes."

Yates told everyone to stay at the table. Then he went upstairs to join Eldon. They did a cursory check of the entire house, the greenhouse, and the teepee, but saved a thorough search of Adrienne's and Ray's bedroom for last.

Along with a pack of rolling papers, they found the SDS flyer and Stoopid's socialist newsletter that Ray had picked up at Max's Tavern. They were nearly done when Eldon found a folded piece of paper in a pair of Ray's blue jeans. It was the page torn from the encyclopedia that Ray had found in Jack Spikes' rental. He unfolded it. Ray had saved it for Adrienne because of the piece on moles. But on the other side of the page, unnoticed by Ray or Adrienne, and following in alphabetical order, was the description and drawing of a Molotov cocktail. Eldon showed it to Yates.

"This isn't good," said Yates.

"This whole house could be involved," replied Eldon.

Yates thought about Rain. "Boy, I hope not. Let's see what the young man's girlfriend has to say before we jump to any conclusions."

They went downstairs and joined the group in the dining room. Yates placed the page from the encyclopedia on the table and pointed to the piece on Molotov cocktails. He looked at Adrienne. "We found this in a pair of jeans in your bedroom. I believe they were Ray's. Know anything about it?"

Adrienne picked up the page, frowned, then turned it over. "Yeah, Ray brought me this." She pointed to the piece on moles. "He knew I was having trouble with moles in the garden. That's what this is about."

"Where were you when Campbell Hall was bombed?" asked Yates.

"At Max's Tavern with Ray. We were at the bar when we saw people running toward the university. We both went to watch the firemen put out the fire."

"Can anyone support your story?"

"Tim O'Malley the printer. He was sitting next to us."

Yates nodded, thinking of Tim's appearance at First and Madison two days earlier. He put Stoopid's newsletter on the table. "Where'd this come from?"

Adrienne was struggling with the questions, but she maintained. "He got that at Max's the night of the bombing. The old man who was killed dropped it off with Tim the printer."

"What about this one?" He placed the SDS flyer in front of Adrienne.

"Same thing. We got this from Tim one night a Max's."

"Was Ray collecting this kind of propaganda?"

"No, they were both at the bar for the taking. Ray wasn't interested in politics at all. The man, Tim, interested him. He wanted to see what he was printing."

Yates looked around the table. "Anyone want to add to this?"

After a long pause, Rain flashed her eyes at Yates, swept her hair over her left shoulder, and softly said, "Ray was not political. Neither is Adrienne. I'm the only one in this house who has made a personal stand against the war and ROTC on campus. Tai is against the war also, but not with my conviction. And these others—Marsha, Van, and Janice—they aren't political at all.

Again the tenor of her voice and her composure struck Yates as sincere.

Eldon asked the next question. "Any chance this young man hung himself because he planted the bomb—and then regretted it when he learned the janitor died?"

"No," snapped Adrienne. "I was with him. He had nothing to do with the bomb."

"But he had this description of a Molotov cocktail. That's what we found at Johnson Hall. Where was Ray that night?"

"I don't know. What day was it?"

"November twenty-second," said Eldon.

Adrienne started to respond with another *I don't know*, then stammered and began to cry. Rain interceded. "I understand that this encyclopedia page reflects badly on Ray, but Ray was not the one, nor was Adrienne. Ask Tim O'Malley about the night Campbell Hall was bombed. If they were with him, he'll say so."

Yates knew he should be taking Adrienne in. Instead he decided to trust Rain. "I know O'Malley. I'll talk to him." He looked at Adrienne, but his words were meant for all of them. "If you say anything to O'Malley before I do, it will further incriminate you." He turned to Eldon. A glance to the door suggested it was time to leave.

Eldon nodded.

Yates faced the group at the table. "I'd like you all to stay in town until the autopsy is done. It will be a few days." He looked straight at Rain as though he couldn't resist her beauty. "And be careful out here. I'd hate to be escorting another ambulance down your driveway."

Yates and Eldon walked out to the squad car. The ambulance had already left.

Crow crept in the back door within minutes of the officers' departure. No one had left the table. The mood was thick as glum pudding. "What'd they say?"

"They think Ray might have done the bombings at the university," said Rain. "And that's why he killed himself."

Adrienne laid her head on the table.

Crow pulled out a chair and sat down stunned. "Now what?"

Adrienne lifted her head.

"Back to the teepee," said Tai. "To hell with politics, we've got stranger fish to fry."

"Gloria's request comes first," said Rain. "We'll get her ashes tomorrow and give her a proper memorial service—then we can figure out what's next."

CHAPTER 89

Bob Yates and his partner Eldon stopped by Tim's print shop on the way back to the police department. During the ride, Yates told Eldon the story about the bikers, Spikes, and Tim. They knocked on the print shop door, and Tim responded the way he always did, "It's open. Come on in."

Tim was seated on a lawn chair in the corner smoking a joint when the two officers came through the door wearing their uniforms and holstered revolvers. Tim crushed the joint between his fingers as he stood up, then casually dropped it on the floor.

"Mr. O'Malley," said Yates, ignoring the heavy smell of pot. "I came by to thank you for helping resolve that little confab two days ago. It could have gotten ugly."

"You're welcome, officer. It was my pleasure. Hardly anything I like more than assembling motorcycles."

"Well, the timing could not have been better."

Eldon was looking around the shop, noting the anti-war posters and the copies of *Prairie Fire*. He would have busted Tim right there for the pot, but he was the junior officer and followed Yates' lead.

"We've been investigating the bombings at the university," continued Yates. "If I'm not mistaken, the FBI has already talked to you."

"I told them I'd help in any way I could. The man killed at Campbell Hall was a friend of mine. His ashes are right here." Tim pointed to the tobacco can on the shelf. "I'd like to find the bomber as much as you would."

"Where were you that night?"

"Right here until about ten. Then I went to Max's as I do almost every night. I was sitting at the bar when it happened. The bartender will verify that. He knows me pretty well."

"Do you remember who you talked to that night?"

Tim grinned. "Yeah, about twenty people by the time I left."

"What about a young couple? Maybe your age. A pretty little hippie girl and a young man by the name of Ray."

Tim scratched at the hair on his chin. "Yeah, I shared space at the bar with a young couple that night. They chased after the fire engines when word got out about the bombing. I've seen them at Max's a few times. What about them?"

"Just curious. A couple folks we're checking out."

"I don't know those folks except in passing, but I got a good read on them. There's no way it was them."

"Fair enough. That was part of why we came by."

Tim, a little surprised they hadn't mentioned the weed, shrugged. "No problem. Like I said, I'm as interested in finding the bomber as you are."

"Any leads?"

Tim thought of the can of spray paint but felt he needed to know a little more before throwing Mike to the wolves. "Nothing more than's been in the paper."

Yates led Eldon out of the building to the squad car. Within the car, Eldon turned to Yates. "You believe anything that kid said? Hell, he was smoking pot when we walked in."

Yates shook his head. "I'm not sure. That guy's a little different than most. After what he did the other day, I think he's a pretty straight shooter."

"Like that woman Rain?"

The suggestion was obvious. Yates blew past it. "Yeah."

When they got back to headquarters, Yates went directly to Wilkerson's office. He was on the phone. After a moment, he hung up. "What was the deal on that suicide?"

"A little more than we expected. We found this in the young man's bedroom." He handed Wilkerson the page torn from the encyclopedia.

"Shit, Yates. This is important."

"And these." He handed him the SDS screed and Stoopid's newsletter.

"You think this guy killed himself out of guilt?"

"It's possible. But he lived in a house with six others. I quizzed them about it. They made a strong case for it not being him." He paused.

"And I knew the young man. He works for a friend of mine. I would never make that connection myself."

Wilkerson sat back. "What other leads do you have? I know the FBI has none."

"This is it. And I'm not convinced of anything yet—yes or no."

Wilkerson turned to gaze out the window of his office. The skyline of Eugene boasted only one building over five stories, the twelve story Hilton Hotel. He spoke without facing Yates. "The mayor called the other day. He's getting edgy about the Olympic Trials. He told me to find someone to pin the bombings on—even if we can't prove it. The Olympic officials wants to be sure it won't happen again. A decision will be made on the Trials next fall. The mayor wants this thing solved long before then."

Yates shook his head. "I doubt this guy did it, Chief."

Wilkerson turned to face Yates. "Fine. But this," he lifted the page from the encyclopedia off his desk, "is as close to a lead as we've got. I want you to get a little more aggressive on this. And if nothing comes up, this guy's dead. He'll have a hard time proving he's innocent."

Later that evening, Yates called Spikes to tell him that Ray had killed himself. Spikes struggled to believe it.

"I saw the body today, Jack. It was Ray."

"It doesn't fit. That kid was solid as a rock."

"His girl friend said they'd just broken up."

"Oh, shit, he wanted to marry her. That can blow any man's mind."

"Did he ever talk about the war?"

"You mean, against it?"

"Yeah."

"We never talked about it at all. Why do you ask?"

"We found the description of a Molotov cocktail in his bedroom—on a page torn from an encyclopedia."

"Really?"

"Did he say anything about the bombings?"

"No."

"Did he tell you he was there to watch Campbell Hall burn?"

"No. Fuck! What is this? You think he did it?"

"It's something I'm checking out."

A long silence ensued.

"You still there, Jack?"

"Yeah. This makes no sense."

"I find it hard to believe also. Did he do drugs?"

Spikes cursed again. "I never asked, but I'm sure he smoked pot. Every kid in Eugene does."

"Anything else?"

"I don't know."

"We'll get an autopsy in a few days. That might help. Sorry about the news. But I thought I should be the one to tell you."

"Well, thanks for that. I really don't believe he could have done the bombing. But I would have said the same thing about suicide."

"Just think it over. Let me know if you come up with something."

Spikes hung up the phone and wandered into Sheila's office. She had overheard some of the conversation. "Was that Bob?"

"It was." His huge mustache masked the distress in his face, but his eyes told the story.

"What was it?"

"Ray hung himself last night."

"What?"

"Yeah." He shook his head. "I can't believe it."

"Did he leave a note?"

"Not that Bob mentioned. He wondered if it weren't drug related."

"Ray? Really?"

"That's just it, Sheila. We've got drugs everywhere." He stared at the floor. "And that's one more reason I don't want Joey on medication."

"But this would be different than street drugs."

"Then Joey will think drugs solve your problems. He'll be taking them the rest of his life."

"That's an exaggeration, Jack. Come on."

"No, it's true. I saw it in Vietnam. It's what made Mike Rogers the jerk he is."

"Jack."

"And it's all experimental. They don't know what they're doing. I can't possibly go along with it."

"But what else can we do?" Now Sheila was as upset as Jack. "You know as well as I do Joey hates being in those special classes."

"Well, you want a commitment out of me. It ain't happening if you put that kid on speed or whatever it is they give him." He spun around and stalked out of the room. Sheila leaned over her desk and began to cry.

CHAPTER 90

No one slept well that night at Blake College. Rain was the first one to get out of bed. She made coffee at six. She sat alone at the dining room table, sipping her coffee and thinking about what had happened. Two sips into her coffee, she realized her head was clear. She sat there cup in hand studying the moment, plying its depth, feeling for the thing in her head. *It wasn't there.*

Marsha and Van came down from upstairs. It was the first thing they said. "It's gone."

Crow was next with the same observation. Tai followed. "No more aliens."

Adrienne clomped down the stairs and said the same thing.

"I kind of miss it," chuckled Tai.

"Not me," said Marsha. "I'm kind of attached to the privacy of my own thoughts."

"Me too," seconded a forlorn Adrienne.

Tai suddenly stood up. "Hey, I think we've got visitors. Crow move it."

A police squad car rolled to a stop in their driveway. Crow went out the back door, carrying Tai's drug stash. A minute later, Yates and Taylor were on the front porch. Rain opened the door. She was wearing her Japanese kimono with nothing beneath. She couldn't have looked more alluring. "Hello, Officer Yates. Is the autopsy already done?"

"Hardly," said Yates. "The body has disappeared."

Rain's face went white. Van and Marsha, standing behind her, turned to each other, mouths hanging open. In the dining room, Tai and Adrienne also heard it. They immediately joined the group at the door. Janice was still in bed. Crow was hiding in the weeds.

Adrienne pushed breathlessly past Rain. "Ray's body has disappeared?"

Yates nodded. "The corpse we picked up yesterday vanished last night or early this morning."

After what they'd already experienced, it was hard to imagine that things could get any stranger—but they had.

"Ray Harper's body is gone?" repeated Adrienne, emotion heavy in her voice.

"That's right. Do you know anything about it?" asked Eldon. "Any of you?"

While question after question swirled in everyone's head, Rain gathered herself. "My God, no. Why would we?"

"That's what we were wondering," said Yates. "After Gloria Freeman's death, you held her body here for three days before sending it to the mortuary." He looked around at four blank faces. Tears streamed from Adrienne's eyes. "Maybe you wanted to do the same for Mr. Harper."

"No, no," said Rain. "What we did for Gloria was at her request. We felt Ray's parents were the ones who should arrange his funeral."

"We called them yesterday," said Yates. "They're on a plane now headed to Eugene. They had planned to take the body after the autopsy."

Everyone was stunned to silence.

"We'd like to look around," said Eldon.

"For the body?" asked Tai incredulously.

Yates nodded. "We're going to have to."

Rain took a great breath. "Go ahead. Whatever you need to do. But I can assure you it's not here."

"Thank you, Miss Adams." Even with all the odd things he'd encountered at Blake College, Yates couldn't deny the effect Rain had on him. The two men headed to the stairs.

"Wait a moment," Rain called out. "My niece is up there asleep. Let me get her up."

"We'll start in the basement," said Yates, as he watched Rain walk up the stairs. Her kimono was nearly transparent in the morning light. His ex-wife had been big and buxom. He couldn't help admiring Rain's sleek figure before she disappeared onto the second floor.

An hour later, Yates and his partner had completed their search. Ray's corpse was not there.

"Please, let us know what you find out, officers," said Rain as she walked them off the front porch.

"Oh, you can be sure of that, Miss Adams. Sorry for the intrusion."

As the two officers headed back to their car, Eldon turned to Yates. "You've got a thing for that woman, don't you?"

"Is it that obvious?"

"Your eyes were riveted on her ass when she climbed the stairs."

"I'll bet yours were too."

"She's a pretty woman," said Eldon. "It's hard not to look. But I wasn't staring the way you were."

Yates shrugged. "Think she noticed?"

Eldon grinned and nodded. "Oh, yeah. She noticed."

Crow appeared moments after the police had left. Everyone sat at the dining room table in all shades of gloom. Adrienne's head was on the table.

"The autopsy?"

"Sit down, Crow," said Tai.

"What? Did they ask about me?"

"Sit down."

Everyone watched Crow ease into a chair.

"Someone took Ray's body from the morgue."

"What do you mean?"

"His body was gone this morning."

"And where is it now?" asked Crow.

"No one knows. The police came here looking for it."

"Wow! And I thought we might have gotten through the worst of it."

Adrienne left the room. They could hear her crying in the downstairs bathroom.

No one knew what to do. The rest of the morning passed in a tense silence, each person struggling with the horror of Ray's suicide and the conundrum of his corpse's disappearance, while also greatly relieved that the alien presence had vanished or returned to its planet.

Van and Marsha walked down to the river after lunch. They sat on the bank and tossed stones into the water.

"It has to be a mistake," said Van. "Somebody must have moved the body to another room. I'll bet he's just in the wrong drawer."

"I hope you're right."

"What else could it be? Body snatchers? I don't think so."

Marsha lowered her eyes. "After what we've seen, I keep thinking zombies and vampires." Marsha wasn't trying to be funny.

And Van didn't smile. "I'm trying not to think that way. But, you're right, things are not the same."

"And never will be."

They were quiet a long time before Marsha addressed the other issue. "What about the thing in our heads? It's gone. What do you make of that?"

"No idea. All along Rain kept saying it would go away. I guess she was right."

"Do you think it was real?"

"I keep thinking it was the drugs, but that second séance seemed awfully real. Seems like a bad dream now. Thank goodness we all woke up."

"Should we just forget it?"

"I don't think that's possible. I'll remember this last week the rest of my life."

CHAPTER 91

That afternoon Crow and Rain drove Adrienne's truck to the mortuary to pick up Gloria's ashes. Tai took his van into town to get a space heater. The house was minimally heated by a wood stove, and the basement was cold.

Tai went across town to the Eugene Hardware and found a heavy-duty heater that was on sale. He took it to the cashier at the front of the store. Four people were ahead of him in line. He was anxious to get back to Blake College. They would hold the memorial for Gloria as soon as Crow and Rain returned with her ashes, and he didn't want to hold things up.

Another person got in line. Tai glanced over his shoulder. An older man in blue jeans, a tan fleece-lined jacket, and a cowboy hat stood behind him. Something about the man's face struck him. He turned to look again. He unintentionally caught the man's eyes. With a sinking in his stomach, Tai realized this was the farmer who owned the mushroom field out Route 45. He hoped the man didn't recognize him.

But there was no way Maynard Smith was going to forget the blond dreadlocks. One glance at Tai brought back the scene in his field. Maynard had no intention of confronting the man, but he did find himself heating up and thinking of things he might like to say. Tai, who had spent so much time in the man's field trying to be invisible, wished now that he really were.

After what seemed hours, Tai was finally at the head of the line, paying for his heater. Maynard was also in a hurry. He had the exact change ready and hardly stopped at the register. He was ten steps behind Tai when they left the store. Tai saw him in the reflection off the glass door. He decided not to go to his van for fear the farmer would recognize it—like his hair, it was hard to miss.

Maynard saw the van in the parking lot and was surprised that the man in dreadlocks veered off in a different direction. When he got in the cab of his old Dodge, he watched Tai wander around the parking lot as though he might be lost. "Must be the mushrooms," Maynard muttered before driving off.

Crow, Rain, and Tai returned to the house within five minutes of each other. Everyone went down to the teepee. It was a lovely, but cold January day. The sun shone white in a sky of pale blue. Rain carried the ashes in a ceramic vase that had been Gloria's. They stood in a circle around the teepee, too far apart to hold hands, and passed the vase from one person to the next, sprinkling the ashes around the circumference of the teepee. Rain called for a moment of silence. They closed their eyes and thought their best thoughts of Gloria.

Afterward, Rain ducked into the teepee with the others behind. Once inside, everyone would say a few words about what Gloria meant to them. When Rain entered the tent, dimly lit by the sunlight passing through the canvas, Ray was standing in the center of the teepee, wearing a white lab coat over medical scrubs. His neck showed bruises from the rope he'd used to hang himself, and the color of his skin matched that of Gloria's ashes.

Rain caught her breath, stifled a scream, and stood there unmoving as each person entered and was likewise shocked to stillness. Adrienne was last, followed by Moxie and the other animals. Crow and Van caught her when she fainted.

Ray stepped forward to help, but she pushed him away.

"It's just me, Adrienne."

She was angry and confused. "How can you be here?" She looked at the others, then back to Ray. "How can you be here? We saw you dead!"

"I'm not sure what happened," said Ray with unreasonable calm. "All of a sudden I was awake in a drawer at the morgue with a clear memory of the moment I gave into the rope." He looked at Adrienne with sad eyes. "I didn't understand the mistake I'd made until I was dead. It was terrible thing to do—to you. I apologize."

"But how are you alive?" demanded Adrienne.

"I know only what you know. I was dead, and now I'm alive and standing right here." He looked down at his feet. "But I think that blue manta had something to do with it."

"But how can you be so matter of fact?" Tears streamed down Adrienne's cheeks. "This is completely insane."

"I'm not sure, Adrienne. Death is enlightening—if that makes any sense. I saw through to the other side."

Rain came up close to him. "The manta is gone, Ray."

He looked around at the others. "No, it's not."

Van stepped in beside Rain. "How so? It left all of us."

"Not me. It's still in my head, Van. I can feel it now—and I'm beginning to believe it brought me back to life."

"What do you mean?" asked Tai.

"When we were in the teepee that first night, we were possessed by a life form that, apparently, can move through consciousness as easily as we swim through water."

This was the last thing they wanted to hear, but they all moved in close to catch every word.

"When we, you and I, think of aliens," Ray continued, "we imagine spaceships and flying saucers, fabricated devices that travel faster than light and contain little green men. But this entity seems to travel psychically. And it used the moment of Gloria's death and our opening ourselves to the astral plane to get into our heads. When I committed suicide, I relinquished my will and the creature was there waiting, taking advantage of that portal or worm hole or whatever it was that Gloria described to us to fill the vacuum that was me. I'm guessing it left all of you to take greater advantage of me."

Wide, unbelieving eyes flashed around the circle. It was impossible. Ray could not be alive. And yet there he was, much as he'd always been. Only having seen the things they had already seen made it possible to believe that this was happening—without screaming!

"So, are you still Ray?" asked Marsha hesitantly. "Or that manta-thing?"

"It's the same as it was before. I know that it's there. But it has no voice and gives me no direction. All that I've told you is no more than speculation based on what we've all seen." He opened his hands as a sign of helplessness. "I'm just getting used to this myself. I mean, give me a break. I woke up in a morgue sometime last night as surprised to be there as you are to see me now."

Janice muttered, "Bullshit," and ducked out of the teepee. Rain went after her.

"Why should we believe you?" asked Van.

"Because I'm here. Because I'm alive."

"And the thing is not controlling you?"

"Not that I know of, no."

Tai was more intrigued than scared. "So, what are you going to do now?"

"Hanging only asphyxiated me." Ray turned his head from side to side. "The neck's a little sore, but not broken. I'm going to take advantage of being alive—with much greater appreciation."

"Are you planning to stay with us?" asked Marsha.

"You're all I have." Ray turned to Adrienne. "I'd like to get back to my old life."

"With that thing in your head?" Tai made a face. "Good luck with that. Besides, being a dead guy could be a problem."

"The cops came by this morning looking for you," said Van.

"And your parents are due to arrive in Eugene today," added Adrienne. "They think you're dead."

Rain caught up with Janice as she reached the house. "Hold on, Janice."

Janice continued into the house. Rain found her sitting at the dining room table. "I don't want any more of this crazy alien shit," she snarled.

"No one does, Janice, but what are we going to do about it?"

"Figure something out, Rain. If it got into the animals, it probably got into my baby. You got us into this mess, now get us out."

Rain shook her head in exasperation. "But it just keeps getting weirder and weirder."

Crow came into the room. "You ladies all right?"

"Not at all," said Janice.

"Rain?"

"I just don't know anymore."

Tai came in and sat down, then Marsha and Van.

"Where's Ray?" asked Rain.

"Just behind us," said Tai.

"Can we trust what he said?" asked Marsha. "He seems like the old Ray, but having a dead guy around really creeps me out."

"Creeps you out, Marsha," said a traumatized Adrienne. "I used to sleep with the guy."

"I kind of like the new Ray—our own zombie," said Tai, chuckling.

"Not me," snapped Adrienne. "And it's not funny! You saw the thing that's in him. It's awful."

"Easy. All of you," said Crow. "We need to know more about this. Let's give Ray a chance. Give him some space."

They heard Ray come into the kitchen. He joined them at the table. Everyone was uncomfortable in his presence. No one wanted to speak.

"One thing you need to know, and that I'm just learning," said Ray, "is that the entity can pass in and out of your minds as it pleases—allowing me to see into your thoughts. Marsha, you wanted to know if you can trust me. I'm not sure you have a choice."

"What am I thinking?" demanded Janice.

"That I'm Ray. That I've gone insane, and that everything I've said is stuff I've made up."

"Bingo!" exclaimed Tai.

CHAPTER 92

Sometime back, Rain had invited Rebop over for dinner that Sunday evening to give a poetry reading, but after the events that had occurred during and after Gloria's death, Rain had completely forgotten about it. Rebop appeared at the door forty minutes after Ray's unexpected return. Rather than try to make up an excuse and turn her away, Rain invited her in.

Rain and Rebop joined everyone at the dining room table. Rain sat at one end of the rectangular table; Rebop sat at the other end with her sheaf of poems.

Rebop had felt the tension the moment she came into the house. She knew Gloria had died and had read about the suicide in the newspaper. She knew it had been Ray but had never met him. When Rain went around the table introducing her to everyone, including Ray as Ray, Rebop didn't know what to think. No one else did either.

"I'm here to read a few poems," she said, making eye-contact with each person around the table, "but I'm wondering if there isn't something else you might want to talk about before I begin?"

Was there ever!

Marsha, Adrienne, Van, Janice, and Crow turned to Rain. Tai, who had immediately become fascinated by Rebop, whom he had never met before, kept his eyes on the scintillating Cuban woman.

"As you know, we've had a difficult week," said Rain. "So difficult in fact, and I apologize for this, Rebop, we weren't properly prepared for you to be here tonight."

"I almost didn't come but decided you might need some support."

"We do—even more than that, we need someone from outside the school to talk to. It's gotten pretty weird out here, and I can't think of anyone more open-minded than you." Rain looked straight at Ray. "Ray, you okay with this?"

Ray nodded. "Why not?"

Rebop was surprised that Rain had deferred to Ray, but she was a subtle being in her own right and remained entirely composed. "Well, of course, I'm completely open to listening. I have one question though before you begin." She glanced around the table. "I'm a little confused. Who was it that committed suicide yesterday? I thought it was Ray."

"It was," said Ray without hesitation. Van, Marsha, Janice, and Adrienne looked down at the table. Rain and Crow watched Ray watching Rebop, while Tai continued to undress Rebop with his eyes.

Rebop tilted her head. "I see. Then maybe you should start at the beginning."

Rain recounted the events of the last week—everything. Rebop listened quietly, and no one else spoke or interrupted. The story ended with Ray's resurrection and unannounced return. A long silence followed as the members of the school waited for Rebop to explain what they could not.

Rebop stood up from the table and walked into the living room and back, giving herself a chance to think about the situation. Rather than sit down she stood. "My first thought is that it's the drugs." Rebop paced as she spoke. "I've heard of it before. When a group of close friends takes LSD or some other hallucinogen together, they often find their thoughts synchronized for several days afterward. They might even see the same hallucinations during the trip or later in a flashback. Even the sense of sharing your consciousness with each other could be something imagined during or after a strong trip." She stopped her pacing and looked at Ray. "But none of that accounts for Ray's…return to life."

Ray smiled a wide confident smile. "I thought it was the drugs at first also, but after we saw the creature, I freaked out. I worried that Tai's potion had done something permanent to my brain." He looked at Adrienne with sad eyes. "And when I committed suicide, the thing reanimated me."

"Maybe you're mixed up about that, Ray?" ventured Adrienne, refusing to believe that Ray was not Ray. "I mean, who wouldn't be if they woke up in a drawer at the morgue?"

"No, I was dead. I saw the spirit world beyond."

"Maybe you had a near-death experience, Ray," said Rebop, "and it shocked you or changed you in a fundamental way. That often happens. People come back believing in things they hadn't before. That makes more sense than contact with another world."

"Unless you're a spiritualist," said Tai. He looked at Rain. "Some of us believe that contacting the spirit world is possible—and, in my opinion, could lead to connection with spirits from other parts of the universe."

"There is something more than ordinary reality," seconded Crow. "We've all experienced that several times now. There is more."

"And what about the animals?" asked Tai. The animals—including the chicken—and the spider that no one had noticed, hanging from a web attached to the light fixture—had gathered around them and seemed to be listening to their conversation.

Rebop glanced at the animals then her friend Rain. "That's crazy."

Tai shook his head. "You haven't seen the things we have."

"And we all saw Ray dead," said Van.

"And we guessed Van's number," added Janice. "That was real."

"I don't know what else to tell you," said Rebop, pacing back and forth. "You believe what you believe, and if you don't believe Ray, try another séance." The silence at the table provided her answer to that suggestion. "This stuff is beyond me, but that's my advice. Go back to the teepee or take Ray to a psychiatrist."

Ray lifted his eyes to the ceiling.

Rebop stopped pacing and looked at the faces around the table. "But there's something important that you haven't followed up on. It won't give you an answer to Ray's possession, but it might help you with something else."

"Go on," said Rain.

"You mentioned a page torn from an encyclopedia. It contained a description of a Molotov cocktail. You said the police found it in Ray's jeans." Rebop faced Ray. "Where'd that page come from?"

"Yeah," hushed Rain.

"I found it in a rental that I was cleaning. I saw nothing about a Molotov cocktail. It was an article on moles. It was for Adrienne."

"Who lived in the rental?" asked Rebop, now trying to put together pieces from the other mystery.

"It was a woman, Karen, and her boyfriend, a biker, Mike Rogers."

"Could he be the bomber, Ray?" asked Rebop, looking at Rain.

"He's a crazy biker—and against the war, but I haven't a clue."

"No," said Rebop. "That page you found is a clue."

"This isn't helping us at all," moaned Janice. "Who cares about damn Campbell Hall? We need to figure out what to do with Ray."

Janice stood up from the table. "I'm going to make dinner. Who's got the shift with me?"

"I do," said Marsha. "Let's make dinner. I need a break, too."

CHAPTER 93

That same Sunday night, Gino decided to track down Mathers and Ball to give them some of their own medicine by going undercover himself. Instead of wearing his tuxedo pants, pork pie hat, and white guinea shirt, he put on a dress, a little makeup, and a woman's blond wig. He got on his bike and rode to the Odyssey to see if the agents were hanging out there. When they weren't at the coffee shop, he went to Max's Tavern. Again with no luck, though one dumb drunk made a pass at him.

Next he went to the Vet's Club. The place was dark as usual, but Gino saw them right away, drinking beer in a booth opposite the bar, listening to the swing band that was there that night. Gino took a stool at the end of the bar where the drinks were made, bought a beer, and watched the two men through the bar mirror.

Gino knew what he wanted to do but wasn't sure how he would carry it out. The men had told him they were interested in getting some LSD. Gino thought they should try it first. He had four hits of blotter with him. His plan was to wait for them to order another beer, then shred the tiny squares of paper into their beers when the bartender set them on the bar for the waitress to deliver. But they didn't order another beer. They got food instead, which meant it would be placed in the kitchen's service window, not where Gino was sitting.

Paying as close attention as he could, he watched the waitress post their order above the service window. He tracked each order as the cook placed them in the window. When he saw the cook put the agents' order up, he slipped off the bar stool, went behind the bar as though he worked there—the band providing the perfect diversion—and placed two hits in the burger and two in the turkey sandwich. Then he was back on his stool, sipping beer, without anyone noticing.

Gino watched the waitress get the order and place it on the agents' table. He remained at the bar until they had cleaned their plates and stood to leave. Gino followed them out of the building. They were on bicycles, so he got on his and rode after them, eager to see how they would react to his little gift.

CHAPTER 94

After the meal, Rebop read some of her poems, but her audience was distracted, and only Rain and Tai engaged in the discussion afterward. Rain was complimentary. Tai put the full court press on Rebop, praising her poetry, hoping to pave the way for a date in the future.

When Rebop left, Rain walked her out to the porch for a few words in private. "I know this looks crazy, Rebop. But I've seen too much to write this off as drugs. Something happened."

"I'm sorry, Rain. I'm trying to be straight with you. It's simply too much for me to believe that Ray is possessed by an alien. He seems completely normal except for that nutty idea. I don't know what else to tell you. I hope you don't think I've failed you." She looked out across the yard then back to Rain. "This is something you need to work out among yourselves. But I wouldn't rule out some kind of psychiatric counseling for Ray." She embraced Rain, kissed her on the mouth, and walked off the porch.

Rain respected Rebop as much as anyone she knew, but she also understood that what they had told her was far out by any standards— very far out. No one would believe them. When she went back into the house, everyone was still at the table.

"Well," said Van, looking at Rain and then around the table. "Was she right? Was it just the drugs?"

"No," said Ray. "And I'll prove it."

"I won't go back to the teepee," said Janice.

"Neither will I," said Adrienne.

"Will you hold hands around the table?" asked Ray. "I think it's important."

Although their past experiences in the teepee had invoked real fear in both Janice and Adrienne, they did agree to hold hands around the table and meditate as they'd done so many times with Gloria. They turned off the dining room light and placed a candle in the middle of the table. Rain started it with a steady *om*, so pure and steady they could hear Lena purring along with them.

The meditative state came on easily and quickly opened into the astral world of extended consciousness. Psychic entities that had been invisible prior to the trance now glided around them. This included verification of what Ray had been saying. The manta-like creature they'd seen in the teepee now hovered over Ray's head like a luminous blue sombrero. The creature's three protruding eyes sat on top, watching in all directions at once. Its tentacles extended from beneath its flat body and drifted through the air like luminous strands of smoke, reaching out and winding around the heads of the others at and around the table.

CHAPTER 95

Working in the woods, either harvesting trees or replanting them, was a critical part of the economy in western Oregon. The work was hard. It started early in the morning and didn't let up all day, setting chokers or manning a chain saw or hauling a bag of one hundred seedlings up a hill for replanting. It was a grueling day, and the men and women who worked in the woods felt a certain pride doing the hard work that was at the foundation of just about everyone's job in Oregon except the farmers.

The work force in the woods was driven by the needs of huge logging companies and lumber mills like the ones owned by Walt Arnold. These companies either harvested the timber themselves or contracted the work out to cheapo outfits that bid on logging jobs all over the state. Loggers made a decent wage for the region, but the sense of working in the woods carried a little macho heft, and a lot of the country boys who didn't go into farming or into mills liked the brisk outdoor life of felling trees. Seeing the crummies, as they were called— oversized suburban station wagons with eight or ten crew members packed in with their chainsaws, hardhats, and work boots—passing through town and into the woods was a cultural perspective on the Northwest all its own.

The standard practice was clear cutting. That meant stripping all the trees off the side of a hill or portion of forest. This was hard on the land and could lead to serious erosion problems and water contamination. Conservation laws required logging companies to replant these clear cuts, work they contracted out to tree planting outfits much as they did the logging.

In Eugene, one of these tree planting outfits, called the Hoedads, after the hoe-like tool they used for replanting, was a group of hippies. As in other parts of the alternative community, they organized themselves into a collective. They bid on jobs just like all the other companies, but split the profits equally among the co-op members, usually resulting in a better wage for everyone. With their long hair and untamed mustaches and beards, they were a wild bunch, alternative in their thinking, but also pumped up on the physical nature of their work. When a crew of Hoedads, which might include a few women, returned to Eugene with paychecks in their pockets after a week or ten days in the woods, they would fill the local bars like dusty cowboys—and cowgirls—returning from a roundup.

Max's Tavern was one of the Hoedad's favorite landing spots. Any night of the week eight or ten members of a crew might crash the place and stay there drinking until closing time, with no other purpose than getting bombed. Word of a crew's arrival invariably drew a good number of street hippies to the tavern, who were also looking for a wild time.

On the same night that Gino was cross-dressing, two Hoedad work crews descended on Max's for the evening. With sixteen men and four women straight from the woods, the place rocked and rolled like it was Saturday night twice over.

Tim O'Malley was there that night, standing with his elbows on the bar, when Ball and Mathers walked in. Tim pretended not to notice them as they ordered a beer and settled into the only empty booth in the loud, crowded bar. Shortly afterward, Gino came in and took a stool beside Tim at the bar.

Gino nudged Tim. "Hey, good lookin', wanna buy me a beer?"

Tim looked at him and grimaced. "What are you doing in a dress?"

"How'd you know it was me?"

Tim looked up at the ceiling. "I recognized your bike when you pulled up out front. Besides, there's no woman in Eugene as ugly as you."

Gino crossed his eyes.

"I'll buy you a beer if you promise not to go home with me."

"Fuck you."

"Did you see who's here?" Tim tipped his head toward the FBI agents.

"Yeah. Keep a close eye on them."

"I always do," said Tim. "I'm more worried about you."

"I fucked up once, but I've got them this time."

Tim's eyes narrowed. "How is it that *you've got them*? Is it the dress?"

Gino grinned. "I dosed them at the Vet's Club."

"Dosed them with what?"

"Vitamin A. Two hits each."

"You dumb fuck, that could get you twenty years in Federal prison."

Gino shook his head. "I don't think so. They never saw me."

"But who else could have done it? You're the one who tried to sell them the stuff, you idiot."

Gino tipped his head, then frowned. "Damn, I hope you're not right."

"Me too. They'll probably drag me into it."

"I'll confess if that happens. This is all on me, not you."

"I wish it were that easy. Remember, I do the printing for all the radicals in town. You know they'd love to get me off the street."

"Think we'd be better off if we left?"

"No, if we're headed to prison, we might as well see what we're in for."

CHAPTER 96

They were part of a huge flock of the blue, manta-like creatures, three hundred or more, gliding over the surface of the alien planet. It was exhilarating and lovely beyond words. But it wasn't really them flying—the members of Blake College—as individuals—but them conjoined with the mantas, operating as a single consciousness, turning and twisting, darting here and there as one unified entity, like a flock of starlings. They flew over vast stretches of open desert, swooping down low, past the sandy mounds that appeared in clusters. Human-size, multi-legged, insects-like creatures marched in long lines like ants between these simple pyramidal structures that they appeared to be building. After circling a colony of these mounds twice, the flock lifted high in the air and headed to a ridge of mountains on the horizon. Upon reaching the mountains, the flock dove into and out of one mountain valley after another, dragging their tentacles through tall, luxurious grasses of different colors and smells and textures and tastes, feeding off the seeds.

Nourished, the flock rose in a V-formation up through the sky into the outer reaches of the atmosphere until the vision vanished, leaving the school members sitting around the dining room table, staring at each other.

Janice immediately began waving her hands around her head as though she were being attacked by bees—and screaming, "Get those tentacles away from me. Get them away."

Rain took her in her arms, trying to her calm her down, but Janice continued to swing her arms and scream. Tai produced two valiums from an amber plastic container and convinced Janice to take them. But it wasn't just Janice. Everyone at the table was blown away. The alien creature had not left at all. And once Janice had calmed to contained hysteria, their distress focused on Ray, sitting at the far end of the table like the Cheshire Cat. "Do you believe me now?"

"Did you know what we would see?" asked Crow.

"Only that you would see the manta over my head."

"No shit," muttered Tai, twirling a dread lock between his fingers.

"And yet," continued Ray, "I feel no purpose connected to it. No motive." He passed his hand over his head. "I can't feel it on my head. I just know it's there inside—like a lingering cold."

"But why aren't you freaking out?"

"I'm not sure, Adrienne." Ray shrugged. "I guess I'm getting used to it."

"When one of its tentacles wraps around our heads," asked Van, "you can read our minds?"

"Only in a very general way. It seems haphazard. I don't have any control over the creature or its tentacles. I think it's how it appears. I'm only a vehicle for the thing."

"How do we know that?" demanded Janice, who had been glaring at Ray, imagining the damn blue manta fluttering over his head the entire time. "How do we know you're not crazy and plan to kill us during the night?"

"You don't. But I won't." Ray looked around the table. "Does it feel like I'm trying to control you now? Any of you?"

No one could say yes.

"But it looked that way," blurted out Janice.

"Do you think I'm a threat?"

"With that thing on your head—yes!"

When no one countered with a *no*, Ray took a deep breath, then asked, "Do you want me leave?"

"No," said Crow emphatically. "If Blake College is what we think it is, we should come together on this just like we did for Gloria."

Janice looked up at the ceiling in frustration, then pointed at the light fixture. "Is that the same spider we saw in the teepee?"

Everyone looked at the fixture. "No," said Marsha, "there's loads of those spiders on this property."

"It's the same one," stated Ray.

Looks flashed around the table.

"So, what do we do now?" asked Tai.

"Turn him over to the FBI," said Janice.

"I think it's the CIA that would want him," said Van.

"No, no. Stop. I'm with Crow," said Rain. "Besides, no one will believe us anyway. Rebop didn't even believe us. If we tell the authorities what we've seen, they'll lock us all up. I think this is our problem to solve among ourselves."

"So, Ray, what do we do now?" repeated Tai.

Ray looked down at the surface of the table, then up at those awaiting his response. "I'm beginning to believe these creatures contacted us for a reason, and that they are trying to tell us something."

"What do you mean?" asked Rain.

"Well, for instance, I don't think it's just one of them that's in my head. It's all of them, the whole flock."

"What makes you say that?" asked Van.

"That's what they were showing us. The entire flock, though many physically separate entities, operates as a single unit with a single guiding motive." Ray struggled to find the words. "That's how they fly in such perfect synchronization. And that's how it felt to me. I was part of a single collective consciousness."

Everyone at the table nodded slowly. They had also felt that.

"And though we only see one as an astral presence fluttering over my head," said Ray. "I think it's all of them together as one unified psyche." He tapped the side of his head. "All here inside my head."

Marsha sat up. "Are you suggesting they took us on a tour of their planet as a way to communicate with us about their life?"

"Yes, I think so," said Ray. "They don't communicate with words, but they can show us things. Like their planet—wasn't it beautiful! Or how they graze off the mountain grasses without ever landing."

"And those other insect things that live on their planet and their giant ant hills," added Van. "I bet they live beneath the ground just like ants on Earth."

"Bullshit," snapped Janice, valium and all. "You can romance about this all you want, but I don't like it. There's something in Ray's head and none of us knows what it is or what it wants." She glanced at Adrienne. "Who knows? By tomorrow all of us might have decided to string ourselves up."

Adrienne began to cry. Even Rain, ever cool, was exasperated and had little to offer. When they went to bed that night, with no answers to their questions, and really no idea what to do next, Janice slept in Adrienne's room, and Ray slept alone in Janice's room.

CHAPTER 97

Rebop knew plenty of crazy hippies. She wasn't into drugs, but she'd seen her share of the wasteland. When she left Blake College that evening, she was more interested in the page torn from the encyclopedia than the story of alien possession. Instead of going home, she decided to stop by Max's Tavern on the off chance Tim O'Malley might be there.

Max's had been hopping with Hoedads for hours by the time Rebop arrived. The tree planters threatened to drain every keg in the place the way they were tossing down pitchers, and, of course, Tim and Gino had been dragged, kicking and screaming, into the party atmosphere. Hell, what could be better than being forced to drink beer with Eugene's wildest collection of hippie woodsmen and woodswomen?

"Check'em out," said Gino, his wig slightly off center, nudging Tim in the ribs, and tipping his head twice in the direction of Ball and Mathers. "I think it's coming on."

It had been two hours since Gino had dosed them. Instead of drinking their beers, Mathers was looking around the bar, gawking at the freaks like a child at the zoo, and Ball was staring at the veins in the back of his hand.

"Yeah, telltale signs." Tim pulled out his tobacco pouch and set to rolling a cigarette.

Gino took something out of the purse hanging from his shoulder and stuck it in his mouth as Rebop stood up to the bar next to Tim.

"Hey, Rebop." Tim bobbed his head a couple times. "What brings you into this madhouse?"

"I got a lead for you," she said as softly as she could and still make herself heard over the noise.

Tim completed rolling his cigarette, put the whole thing in his mouth, and drew it out between his lips. "Fill me in."

But Rebop's attention had been drawn to the "woman" next to Tim. Although it was too dark and smoky to make a clear assessment, Rebop was pretty sure it was a man in women's clothing. Gino saw her staring at him and faced her straight on. His stupid grin revealed the set of plastic vampire teeth he'd put in his mouth.

Tim broke into laughter. Rebop just stared. When Gino winked at her, she saw through his disguise and shook her head. "A new persona, Gino?"

He took the fangs out to talk. "It's a disguise. I'm doing a little undercover work." He put the fangs back in and stuck the squeaking red ball on his nose. "Watch this-s-s-s," he hissed through the plastic mouthpiece. Gino slid off his stool, beer in hand, and sauntered across the bar to the booth of interest.

Tim winced. "Oh, shit."

Without a word, Gino sat down beside Mathers so that he faced Ball.

Rebop recognized the FBI agents and turned to Tim. "What's he doing?"

"Damned if I know. Keep an eye on him. This is going to get very funny or very ugly, very fast. Don't stare. Use the mirror to watch. What's your lead?"

"You know a biker by the name of Mike Rogers?"

But Tim wasn't listening. He was staring in the mirror watching Gino, knowing if this went badly, he could get dragged into it. Instead of repeating the question, Rebop found herself staring in the mirror also.

Gino winked at Mathers, then leaned across the table and smiled at Ball. The cheap wig, the Saint Vincent DePaul dress, the sloppy eye makeup and smeared lipstick—accented by the vampire teeth and clown nose—all of which appeared completely ludicrous to ordinary eyes—had an entirely different effect on the two men well into their first psychedelic trip. To them, Gino's face appeared to be moving, like three faces superimposed over each other, with three sets of eyes, three sets of blood red lips, and a hideousness that made Gino look like a real vampire. And it scared the shit out of them.

Ball got up from his seat, mouth wide-open, and backed away from the table, right into a big, well-lubricated tree planter. The man shoved him. Ball stumbled and fell onto the floor. Mathers pressed himself into the corner of the booth as far from Gino as possible. When Gino inched closer and gave him another big grin, he climbed onto the table, took a leap, and landed on Ball as he was trying to get up. The two men ricocheted from one flailing dancer to another, trying to get off the floor. One woman stopped mid gyration, pointed at Mathers, and shouted out the secret that everyone on the streets of Eugene already knew, "This guy's an FBI agent!"

Ball and Mathers looked around in absolute terror and ran from the bar. Gino followed them to the door to watch them fumble onto their bicycles. Mathers fell twice before the two men were out of sight.

Gino returned to the bar and bowed before Rebop and Tim to a rousing applause. Gino took a drink from Tim's beer and headed to the bathroom. Tim and Rebop watched him go into the men's room, then come flying out. He pulled off his wig and clown nose and went right back in.

Rebop turned to Tim. "Who said drugs weren't dangerous?"

Tim was laughing so hard he was nearly in tears.

"Tim, do you know a biker by the name of Mike Rogers?"

Tim sobered as much as he could. "Yeah, I do. I helped him rebuild his Harley."

Rebop told him about the page from the encyclopedia that Ray had found at First and Madison. She didn't confuse the matter by telling him the rest of the Blake College story.

"You know, Rebop," said Tim, adding this clue to what he already knew, "this is big. I'm going to follow up on this right away. Thanks. Thanks a lot."

Rebop nodded. "Keep me in the loop."

CHAPTER 98

Rebop's tip had Tim buzzing. It was eleven-forty-five. Always one to act in the moment, Tim figured it was a fifty-fifty chance Mike Rogers would be at the Alibi Club. Tim finished his beer, told Gino he'd had enough fun for the night, then headed outside to his motorcycle.

Fifteen minutes later he parked the Indian out front of the Alibi Club and strolled in. Although the cigarette smoke was as dense as the smog in LA, the place was relatively quiet compared to Max's. Tim saw Mike at a table in the back, sitting alone with half a glass of beer and an empty pitcher. Tiny, Mike's father, was behind the bar. Tim bought a pitcher of Blitz and approached Mike's table.

"Mind if I join you?" asked Tim, hefting the pitcher in his hand as an offering.

Mike curled a drunken grin at Tim. "Not at all. Always a pleasure to see you, O'Malley. Man, I hope you didn't pay for that beer. I owe you big time for helping me on that bike. Did Tiny charge you?"

Tim nodded. "He doesn't know me."

"He's a dumb shit. I'll get the next one."

"I'm only here for one. Maybe another time."

"What brings you to this watering hole?"

Tim grinned. "I was looking for you."

"Really. How can I help you?"

"Start by pouring us both a beer."

Mike tipped his head in acknowledgment and filled his and Tim's glasses. "What'd ya need?"

"Nothing. Just wanted to know how your bike is running."

"Runs perfect. You're an ace, dude." Mike placed his right hand on his left side. "But after taking that bullet, I can still feel it when I ride."

Tim bobbed his head a couple times. "Were you living in that house where we assembled the bike?"

"Yeah, for about two months—until that little dust up with the Free Souls. They don't much like my politics. Me being a vet and all." Mike glanced at the front door as though he were expecting someone. "I've got one last caper to pull off for a friend, then I'm leaving town. Can't be looking over my shoulder all day for fucking bikers."

"I can't imagine a stronger statement against the war than when it comes from a vet. I admire you for getting out front on that."

"I got a habit in Nam, and it fucked me up good." He looked down at the floor. "We don't need to be sending any more of our boys over there. You either get killed or get your brain twisted. Look at me!" He grinned, big and wild. "I'm half-crazy and have nightmares every night."

"Only half, uh?"

Mike laughed. "Only half as crazy as you. Somebody told me about your getting a bunch of look-alikes together to fuck with the FBI. Pretty damn smooth for a fucking hippie, O'Malley. Pretty damn smooth."

Tim took a slug from his beer and grinned. "That was supposed to be a secret."

"That slinky Cuban dike friend of yours brought those two undercover boys in here one afternoon. Did you hear about that?"

"No, she didn't say a word to me."

"They got the full hippie welcome from the rednecks that drink here. Got quite weird according to fatso over there behind the bar. Ever see the bathroom stall in here?"

"Oh, yeah."

Mike laughed and took another long swallow of beer. "What's with the FBI?"

"They're looking for the group behind the bombings."

"Group?"

"They think it's the SDS. Or me!"

Mike grinned his ugly grin. "Ain't never asked me about it." He laughed drunkenly. "Kind of makes me feel forgotten."

"I've got no idea who did it," lied Tim. "But a friend told me he saw a diagram for making a firebomb in the encyclopedia. Believe that?"

Mike returned a wide smile. "Oh, yeah." He licked his lips. "I've seen that, too."

"Really?"

"Fuck, O'Malley. They got everything in the encyclopedia. Just look it up. Molotov cocktail. Explosives. Detonators. The history of Harley-

Davidson motorcycles. Anything you want." He lifted his glass and took a drink. "Ain't no fucking secret."

At this point Tim had no doubt Mike had done the bombing. Despite his seeming good humor, he raged with anger. This dumb biker had killed his friend out of pure ignorance. But now was not the time to confront him.

Mike sat up in his chair, his eyes trained on the front of the tavern. "What do you know? There's Uncle Walt. He said he'd come in here about midnight."

Tim looked over his shoulder and recognized the bigtime lumberman at the bar talking to Tiny.

"I don't mean to be rude, Tim, but I've got some unfinished business with that man. And he ain't likely to take to you so much— with the red shoes and all." He laughed with little restraint. "Finish your beer. I've got to talk to him in private. He owes me some money. Comprende, amigo?"

"No problemo. I only stopped by to see how the bike was running." He turned to appraise Walt Arnold again, thinking of Dick Danger's comment about following the dynamite—either road construction or *big-time logging*. "That guy have anything to do with that one last caper?" He curled his own ugly little grin at Mike.

Mike nodded slowly. "Yeah, me and Walt Arnold, a true odd couple."

"How soon you leaving town?"

Mike shrugged. "Depends on my conversation with Uncle Walt." He winked. "Could be as soon as this week."

CHAPTER 99

"Van, I'm not sure I want to stay here any longer," said Marsha. The light in their bedroom had been out for a while, but they were both awake, lying side by side in bed. "Ray's return is just too strange, and it scares me."

"I've been thinking the same thing, but what would you do?"

"While I was home over Christmas, I applied to Stanford again. My parents were pushing me, and I did it to please them. But now, Stanford seems much more attractive than it did a month ago."

"Maybe I should do the same. When is the application due?"

"The middle of February. With your SAT scores you'll get in for sure."

"I wouldn't want to go unless we both got in."

"We can't know that until April. And I'm thinking of leaving much sooner than that."

"You mean like both of us packing up and sneaking out tonight?"

"Seems crazy, but yes."

"Crazier than staying?"

Marsha took a deep breath. "No."

"Where would we go? I don't want to go home."

"And I don't either."

"We'd need some money. And would probably have to tell our parents."

"Tell them what?" asked Marsha. "About Ray?"

"No way. Can you hang on a few more days? I feel like we've made a commitment to the others. Maybe we play it day to day and see what happens."

"Might be easier than trying to find a place to stay tonight."

"Let's give it some time, Marsha. But I'll apply to Stanford regardless."

"Okay, let's see what happens."

In the morning they were at the dining room table with Janice, Rain, and Crow, when Adrienne entered the house through the kitchen even more lost than the day before. "Ray's gone again. I just checked Janice's bedroom and the greenhouse and the teepee. He's not here."

Everyone slumped in their chairs. Crow muttered a low, "Fuck, he's got to be here. Where else could he go?"

"Back to the morgue," said Tai, coming up from the basement to join the discussion.

"Maybe we just dreamed he was back," said Janice, still obsessed with feeling the sides of her head.

"Yeah, perfect," sneered Tai. "We all dreamed the same thing."

"Eat me, Tai," spat Janice. "After what we've seen this week, why not?"

Ray had gotten up with the sun and deliberately put on a long-sleeved turtle neck to hide the marks on his neck. He ate a bowl of Blake College granola, then got on his bike and pedaled to Twelfth and Jefferson. Although his initial contact with the creatures had caused him to doubt himself, he was getting increasingly comfortable with what he imagined to be the unified psyche of scores of mantas dwelling in his head. And if he wasn't dead, he might as well go to work.

Ray had been sitting on the curb beside his bicycle for half an hour when Spikes drove up in his pickup. He climbed from the cab slowly and approached the young man as calmly as he could. This was a man who had won two purple hearts, had seen many hundred dead, including several of his army buddies, and enough devastation for three lifetimes. But he was so unsettled by the sight of Ray he was shaking. He even wondered—like everyone else—if he were dreaming.

"Howdy, Jack," said Ray as though it were just another day at the coal mine.

"Uh, that you, Ray, or are you his twin brother?"

Ray laughed. "What do you mean? I don't have a twin brother."

"I heard a rumor you were dead."

"Must have been a different Ray."

"No doubt about that. What do you think about the war, Ray?"

"As little as possible. I don't know. Why?"

"Just curious. What about ROTC on campus?"

"It's a way to get your schooling paid for."

Spikes nodded. "That's what I'd say. Let's get to work."

To move the house, they had put plywood over the windows and several structural supports inside. They worked all morning removing the plywood and the internal supports. Ray said very little, and Spikes was happy Ray was back—and thankful Yates had been wrong.

At noon, Spikes and Ray went to Burger King for lunch. Spikes told Ray he needed to call Sheila and went to the payphone at the corner of the lot. He called the Eugene Police Department and asked for Yates.

"Hey, man, you fucked with me badly. Ray's not dead at all."

"What do you mean?"

"He showed up for work. Worked four hours and just ate lunch with me."

"You saw him? Alive?"

"Just like always, yeah."

"Where is he now?"

"He's in the truck waiting for me to get off the phone."

"What's next?"

"What'd ya think? Back to work."

"At Twelfth and Jefferson?"

"For the next two or three months, yep."

"I'll be there in thirty minutes. Don't let Ray out of your sight."

"Shouldn't be hard. He'll be working right next to me."

CHAPTER 100

Janice went into town that morning after breakfast. She walked around Skinner's Butte to the print shop where Gino's panel truck was parked. She looked in the back window. Gino was inside asleep—alone. Janice banged on the window. Gino rolled over. She banged again. Gino put a pillow over his head. Janice yanked both doors open and Gino sat up. He hadn't seen Janice in six weeks. He blinked twice, struggling to gather his thoughts. "Oh, hey, Janice. Kinda early, isn't it?" Then he remembered their agreement. "You ever set up an appointment with a counselor?"

"I changed my mind. I want to abort it. It's been nearly four months, and we're running out of time. I need some money."

"Okay." Gino scratched his head. "How much you need?"

"Five hundred dollars."

"Haven't got that much."

Janice leaned into panel truck and got up close Gino. "You've got to help me with this, Gino. The baby's been possessed by aliens."

"What? Aliens? You sure I'm the father, not some guy on Neptune."

Janice started crying and fell into the bed beside Gino, helpless to her emotions.

"Okay, okay, Janice. Don't cry. Tim knows a hip doctor who'll do it. It's more money than I have right now, but maybe I can work out a deal with the guy."

Janice sat up, wiping tears from her cheeks. "I want to do it as soon as possible."

"Okay. We'll have to talk to the guy first. I'll get his name from Tim."

Janice began to cry again. Gino held her and eased her down into the bed. He pulled the doors shut with his bare feet and stroked Janice's back until she began to relax.

CHAPTER 101

Tim woke up late but got moving right away. He found Gino asleep in the back of his panel truck. Janice had left. Tim pulled open the truck's back doors and handed Gino a lit joint. Gino sat up, took a toke, and lay back down.

"I've got water on in the house. Meet me in the shop. I'll have a cup of coffee for you."

"Fuck, I need some shuteye."

"It's ten-thirty, Gino. Get up. This is important."

A cup of hot java in each hand, Tim used his hip to open the shop door. Gino was in a lawn chair smoking a cigarette. Tim handed him the sugar-no-cream. Tim sipped the cream-no-sugar then rolled a cigarette before revealing his scheme. "I got another lead on the bomber last night." He was as serious as he ever got.

Gino, who was the only one Tim had told about the spray paint, felt it and squinched his eyes trying to focus.

"Remember the guy with the cute girl that night I broke up the biker fight?"

"I remember the girl, yeah."

Tim told him Rebop's story about Ray and the encyclopedia page. "After I saw you last night, I went to the Alibi Club." Tim took a pull from his smoke and exhaled. "I had another talk with Mike."

"Did you ask him about the spray paint?"

"Didn't need to. I'm all but certain he's the one."

"He's crazy enough that's for sure."

Tim recounted his conversation with Mike. "He didn't say it outright. But he was bragging about something, then Walt Arnold, the big lumber guy, who's Mike's uncle, came into the bar."

Gino nodded that he knew the name.

"Mike said he had a job to do for his uncle and needed to talk to him about some money."

"And?"

"I've got a sneaking suspicion Walt Arnold paid Mike to do the bombing."

"Why would he want to bomb the university? I can see Mike getting drunk and doing it for no other reason than he's against the war and he's an asshole. But why this Arnold guy?"

"Yeah." Tim crumpled up his face. "It doesn't make much sense. But I know they were doing some kind of business deal. Shady business that Mike openly told me I couldn't hear about. Pretty suggestive. I don't think Mike knows how much Stoopid meant to me. That part didn't come up. But I felt my blood boiling. I'm sure he did it, Gino. And you know me."

"Don't cross easy-going O'Malley." Gino grinned wide and crazy. "So, why'd ya have to wake me up to tell me this?"

"Whatever Mike's about to do—a bombing or some other stupid shit—he implied it might happen this week. And that afterward, he's leaving town."

"Sounds suspicious."

"And since we have nothing else to go on, and I don't want him getting away, we're going to start following Mike. Day and night, highest priority. Starting now. My gut says he did it, and I want to put a lock on this case for Stoopid's sake—then turn that fucker in."

Gino grinned. "Sounds like an around the clock job. Got any acid?"

Tim laughed. "I think I can find some. Whatever happened to those FBI agents?"

Gino looked at the ceiling and grinned. "Now that they know the whole street is on to them, I figure they'll turn in their badges and start reevaluating the meaning of life." Gino took a hit from his smoke and exhaled. "But I've got a problem of my own. What's the name of that abortion doc you know?"

"Tom Rosenburg. Why?"

Gino stared at Tim.

"Okay. Who is she?"

"That stocky blond with the big butt. She says the fetus has been infected by aliens."

"Mexicans?"

"No men from outer space."

Tim laughed. "What'd she expect? She's been doing it with you."

"Fuck you. She really believes that."

"Has she been eating psilocybin mushrooms?"

"What do you mean?"

"We ate a lot of mushrooms when I lived out at the Lorane commune. When we got them from this one field, we thought they made us dream of aliens and UFOs."

"Never happened to me."

"You had to be there at the commune to understand. One day a friend and I picked two thousand of the little guys at this field. We went back to the commune and shared them with everyone. Dick Danger was passing through at the time." Tim laughed. "We ate them all in one day—about eighty 'shrooms per person. Wild times. When we started sharing our unusual dreams, Dick said a farmer told him that mushroom field was a sacred site for the Kalapuya Indians—and that it contained powerful medicine linking the spirit world to the mushrooms."

"Sounds like you're the one taking too many psychedelics," laughed Gino.

"Fuck you. Like I said, you had to be there. I just try to stay open to anything—even this Walt Arnold-Mike Rogers connection."

CHAPTER 102

Ray's parents had arrived in Eugene. Yates spent the morning talking to them. That Ray's corpse was missing didn't go over too well. Ray's father came unglued and his mother wept. Yates assured them that a mistake had been made. They should go to their hotel, and he would contact them as soon as they found the body.

Yates was still searching for the body when Spikes called. Yates' first thought was to call the parents. After all the strange twists in the investigation, however, he decided to talk to Ray first and get the story straight before facing the parents again. At least he would be giving them the good news that their son was alive. Then he would have to address the issue of the bombings.

Yates had told the FBI about finding the page torn from the encyclopedia. Now, having found out that Ray was alive, he decided to call Bascomb to update him. Bascomb surprised him. He wanted the first opportunity to question Ray. This led to a pissing fight over the phone about jurisdiction. Bascomb went over Yates' head to Wilkerson. Wilkerson overrode Yates, who would still have to deal with Ray's parents.

A black, unmarked sedan pulled up alongside the curb at Jefferson Street. Spikes and Ray were both perched on ladders, removing sheets of plywood. Spikes saw the car first, noting it was not a Eugene police vehicle. He climbed off his ladder and met the two men in black suits and hats as they came up the driveway.

"Can I help you?"

Bascomb flashed his badge and introduced himself and his partner. "We're looking for Ray Harper. We spoke with officer Yates of the Eugene Police Department. He said we could find him here." Bascomb pointed to Ray. "Is that him?"

Spikes didn't know what to say. He knew Ray was a suspect in the bombings. He didn't believe it, but Christ, this was the FBI. He called to Ray. "These men want to talk to you, Ray. They're from the FBI."

Ray climbed off his ladder and joined the men in the driveway.

"Mr. Harper, I'm Agent Bascomb." He flashed his badge. "This is Agent Franklin. We have a few questions we'd like to ask you."

Ray looked at Spikes and shrugged. "Ask away."

"We'd like to do it downtown at our office. If you don't mind, we can drive there right now." Bascomb motioned to the car.

"Well, I'm working at the moment. I believe my boss needs me. How about five or so this evening?"

Bascomb looked straight at Spikes. "We're investigating a federal crime, sir. Our request takes priority."

Spikes did not like it, but he'd been intimidated by Bascomb's manner and his badge. "You better go, Ray. Give me a call this evening. Let me know how much you can work this week."

"No problem." Remarkably calm, Ray climbed into the back seat of the black sedan with agent Franklin. Bascomb took the wheel.

Not five minutes after they'd left, Yates came speeding up in his cruiser. He jumped out of the car and ran over to Spikes, who was still sorting out what had happened.

"They took Ray?"

Spikes shook his head in confusion. "It was weird, yeah. Ray seemed alright with it. I don't know."

"But it was Ray?"

"You mean not a corpse. It was Ray. Alive. Hooting and honking."

"Did you ask him about the suicide?"

"I told him I thought he was dead."

"Yeah?"

"He just laughed and said it must have been another Ray."

"Any explanation? I mean, I saw him hanging from a rafter. And I'm sure it was him."

"That's all he said. It was too stupid asking a living man if he was dead, so I let it go. But you saw him dead, not just unconscious?"

"Fuck, I don't know. He was dead. But people can be dead for a couple of minutes and then come back to life. I've heard of that. But worst of all, I've got to tell his parents that he's alive—and that he's in the custody of the FBI."

"Any progress with your hippie girlfriend?"

Yates looked to the sky. "She's not my girlfriend, dipshit, but I did see her again. And I'm still fucked. I fall all over myself in her presence. It doesn't make sense to me that Ray did the bombing, but I'm worried that my feelings are tainted by…"

"The head of your penis." Spikes laughed. "Do the right thing, buddy. And don't ask me what that is." He laughed again, even harder.

Yates didn't laugh. "I've got talk to Ray's parents. But not until I hear what those FBI fucks have to say."

CHAPTER 103

Ray's parents were at the Eugene Police Department when Yates returned to headquarters. Forest Harper, Ray's father, a noted architect in the Durham, North Carolina area, was livid. Yates could hear him yelling at the desk clerk the moment he entered the building. Using Yates' name in vain several times, Forest demanded to talk to Wilkerson.

There was no avoiding it now. Yates knew it would either be him or Wilkerson to give the family the good news—which, of course, would unleash another flood of acrimony. Yates walked up to the clerk and told him he would handle it.

Forest didn't waste a second. "What the hell is going on? Have you found my son's body yet or is it still lost?"

Yates calmed himself and said it slowly. "We made a second mistake."

Forest's eyes went wide with anger.

"Ray is alive."

Vera, Ray's mother, burst into tears. Forest hugged his wife to calm her down. He shot a searing glance at Yates. "Where is he?"

Wilkerson came out of his office. He'd been on the phone with Bascomb. "He's with the FBI, Mr. Harper. They're holding him at their office for questioning."

Vera's elated crying suddenly transformed into anger. "What? The FBI? Questioning him about what?"

"His death?" snarled Forest. "I want to see my son. No matter where he is."

Wilkerson nodded. "I understand, sir. We made a terrible mistake." His eyes slid to Yates and back. "The good news is your son is alive. The bad news is he's a suspect in the investigation of two bombings on the University of Oregon campus. The FBI considers him a suspect."

Both parents were stunned. "A suspect for a bombing? Ray?" said his father. "No way. Where's the FBI office?"

"Officer Yates will take you there."

"And we'll get to talk to our son?"

"Yes, Mrs. Harper. I'm sure you'll have a chance to talk to him."

"A chance?" snapped Forest. "It better be more than that."

CHAPTER 104

In the forty hours since his resurrection, Ray had steadily grown more and more comfortable with the entity—meaning the collective psyche of the mantas—that shared his consciousness; moreover, he was learning to work with it. Now he could enter the mind of anyone, including the FBI agents', and read his or her mind.

He sat across a small table from Agent Bascomb. Agent Franklin stood a few feet away, leaning into a corner of the compact interrogation room. The page torn from the encyclopedia lay on the table, showing the diagram of a Molotov cocktail. Alongside the page was a portable tape recorder with the red recording light on. They had already talked about the bombings, the torn page, Stoopid's newsletter, the SDS flyer, and Ray's politics. Though Ray had been completely honest with them, he knew they hadn't believed a word he'd said.

"Why did you try to kill yourself?" asked Bascomb.

Ray stuck to the truth. "I'd been possessed by an entity from another planet. I thought it was taking over my mind. Death seemed a better choice than life."

Bascomb looked over his shoulder at Franklin, then back to Ray. "Did that same entity inspire you to bomb Campbell Hall?"

"No. As I've gradually discovered, it's only using me to observe life on Earth, and it's no threat to me or anyone else. Neither it nor I had anything to do with bombing either Campbell Hall or Johnson Hall."

"Does this entity still possess you?" asked Bascomb, again with a crooked look at Franklin.

"Yes, and at one point all the others in our house, plus the animals," said Ray. "It brought me back to life and allows me to read your thoughts, even alter them if I were so inclined."

"Oh, really? So what am I thinking?"

"That I'm nuts, and if I had such powers, why haven't I already walked out of here."

"Got me there," said Franklin from across the room.

"So why are you still here?"

"I've done nothing wrong. I have nothing to hide."

Bascomb turned to his partner. "What do you think?"

Franklin shook his head. "He's certifiable. Next he'll be telling us he has a six-foot rabbit for a friend."

Bascomb put his hands together, made a steeple with his fingers, then leaned his chin against the steeple. After a moment, he reached out and turned off the tape recorder.

"Okay, Mr. Harper, that's enough for now."

CHAPTER 105

Bob Yates drove Vera and Forest Harper twenty blocks west on Sixth Avenue to the FBI's rented office space. The office was small and unmarked. The door was locked. Yates knocked. He knocked a second time before Agent Franklin opened the door.

Yates was in uniform. He introduced Ray's parents. "As you know, it was initially believed that Ray Harper was dead. His parents came to Eugene to get his body. Now that they know he's alive, they want to see him. I'm hoping that won't be a problem."

Franklin nodded. "Come in. Agent Bascomb's in the back with Mr. Harper. I'll let him know you're here."

Vera and Forest remained angry and tight lipped. Franklin offered them a seat in an office that had only three chairs, a desk, and two telephones, then left the room, leaving Yates pacing back and forth.

"What's this about these bombings?" asked Ray's father. "I saw one of them in the newspaper when it happened. But surely Ray had nothing to do with that."

Yates told them about the page torn from the encyclopedia. "I haven't spoken to him about the bombing yet. I'll be interested to hear what he says to the FBI." He looked straight at Vera. "Ray works for a friend of mine, who always speaks highly of him, and the woman he lives with says she was at a bar with him the night of the first bombing." He turned to face Forest. "Let's just say I'm trying to keep an open mind."

"The woman he lives with?"

"You'll have to ask your son about that, Mrs. Harper."

"So, it's just this piece of paper that's gotten him into trouble?" said Forest.

"And the fact that I found him hanging from a rope two days ago— looking dead enough to take to the morgue. That was pretty strange— and why I'm still suspicious."

"You found him?"

"The people at the house where he lives found him. I arrived with the ambulance."

The door to the back room opened. Ray came out with Bascomb and Franklin. He was handcuffed, wearing his work clothes, looking hangdog. This was not the way he wanted to reunite with his parents. He hadn't seen them since he left school nine months ago. He'd spoken to them four times on the phone and had never explained to their satisfaction why he had dropped out of the University of North Carolina.

Vera stood up, glanced at the two agents, then rushed forward to hug her son and cry. Bascomb and Franklin stood back to give Forest a chance to say something. He looked lost. "Ray, we're here because we were told you committed suicide. Now we've learned that you're alive— and under suspicion for two bombings. What's happened? Are you okay?" He was almost in tears.

Ray said that he was fine and that there had been a mistake.

Forest looked into his son's eyes. "This officer said he found you hanging from a rope. That can't be right."

Ray looked down at the floor.

Yates stepped forward. He used his index finger to pull back the turtleneck Ray was wearing. The rope burns on his neck were still raw. "I'm wondering how he got out of the morgue," said Yates.

Ray continued to look down.

Vera was staring at the handcuffs. "Is he under arrest?"

Bascomb presented his best stone face. "Yes, but we're also concerned about his mental health, Mrs. Harper. We don't have the facilities here, but we're going to ask Officer Yates to find a solitary cell for him in the city jail."

"Is this because of the suicide attempt?" asked Forest. Beside him, Vera got a Kleenex out of her purse and dabbed at her eyes.

Bascomb looked at Yates, then back at the parents. "Not exactly. He told us he hung himself because he had been possessed by an entity from another planet."

Forest's and Vera's faces went blank. "What?" they chorused.

Ray looked up. "And it brought me back to life." He gave his parents a weak smile.

Their blank faces blanched to a whiter shade of pale.

Yates couldn't help himself. "You mean, you were dead until this entity brought you back to life?"

Ray looked right at him. Sincere as the sun. "Yes."

Bascomb glanced at Franklin. "He also said the entity had possessed all the others at the house and the animals as well."

Vera began to cry again.

"Don't worry, Mom," said Ray. "It's harmless."

Forest just stood there, mouth agape, staring at his son in disbelief.

CHAPTER 106

Tim didn't know where Mike was living—it was something he should have asked him the previous night, but he did know that Mike would be looking for dope in the usual places and that the Free Souls had a mark on him. Tim told Earl at Lucky's, Horace at the bike shop, Rebop, Pat Riley, and several other folks on the street that he thought Mike Rogers might be the bomber. "Keep an eye out for him. Starting now. He'll either be in bars or garages with other Jokers or at the Alibi Club. Those are safe spots for him. If you see him anywhere else, he'll be taking a chance. That's when I want to know about it. All messages go through the phone at my house—345-6748. Talk only to Jeannie, me, or Gino. I've got a CB radio on my Indian, and there's one on the second floor of the house. Jeannie will be able to contact me at a moment's notice."

Tim did not mention Walt Arnold to his watchers, as Gino had said that seemed too far-fetched to start spreading around. Tim would simply continue his detective work, and once he felt he had an air-tight case, he'd let the Eugene Police Department or the FBI take care of it.

Tim told Gino to hang out at the coffee shop across the street from the Alibi Club and to call if Mike showed up. Tim went to the U of O to do some research on Walt Arnold, focused on one question: Why would a big-time capitalist like Arnold be paying Mike to set off bombs? Tim secluded himself in the library basement, searching for anything he could find about the lumber tycoon—newspaper articles, interviews, notes from City Council meetings, letters to the editor, anything. What could have turned Walt Arnold against the war or the university?

CHAPTER 107

Prior to taking Ray to a holding cell in the Eugene jail, the FBI agents allowed his parents to talk to him in private. Ray described what had happened when Gloria died and during the days afterward. His parents thought he was out of his mind. When they briefed Yates on what Ray had said, he promised to talk to the others who had taken part in the "funeral ceremony" with Ray. Determined to beat the FBI on this one, Yates went straight to Blake College without stopping at headquarters to get Eldon. He had no idea what to expect from the members of Blake College, but he wanted to hear the story from Rain before anything else came down.

Van spotted the patrol car coming down the driveway and immediately ran to the kitchen, where Crow and Marsha were packaging granola and Rain and Adrienne were cutting vegetables for dinner.

"Fuck!" shouted Rain, who rarely cursed. "What are we going to say?"

The others answered in unison, "Don't mention the mantas." Then Crow dashed out the back door. On his way to the river, Crow alerted Tai and Janice who were smoking pot in the teepee.

Van opened the front door as Yates climbed the porch stairs. "Officer Yates, this has to be about Ray."

"You know he's alive?"

"He came here last night after you told us he was missing."

"And you didn't call me?"

"We intended to," lied Van, "but he left as soon as he arrived."

"When was that?"

"This morning before anyone got up."

"This morning? Jesus. I want to talk to everyone here at the house. There's a lot of questions that need answers."

"Yes, sir. We've got a few questions of our own. Come on in."

Rain came out of the kitchen wearing an apron. Her smile melted Yates, but he stayed upright. "Miss Adams, sorry to bother you. Can you gather everyone in the dining room? We need to talk about Ray."

"Of course, officer. Sit down. We'll be right with you."

Five minutes later, everyone but Crow was at the table. Rain sat at one end, Yates at the other. He didn't waste any time getting to the point. "As you know, your housemate Ray Harper is alive." He glanced around the table. "Van told me he came by yesterday after I did. I'm disappointed you didn't call me immediately." He looked directly at Rain. "Understandably his return was shocking, but you had to know I needed to know he was here. You had to know that." He shook his head to emphasize the point.

"Ray is still a suspect in the bombings," Yates continued. "He's currently in the custody of the FBI and being held in a jail cell downtown."

Yates watched the others exchange looks. Adrienne spoke out. "He had nothing do with Campbell Hall. I was with him that night. We watched the building burn like lots of people around the university. But he had nothing to do with that bombing or the other one. I'll swear to that in court."

Yates nodded. "I'm still gathering the facts, Adrienne. But the FBI believes he did it and will likely be out here to talk to you very soon."

"But they were already here," said Rain.

"They hadn't talked to Ray yet."

Again, looks flashed around the table.

"Ray told them the entire story." He watched Rain's reaction. "The funeral ceremony. Taking some kind of hallucinogenic potion. Seeing Gloria's spirit leave her body. And then being possessed by an alien entity—that's responsible for bringing him back to life, and that at one time possessed all of you—including the animals." Yates looked at Moxie on the floor gazing up at him, Lena on the sideboard staring at him in the cat way, and the two young foxes peeking over the edge of the table from Adrienne's lap. He didn't notice the chicken roosted on the window ledge, looking in from outside, or the spider overhead.

"Yes," Rain sighed, "that's what he told us also."

Yates continued. "The FBI doesn't see him as a political radical, they see him as a nut. They think he's emotionally disturbed—or worse. They probably think the same thing about all of you, and that this school is a front for some kind of Manson family anti-war cult."

Yates let this settle in. "Last time I was here, you didn't tell me about the ceremony or the possession. I'm not sure if you were hiding something or just trying to protect Ray, but I want to hear the story from all of you."

Rain retold the story. Each of the others threw in their personal insights. They stopped short of saying they had been possessed but admitted that Ray had told them he was.

"Do you believe that?"

Van began. "Initially, I thought something had really happened at the ceremony. Now I think it was the drugs. As far as I'm concerned, there are no alien entities, and I think the rest of us feel the same way."

Marsha followed. "I agree with Van, but I don't understand how Ray came back to life. I saw him hanging in the greenhouse dead. It's seems impossible that he could be alive."

"We ate mushrooms that I picked in a field west of Eugene," said Tai. "I didn't think they were that strong, but maybe they affected Ray differently. His fascination with this alien thing is plain crazy. I always thought he was a little quirky. Maybe the drugs tipped him over the edge." He glanced at Adrienne. "As to him coming back to life? I've read a lot about near-death experiences. I think that's what this is."

Yates took a deep breath. "Rain, what about you?"

Rain ran her hand through her hair. "I believe in the spirit world, officer. What happened during our funeral ceremony was real to me, regardless of the mushrooms. I did see Gloria's spirit leave her body." She smiled. "That might qualify me for the nut house also. But that's what I believe. Regarding Ray, I think the experience unsettled him. He saw something outside his belief system. He thought it was aliens. I don't know how he survived the hanging, but when he woke up in the morgue, he had to have been badly scared and lost. I think that's what we're seeing in Ray now. He needs some time to pull himself together. Maybe he should get some counseling."

"I saw Gloria's spirit leave her body also," said Janice. "And I believe it was real. I'm with Rain. I think it was too much for Ray. He blew a circuit rather than accept the spirit world."

Adrienne was last. She was struggling emotionally with the comments that had been made about Ray. "Officer, all I know is Ray was a really good man when I met him in September. Something happened to him and I can't explain it. Maybe it was the drugs. I don't know. But it's the bombings that I do know about." She looked around at the others, then right at Yates. "Something came up last night when he returned. Because of what you'd said about the page torn from the encyclopedia, we asked Ray about it."

Yates leaned forward.

"He said he found it cleaning one of Jack Spikes' rentals. I believe you know Jack."

Yates nodded.

"Ray kept it because of what was on the other side, the article about moles. It was for me. I'm the lead gardener here, and we have an ongoing mole problem. He didn't even notice what was on the other side and neither did I."

"Did he say where he found the piece of paper?"

"Some place where a biker lived. Mike somebody."

Yates knew immediately that this was a lead he needed to chase down, but he kept that to himself. He just nodded his head and told them he was satisfied with their comments. He advised them not to eat anymore mushrooms, and if they had any, they'd be wise to get rid of them before the FBI showed up. "They won't be as understanding as I am."

Rain escorted Yates to the door. He looked into her eyes while standing on the porch. He felt a tiny throb in his chest. He knew that Rain would never go for him. He still wanted to ask her out when this was over—*even if she did believe in ghosts and eat magic mushrooms!* But right now, he needed to focus on Mike Rogers.

Rain came back into the house and closed the door. She thought a moment about all that had happened, then returned to the dining room. Crow had come in and taken the seat where Yates had been.

Adrienne whistled. "Boy, Officer Yates sure has an eye for you, Rain."

"He's been very generous to us." Rain had grown to respect Yates for his openness to all of them.

"I think you're the reason why," said Marsha.

"Offer him a roll in the hay, and he'd probably let Ray out of jail."

Rain gave Tai the finger and flopped into her chair. She stared down at the table to gather her wits, then recounted Yates' visit to Crow.

"Basically, we lied," she concluded. "We said Ray was nuts and denied any existence of aliens."

"And what will Ray think when they tell him that?"

"That we betrayed him," said Adrienne.

"You know, folks, this might not be a good place for me to be any longer," said Crow uneasily.

"Van and I also talked about leaving," admitted Marsha.

"Except for Crow," said Rain, "I think we'd be wise to stay around until the FBI solves this bombing. They know our names and our best hope is to cooperate."

"And if they ask," said Janice, "what do we say about the possession?"

"Let's stick to denying it as long possible," said Tai. "No one would believe us anyway."

Van looked around the table. "So, what do we do now?"

No one had an answer. After a long silence, Adrienne stood up from the table. "I'm going downtown. I want to talk to Ray. I need to know if he's okay."

"They usually have visitors' hours," called out Tai, as Adrienne took a hooded sweatshirt from the coat rack beside the door.

"I'll take my chances." The door slammed behind her.

Marsha spoke up. "Should someone go with her?"

"No, let's give her some space," said Crow. "She and Ray have some shit to work out. I hope she actually gets to talk to him."

Fifteen minutes later, the group was still hashing it out at the dining room table. Suddenly Tai stood up. "Was that footsteps on the front porch?"

Crow jumped up from the table and ran to the back door. Agent Bascomb came through the front door and into the dining room as Agent Franklin led Crow in from the kitchen—followed by the chicken.

CHAPTER 108

Tim spent two hours in the library but didn't find anything helpful about Walt Arnold. On his way back to the print shop, he saw a bicycle coming in his direction with a rider who looked just like him. He pulled the big Indian over to the curb.

"Like them shoes," joked Tim, as Pat Riley rolled up.

"Just following your orders, boss. You told me to ride around in this crazy get up."

"Well, I appreciate that. But you don't have to do it anymore. The undercover agents got uncovered last night."

"Good. You don't know how many times I've been offered marijuana riding around in this outfit."

"Hope you didn't turn it down."

"Of course, I did. I don't smoke that shit."

"Damn," chuckled Tim, "you're going to ruin my reputation around here."

"No, I think it's my reputation that's in trouble."

"What do you mean?"

"I've decided to give up the co-op."

"No way. It's the best one in Eugene."

"But I've been making it work by covering the shortages with my own money."

"Really?"

"You know how it goes. All the co-ops run on a shoe string. I just stretched it out too far. Laura gave me an ultimatum last week. It's either her or the co-op."

"Damn. Can you find someone else to run it? Maybe you and Laura could just be members."

"Well, yeah, if I can find someone to take over for me. But there's no one crazy enough to put in the hours I do."

356

"Bummer. Can't you change the business model or something?"

"I've been trying for the last three weeks. Everything I come up with involves so much change, no one could do it but me. Mostly Laura wants our house back—and she wants a family." Pat looked down the street, then back at Tim. "That means finding someone who can use their own house and start from scratch. It's over. I feel like I've failed the community."

"Come on. You've done more than anyone in Eugene to get the co-ops up and running. Don't get down on yourself. Something will come up."

"Maybe Laura will get pregnant." Pat glimmered a weak smile.

Tim's citizen band radio squawked. He keyed the mike. "Breaker, one-three, Buzz Aldrin here. Over."

"Got a call from Gino, Buzz."

"I'm a couple blocks away. Let's talk when I get there."

Pat watched him replace the mike. "What's going on?"

"Long story. Hey, do you know who Walt Arnold is?"

"Yeah, he's owns a big mill and a bigger logging operation. Might be the richest guy in Lane County."

"You know anything about him?"

"More than I'd like. I think about trees almost as much as I think about food. I've gone to some of the recent logging conferences organized by the state. They usually get a good mix of people trying to protect the trees and folks like Arnold who want to cut them down. Yeah, I know him."

"Can you imagine a guy like him wanting to blow up a building at the U of O?"

"Not at all. He's gung-ho for the war and has no grudge against the university that I know of." He chuckled. "Unless he wants to prevent the Olympic Trials from coming to Eugene?"

"Olympic Trials?"

"Yeah, it's been in the paper a couple of times. Eugene is trying to get the Olympic Track and Field Trials for the summer of 1972. It's a big deal to the businessmen and developers. They believe it'll bring a lot of money into Eugene. The rumor I heard was another bomb or two and Eugene would be out of the running."

"That's interesting, but I don't see the connection to Arnold. He must want the Trials like every other big roller."

"Unless he doesn't want the attention the Trials would bring to his operations in the forest. He's become sensitive to criticism of the timber industry and changing attitudes about logging practices. A more cosmopolitan Eugene would bring more attention to the sins of clear cutting and over-harvesting."

"Seems unlikely. I'll have to think a little more about that. But I've got to get going." He grinned. "And don't forget, I want those shoes back."

"Gladly."

"Don't get down on yourself, Pat. You've done too much for this town already."

"Yeah, now it's time to focus on Laura. She deserves it."

Tim was at the print shop five minutes later. Jeannie caught him as he unlocked the door.

"Gino says Mike is at the Alibi Club. He'll keep in touch through the phone."

"Damn, I wish I'd talked to him. Was he at the Aroma Coffee Shop?"

"That's what he said."

"I hope he's careful. Mike could be dangerous if he thought he were being followed. How often does Gino call in?"

"That was his only call."

"I'll be in the shop. Next time come get me. I want to talk to him."

CHAPTER 109

Rain and the others at Blake College had convinced Yates that Ray might be badly confused or emotionally disturbed, but that he was not the bomber. And if Ray had found the encyclopedia page in the house at First and Madison, Yates figured the man of the hour was Mike Rogers. Upon leaving Blake College, he drove straight to Twelfth and Jefferson. Spikes' utility truck was parked at the curb. Yates walked into the house and yelled for Jack. Spikes yelled back from beneath the house. He and Henry were attaching the main plumbing lines.

Yates met Spikes at the entry to the crawl space. Spikes slithered out of the opening, filthy from crawling around beneath the house. "What's the latest on my boy Ray?"

"He's in a cell downtown. The FBI thinks he's the bomber."

"You're kidding. Do you believe that?"

"No, but Ray didn't help his case. He told them he had been possessed by an entity from another planet."

"Another planet?"

Yates told him the whole story.

"Jesus Christ, I thought a lot of that kid. You think it was a bad drug trip?"

"Must have been."

Spikes shook his head. "Is that why you're here?"

"No. What do you know about your one-time renter Mike Rogers? I'd like to talk to him."

"I don't know him any better than you do. He's a vet and part of the Gypsy Jokers anti-war clan. Pretty sure he's a junkie."

"Did he leave a forwarding address?"

"No."

"Did he have a job?"

"I doubt it. But his girlfriend Karen did."

"Where?"

"I might have it here." Spikes led Yates over to his pickup. He dug into the trash on the passenger's side of the cab. He pulled a coffee-stained sheet of paper out of the mess. "Here it is. The original rent agreement." He handed it to Yates.

"I like your filing system."

"Fuck you. I found the damn thing didn't I."

Yates quickly read through the application. "Here it is. She works at Burch's Shoe Store downtown. I guess that's my next stop." He returned the piece of paper to Spikes.

Spikes dropped it back into the heap of trash in the cab. "What do you want Rogers for?"

"According to Ray, he found that encyclopedia page in your rental at First and Madison. I'd like to ask Mike about it."

"You think he's the bomber?"

"I'll know more after I talk to him."

"And that would get Ray off the hook?"

"But still leave him on distant planet far, far away."

CHAPTER 110

Bascomb and Franklin checked everyone's ID. Tai only showed them his driver's license. Rain covered for Janice, and Crow got busted. Bascomb immediately called the Eugene Police Department, asking them to run a background check. It didn't take long. Crow's real name was Cliff Walker. As Crow had told Gloria and Rain, he'd killed a man in a car accident in Illinois. He had served ten years for manslaughter, then the year after his release, he'd skipped out on his parole officer. He had been on the lam ever since. Franklin handcuffed Crow who would be held in the Eugene jail before being shipped back to Illinois.

Bascomb had everyone sit at the table as he paced around the room asking questions. Franklin leaned against the kitchen doorjamb with a pad of paper and took notes.

"Ray Harper, the man who had been thought to be dead, was apprehended earlier today," began Bascomb. "We spoke to him at length."

Rain interrupted. "Officer Yates was here before you arrived. He told us what has happened." Her voice was calm and respectful.

"Yates was already here?"

"He was."

"What did you tell him about Harper?"

"That we knew he was alive," Rain looked around at the others, "and that he claimed to be possessed by an alien of some sort."

"He told us that this thing had possessed all of you."

"He told us that, too."

"He also claimed the animals were affected as well."

Van chuckled.

"I wish it were funny, Mr. Hammond. This is serious. We believe that crazy or not Ray Harper was involved in the campus bombings. He will be seeing a psychiatrist tomorrow. But I'm here now because I need to know if he got help from any of you."

"Ray Harper told us that you had a ceremony out here involving drugs," added Franklin. "Is this some kind of cult you've got going?"

Rain sighed. "No, nothing of the kind. We run a school here. We call it Blake College. When Gloria, our yoga teacher, was diagnosed with terminal cancer, we decided to focus all of our efforts on helping her through her last days."

"And that involved hallucinogenic drugs?"

"Local mushrooms, Mr. FBI," said Tai. "It's not like we were using LSD or anything like that. This stuff was natural, organic, and legal."

"We were trying to recreate a Buddhist Funeral," said Rain.

Bascomb's glance to Franklin was fraught: *How fucking nuts are these kids?*

"I think we should take them all downtown," said Franklin. "The drug use alone makes them suspicious, and I'm not so sure these local mushrooms are legal. There have been some recent law changes—hey—hey!"

Moxie stood beside him, leg uplifted, pissing on his pant leg. Franklin abruptly kicked Moxie aside. Janice screamed. The two foxes in her lap went for Franklin's ankles. Trying to dance away from the little critters, he stumbled and fell backwards onto the kitchen floor. At the same time, the spider on the ceiling dropped down on a thread of silk and dangled in front of Bascomb. When he swung at the spider to bat it away, the chicken that had roosted on the windowsill went straight for his face. Bascomb barely got his hands up in time to fend off the beating wings and slashing talons. As he backed up fighting off the chicken, Lena wound through his legs, causing him to also fall to the floor.

Crow didn't hesitate. He lifted the dining room window sash and dove out. He did a forward roll when he hit the ground and ran off as fast as he could. By the time Rain and Marsha had corralled the animals, Crow was out of sight, long gone, like a turkey through the straw.

CHAPTER 111

Adrienne had been lucky. She arrived at the jail thirty minutes before visiting hours began at five. She filled out a form and requested an opportunity to talk to Ray. When the time came, she was escorted into a room with ten double-sided booths, each separated by a wire-mesh window and connected by a direct phone line. Ray, in an orange jumpsuit, was seated in one of the booths. He lit up upon seeing her. Adrienne's response was more muted—even though it was invisible, she couldn't help imagining the blue manta hovering over his head.

"Thank you for coming to see me, Adrienne," said Ray through the phone, smiling at the young woman whom he still loved.

"I had to Ray. I know I've been distant, but I think you understand why. The image of you hanging in the greenhouse causes knots in my stomach whenever I think about it. You scared me badly, and for a while I hated you for it. But not anymore. I know it's more complicated than that. Mostly I needed to know, as a friend, if you're all right."

"There's nothing to worry about, Adrienne. I'm fine."

"But the FBI thinks you're the bomber."

"And they are mistaken."

"Do you have a lawyer?"

"Yes. My parents are in town, and they have enlisted the help of a lawyer—and a psychiatrist."

"Because of the attempted suicide?"

"Because I told them the truth. That I share consciousness with an alien entity."

Adrienne nodded slowly. "And they think you're crazy?"

"Or I've had my brain scrambled by a psychedelic trip."

"Who am I talking to now? Ray Harper or those mantas?"

"That's not so easy to answer. After seeing my parents, and now you, I'm certain that I'm still the same person with the same feelings I've always had. But I've also been learning more about this thing or things I'm sharing my mind with." He looked around at the other inmates talking to their visitors. "I'm learning to work with them."

"What do you mean?"

"I'm beginning to believe the mantas are a good thing, and they might even help get this whole mess straightened out."

"They think you're crazy, Ray. And that you're the bomber. You're in deep trouble—and maybe the rest of us are too."

"But I can help with that."

Adrienne was at a loss. "How?"

"If, in fact, what contacted us was the collective consciousness of the entire flock—and more and more I believe that's true—that means several hundred of them unified as a single psyche. That's a much more subtle and potent thing than just a single entity. Do you understand what I'm saying?"

"Kind of. But how does that change anything or help us?"

"I'll come visit you tonight at the house and show you."

"Are you getting out on bail?"

"No bail. I'm considered unstable."

"No doubt."

"Trust me. I'll come to you."

"You mean in a dream or telepathically?"

"No, in person. Just wait and see."

Adrienne rolled her eyes, then forced a smile. The inmate next to Ray got up and left the visitor's room.

"Our time is running out, Adrienne. Don't be frightened when you see me."

Adrienne kissed two fingers on her right hand and pressed them against the glass between them, then stood and walked out.

CHAPTER 112

Yates went to Burch's Shoe Store in downtown Eugene. He was still in uniform. He walked around the store looking at the shoes that were on display, then took a seat as though he were going to buy a pair. Karen didn't recognize him from the incident at First and Madison and approached him as she would any customer.

"Is there a shoe you'd like to try on, officer?"

Yates looked the woman in the eye, trying to evaluate her. She was attractive but had a lot of makeup on and was packed into a rather tight skirt. "No. I wanted to talk to you. Can we talk right here?"

"Here?"

"Otherwise we go downtown."

Karen looked around to see who else was in the front of the store. The other salesperson, a middle-age woman, was helping another customer

"Sit down," said Yates. "Grab one of those sizing devices. Act like you're selling me shoes."

"Okay. Let's make it quick if we can."

"That will depend on you."

"This is about Mike, isn't it?"

"Where is he right now?"

"Mike scares me. He can get angry."

"Where is he?"

"He'll hurt me."

"Then report it. Where is he?"

"He'll know it was me if I tell you."

"Do you want to go downtown?"

Across the store the other salesperson went into the back. Karen fidgeted with the shoe scale and dropped it. She picked it up and looked straight at Yates. "There's a little cabin at the back of the Christmas tree

365

farm off Route 45. There's a big sign. Take the gravel driveway to the end. You'll see the cabin. That's where we've been staying. His uncle owns the place." She looked around. "What'd he do?"

Yates hesitated. "Did he ever talk about dynamite or firebombs?"

"Not to me."

"Ever see him looking at a page torn out of an encyclopedia?"

"Encyclopedia? I don't think he could even pronounce the word."

"Will he be out at the cabin now?"

"I have no idea. But what am I to do? Where do I go?"

"Get a hotel room in town." He handed her his card. "Call me when you've got a place. I'll have the police department pay for it."

Karen looked at the card, then up at Yates. "I'm scared."

"Trust me and everything will be fine."

It was dark when Yates pulled out of Burch's parking lot. He decided to go after Mike Rogers right away. He stopped at the police station to get Eldon. He told Eldon the story on the way out to the Christmas tree farm. Yates knew where it was. He'd seen the sign fifty times or more driving west on 45.

They motored up the driveway about half a mile before they saw the cabin in their headlights. No cars or motorcycles were in sight. Both officers got out of the car. They looked around briefly before knocking on the door. When no one answered, Yates tried the door. It was open. The place was a mess with pizza boxes, cigarette butts, liquor bottles, and beer cans. Clearly someone was living there in a temporary fashion. On closer inspection, Yates and Eldon found two syringes and a couple of roaches, but no explosives, no sign of bomb making.

"What do you want to do, Bob? Stay here until the guy comes back?"

Before Yates could answer, they heard a car coming up the driveway. They were outside when the headlights flashed across the cabin. The driver's side door swung open and Walt Arnold stepped out of his Land Rover. He'd met Yates before, but not Eldon. "What's going on up here? Yates, I believe. That right?"

"Yes, that's right, Mr. Arnold. This my partner Eldon Taylor. We're looking for someone. What brings you up here?"

"I own this place. My foreman saw your cruiser and gave me a call. I thought I should see what's going on."

"Do you know Mike Rogers?"

Arnold nodded. He was a large man, not used to kowtowing to anyone—even the police. "Unfortunately, he's my nephew. I let him stay here for a while to recover from a wound he received in a gang fight."

"Will he be back here tonight?" asked Yates, struggling to read the other man.

"Who knows? The guy's a mess. Drugs, everything. I told him I wanted him out of here three weeks ago. Out of Oregon would be even better."

"I need to talk to him before he goes anywhere. Can you let me know when he comes back?" He handed Walt his card. "Maybe give me a call."

"I can't see the cabin from my place and my foreman's about to leave for the day. What is it? More trouble with the Gypsy Jokers?"

"A couple of bombings at the university." Yates noted that this seemed to surprise Walt.

"Well, yeah, sure, everybody knows he's been a little crazy since coming back from Vietnam. You really think it was the Jokers?"

"Maybe just Mike. That's why I need to talk to him."

"If I see him, I'll call."

"Thanks, Mr. Arnold. I hope this doesn't make any trouble for you."

Walt tipped his head. "The kid's been trouble for a long time. And everyone knows it."

"Well, don't be surprised if we come back."

"Do whatever you feel is necessary."

Walt watched the squad car taillights disappear down the driveway before he got into his Land Rover. He'd decided to call the Alibi Club when he got back to his house.

Yates wanted more immediate notice if Mike returned to the cabin. As he eased out onto route 45 from the driveway, he noticed a lit farmhouse on the hill across the road. He powered the cruiser up Maynard Smith's driveway and knocked on the door.

Nearly a minute passed before the door opened. Maynard appraised his visitors in blue uniforms. "What can I do for you boys?"

"Officers Yates and Taylor, sir. I have a favor to ask."

"What's that?"

"Judging by the position of your living room window, I'm guessing you can see if anyone goes up that driveway across the way—the one that leads to the Christmas tree farm."

Maynard nodded. "That's right."

Yates handed him his card. "Would you mind giving the Eugene Police Department a call if you see a motorcycle turn in that driveway?"

Maynard looked at the card. "This about that boy Mike?"

"It is. What do you know about him?"

"I don't like him around."

Across Route 45, Walt was at home on the phone with his nephew.

"What do you want, Unk?" Mike stood behind the bar at the Alibi Club.

"The police were just out at the cabin. They're gone now, but they're on to you. Do it tonight. And then get out of town."

"What do you mean tonight?"

"I mean tonight—now! I spoke with two police officers. They want to ask you about the bombings. I paid you ahead time. So do it and get lost. Fast. Got it?"

"Yeah, Unk, I got it." Mike slammed the phone onto its cradle. "Fuck." He threw down what remained of his beer, then drew himself another from the tap.

CHAPTER 113

Tim got anxious waiting for Gino to call, so he called the Aroma Coffee Shop and asked for Gino.

"You still got an eye on Mike?" asked Tim when the clerk gave the phone to Gino.

Gino could see the Alibi Club through the window. "Yeah, he's been in the tavern about an hour now."

"I'm on my way. Don't go anywhere."

"Unless Mike takes off."

"Yeah, then follow him, but let me know. I'll be on the Indian. I'll park behind the coffee shop. If he leaves, we'll follow him in your panel truck. My Indian is too obvious. See you in fifteen minutes."

"Got it."

Gino was nowhere to be seen when Tim came in the back door of the coffee shop. He paced back and forth, then crossed the street and went into the Alibi Club. Neither Mike nor Gino were there. He ordered a beer then rolled a smoke. He lit the cigarette and went to the phone booth in the back. He called Jeannie. She picked it up on the first ring. "Heard from Gino, Jeannie?"

"No calls since you left."

"Shit. I've lost him. Stay by the phone. He'll call eventually." Tim hung up, then found a seat at the bar to drink and think. He knew Tiny was Mike's father. He took a chance. "Was Mike in here today?" he asked the rotund man behind the bar.

"What's it to you?"

"I'm the mechanic who put his Harley together. Just wanted to see how it's running."

Tiny picked his nose and looked to the front door. "He just left."

Tim bobbed his head. "Going back to Eugene?" It was a guess.

369

"Yeah, as far as I know." The man turned away to serve another customer.

Tim threw down the rest of his beer, jogged across the street and down the alley beside the coffee shop. He hopped on his Indian and hightailed it back to the print shop, hoping Gino would put in a call to Jeannie before he got there.

CHAPTER 114

Gino followed Mike through Springfield, then west across Eugene on Sixth Avenue, then north on Highway 99. A couple miles down 99, Mike pulled off the road into a fenced yard of storage units. Gino waited a quarter mile down the road. He pondered running into the Seven-Eleven across the street to call Tim, but before he could decide, Mike strode out of the storage facility carrying a red metal tool box. Mike strapped the box to his bike and fired her up. He continued north on 99 before turning left on route 45.

Gino had never secretly followed anyone before. Mike was riding a motorcycle; Gino was in 1948 Chevy panel truck that shook pretty good when it topped fifty miles an hour. Gino drove as fast as he dared, giving no thought to being seen, while Mike, high as a kite on meth, didn't look once in his rearview on the way to the Christmas tree farm. He turned up the driveway, spraying a rooster tail of gravel all the way to the cabin.

Gino pulled off the road and walked up the driveway until he saw Mike's Harley and a light on in the cabin. He crept up to a window and peered in over the sill. Mike stood, head down, at the kitchen counter with the tool box open beside him. He appeared to be working on some kind of mechanical device with a lot of wires.

This was exactly what Tim was worried about, but Gino had no way of reaching Tim. He decided to go back to his panel truck and wait for Mike's next move. As long as Mike remained in the cabin, he couldn't cause any trouble in town.

Meanwhile, Maynard Smith had already called the Eugene Police Department. He left a short message for Yates: *Mike Rogers is back at the cabin.*

Yates and Eldon were coming into headquarters when the switchboard operator told them of Smith's call. They returned to the squad car and headed back to where they had just come from.

CHAPTER 115

Back at Blake College, Bascomb charged everyone with aiding and abetting a criminal. They were all going to jail. Franklin took Van, Marsha, and Janice in the black sedan, and Bascomb rode with Rain in Tai's van, with Tai behind the wheel. They filed into the police station at six-thirty. Bascomb conferred with Wilkerson. He told him that Crow had escaped and that the others had been helping him hide. He said he was concerned that the whole group, including Crow, was a drug cult with anti-war leanings. They decided to book everyone and hold them in the Eugene jail.

Meanwhile, Gino sat anxiously in his panel truck, parked along route 45 with the headlights off. He rolled a joint and smoked it to relax. After he finished the joint and stashed the roach in the ashtray, he retrieved the squeaking red nose from his pocket and put it on. He was looking at himself in the rearview mirror, trying out funny faces, when he heard the crunch of gravel coming from behind his truck. He peered into the side view mirror. An older man in a cowboy hat and a fleece-lined jacket was walking up to the window.

Heavily stoned, Gino sat up and tried to focus. Maynard Smith tapped on the window. Gino cranked it open.

Smith peered in and appraised Gino and his red nose. "What are you doing out here, young man?" asked Smith, making the presence of his shotgun obvious.

"I had little engine trouble," lied Gino, pulling the clown nose off with a little squeak. "I thought I'd let the motor cool down a bit before limping this buggy into town."

"I live up on the hill over there." Smith pointed. "You've been here quite a while. You got anything to do with Mike Rogers?"

"No," said Gino. "Don't know the man."

"Well, from my angle it looked like you followed him here. And I already know the police are looking for him."

"Just a coincidence, sir. But, you know, I could use a favor."

Smith had smelled the pot right away and had no good use for pot smokers with rubber noses. "Yeah?" he growled.

"If you have a phone up there at your house, could you make a call for me?" Gino grabbed a pencil and a slip of paper from the glove compartment and began writing down the number at Tim's house. Before he finished, the sound of a large, powerful motorcycle made both men turn to the driveway entrance. Mike roared out of the driveway without the slightest hesitation, turned right on 45, rose up on his back wheel, burned rubber, and screeched back toward town.

Smith and Gino looked at each other.

"God damn, I hate that shit," cursed Smith way out of character.

"Yeah, me too," said Gino. He extended the piece of paper to the man and started the truck. "Call this number and tell whoever answers that Gino's coming into town on Seventh Avenue from Highway 99— and that I'll call when I reach town."

Smith frowned. "Why should I do this?"

Gino put the truck in gear. "You've got a problem with Mike Rogers, and so do I." Maynard stepped away from the truck as Gino let out the clutch.

"Hey! I thought you didn't know him," shouted Maynard, as Gino pulled onto the highway. "And had engine trouble."

"Call that number," yelled Gino out the window, as his single tail light vanished into the night.

Maynard had not been impressed by Gino but was more concerned about Mike Rogers leaving. He hiked back up to his house and called the police station. Then, for reasons he couldn't pin down, he also called the number Gino had given him.

Tim answered the phone. "That you, Gino?"

"No, but I just spoke to him. He's headed into Eugene on 99. He'll call you went he gets into town."

"Hey, thanks, mister. Where you calling from?"

Maynard wasn't sure he wanted say, but he did. "Out route 45. It'll be fifteen minutes before your friend reaches town."

"Got it. Thanks again."

CHAPTER 116

No one was at Blake College when Adrienne returned. She turned on the lights in the kitchen and the dining room, then filled a bowl with granola and sat down at the table with all the animals around her and the spider dangling from above. Several spoonfuls into her meal she heard the back door open. Moxie's ears went up, but he didn't growl or bark.

Crow peeked around the edge of the kitchen doorjamb. "Anyone else here?"

"No, I just walked in. Where are the others?"

Crow showed her the handcuffs, then related the story.

"The animals saved you?" Adrienne looked around the room at the whole menagerie.

"That's what it seemed like. But everybody else is downtown in the custody of the FBI."

"You ought to get out of town quick."

"I know, but I fell for you guys. I don't want to leave." He paused and looked up at the spider. "And I'd like to get some resolution on this alien thing."

Adrienne told him about her visit with Ray. "We had a good visit, but I left wondering if I had been talking to Ray or those creatures." She closed her eyes and started to cry.

Crow did his best to console her, but it was all beyond him, too. "I shouldn't be in the house, Adrienne. Let's find some tools and get me out of these handcuffs. Then I'm going down to the teepee."

Thirty minutes later, Crow freed from the cuffs, Adrienne sat on the front porch steps with Moxie at her feet. She was trying not to cry. Moxie lifted his nose, then got up and ran out into the dark.

"Who's out there, Moxie?" whispered Adrienne into the darkness. She heard footsteps crunching down the driveway. She saw a man's silhouette and Moxie alongside. Adrienne stood up. "Ray!" Although invisible, in her mind's eye the blue manta floated over his head, tentacles and all. Adrienne took two hesitant steps off the porch, then rushed out to meet him. "How'd you get out?"

"I told the guard I had a date with the most beautiful woman in the world." Ray wore an orange jumpsuit. "What could he do but give me a pass for the evening?"

"Did your parents pay the bail or something?"

"No," said Ray, as he led Adrienne around the house, down to the river. "I want to prove to you that what found us the night Gloria died—the collective psyche of those mantas—is not a bad thing, but, in fact, is a good thing. It's given me tremendous psychic power that I'm still learning how to use."

Adrienne stopped walking.

"Well, wouldn't you expect that from someone who's been possessed by aliens?" Ray laughed. "It or they can move from one consciousness to another as easily as extending a tentacle. That's why the jailer let me out. I got into his head."

"You can get into the mind of anyone?"

"The mantas' collective consciousness can, and it takes me along for the ride. I don't know what it means or how it works, but they allow me to see into people's thoughts. Sometimes the thoughts are too confusing to understand. Sometimes they're focused, and I can read them."

"I don't like it."

"It's nothing to be frightened of, Adrienne. That's what I came here to tell you. These mantas hum when they're pleased—kind of like a cat purring—and as a way of communicating. In fact, I think it was our chanting that drew them to us in the first place."

"Like a language they recognized?"

"More or less. And when they get into another mind, if the situation is right, they purr very softly—as an offering of some sort. It creates a bliss state in the individual."

"And then the person will do whatever you ask them to?"

"They feel too good to care. That's how I got out of jail. I hope to use these powers to straighten everything out—all the confusion and misunderstandings."

"How?"

"I don't know yet. First I have to prove I'm not crazy!" He laughed wildly. "Come on, let's sit by the river. Mostly I wanted to spend some time with you."

"Just stay out of my head." Adrienne reluctantly accepted his hand, and they continued down to the river to sit on the bank. A full moon lit up the river like the surface of a wavy mirror.

"Don't be afraid, Adrienne. That's my main point. The mantas are showing you and me and the others the extent of our psychic mind. They seem very wise to me, almost Zen-like."

"But the possession was why you committed suicide."

"Only because I didn't understand what was happening until I died. Then they brought me back to life, which suggests to me they might have some capacity for healing. That has to be a good thing, right?"

Adrienne looked out at the river, then back to Ray. "Yeah, but it sure has made things complicated."

"Trust me. I will uncomplicate everything."

Adrienne finally gave in and laughed. "Either you are completely out of your mind Ray Harper or you're truly something special."

"No, it's the mantas—they're truly something special."

CHAPTER 117

As Yates and Taylor turned left off Highway 99 onto route 45, headed back to the Christmas tree farm, the police radio announced the disappearance of inmate Ray Harper.

"What?" screamed Yates. "That can't be!"

"That's one slippery dude, Bob. I'm glad we're only chasing a damn Gypsy Joker. Not a fricking alien."

"No shit," said Yates, then he laughed. "How crazy can it be?"

A few minutes later, Maynard Smith's message came in from headquarters: *Mike Rogers has left the Christmas tree farm.* Ten seconds after that a motorcycle came out of the next curve and sped past them going the other way into town.

"That's Rogers!"

Yates pulled the cruiser off the road to the right as far he could, then turned hard left into a U-turn—as Gino's panel truck came chugging around the curve. Yates saw the truck at the last second and pulled off the road into the drainage ditch. Gino saw it was the cops and just sped by stoned as a meadow lark.

While Yates spun his wheels trying to get out of the ditch, Gino raced after Mike Rogers, steadily losing ground to the speeding motorcycle. By the time Gino reached the edge of Eugene, he had no idea where Rogers had gone. He pulled into a gas station and called Jeannie at the house. "Tell Tim I found Mike at the Christmas tree farm out route 45. I think he was making a bomb. I chased him back into town, then lost him where ninety-nine turns into Seventh Avenue."

CHAPTER 118

Tim, responding to Maynard Smith's phone call, was already headed west out of town. He got Gino's message from Jeannie while sitting at a stoplight on Sixth Avenue. With his bike throttled down to talk on the CB, he heard another motorcycle coming from the west. He saw Mike's KHK speed through the intersection a block south on Seventh. Tim gunned the Indian, made a quick left, and then another onto Seventh. Mike was a block and a half ahead of him going east.

Two blocks behind Tim was Yates, who had powered his cruiser out of the ditch and driven into town at a hundred miles an hour. He saw Tim's bike from a distance and thought it was Rogers. Instead of pulling him over, Yates slowed down in order to follow him without being seen.

At Chambers Street, Mike turned right, headed south. At Thirteenth, he took a left and continued east six blocks to the open field where Ray and Spikes had dismantled the Quonset huts. Because of Gino's message, Tim figured it out immediately. Mike's target was the armory. Heavy security had been installed day and night at the university since the bombing of Johnson Hall. The armory on the west side of town was not guarded at all, but it was clearly an anti-war target.

Tim watched Mike pull off the road into the empty lot and come to a stop. Tim cut his motor and coasted up to the curb a few blocks short of the armory. Behind him, Yates and Taylor did the same.

The full moon lit the grassy field a luminous gray. Tim could see Mike's silhouette as he lumbered across the field to the big brick building. Tim followed, skirting through the shadows at the edge of the field—with Yates racing after him as quietly as he could and Eldon bringing up the rear.

There were no floodlights around the building. The only exterior lights were single bulbs, one above the front door and one above the side door that opened onto the parking lot. Tim saw Mike crouch down behind the building, presumably to set up his bomb. Clearly, it was too late for Tim to call the cops. He had to intervene, and it had to be now. He decided to use his natural charm. He walked out of the shadows directly toward the building. From about ten feet, he quietly asked, "What's going on, Mike?"

Mike popped to his feet like a jack in the box. "Fuck! O'Malley, you scared the shit out of me. What are you doing here?"

"I saw your bike breeze through town. I was on the Indian. I was trying to catch up with you. What have you got there?" He knelt down and looked at the device Mike was working on.

"That looks like a bomb to me," said Yates, coming up from behind. He pointed his revolver at Tim and Mike. "Hands in the air. Step away from the building."

Mike knew instantly that being caught now would link him to the other bombings and Stoopid's death. Instead of raising his hands, the amped up biker tried to slap the gun out of Yates' hand. Yates shot him twice in the chest. Mike fell to the ground at Tim's feet, tried to talk, but burped up blood.

Eldon appeared out of the shadows. He looked down at Mike Rogers and shook his head. "I saw it, Bob. He went for your gun."

Yates nodded at Tim. "Handcuff this man."

"But I was here to stop him, officer."

"Cuff him," repeated Yates.

As Eldon slapped the cuffs on Tim, Yates knelt to inspect the contraption on the ground. He stood up and backed away. "Eldon, put that guy in the squad car and get on the radio fast. We need an ambulance and an explosives expert as soon as possible."

CHAPTER 119

Ray leaned up close to Adrienne's face with his lips puckered. Adrienne looked him in the eye. "I'm thinking of kissing you, Ray Harper. Is that me or are you using the creatures to soften me up?"

Ray backed off, holding up his hands and wiggling his fingers as though they were tentacles. "All you. I promise."

Adrienne smiled with all her youthful beauty. "Good." She kissed him on the lips. He embraced her. They lay down on the ground and gave in completely to the physical forces that had once so deeply connected them. Afterward they walked back to the house. Instead of going in, Ray asked Adrienne to drive him back to the jail.

"But why?"

"I can't be with you as an escaped convict. I've got to get back to my jail cell and act like I never left."

Adrienne made a face. "You can do that?"

He nodded, then asked, "Do you still like me?"

She looked up to the heavens in mock exasperation. "Do you think I would have gotten naked with you just now if I didn't?" She grinned, then shook her head. "I don't know what's going on, but none of this makes sense if I can't trust a guy who can read my mind. Come on, I'll take you back to town."

They climbed into Adrienne's pickup. Ten cranks on the starter got it going. Adrienne dropped him off a few blocks from the jail. He kissed her and made her promise to visit him the next day.

"What about the charges against you for the bombing?" asked Adrienne before he left.

"I'm not worried. You were with me. It's nonsense. They'll find the right guy—then all I'll have to do is deal with a psychiatrist."

Adrienne laughed. "That should be interesting—especially if you can read his mind."

381

Ray walked to the jail. He entered the building in his orange jumpsuit and should have been arrested immediately. And yet with the help of the mantas' powers, Ray walked past the officer at the desk, who simply smiled blissfully, then past the attendant at the door to cell block two, who did the same. No one said a word or would remember what had happened. Ray entered the first cell he came to that was vacant, slid the door shut, and lay down on the bunk as though he had never left.

CHAPTER 120

Bascomb and Wilkerson had a screaming, knockdown argument at police headquarters about Ray's disappearance. When the two men calmed down, Wilkerson drove Bascomb to the city jail to talk to the attendants. Upon entering the building, they asked to see the man in charge of the cell block where Ray Harper had been held. They were directed to the back of the building.

The attendant met them at the door to cell block two. "I must have made a mistake," he said as soon as he saw Wilkerson.

"I would say so. You lost our main suspect in the most important case we've had in years."

"No, sir. I mean a mistake about the inmate's being missing. I just went back there. He's in a cell, but it's not the one in the books. There must have been a transcription error."

Bascomb looked up at the ceiling.

Wilkerson appeared ready to explode. "Ray Harper is here—in a cell?"

"Yes, sir. It was my oversight and my error. But he's here. Nothing really happened."

The attendant took the two men into the cell block. Ray was asleep on his cell's bed. They didn't bother to rouse him.

As Wilkerson and Bascomb exited the building, Yates and Taylor were leading a handcuffed Tim O'Malley across the parking lot.

"Who's this?" asked Wilkerson.

"One of the radicals responsible for the bombings," said Eldon proudly.

Tim shook his head slowly in denial.

"One of them?" said Bascomb.

"I caught this man and his friend setting up a bomb at the armory on Thirteenth Avenue," said Yates. "His friend went for my gun."

Eldon nodded.

"I shot him twice," continued Yates. "He's at Sacred Heart Hospital in critical condition. They don't expect him to make it."

"What about Ray Harper?"

Yates took a deep breath. "He's not our man. He might be crazy as a loon, but I don't believe he had anything to do with the bombings. This guy and his friend are our men."

Wilkerson addressed Tim. "Is that true?"

"Ray had no part in any of it," said Tim. "But neither did I. It was the guy who got shot. He did all the bombings."

"Then what were you doing at the armory?" snapped Yates.

"I know Mike. You know that. I was there trying to stop him. I might be against the war, but I'm not for meaningless violence."

Wilkerson laughed. "Put him in a cell. No visitors." He looked at Bascomb. "We'll hold him, but this is your case. Do as you please."

"What about Harper?" asked Yates.

"Put bail at two hundred and fifty dollars. Have his parents pick him up. Tell them we'd like a psychiatric evaluation before they leave town."

Wilkerson and Bascomb walked off. Yates and Eldon led Tim into the jail. They put Tim in a cell by himself in block one, then woke up Ray in block two and told him they had caught the bombers—two bikers. "Wait in the reception room," said Yates. "Your parents will be here shortly."

Van and Tai were in a cell three doors down from Ray. They saw Yates and Eldon walking out. Tai called to them, "Officers, did I hear that you nabbed the bombers?"

Yates stopped. "What are you two doing in here?"

"The FBI came by our place right after you did. They questioned us about Ray and booked us. Rain's here too. Talk to her."

"I will, thanks."

Yates went to the front desk and looked through the daily log. Yes, Rain, Van, Tai, and two young women were being held for the FBI, but not for the bombing, for aiding a man who had broken parole. This made no sense to Yates, so he asked to see Rain. He was taken to the cell she shared with Marsha and Janice.

He took Rain to one of the interrogation rooms. He told Eldon he wanted to do this on his own. Eldon winked at him and told him he'd be at the front desk getting a cup of coffee.

After Yates told Rain that Ray had been cleared of the bombings and released to his parents, he asked her about the FBI's visit to Blake College. "Who was this man Cliff Walker? We never saw him there."

"He was part of the school. We knew he had a record, but not that he had broken parole. He always left when your patrol car pulled up."

"And you didn't think that was suspicious?"

"He was our friend. We gave him the benefit of the doubt."

"But Bascomb also thought you might have been helping Ray."

"Only because we were worried about his mental state, nothing more. He didn't do the bombing. You know that now."

"But you helped this man Walker get away."

Rain pushed her hair behind her ear. "No, not really. It was the dog and the chicken."

Yates gathered himself. "The animals that had been possessed by the alien."

"If you believe Ray."

Yates looked up at the ceiling, then nodded slowly. "Right."

Rain smiled through it. "You've been awfully nice to us so far, Officer Yates, but is there any way you could convince them we don't need to be in jail? We had nothing to do with the bombing, and Cliff Walker was just a traveler in Eugene who happened by Blake College."

Rain's poise had impressed Yates from the first time he'd met her. Even after all the craziness at Blake College, he still trusted her and felt she was the kind of woman he wanted know. "I'll call Bascomb and see what I can do. No guarantees. But the FBI owes me one."

"Any way you can help, Bob." She deliberately used his first name.

Yates didn't miss it. "I'll call him now."

Thirty minutes later, Yates had them all released. He got the keys to Tai's van and walked them out to the parking lot. Rain was the last one to get in the van. "Thank you, Bob." She placed her palms together and bowed to him. "You were more than kind." Then she smiled. "I guess I owe you one now."

Yates closed the van door after Rain climbed in. He watched them drive off, but as he walked back to the jail, he felt a tingling all the way down to his toes. When this was over, he was going to ask her out and she would say yes.

CHAPTER 121

The story of the attempted bombing was in the morning paper. That Tim was in jail for the crime ran through the alternative community like spilled quicksilver. Tim was not allowed visitors, so Gino went to Rebop to tell her that Tim had tried to stop the bombing and was simply a victim of bad timing. Rebop called Rain and asked her to meet her at the SDS office at the university. She wanted to powwow with Dave and Sue.

Only Dave was there when Rain and Rebop squeezed into the tiny closet-size office. Rebop related her conversation with Gino to Rain and Dave. "Gino knows that no one will listen to him, and he's afraid to go forward because of his previous run-ins with the FBI. I'm sure they won't listen to me or either of you, so Mike Rogers is the only person who can clear Tim. But he's in a coma in critical condition. If he dies, Tim will have a hard time getting out of this."

"Damn," said Dave. "We've got to help Tim somehow. He's the glue that keeps this community together. What should we do?"

"I don't know," said Rain. "Pray that Mike Rogers doesn't die."

"I don't believe in God," said Dave.

"Neither do I," said Rebop, "but do it anyway."

Les Anderson put in a call to Bill Bowerman from City Hall. Bill's wife Barbara answered the phone. Bill was working on a pair of shoes in the garage.

"I take it you saw the paper this morning, Bill."

"Oh, yeah, great news. It's going to make my job a lot easier if I can tell the committee that the culprits have been locked up."

"No kidding. I talked to Clark at the university a little while ago. He's been under a lot of pressure. This will help him with the trustees."

"I think he's been too easy on these war protesters. I would have done it quite differently."

"Well, let's just hope this is the end of it."

"With Nixon starting to pull troops, I think the worst is over."

"How about your new shoe design? Making any progress?"

"Little by little. Our goal is to get a couple competitors wearing them in the Trials. And I think we have a good chance at that—especially if the Trials are here in Eugene."

"Fantastic. Let me know when they formally announce the committee."

"Oh, I will, believe me. No one's more excited about the Trials than I am."

CHAPTER 122

While the rest of Eugene, not counting Tim's friends, were talking excitedly about the capture of the bombers, Walt Arnold was in his office stewing, hoping to hell that Mike would never come out of his coma. As far as he knew, no one had connected him to Mike or the bombings. He didn't know the other biker who had been arrested, but he had given Mike specific instructions to never mention his name. Could he trust Mike? He wasn't sure. Still, he felt that as long as Mike remained in a coma, he'd be fine—but he'd surely breathe a lot easier if his nephew simply died.

CHAPTER 123

Ray's parents were staying at the Hilton in downtown Eugene. They got a second room for Ray to share with his father. His mother slept in a connecting room. When they got up in the morning, they ate breakfast together in the hotel dining room. At eleven-thirty they would sit down with a local psychiatrist for an introductory consultation. No one said anything during breakfast about aliens or Ray's sanity. His mother asked about the girl he had been seeing, and his father asked him about work. Ray revealed little to his mother about Adrienne other than her name but talk of work perked him up. He told his father that he would like to introduce him to Jack Spikes and show him the house they had moved. Vera had little interest in meeting Spikes, but Forest, the architect, thought it sounded interesting. It was only nine-thirty. They had two hours to kill, so Ray and his father drove to the work site.

On the ride to Twelfth and Jefferson, Ray did all the talking, going on about the things he'd learned working for Spikes and how he would like to do the same kind of work for a living. This was not what Forest had initially imagined for his son, but with the visit to the psychiatrist pending, he just hoped his son's future included a job of any kind.

Spikes had rented the Bobcat again and was pushing dirt around the lot, filling in the excavation around the new foundation, when Ray and his father pulled up in a rental car. He saw Ray get out on the passenger's side and immediately cut the Bobcat's engine. He assumed the other man was law enforcement and was glad when Ray introduced him as his father.

"Nice to meet you, Forest," said Spikes, with lots of questions banging around in his head.

"Yes, it's a pleasure for me, too," said Forest, at a time when pleasure was the last thing on his mind. "Ray gave me a blow by blow description of moving this house. Mighty impressive."

"Now all I have to do is get it ready for renters—two more months of work." Spikes walked them through the house and told Forest about the changes he planned to make. When they went outside, their conversation stalled. Spikes, still brimming with questions, looked at Ray. "So, what happened, uh, with the stuff downtown?"

"You meant with the FBI?"

Spikes glanced at Forest. "Yeah. What happened after those guys picked you up?"

"Well, they had it all wrong." He explained the issue with the page from the encyclopedia.

"Yeah, Yates told me that cracked the case. I'm sure you saw it in the paper this morning."

"I haven't seen the paper," said Ray. "But I saw Yates last night after he made the arrest. That's why I'm out now. They caught two bikers—and one was Mike Rogers."

"The other guy was that crazy printer with the red shoes and the Indian motorcycle."

"Tim O'Malley? No way," said Ray. "He wasn't part of it. They must have made a mistake."

"Read the paper. They caught him right there at the armory with Rogers, helping set up the bomb. Rogers got shot during the arrest. He's in a coma and likely to die."

"Wow! I was sitting next to Tim in Max's when Campbell Hall was bombed. A friend of his was killed in the blast. He was as mad about the bombing as the university was. Something's wrong here."

"I don't know anything about that. What are you up to now?"

Forest decided to clear the air. "Meeting a psychiatrist."

Spikes nodded his head slowly.

"I did hang myself, Jack." Ray looked at the ground. "I had to explain that to your friend Bob and the FBI—and now I guess to you." Ray looked at his father, then back to Spikes. "No one likes my explanation, Jack. You won't either."

"Try me." Spikes had already heard the worse of it, but he wanted to hear it from Ray.

"I'd been possessed by an entity from another planet. It was driving me nuts, so I killed myself."

Spikes glanced at Forest. Forest lifted his eyebrows.

"But the thing brought me back to life and gave me telepathic powers. I can enter another person's consciousness." Forest rolled his eyes, Spikes' widened. "And read their thoughts."

Forest was now staring at the ground.

Spikes looked as though someone had hit him in the face with a two-by-four. "Really?"

"Want me to tell you what you're thinking?"

"Uh, no. I'll trust you on that."

But Ray had already read his mind. Jack's issue with Joey taking meds was front and center. He recalled Jack's conversation with Henry many weeks before about learning disabilities. It was obvious how much this was bothering Jack. Ray kept it to himself. "Sorry to trouble you with all this, Jack. I just hope we can find a psychiatrist with an open mind." His smile was a weak one. "Still willing to hire me?"

"Well, uh, sure, of course, I never ask anyone what religion they are before I hire them. So, believing in aliens should be no different, right?"

Forest lifted his head.

Ray opened up with a real smile. "Absolutely."

"We should let Jack get back to work, Ray," said Forest. "He looks like a busy man to me."

Ray agreed. "I'll come back when I can, Jack."

Spikes shook Forest's hand and started back to the Bobcat, then stopped. "Hey, Ray, if you have these telepathic powers." He grinned in his bold way. "Maybe you could get into Mike Rogers' head and pop him out of the coma. Might be a way to help your friend Tim—if he's really innocent."

Ray scrunched up his face in thought.

"Don't pop a blood vessel," laughed Spikes, drawing a chuckle out of Forest—and the finger, then a grin, from Ray.

CHAPTER 124

The meeting with the psychiatrist didn't go well. Vera and Forest didn't like him any more than Ray did. Afterward, they decided to find a place to eat. Vera continued to ask Ray about Adrienne and pressed him to invite her to lunch. Even having made love to Adrienne the night before, Ray knew his relationship with Adrienne was unclear. Introducing her to his parents seemed a little premature, but he decided to call her. He got Janice on the phone. She found Adrienne in the backyard. Adrienne surprised him by saying she'd like to meet his parents.

They met at the International House of Pancakes. It was Ray's suggestion. He knew Adrienne, for all her organic beliefs, had a weakness for waffles. Talk at first was stiff. The subject of Ray's sanity was studiously avoided by Vera who led the conversation. Adrienne was charming and managed to loosen things up. She talked about Blake College and her love of gardening. After the meal, Ray walked her out to her truck.

"What are you going to do, Ray? I'm worried about you."

"At least they don't think I was the bomber." Ray looked down at the ground. "But I still have to get past the psychiatrist." He lifted his eyes to Adrienne's. "I guess I could lie. I could say I made it all up or it was the drugs. I don't know. Does that make sense? You're in this with me and so are all the others."

"I just wish the mantas would leave."

"They've certainly changed the way I see things." Then Ray remembered his conversation with Jack. "Hey, what's this about Tim getting arrested? He didn't have anything to do with those bombings."

"I got the story from Rain. He was trying to stop that biker guy Mike when the cops showed up. Totally bad timing. The only person who can clear him is Mike, who's just as likely to die as come out of his coma.

We want to do something for Tim, but we don't know what to do. What about you, Ray? You said the mantas could help. Now would be a really good time."

Ray recalled Jack's comment about getting into Mike Roger's head. "Yeah, maybe I could do something. I'm not sure. But for now, I've got to stay with my parents until the psychiatrist clears me—or puts me in a mental hospital." He grimaced. "That complicates things."

"You said you could fix things." Adrienne gave him a hug then climbed into her truck and leaned out the window. "This would be a good way to prove it." She grinned when the motor caught on the first try, then threw Ray a kiss as she motored out of the parking lot.

CHAPTER 125

Agents Bascomb and Franklin had spent the morning at the jail in an interrogation room, trying to break Tim. Tim told them everything he knew, including that he thought Walt Arnold was involved. Neither FBI agent believed him. When they confronted him on the failed LSD sale to Mathers and Ball, he said he'd taken LSD over three hundred times—but only before it had been made illegal. Now he didn't believe in selling it because it was too dangerous. When they pointed out that they had seen copies of *Prairie Fire* in his shop and that it was anarchist literature, he said, "So what? I didn't write it. I only printed it. Printing is what I do." When they revealed that they had searched the print shop and found the can of yellow spray paint, he told them where he'd found the aerosol can and the nozzle. "That was the reason I tailed Mike to the armory." None of this passed muster with Bascomb and Franklin. They were convinced they had the right man.

Later that afternoon, Bascomb called Yates. He told him about finding the aerosol can at the print shop, then summarized his interrogation of Tim, including Tim's comments about Walt Arnold.

Yates liked Tim. He had been impressed with him, despite his politics and his use of marijuana. He had believed Tim the first time he'd asked him about the bombing and had been surprised and disappointed when he'd found Tim at the armory with Mike Rogers. Yates did not believe Walt Arnold was involved in the bombing, but he made a couple of phone calls anyway—one to Les Anderson and one to Bluto Harris. Les had nothing good to say about Walt, but also nothing incriminating. Bluto considered Walt a friend and said Walt was the most competitive person he'd ever met, and that making money was what made him tick.

"Can you imagine any reason he might want to blow up buildings at the university?" asked Yates as the conversation was ending.

Bluto laughed. "No. That's about the last thing I can imagine." Then he paused. "Unless he wanted to undermine the Olympic Trial bid."

"How's that?"

"He didn't want the publicity coming to western Oregon. He thought it might cramp his style."

"Meaning what?"

"Clear cutting. He hates the tree huggers."

Yates thought about this for several minutes after hanging up the phone, then dismissed it as too unlikely.

CHAPTER 126

Tai saw Rebop as soon as he entered the Odyssey Coffee House. She sat alone at a table beside the window, with a cup of coffee and her notebook. Tai got a cup of herbal tea and approached her table. "Mind if I join you?"

Rebop looked up from her notepad. She took a moment, then said, "No, it's fine."

"My name is Tai," he said, taking the other chair at the table. "You might recall we met at Blake College."

"How could I forget?"

Tai smiled, thinking she meant because he was so unforgettable, when she was referring to the unusual conversation they'd had that night. "I really did like your poetry. Is that a poem you're working on now?"

"Thank you, but no, this is an editorial for my newsletter." She refocused on her notebook and began writing.

Tai took a sip of tea and tried to read her writing upside down. "What's the topic?"

Rebop lifted her eyes long enough to say, "You can read it when the issue comes out."

"Fair enough," said Tai, not picking up on the brush-off.

Ten minutes passed. Rebop lifted her pen from the paper and looked out the window toward the train station, taking a moment to collect her thoughts.

"I gathered from your poems, Rebop, that you prefer women to men."

She faced him.

"Do you swing both ways?"

Rebop knew exactly where this was headed. She tilted her head as though appraising Tai. "In special circumstances."

Tai smiled, knowing how special he was. "Would you consider dinner with me tonight? Any restaurant you like."

"No, thank you, Tai. I already have plans."

"Another night, perhaps?" He batted his pale blue eyes at her.

Rebop turned again to look out the window. After a moment, she looked down at her notebook then up at Tai. "I don't think so." Her smile was forced.

"But you might think about that some more?"

"I already have. No." She returned to her writing.

"Is it the alien possession?" he asked, knowing she hadn't believed anything they had told her about Ray.

She didn't look up to answer. "No, I heard you had a thing for younger women."

"Age is irrelevant."

She lifted her head to look him in the eye. "Not if they're underage."

Tai didn't say another word. He remained at the table until he finished his tea, then quietly got up and left.

CHAPTER 127

Two nights after being released from jail, Ray was still sharing a room with his father at the Hilton. When his father fell asleep at ten-thirty, he left the room. Mike Rogers was in Sacred Heart Hospital, about twenty blocks from the hotel. Ray walked to the hospital in a light rain. Using the mantas' ability to enter other minds, he navigated the interior of the hospital looking for the intensive care unit. On the way, he snagged a set of scrubs from a laundry hamper and pulled them on over his clothes.

He found Mike rather quickly. His room was identical to that of Stoopid's when he had been so badly burned. Mike, who lay motionless in a coma, was not allowed visitors, but his room, which was closely monitored, had a large window for those wanting to come by to see how he was doing. Ray approached the window and noted the number of tubes and flashing screens arranged around Mike's bed.

While Ray stood at the window contemplating his next move, he saw a middle-age man coming down the hall in street clothes. Not wishing to be noticed, Ray walked down the hall toward the man as though he were going to another part of the hospital.

Ray, already in stealth mode, dove into the man's mind as they passed, curious who would be coming to visit Mike this late at night. Although he did not know who Walt Arnold was, the man's thoughts were clear. He was there to end Mike's life. Though shocked by what he'd learned, Ray continued down the hall, then reversed direction to see what the man would do.

Walt had timed his visit to coincide with the change of shifts at the hospital. He walked directly through the nurses' station and into Mike's room. Ray reached the window as Walt, wearing rubber gloves, took hold of a pillow to suffocate Mike.

Ray hurried into the room. "Hey, mister, this room is off limits to all but hospital employees."

Stunned by Ray's sudden appearance, Walt dropped the pillow and backed away from Mike's bed. "Oh, I'm sorry. No one was here, so I came in to see my nephew."

Ray knew he was lying. "An honest mistake, sir, but please leave."

Walt didn't fight it. It had taken him four martinis to get the nerve to come to the hospital, and now nearly shaking with anxiety, he simply left the room and walked away as fast as he could.

With Walt gone, Ray was alone in Mike's room. Working in conjunction with the mantas, Ray entered Mike's mind. In much the same way as they had sparked Ray back to life a week earlier, the creatures immediately began to purr. After just a few minutes of this blissful and healing hum, Mike's eyes fluttered, then opened. Ray quickly backed out of the room and softly closed the door. He reached the hallway as the midnight shift arrived.

While the two attendants poured over the paperwork left by the previous shift, Ray stood out in the hall watching Mike through the window. Mike turned his head right and left, trying to figure out where he was. Then he suddenly sat up, pulling an IV stand onto the bed. One of the attendants raced into the room. Ray quickly hustled down the hallway, ditched his scrubs, and left the hospital.

CHAPTER 128

Word of Mike Rogers' awakening reached police headquarters early the following morning. Wilkerson immediately called Agent Bascomb, then informed Bob Yates, letting him know that Bascomb would be interrogating Rogers in his hospital room at ten o'clock. Yates quickly called Bascomb and convinced him to let him sit in on the interrogation, arguing that his knowledge of the community would be invaluable during the questioning.

Yates met Bascomb and Franklin in the hospital lobby. Prior to his arrival, Yates had called the hospital and asked them to hold off on pain meds for Rogers. He knew the biker was a junky and hadn't had a fix in several days; it might be a useful point of pressure in the interrogation. He told this to Bascomb and Franklin, suggesting they be prepared to stretch the interrogation out as long as possible.

Mike had been transferred to a private room on the third floor. Yates and the FBI agents saw two hospital security guards stationed outside the room as soon as they stepped out of the elevator. The men moved aside when Bascomb and Franklin flashed their badges. Yates, in uniform, followed them in.

Mike lay in bed, with the head of the bed cranked up so he was in a reclining position. Although awake, he was very weak and attached to an IV drip for fluids. He had not been given any notice of the interrogation, and his eyes glared in defiance when he recognized Yates and understood why the men were there.

"Nice to see that you're still alive, Mr. Rogers," said Yates, without any sense that he meant it.

"Fuck you, Yates. And who are these assholes?"

Bascomb introduced himself and Franklin, who set up a portable tape recorder and read Rogers his Miranda rights. "We're here to ask you a few questions," began Bascomb. "We understand that you are not fully recovered from the gunshot wounds. We will do our best to make this as easy as possible."

Mike gave him the finger, then ran his finger across his lips as though zippering them shut.

Bascomb turned to Yates, tipped his head, then faced Rogers. "Do as you please, Mr. Rogers, but be fully aware that you were caught in the act and are facing some serious jail time. Your cooperation today could be beneficial when the time comes for sentencing."

Mike glared back at him, his eyes shifting to Yates, then back to Bascomb.

"There were two bombings at the University Oregon in the fall of last year. We believe you were responsible for both of them. What can you tell us that might convince us otherwise?"

Mike continued to stare daggers at Bascomb but had no other response.

"Were these bombings part of a coordinated effort by the Gypsy Jokers?"

Mike said nothing, while Yates watched from a few feet away and Franklin monitored the recorder.

"Right now, Mr. Rogers, all your gang's members are considered suspects. A few words now might make things a lot easier for them."

Mike made no response.

"Just a few words would save us a lot of trouble. We'll be bringing them all in one by one after we leave here if you can't help us out."

Mike raised a single finger.

Yates leaned forward and whispered to Bascomb. Bascomb nodded. "Officer Yates, here, found you at the armory with another man, Tim O'Malley. He was also arrested and is now in the city jail. What was his part in these bombings?"

Mike's eyes narrowed and flashed to Yates and back to Bascomb. "None."

"But you had a part in the other two?"

"Don't put words in my mouth. You caught me at the armory, that's all. And I have no idea why O'Malley was there. He's a friend. He saw my bike and chased me down."

"Then why did we find a can of yellow spray paint in O'Malley's print shop? Was he part of the other bombings?"

"How would I know?"

"Because we believe that you do know."

Mike just stared back at Bascomb.

"What about the other Jokers? You've no interest in taking some of the heat off them?"

"Did you see any of them at the armory?" snapped Mike. "What do you think?"

"We're investigating the other bombings as well. Were they part of either of them?"

"You just asked me that, asshole."

"But you didn't answer."

Knowing that time would eventually weigh on Rogers, Bascomb continued to question him, getting nothing out of him but his statement about Tim. This went on for another hour with no success. At noon, the three men took a lunch break, giving specific orders to the attendants not to give Mike any pain meds. When they came back at one, the lead nurse said Mike had been beeping for morphine since they'd left and had recently been screaming to get her attention.

When they entered the room, little beads of sweat dotted the edges of Mike's shaggy hairline, and his attitude had changed from silent stoic to fidgety addict. "Where the fuck are those nurses?" he shouted. "I'm hurting right now and need some relief."

"We'll make sure that happens once you've given us a few answers."

"You can't do that."

"Sorry, Mr. Rogers, we need some information. We'll do whatever we want."

The game went on for another forty minutes with Mike getting more and more testy and Bascomb getting agonizingly more patient. "How about a simple yes or no? Did any Gypsy Jokers participate in the other bombings?"

Mike was sweating badly and getting physically agitated. "Fuck," he screamed. "No. Those assholes wanted nothing to do with it. It was me. No Jokers, no Tim, just me. I did all three on my own. Now get that nurse in here!"

"You were responsible for bombing Campbell Hall and Johnson Hall. Is that correct?"

"What did I just say? Damnit! Yes."

Bascomb looked at Franklin, then Yates. "What do you think?"

"I think we've got what we need," said Franklin. "Call the nurse."

Yates stepped forward. "Not yet."

Mike gritted his teeth and seethed hatred through his eyes at Yates.

"Ask him where he got the dynamite. That's something we need to know."

"What about it, Mr. Rogers?" asked Bascomb. "Where'd the explosives come from?"

Mike seemed to swell up with anger, but he was also sweating heavily and clearly in pain. "Shit, I don't know."

"You don't know?"

"I'm too fucked up to think. Give me some morphine. That'll clear my head."

Yates spoke up. "Not until he talks. It's not a question that involves a lot of thinking."

Mike's face glowed red and his eyes nearly popped out of their sockets. "Fuck you, Yates."

"Is it time for a break?" asked Franklin. "Let's come back in an hour."

"NO," shouted Mike. He lowered his head like a mad dog and glowered at the three men facing him. "I got it from my uncle, damnit. Walt Arnold."

Yates came up close to him. "Did he know what you were using it for?"

"GOD DAMN, YES. He paid me to fucking do it! It was his idea!"

Yates nodded to Franklin. Franklin pressed the buzzer for the nurse.

By the end of the day, Tim had been released from custody and Walt Arnold had hired a lawyer.

CHAPTER 129

News of Tim's exoneration spread through the alternative community like the latest delivery of sinsemilla from Mendocino County. Although Tim's release received little attention in the mainstream media of Lane County, he was celebrated as a hero in the Eugene counterculture. He had been instrumental in solving the bombing case and in doing so had removed some of the stigma of violence from the anti-war movement in Eugene.

Tim met Gino at Lucky's the day he got out of jail. As was their habit, they smoked a joint in the alley, then went inside to hassle Earl for a table and a rack of balls. Earl was so glad to see Tim out of jail, he spotted him a free pitcher of beer and a table for the day. Four games of snooker later, and a second free pitcher, Gino leaned over the table to line up a shot, then abruptly stood up and muttered, "Oh, shit."

Linda Sheedy and John Walters strode the length of Lucky's straight to Tim, who was studiously chalking his cue and looking the other way.

Linda hugged Tim. "Thank goodness, you're out of jail."

When Linda let go of Tim, John shook his hand. "I never did believe you did it."

Tim laughed. "Thank the Lord for that! Shit, John! I was tracking the man down. I'm no vandal. I may be crazy," he grinned, "but it's in a good way."

"We're here because we know that, Tim," said Linda.

"So, what's up with the market? Make it quick. I've got three days of pool to catch up on. I'd hate to lose my touch."

Gino belly laughed. "Ask him who won every game today." Gino tapped himself on the chest with the tip of his pool cue.

Tim took a sip from his beer. "And that's about to change." He leaned over the pool table to line up a shot.

"Hey, out of the way, Bozo. It's my turn."

"Oh, yeah. That's right." Tim smirked, then focused on his friends.

"We blew the City Council away with the economics angle," said John. "You were right. We're job creators and tax payers. You could see the lights go on in their heads the moment we said it."

"But they still won't give us the park blocks," said Linda, "and we're scheduled to open the second week of April."

"With no available location," added John.

"Then we thought, let's ask Tim. He always has an idea."

"Your turn, chump," called out Gino as he refilled his glass.

Tim stroked the whiskers on his chin, screwed up his mouth, and, deep in thought, lifted his left brow.

"Damn, dude," jived Gino, "don't blow a gasket. Have another sip of beer." He handed Tim his glass.

Tim drained it, then slammed it down on the table. "I've got it."

"Easy back there, boys," shouted Earl from the bar.

"You know that parking lot west of the County Courthouse?"

"The parking lot for the court," clarified John, "for the judges, jury, and anyone with business in the court."

"It's filled all the time," said Linda.

"The county owns it, and it's only half full on the weekends. It's also got two levels. Go to the County Commissioners. Tell them you want the top level on Saturdays."

"It's pretty big. More space than we had last year."

"And it's in the middle of downtown," followed John.

"But it's sloped."

"So it drains, Linda. If you have no place else to go, I'd drop that one on the commissioners."

The idea had both John and Linda running through the obstacles and options in their heads. After a moment, they looked at each other, knowing they agreed. "I told you, John, there ain't no smarter hipster in this town than Tim O'Malley. I think it's worth a try."

"They just might go for it," said John, shaking Tim's hand in thanks.

"Your turn, dude. Get with it," jazzed Gino.

Tim lifted his cue as a salute to John and Linda. "Hope it works out. I've got a game to win."

"We'll let you know," said Linda as they left.

"Next time," shouted Gino, "find him at the print shop when he's not doing anything important."

Linda turned around and gave him the finger.

CHAPTER 130

Two days after his confession, Mike Rogers was sitting up in bed and eating regular food. Three days later he was well enough to be transferred to a jail cell. The doctors called it a miracle.

That same week Ray returned to Blake College without the company of his parents. He walked in the front door as dinner was being served. No one said a word as he took a seat at the table, grabbed a plate, and began loading it with fresh salad and a tofu dish that Janice, looking considerably more pregnant, had prepared.

Although Adrienne was glad to see Ray, she, like everyone else at the table, could not help imagining the blue manta floating over his head, and a certain uneasiness came with his unannounced arrival.

Ray was the first to break the spell. "Where's Crow?"

Adrienne answered, finally giving Ray a smile. "He left Eugene a few days ago."

Rain described the day the FBI had surprised them at the house, and the events leading to their finding out that Crow had broken parole. As she told the story, things gradually began to loosen up at the table, and the others joined in.

"Where are your parents?" asked Marsha. "Aren't they supposed to be with you?"

Ray smiled at the question. "The psychiatrist released me. I'm on my own."

"How'd that happen?"

"I told the shrink that the aliens weren't real. I said they were a by-product of the drugs and that the effect had worn off."

Tai got up from the table to take his plate into the kitchen. "And he accepted that?"

"Not immediately. We had two more sessions before he released me. The second was earlier today. He said he'd write a report and send it to both the Eugene Police Department and the FBI."

Van glanced around the table. "So, you don't believe the manta possession was real?"

"You all saw what I saw." Ray opened both hands in an expression of *come on now!* "The possession was real—and it's still happening. I got into the guy's head and convinced him otherwise."

The others at the table looked like a chorus the way their mouths all opened at once. "Really?" asked Marsha.

"Really. You'd be surprised what I can do."

Tai came back into the room. "Like what?"

"Stop," demanded Janice. "I don't want any more of this alien shit running through me or my baby. Talk about this when I'm not around."

They all deferred to her request and agreed to talk with Ray later.

After the meal, Ray asked Adrienne to walk down to the river with him. Standing side by side in front of the teepee, they stared at the stars twinkling off the surface of the river for a long time before Adrienne spoke.

"I wish they were gone, Ray. I do."

"I think I can change your mind about that."

Adrienne shook her head. "Doubtful."

Ray reached out and took hold of her hands. "Close your eyes."

Suddenly they were both flying through the sky of the alien planet as part of a flock of blue mantas. As they had before, they flew high over vast stretches of desert and numerous colonies of the pyramidal mounds. At lower altitudes, they could see long lines of the insect-like creatures, coming and going from the mounds like columns of soldiers. Twice they dipped into small desert lakes, collecting moisture with their tentacles. When they reached a mountain range, they swooped down through the luxurious valleys, dragging their tentacles through the tall grasses gathering seed. Then they soared high into the aquamarine sky, performing dramatic aerial acrobatics as a unified flock.

When Ray let go of Adrienne's hands, they were standing face to face on the river bank. As the expression of awe eased form her face, Adrienne muttered, "Oh, my gosh, Ray."

He nodded.

"Can you do that whenever you want? Without the chanting or anything else?"

He nodded again, suppressing a grin.

"The astral traveling is certainly exhilarating," said Adrienne, "but the mind reading still makes me uneasy."

"Try to think of it as a good thing."

"I've tried—and struggled. You saw the expressions on our faces when you arrived this evening. Your ability to get into our heads makes everyone uncomfortable."

"I used it to save Tim."

"What do you mean?"

"I got into Mike Rogers' head and broke the coma."

"What?"

"You asked me to help." Ray grinned. "Remember, we're talking about the collective consciousness of several hundred of these mantas. It's a powerful effect. When they get inside a wounded psyche, they can use their purring to heal it—and that includes waking someone from a coma."

"And bringing you back to life!" Adrienne hugged Ray then kissed him. "That's cool. That's really cool. But also kind of scary."

"Only if you're afraid of them—and I'm not and you shouldn't be."

"Will they stay with you forever?"

"I don't know. I expect them to leave at some time, but it's nice I was able to help Tim without anyone noticing."

"Too weird, Ray."

"Too weird to have me as a friend?"

Adrienne shook her head and hugged him. "Not at all. Take my hands again. Take me across the universe."

And he did.

When they returned to the house, only Tai and Rain were still at the dining room table. Tai immediately asked Ray about the mantas. "So, what else can you do besides read minds?"

Ray glanced at Adrienne.

"Go ahead Ray. They've been part of this from the beginning."

Ray told them what he'd told Adrienne about the mantas' purring and the night he'd left the jail. Tai and Rain were both astounded. Then he told them about bringing Mike back to consciousness.

Rain shed tears of joy. "My God, that's incredible, Ray, and thank you for doing that. You saved Tim."

"I think it was the mantas that did all the work."

"Anything else?" pushed Tai.

Again, Ray looked to Adrienne. She nodded.

"Join hands."

Adrienne took Ray's left hand, Rain took his right, and Tai clasped hands with Rain and Adrienne.

"Now close your eyes." Suddenly, just as before, they were flying with a flock of mantas, banking and wheeling over the surface of the distant planet, part of one collective mind.

The following night, when Janice didn't show for dinner, Van asked Ray about the mantas. Tai and Rain exchanged a grin. Ray told Van and Marsha what he'd already told the others, then asked everyone to join hands.

After yet another stunning trip to the mantas' planet, Marsha and Van sat across the table from Ray awed to silence. Tai spoke up. "How is it you can do this, Ray? Before when they were in all of us, it took a group effort and we had to chant."

"I'm not really sure, but I think it's because of my suicide. When they were in all of us, they were along for the ride. They connected us, but we had none of these other powers. When I ended my life," he turned to Adrienne with a sad look, "I believe that was a unique opportunity for them, an opportunity to fully enter and share a human mind—something much more powerful than what they were able to do with the eight of us. Then it took me a while to learn how to work with them."

No one knew if this were true or not, but they accepted it. Tai then asked the obvious question: "What will you do now, Ray?"

Ray glanced at Adrienne. "I don't know. Mostly I don't want a lot of attention or to be seen as a freak. When I told the FBI, I ended up in jail, then in a psychiatrist's office."

"But you have the ability to heal people," said Rain. "You've been given a gift. There's a responsibility with that."

Ray looked down at his hands.

"It's true, Ray, you could help a lot people," said Adrienne.

Ray lifted his eyes. "But I'm not really sure how all of this works—or if there are repercussions—or side effects—or when it will end. I understand what you're saying, but I'm not there yet. And I don't want to do something stupid or sensational or be on TV—or any of that. It's too much right now. If it gets out that I came back to life, people will start thinking I'm Jesus Christ or something. I definitely don't want that."

Van agreed. "That's fair. We don't really know what's going on. Being cautious is smart—and having been part of this since the beginning, we should support Ray—whatever he decides."

Rain wasn't convinced, but she let it go.

"Just remember," emphasized Ray, "this is our secret. It doesn't go beyond Blake College."

"But Ray, this is too fantastic to keep secret," argued Tai. "We've contacted life on another planet. That's a cosmic breakthrough of tremendous importance. Psychic mind pervades the universe, and we've found creatures that can travel through it—and take us with them. This changes how we understand life and the universe and the mind! The world needs to know."

"No, I don't want it going anywhere. If it gets out, I'll be the one who takes the heat, not any of you. I'll simply deny it. And without me, there's nothing but your word."

"But damn, Ray, there might be money in this!"

"And money fucks up everything," said Rain. "Tai, you've just given us the best reason possible to keep it quiet."

"So, we're just going to hold on to this for ourselves?"

"There can be no other way, Tai," said Ray. "You're either with me or you're not."

Tai frowned and looked around the table, then said a flat, combative, "Fine."

"So, do you all agree? Not a word to anyone."

"What if they leave?" asked Tai.

"Then it won't matter. Tell anyone you want. It makes a good story but nothing more than that without proof. Everyone good with this? Our secret to keep."

"Yes," echoed around the table, Tai last.

"What about Janice?" asked Marsha.

"It clearly makes her uncomfortable," said Adrienne. "Until she shows interest, let's leave her be."

"Good idea," said Rain, "she has other things on her mind."

CHAPTER 131

Gino and Janice met outside Lucky's Monday morning. They were both on bicycles. Gino led Janice across town to an old Victorian house that had been renovated and converted into medical offices by five partnering doctors. They used the house as a clinic and performed their surgeries at Sacred Heart Hospital ten blocks east.

The homey feel of the old house made Janice relax as soon as they entered. Janice sat down in the living room that was now a waiting room, and Gino signed them in. A few minutes later a nurse escorted them to an examination room. The nurse took Janice's temperature and blood pressure, then left her with a health history to fill out. While Janice worked on the form, Gino delved into the cabinets and drawers, putting on pairs of latex gloves, pantomiming rectal exams and trying to be silly. His antics made Janice uptight. She got angry and told him she wanted to talk to the doctor alone. Gino didn't really want to be there. He said he'd be in the waiting room and would pay the bill. He showed her a wad of cash.

Doctor Rosenberg came in minutes after Gino walked out. His hair was long and dark, pulled back in a neat ponytail. A thick brown mustache wrapped around his mouth. He considered himself part of the counterculture and made time to do work in the community, often volunteering at White Bird, Eugene's free clinic. He also knew Gino and wasn't surprised by his absence. Tom Rosenberg was a decent man, and Janice got that vibe right away.

He looked over Janice's health history while standing, then he sat down in his chair and leaned forward. "Have you seen any other doctors about this pregnancy?"

"No."

"Then you haven't been examined at all."

She shook her head.

"That's where we need to begin."

Janice knew this would be necessary. The doctor performed a complete examination. When he was done, and she had dressed, she sat, and he stood. "You are pregnant, Janice. No doubt about that. You seem to be healthy and so does the child from what I can tell right now. Do you know the date of conception?"

Janice had not liked being examined, but the doctor had been remarkably respectful. "It was about four months ago."

"And Gino is the father?"

Janice looked down at her hands. "I believe so."

"And he agrees?"

She lifted her eyes. "Because I told him it's his."

"He said you wanted an abortion. Have you sought any advice on this?"

Janice's conversation with Gloria came back loud and clear. "Yes, with an older woman."

"And she thought an abortion would be a good idea?"

"Not really."

Doctor Rosenburg nodded. "Four months is a little late for an abortion, Janice, but the law allows five. Is this something you really want to do?"

"I think so." Janice would have been irritated by anyone else questioning her like this, but the man seemed so clear about what he was saying and so sincere, she knew she needed him as an ally. Initially she had wanted the baby, then after the possession she didn't. Now she realized she didn't know what she wanted.

"Have you considered adopting the baby out?"

This caught Janice by surprise, and right away it seemed much better than aborting the child.

When she didn't answer immediately, the doctor went on, "If you want the abortion, we would have to do an ultrasound first. I could schedule one in two days."

She stared at him, not knowing what to say.

"That gives you a day or so to think about adoption. I know a couple who are looking for a child. They'd like a newborn."

"I never thought about adoption," said Janice softly. "Maybe I should."

"Be back here in two days, and we'll do the ultrasound. At that point, we'll talk again."

Janice nodded.

She met Gino in the waiting room. As they walked off the building's front porch, she told him she wanted to adopt the child out. Gino knew it was a cheaper way to go and was all for it. Janice made the phone call to Doctor Rosenberg the next day.

CHAPTER 132

When Ray's parents left Eugene, Ray went back to living at Blake College. During the evenings, if Janice wasn't there or left the dining room after the meal, the conversation would often turn to the mantas, and sometimes they would join hands and visit the distance planet—because it didn't scare them anymore—and it was thrilling.

One evening, after another trip across the universe, Marsha wondered aloud, "Why are they here? Why us? I don't get it."

"Maybe there's no reason," said Rain.

Tai nodded. "Cosmic coincidence."

"Or maybe it's what I suggested before," said Ray. "They do have a reason for being here, and they're trying to communicate that to us."

"But what is it?" pressed Marsha.

Adrienne sat back from the table. "Is it possible our flock of mantas is the only one on their planet? We've been there more than ten times now and, if I'm not mistaken, we haven't seen any others."

"It seems unlikely," said Van, "but you're right, we've only seen the one flock."

"That seems strange to me." Ray looked around at the others. "Want to go again? Right now? To check it out."

"Why not?" was the unanimous answer.

They joined hands and once again they were soaring with the mantas. This time it seemed the mantas had read their thoughts, and without words, gave them a tour seemingly designed to answer their questions. They flew high and for long distances, covering vast stretches of ground. The planet was small and mostly open desert. With two suns it was always daylight. They saw only a few mountain ranges; some were barren, some with grassy valleys—but no other flying creatures—mantas or otherwise. They swooped down close to one of the insect colonies. They traced one of the insects' long columns all the way to the

414

edge of the mountains; where on closer inspection, they could see that these creatures also fed off the grasses, swarming over them in huge numbers and carrying the chewed mulch back to their mounds like ants.

When the trip was over, everyone was aghast, Ray as much as anyone. "You were right, Adrienne! That flock is the only one, and they're competing with those insects for food."

"And it looked like the insects are winning," said Marsha.

"And stripping the planet of vegetation," added Van.

"Maybe that's why they came to Earth," said Ray, getting excited. "They need our help."

Tai looked up from rolling a joint. "But we can't do anything for them from here. That's crazy."

"Unless they're looking for a new home! And they're using me as a roving observation device—as I've always thought. To check out Earth as an alternative. Wow! That's helping them, right?"

"Seems a bit far-fetched."

Marsha chuckled. "More far-fetched than them being here at all, Rain?"

"With their ability to travel psychically," continued Ray, now standing and pacing around the room. "I'll bet they've gone to other planets as well, looking for the proper place to relocate."

Van wasn't so sure. "They might have that capacity psychically, but how would they relocate physically? They can't fly to Earth or any other planet. What could they do? It doesn't make sense."

"Maybe a physical presence is secondary to them." Tai lit his joint and took a toke. "Maybe they only hope to transplant their collective psyche. Maybe that's their only choice—to share consciousness with some other life form—as they've already done with Ray."

Tai extended the joint to Ray. He waved it off.

"What if they decide to stay?" asked Marsha. "What would that mean? How would that impact Earth?"

Rain also declined Tai's joint. "You mean, like introducing jack rabbits to Australia? No, I think you're off target. If they're here to tell us anything, it's more likely they're trying to show us what could happen here on Earth if we're not careful. It's not so much a cry for help as a warning."

"Like a psychic reflection of our future." Tai took another pull off the joint that only he was smoking. "That's more reasonable than thinking they could actually physically transplant to another planet."

"Back up, everyone," said Van. "This is all very interesting, but also blind speculation—based on the very little we know. Let's do what we should have done from the beginning. Instead of freaking out, let's take this on as a school project and go one step at a time. I suggest we continue to visit the planet just as we have, and each time assess the number of mantas and the conditions they're facing. If it appears they really have a problem or a message for us...well, we'll worry about that then."

No one had a better idea, so that's what they agreed on.

CHAPTER 133

Yates met Spikes at the Vet's Club the following evening after work. They hashed out all that had happened, laughing quite a bit.

"You know," said Yates, "I was really glad Tim O'Malley was cleared."

"How come?"

"He's good guy. A hippie, yes. And a total stoner. But I got a good feeling from that man every time I saw him—except when I caught him with Rogers. And as it turned out, that was a mistake."

"Yeah, he seemed okay to me. The red shoes are a bit weird for a grown man, but he did show up just when I needed him. And that was crazy. I watched him put the motorcycle together. I'm no mechanic, but he was good."

"He was lucky Rogers came out of the coma. Those FBI guys didn't want to let him go."

Spikes nodded slowly, thinking. "You know, this sounds stupid, but I…never mind."

"What?"

"Ray said he was certain Tim had nothing to do with the bombing."

"The others told me that, too."

"He also told me he could enter another person's head."

"Oh, no, you're not going there are you?"

"I joked with him about it. I told him if he had the power to get into someone's head, he should get into Mike's and wake him up. Maybe he'd confess and let Tim off the hook."

Yates raised his hand to get the bartender's attention. "Another pitcher here," he called out. "We've got a man in need."

Both men broke into laughter.

Halfway through the pitcher, Yates looked at his friend and grinned.

"What is it?" queried Spikes.

"I've got a date with Rain."

"Oh shit, no way. That's going to fuck you up big time."

"I'll soon find out. We're going out Friday night."

CHAPTER 134

Bob Yates had shown remarkable, barely legal, restraint in his dealings with the members of Blake College. When he called Rain to ask her out for dinner, she knew this and felt compelled to say yes. He was not her type—if she really had one—and with her position on the war and capitalism, not to mention the continued presence of the mantas, going out with a police officer felt like a betrayal of her beliefs. But she prided herself on being open, and all things considered, Yates had proven himself to be a decent man.

Rather than have him pick her up at the house, she decided to meet him downtown at the Excelsior Restaurant, where Yates had made reservations for six-thirty. He was seated in the foyer in a sports coat, a dress shirt, and blue jeans when Rain came in. He immediately stood. She surprised him with a hug and an air kiss to the cheek. He helped her slip out of her second-hand, black wool coat, then could not resist stepping back to admire her. She wore black slacks and a hip length, traditional Chinese jacket of brilliant red satin, with a mandarin collar, open sleeves, and cloth ties. Mirror image dragons were embroidered in black and gold on either side of the ties. Add her auburn hair that fell in loose waves over her shoulders, the smattering of freckles across the tops of her cheeks, and her startling green eyes, and Yates felt as though he'd been transported back to high school to escort the homecoming queen to the prom. He struggled to speak and simply followed Rain and the hostess to a table in the corner. He pulled out one of the chairs— like he never did—to let Rain sit down. He helped her slide the chair up to the table, then took the chair opposite her, banging into the table in the process.

"This is nice, Bob," said Rain after they'd picked out a bottle of wine. "I've never been out with a police officer before." She smiled with humor.

"I think we're just like everyone else."

"I'm not so sure about that, but I do think you're an exception."

Bob tilted his head.

"You could have come down much harder on Blake College than you did. I remember when you arrived at our open house. Things could have been a lot different. I'm here tonight because of that."

"Well," confessed Yates, "I think your impact on me that night had a lot to do with it."

"You mean, you were angling in on this date from the beginning?"

Yates looked down at the table, then up at Rain. "You probably knew that all along, didn't you?" He chuckled. "That's what Eldon told me, anyway."

"I knew. But I also grew to respect you. You could've gone about things much differently."

"And you would never have accepted this date."

Rain shrugged. "Probably not."

The waiter arrived with their bottle of wine. He opened it, allowed Bob to taste it, then poured them each a glass. When the waiter walked away, they clinked their glasses together and took a sip.

A period of silence stretched out too long. Rain, always composed, brought it to an end. "Ray told us you're a veteran."

"That's true."

"Then you must know more about the war than I do. What do you think about it?"

Yates knew this was something they had to talk about if he were interested in a second date. It was a tough topic for him. He took a breath and let it out. "I'm not gung-ho like I used to be, Rain. The experience changed me. It's why I became a cop. I wanted to make a difference, and I knew I could deal with things others might not be able to because of my experience in Southeast Asia."

"What do you think of people like me who protest the war? Does that put me on the other side?"

"No." He took a sip of wine. "Protest is part of our democracy. I respect that. I don't like the violence, and the screaming students can push my buttons. But I understand. There's a fair debate about why we're in Vietnam. I try to listen."

"At least you're open, Bob, that's really important."

The salads arrived, and they slipped into silence while they ate.

"Are you going to continue with the school?" asked Yates after the salad plates were taken.

Rain smiled at the question. "It's hard to say. We don't own that house. The owner could return at any moment and throw us out. Or the bank might not like the non-arrangement we put together. We'll finish this year and see what happens."

"I heard you wildcraft to support yourself. Tell me something about that."

Rain told him what she did and how she sold her products at Saturday Market. "I really like the outdoors and the opportunity to hike and explore with a purpose."

"I got a little too much sleeping on the ground in the army to enjoy camping anymore, but I still love the peace and quiet of the forest. Would you consider letting me join you on an outing?"

Rain lowered her eyes, then gave him a smile. "I think we could work that out."

When they had finished their meal and the bottle of wine and one piece of chocolate cheesecake, Yates found himself anxious about the conclusion of the date.

"I walked into town this evening, Bob. Would you mind giving me a ride back to the school?" This was something Rain had been weighing all evening. How far did she want this date to go?

"I might be a cop," laughed Yates, "but I'm no barbarian. Of course, I wouldn't mind. It would be a pleasure."

Little was said as they drove north through Eugene. It was a short drive, no more than ten minutes. Bob got out of the car when they arrived and went around to the other side to open the door. Rain was already out. They stood beside his Oldsmobile a moment. Yates wanted to kiss her good night and then ask her out again. Instead, Rain took his hand and led him around the house and down to the river. It was cold. They stood on the river bank a short time, staring at the wind-blown surface of the Willamette. Rain leaned up next to him and whispered, "Let's go inside the teepee. It's warm in there."

Yates had not anticipated anything more than a kiss. His greatest hope was a second date. But Rain was way ahead of him. She had enjoyed her time with him. He was different than the array of artists and hipsters she'd spent time with over the last few years. She'd known by the second time they'd spoken that he was attracted to her. But he'd always been courteous. He never got weird. No insinuating comments.

No aggressive behavior. Something very solid ran through the man. They spent the night in the teepee. They got up early, before anyone else was awake, and went into the house. Rain made a cup of coffee for Bob and a cup of tea for herself. Afterward, Rain walked Bob out to his car.

"Would you like to get together again sometime?" asked Yates.

Rain tilted her head. "After last night that should be obvious." She gave him her most radiant smile.

Yates beamed. "How about next weekend?"

"That would be nice." Rain kissed him on the cheek and headed back to the house.

Yates didn't remember driving home or anything he did Saturday morning until going into work at noon. The phone on his desk rang fifteen minutes after he sat down.

"How'd it go, Romeo?" It was Spikes.

"I was right all along."

"How's that? It's never going to work."

"She's perfect. We've already got a second date planned."

"Did you get some?"

Yates didn't answer. He just laid the phone back in its cradle. The phone rang again. He picked it up.

It was Spikes. "You did, didn't you?"

Yates hung up the phone, leaned back in his chair, and smiled to himself. When the phone rang again, he let it go.

CHAPTER 135

That night Oregon Sports Awards held their annual Bill Hayward Banquet of Champions to celebrate amateur and professional athletics in the state of Oregon. Bill Bowerman sat in the audience at the Sheraton Hotel in Portland with his premier long-distance runner Steve Prefontaine, who was halfway through his sophomore year at the University of Oregon.

After several lesser awards were presented and the energy was building in the audience, Bill Mulflur, a sportswriter for *The Oregonian* newspaper, stepped up to the podium to present the prestigious Bill Hayward Award, given to the top amateur athlete in Oregon. Mulflur began with a little background on the award.

"Oregon sports really begins with the track coach Bill Hayward. He spent forty-four years at the University of Oregon and was the United States Olympic track coach six times." As he spoke, Mulflur couldn't help looking into the crowd for Bill Bowerman. Bowerman had followed Hayward as the track coach at the U of O—meaning only two track coaches over a period of nearly seventy years.

"When Bill Hayward died in 1947, Oregon sports writers and sportscasters decided to present the first Bill Hayward Award the following year, meaning there have been twenty-two award recipients to date. Some of the recipients are in the crowd tonight—Terry Baker, the Heisman Trophy winning quarterback at Oregon State, Dick Fosbury, Olympic Gold Medalist in the 1968 Olympics—another Beaver, Don Schollander, five-time Olympic Gold Medalist from Lake Oswego High School, and the man who followed Bill Hayward at the University of Oregon, Bill Bowerman." The crowd responded with applause after each name was mentioned, then stilled in anticipation of the announcement of the award winner for 1970. There was little doubt who that would be.

"The twenty-third recipient of the Bill Hayward Award for Amateur Athletics in Oregon," said Mulflur, opening the envelope containing the winner's name, "is the spectacular distance runner for the University of Oregon, Steve Prefontaine—the NCAA Five Thousand Meter Champion last year and the NCAA Cross Country Champion this year—who, by the way, just turned twenty years old last week. I'll bet he has a few more races yet to win. Come on up here, Pre. This award's got your name on it!"

Applause exploded from the crowd. Bill Bowerman stood when Prefontaine did. Bill gave his prize runner a handshake and then embraced him before the young man went up to get the award.

Afterward, as the celebrities and attendees milled around at the post-ceremony reception, Bill Mulflur found Bill Bowerman and clapped him on the back. "That's quite a runner you have there, Bill."

Bowerman nodded. "He might be the most competitive person I've ever met—next to me." He grinned, then laughed.

"Any news on the Trials?"

"They're a long way off. But I got a letter yesterday confirming that I'll be on the selection committee."

"That might help Eugene."

"I can't say a word until the site's been chosen." Then he glanced across the room to where Pre was surrounded by other sports writers. "But wouldn't it be great to have the Trials at Hayward Field with the latest Hayward Award winner as part of the competition."

CHAPTER 136

Early in February, Ray went to Twelfth and Jefferson to talk to Spikes about working again. Spikes had always liked Ray, and after a long conversation, Ray convinced him all his problems had come from one bad drug experience, and that the psychiatrist had helped him overcome the related issues. Spikes accepted this. Ray worked with him the rest of the day, and by the end of the week, it was as though nothing had ever happened. Neither the alien possession nor the suicide attempt was mentioned again.

The third weekend in February, Spikes asked Ray to work Saturday morning at Twelfth and Jefferson for half a day. Spikes brought Joey with him and gave him the job of reorganizing the utility truck's built-in tool boxes. This meant Joey would remove everything from the tool boxes and then put it all back in.

Spikes called for a mid-morning break to share a piece of coffee cake Sheila had added to his lunch bag. While the three of them sat on the front porch stairs eating Sheila's treat, Spikes told Joey the story of moving the house to Twelfth and Jefferson.

Ray could feel the submerged tension in Jack while he spoke. He did not like entering his friends' minds—he saw it as an intrusion of privacy—but on this occasion, because of his fondness and concern for Jack, he allowed the mantas to wrap a tentacle around Spikes' head. Although reading another's thoughts could be difficult or confusing, one painful issue dominated Jack's thoughts—the impact of Joey's mental health on his relationship with Sheila.

Ray shifted his attention to Joey, sitting beside him on the stairs, intent on Jack's story of the house. Ray had never entered a child's mind, but he felt compelled to now because of what he'd read in Jack's. It was like tuning in a radio. And Joey broadcast a lot static, little clarity, and a lot of blur. Buried in the fog of it all was one clear image, the punch that had caused Joey's left eye to droop.

Ray could see and feel the impact of the incident on Joey's psyche, but he could do nothing about it. The mantas were another story. They had brought Ray back to life and awakened Mike from his coma; now Ray couldn't help wondering if he should do what Rain had pressed him to do—use the mantas' powers to help others. After a moment of hesitation, Ray directed the mantas—by merely thinking the thought—to apply themselves to Joey's psyche. With a tentacle already wrapped around the boy's head, they immediately set to purring and continued to do so until Spikes completed his story.

Afterward, when they returned to work, Ray saw no obvious change in Joey or during the rest of the morning. He could only hope that the mantas had done something good.

CHAPTER 137

Throughout the ensuing weeks, Tai, Rain, Van, Marsha, Adrienne, and Ray continued to make regular visits to the mantas' planet to assess the situation. Although they flew with the mantas as a single collective consciousness, they returned with individual memories and accounts of what they saw. Van encouraged them to go at it like scientists exploring a new world, not unlike Darwin detailing the Galapagos Islands. They took a census of anything they could reasonably count—the number of mantas, the pyramidal colonies, the other life forms, the relative size and number of the lakes—hoping to both create an accurate picture of the mantas' planet and what they believe to be its ecological decline.

Rain and Marsha were skilled with colored pencils and water colors. They drew pictures of the terrain and any plant or animal life they saw. Rain drew one remarkable drawing, showing a manta from three views—from the top, the side, and the bottom. From flying with them, she had noted that some of the mantas had only a fringe of tentacles around the edges of their bodies, with gills, like you would see on the underside of a mushroom, filling up the rest of the area underneath. Others had no gills, and the underside was filled with the dangling tentacles. Rain hypothesized that this was a sexual difference—with the gills indicating a female. Marsha made a similarly excellent drawing of the insect creatures that appeared to be stripping the planet of vegetation.

Unfortunately, despite this engaging work, each visit deepened their concerns. The manta numbers were on a slow but steady decrease, falling below two hundred midway through March. They also noticed small fish-like carcasses accumulating around the edges of the lakes, that seemed to shrink in direct proportion to the mantas' numbers. Either they were watching an environmental catastrophe unfold or simply the ongoing evolution of a planet far outside their own solar system.

"This is so sad," said Rain, after their most recent visit to the planet they had named Glorium—for Gloria. "Those insects are changing the face of Glorium, and there's nothing we can do but sit back and watch it happen."

The others were equally upset and frustrated.

"There must be some lowest number of mantas," said Tai, "where they will lose the ability to project their psyche—sort of like the reverse of the hundredth monkey concept."

Marsha made a face. "Hundredth monkey?"

Tai was happy to explain. "There was a study twenty years ago of some monkeys that lived on the islands around Japan. One day it was noticed that one of the monkeys on one of the islands began washing its sweet potatoes before eating them. Shortly after that, one monkey after another on that island realized that the potatoes tasted better this way and began washing them also. When the hundredth monkey on the first island took on this behavioral trait, the researchers discovered that monkeys on the other islands suddenly started washing their sweet potatoes as well—without any physical contact between the populations. It was as though there were a critical mass of collective consciousness— one hundred of these monkeys—when their behavior was psychically transferred to the others, though separated by many miles of ocean."

"Right, Tai," said Van, rolling his eyes. "That's got to be baloney."

Tai shrugged. "There's a scientific paper on it. And even if you don't believe it, it still might apply to the mantas."

"I don't know about the monkeys," said Ray, "but we've seen something like that in the mantas already. And if you're right, Tai, at some point, at some minimum number prior to extinction, they might lose their ability to travel psychically—and lose contact with me."

"That's what I'm thinking. And it might be sooner than later."

"So, what can we do about it?" asked Marsha.

"Nothing. Give it up." Janice stumbled down from upstairs, now very pregnant, and as surly as ever. "You're making too much noise. I'm trying to sleep."

CHAPTER 138

Several weeks into March, Sheila sat at her desk on a Friday afternoon, looking out the window. It was three-thirty. She heard the roar of a school bus, then saw it pass on Highway 99. Joey came running down the driveway ahead of his sister, who walked well behind.

"They put me back in third grade," exclaimed Joey, bounding into the house and into Sheila's office.

"How's that?"

He pulled the pack off his back and delved into the side pocket. "Look." He handed his mother an envelope. "No more special classes."

The envelope contained a note from the counselor Mr. Fairbanks:

> *Joey has shown remarkable progress in the last few weeks. So much so that there is no reason for him to be in a special education class. He will rejoin the rest of his third-grade class starting Monday. I don't know what happened, but a light went on in his head, and he became an entirely different child.*

Sheila stopped reading and looked up at her smiling son. "This is wonderful, Joey." She hugged him so tightly a few tears leaked out of her eyes. She held him out and looked at him proudly, wondering if his drooping eye didn't droop so much anymore. "Nothing could make me happier."

"Except maybe Jack marrying you."

Joey had never mentioned this before. Sheila was taken aback—and gasped, but it also made her smile. She kissed Joey on the forehead. "No, I'd rather have this letter from Mr. Fairbanks."

Sheila let Joey tell Jack when he came in from work. They were at the dinner table. Jack had to hide his tears. The question of meds for Joey had so twisted his thinking about Sheila and everything else that he'd sunk into denial. He had pushed ahead each day with work, promising to tell Sheila *tomorrow* that he couldn't marry her.

Jack and Sheila had enjoyed a wild sex life the first eighteen months after meeting, but over the last few months, the complications of life and the marriage question had turned everything inside out. Sex hadn't been happening very often and the enthusiasm was missing. But Joey's announcement and the counselor's note had taken a huge weight off Sheila's shoulders, and it had been too long since she and Jack had made love. That night, when Jack and Sheila went to bed, she stripped off her clothes, pulled back the covers, and lay back in the pillows, knees up, legs parted. When Jack came in from the bathroom in his skivvies, she was grinning like the Mona Lisa. She reached out and pulled Jack's shorts down to his ankles...

Afterward, when the physical act had dispersed some of the tension between them, Sheila became serious. "Joey's no longer in special ed." She shook her head in wonder. "Can you believe it?"

Jack looked deeply into Sheila's eyes with his own sense of wonder. "There's nothing I could have wanted more." Joey's announcement had affected him deeply. He knew how much Sheila wanted to marry him and that she needed his commitment for the children's sake. He also knew that she had only brought the issue up four times in four months, had always been diplomatic, and had never really cranked up the pressure. If he was anything close to the man he pretended to be, he needed to be just as high-minded as Sheila had been. "I'm sorry I was such an ass when the doctor recommended medication," he said just above a whisper. "Thank God for today."

"It was killing us." Her smile was sad and sweet. She snuggled up to him, just feeling good.

"This may sound lame. But I wasn't coming around on this too quickly—or maybe at all."

Sheila lifted her head to look at him.

"But now that I've proven I'm a bull-headed jerk, is there any chance we could reopen the marriage discussion?"

"Is that a proposal?"

Jack made a funny face. "Well, yeah, I guess it is."

Sheila's mouth fell open, then transformed into a smile and a big kiss. "I accept," she hissed, sliding her leg up onto his belly. "Let's do it again to celebrate."

CHAPTER 139

When Ray learned of the change that had occurred in Joey, it had a powerful impact on him. He knew for certain that he had the capacity to help people in significant ways, but he worried that he might soon lose the mantas' healing powers when their numbers became too low or fell to zero. Perhaps Rain was right; he had the responsibility to do more while he could. But he didn't want to attract attention to himself or explain to others how he could do what he did. So, instead of making a big deal about it, he began volunteering at the Eugene Mission half a day a week as a food server. Each time he was there, he would seek out one or two of the most emotionally disturbed of the homeless men and women and use the mantas' powers to massage their psyches. Although Ray didn't really enjoy going into other people's heads—it could be quite unsettling—he did like helping people in need and felt grateful for the gift the mantas had bestowed upon him. In this quiet way, he did what he could—telling no one but Adrienne.

During this time, the excursions to Glorium had progressed to a weekly routine. One night in early April, after a dinner when Janice was there, they went down to the teepee so as not to intrude upon her space. Tai, Van, Marsha, Rain, Adrienne, and Ray sat in a circle with a single candle providing light. They joined hands and once again sailed off to the distant planet.

On this occasion, the flock flew to the highest peak in one of the barren mountain ranges, where the astral travelers witnessed the remarkable sight of the mantas breeding. As Rain had guessed, the females were the ones with gills on a portion of their underside. Several of them flew upside down, allowing males—more than one—to drag their tentacles across their gills in a beautiful, midair sexual display.

Shortly after this fertilization process, the females, flying right side up, glided low over the rocky promontory, sprinkling the fertilized eggs, like spores, onto the barren ground.

When the group of them released hands, they were all excited about what they had seen. "Maybe there's hope yet," exclaimed Adrienne. "If what we just saw is what I think it was, that's a new generation of mantas. Maybe they aren't going extinct."

"Seems like an unlikely spot for something to propagate?" said Van.

"I think they chose that location because of its remoteness," said Rain. "It's safe from intruders."

The following week, they were again treated to a rare scene, purposely revealed to them by their psychic hosts. They flew with the dwindling flock of mantas to that same barren peak, where now those spores had begun to sprout. Hundreds of thin white stalks had broken through the otherwise barren and rocky soil. Each was topped by a tiny blue bulb—presumably the first developmental stage of the mantas' offspring—looking quite like an eyeball.

Adrienne the gardener was ecstatic. "Oh, God, how cute were those little sprouts."

"They looked like mushrooms to me," said Tai. "How crazy it that!"

"I'm just glad they're able to reproduce," said Rain, who was already sketching a drawing of what they'd seen

"Yeah, but what will they eat when they mature? The flock is already dealing with diminished resources."

They all looked at Van the realist, knowing he was right. He shrugged. "That's why we're charting this. We want to see what happens—good, bad, or indifferent."

CHAPTER 140

After five weeks of deliberations, the Lane County Commissioners accepted Saturday Market's request to use the top level of the County Courthouse parking lot. It was much larger than the lot at Tenth and Oak and could accommodate nearly twice the number of farmers and craftspeople. Both factions of the market were pleased when it opened on April tenth in the spring of 1971.

Mid-morning on the tenth, Tim sat on his balloon tire bicycle, admiring the array of pop-up canopies that filled the parking lot. He played no part in the discussions with the County Commissioners nor any of the efforts led by Linda Sheedy and John Walters, but he felt good about their success and knew it was a huge positive for the community.

Pat Riley came up to him from behind. "It's been too long, Tim. I never got a chance to congratulate you on getting out of jail."

Tim grinned stoned. "Sometimes we get lucky. What's happening with the co-op?"

Pat smiled. "We found a new manager. It's gonna work out."

"Far out. I figured it would."

"And Laurel's pregnant." Pat's face filled with a smile.

"Congratulations." Tim laughed. "That'll give you plenty to do."

"I'm excited. But I've got to go. I saw you here and wanted to say hello."

A few minutes later, Linda Sheedy came out of the motley collection of vendors, headed directly for Tim. She was clearly pleased. "I think this location works pretty well, Tim. Don't you?"

"Yeah. How do you like the slope?" The parking lot, known as the Butterfly Parking Lot, had two wings that sloped toward the center.

"It's a pain," said Linda. "Worse than I thought. But I love the space and figure once we prove ourselves, we'll get the park blocks."

"What's John think?"

"He's pleased, but still mutters about a separate market for the farmers. We'll worry about that another time. Right now, I'm just happy we have a place. And I give all the credit to you." She leaned over to Tim and kissed him on the cheek.

"You did the work, Linda. I only provided an idea or two."

"But ideas are where everything starts, and you are full of good ideas."

Tim wagged his head, not really wanting any credit.

Linda kicked one foot with the other, hesitating. "Tim, any chance you'd go out to dinner with me tonight? I'd like to celebrate, and I can't think of anyone I'd rather do that with than you."

Tim straightened up on his bicycle. He had always admired Linda for her intelligence and energy. "Are you asking me out on a date?"

"I am."

"Well, damn, how could I possibly say no to as formidable a woman as you?"

"I'll take that as a yes."

"You bet. It would be a pleasure."

"I'll come by the print shop at six this evening."

"Perfect."

CHAPTER 141

The charting of Glorium continued into the spring with increased excitement due to the brood of young mantas. Each visit, the flock would swoop low over the breeding site to check the progress of their babies. Although still attached like flowers to their thin white stems, the little blue bulbs were steadily developing the flat manta shape and the protruding eyes. It was both thrilling and fascinating to watch, and almost too much to keep to themselves. But Ray demanded secrecy— while Van meticulously complied the data, all collected through psychic travel, into a remarkable scientific report—that would never go beyond Blake College.

On May fourth, the one-year anniversary of the Kent State shootings, the SDS led a takeover of the ROTC building on the University of Oregon campus. More than one hundred students occupied French Hall, forcing the police to use tear gas to rout them out. There was no violence, and no one was injured beyond what was incurred by the tear gas, but forty-four people were arrested. Mayor Anderson went ballistic, and Dave Berman found himself in jail.

That same week, the members of Blake College began taking the trip to Glorium every night, hoping to see the moment when the young ones detached from their stems and took off in flight. They knew it would be soon and didn't want to miss it. On a Tuesday night, the school members assembled in the teepee—without Janis, now eight months pregnant. Rain lit a candle, then settled into the circle with the others. As soon as all hands were joined, they were soaring above the planet surface with the remaining mantas. As had happened in all the recent visits, the mantas' flight pattern included a fly over to check out their brood.

From a distance, they could see that many of the stems no longer held a young one—and it appeared that this was, in fact, the moment the maturing young mantas were breaking free. But on closer inspection, they saw that a long trail of the mound-building insects wound up the side of the mountain all the way to the top—where they fed on the babies, plucking them from their stems like ripe fruit, to be masticated and taken back to their colonies. The mantas dove as one at the insects, trying to keep them away, but they were plucked from the air as easily as the babies from their stems—and the mantas were forced to fly off in retreat.

No one said a word when they walked back to the house that night, downcast and frustrated. There would be no new generation. The mantas would not survive the ecological breakdown caused by a planet-changing species. The everyday visits stopped.

Five days passed without another trip to Glorium. On Sunday morning, when Ray and Adrienne came down for breakfast, Tai suggested they gather that night to visit the planet. The others agreed, knowing that at some point they would have to go again. It would be after dinner.

That evening Van and Marsha made a stack of bean and rice burritos, guacamole with chips, and a large salad. When they brought the meal to the table, everyone was there but Rain, though Janice only stayed long enough to put a burrito and some chips on a plate and disappear upstairs. The closer she got to her June due date, the more she tended to seclude herself in her bedroom.

As they passed the plate of burritos around the table, Rain came in the front door, apologizing for being late. She took a seat and placed a burrito on her plate, then looked around at the others. "I invited a guest for dinner tonight. He'll be here shortly."

"Not the police officer," groaned Tai.

"Weren't we planning to go to Glorium tonight?" asked Adrienne, glancing at Ray. "Did you want to cancel that?"

"Not at all, and don't worry, Tai, it's not Bob."

"But our trip's not open to others," said Ray, clearly perturbed. "You know that, Rain. Why did you invite someone else?"

"After the last visit, it seemed as though we were lost. I wanted another opinion."

"No way, Rain." Ray was angry. "Did you already tell your guest what we're planning to do?"

"No, but I think you'll understand when he arrives."

"Understand what?"

"That I found the one person in Eugene who might be able to help us."

The conversation suddenly stopped when they heard a vehicle coming down the driveway. "That didn't sound like a car," said Van, getting up to look out the living room window. "It's someone on a motorcycle."

Ray didn't hear Van he was so upset. "What's going on, Rain?"

"Trust me on this, Ray."

"No, this is our secret. You've blown it." He stood from the table. "I'm out of here." Adrienne grabbed his arm, but he pulled away from her. He was two steps from the table when the front door opened. In strode the stork from outer space—Tim O'Malley, wearing his leather headgear and goggles. "Howdy, folks. What's for dinner?"

Neither Tai nor Van nor Marsha knew Tim. But, of course, Ray did, and he had seen Tim in some remarkably difficult and dangerous situations—and resolve them with utter calm. He knew Tim was special—and so did Adrienne. Despite his anger, Ray immediately lit up and turned to Adrienne.

"I thought you might understand," said Rain, standing to welcome Tim into the dining room and introduce him to the others. He pulled off his headgear and took a seat at the head of the table opposite Adrienne.

"I invited Tim over to visit Blake College and have dinner," said Rain. "But if you're open to it, Ray, I think we should unload the whole story on him just like we did with Rebop. At the very least, he should know about Mike Rogers."

Tim put two burritos on his plate. "What's this?"

Everyone turned to Ray.

After a long moment, Ray said, "All right." He looked down at the burrito on his plate, then directly at Tim. "We have a story to tell, and it can't go beyond this table."

Tim shrugged. "I can keep my mouth shut."

"Don't even tell Gino."

"I get it."

Ray told the story up to the second contact with the mantas. "At that point, I thought I'd lost my mind—and that maybe I'd lost

Adrienne, too. I freaked out and hung myself from a rafter in the greenhouse."

Tim, who had listened intently without comment, stopped him. "You hung yourself?"

Ray nodded. "I committed suicide, Tim. Not my best moment. The police came and took my corpse to the morgue."

Tim looked around at the others. "But you didn't really die? Or what? I don't get it."

"The mantas brought me back to life."

Tim bobbed his head and said a flat, "Okay."

"And instilled me with psychic powers, which I still have."

Everyone was watching Tim as Ray told his story, stringing together one impossibility after another. Each time, Tim nodded, seemingly taking it all in without undue drama.

"When Mike was in a coma, I went to the hospital and used the mantas' powers to bring him back to consciousness—with the intent of helping you."

"Really." Tim sat back in his chair, very surprised. "I guess I owe you some thanks."

"Not me, the mantas."

Tim nodded, then tipped his head in thought. "So, all of this began with Gloria's funeral?"

"That's right."

"And you ate mushrooms during the ceremony?"

"Along with some peyote and a little jimson weed," said Tai.

"Any chance you got the mushrooms out on route 45?"

Tai exchanged a look with Rain. "Yes," said Rain, "where several folks have found Native American artifacts."

Tim bobbed his head. "I know the field." He related the story he'd told Gino about picking two thousand mushrooms in that field and eating them all in one day with the members of the Lorane commune. "We had a similar but lesser experience."

Around the table eyes widened and people leaned forward.

"We didn't see any creatures, like you did, but the next day, we began sharing the dreams we'd had during the night—and they all involved some kind of alien contact or a distant planet. Some of the folks said they had the feeling in their heads that you've described.

"When this happened, an older hippie was passing through—a man who would later return to the commune and become its leader. He's there now. His name is Dick. We called him Dick Danger back then because he carried a gun and always had a new paranoid conspiracy theory to twist into people's heads. He painted the mushroom experience in the darkest way imaginable, saying we'd been possessed by brain parasites. Though the effect wore off after a couple of days, we were all badly freaked out. No one wanted to take psychedelics of any kind for months, for fear of being possessed by beings from outer space. Over time we eventually took LSD with no problems, and ate mushrooms from other locations, but no one went back to that one field because of what had happened."

"You mean, you think it was specific to those mushrooms?" asked Tai.

"That's how we explained it then, but it was nothing like what you've told me. It might be a longshot coincidence—our experience and yours, but I've always believed that psychedelic drugs can open the mind in ways that are either difficult or impossible to explain. And both instances fit the bill."

Glances shot around the table. "There's more to the story," said Rain.

Ray proceeded to tell Tim about their regular trips to Glorium, and the mantas' predicament. Van broke out the notes and drawings the group had made. Tim was mesmerized by the detail. "This is amazing. It's like a bizarre mix of art and science."

"We're planning to visit Glorium tonight as part of our ongoing research," said Ray. "Would you like to join us?"

"Absolutely, but I'm hungry as hell, and these burritos are calling my name."

This generated a good laugh, and everyone agreed that they should continue as planned—eat dinner, then take the excursion to the mantas' planet. When the plates were cleared, they gathered around the table. And yet something held them back. Even after the buildup they'd given Tim, there was a palpable reluctance among the members of Blake College to join hands. Ray said what the others were thinking. "Because of our last visit, Tim, when we saw the young ones being eaten, we're a little anxious about what we'll see there tonight. Be prepared. It could be very close to the end."

But when they finally joined hands that was not the case. The mantas' numbers had decreased but they weren't gone, and the astral travelers were able to take an extended flight with about eighty of the blue creatures. When they unclasped their hands, they were back at the dining room table, all eyes on Tim—even the dog's and the cat's.

Tim sat back from the table, clearly amazed. "Wow!"

"I take it you saw what the rest of us did—a mostly barren planet and a flock of blue mantas."

Tim nodded his head slowly. "Yes, I believe I did. Man, that was a trip—a real trip." He shook his head. "Far fucking out is all I can say."

"But we're stuck, Tim," said Rain. "We've been watching the mantas' numbers steadily diminish for several months now—and we're heartbroken and don't know what to do. That's why I asked you over, I felt we needed some advice about our next steps."

Everyone turned to Tim as though he might actually have an answer. Tim got out his tobacco pouch. "Mind if I smoke?" When no one objected, he set to rolling a cigarette while he spoke.

"I don't believe I know anything more about this than you do, but I see a couple of ways to look at it." He lit his smoke, took a drag, and exhaled. "Either it's just as you see it. Life from another planet trying to reach out psychically for help—or maybe, as Rain suggests, to give people on Earth a warning of some sort. No doubt we could use it." He cocked a grin with the cigarette poking out one side of his mouth. "Or maybe this is something quite different—something that's already happened."

"What do you mean?" asked Rain.

"What if the mantas relocated to the mushroom field long ago and that's what this is about."

Van asked what everyone was wondering. "What makes you say that?"

"It's no more than an educated guess but think about it. We don't know if what you're seeing on Glorium is occurring in real time. It appears that way because of how you're experiencing it, but that planet could be light years away and transmission of the thought waves or whatever it is that connects you might include an element of time—minutes or even many, many years."

This got everyone looking at each other.

Tim took a pull off his cigarette. He blew a smoke ring that floated down the length of the table and passed over Adrienne's shoulder. "Meaning, the mantas' extinction could have happened an hour ago or at some time in the distant past."

"Leaving their collective psyche to wander the ethers indefinitely," said Tai, "waiting for an opportunity to relocate."

"Just as the Tibetan priests imagine a lost soul seeking a womb to be reborn to," said Rain, looking around at the others.

"But the mantas' healing takes place in real time," said Ray.

Tim bobbed his head several times. "Suggesting to me that your psychic connection is more likely with the mushroom field—meaning here and now—than with some distant planet in an entirely different time frame. I certainly don't know if that's what's happening, but that's how we talked about it after our experience at the commune. We didn't have all the information you do, and nothing close to the visuals, but we felt that we'd tapped into some kind of ancestral memory—held within the mushroom mycelium and activated by the psilocybin—that dated back to the time of the Kalapuya Indians or before."

"Why so far back?" asked Marsha.

"Because the Kalapuya seemed to know that field was unique long before the white folks showed up. There are plenty of mushroom patches in the valley, but none of the others contain such a high concentration of artifacts. It was sacred to the Kalapuya because it was special to them in some way."

"So, you think what we're watching unfold is a cosmic memory?" said Tai. "A kind of temporal ghost embedded in the mushroom mycelium."

Tim opened his hands as a sign of uncertainty, then took a pull from his smoke and exhaled straight up in the air.

"So, there's nothing we can do or even need to worry about because what we're seeing happened in the past? That seems too easy, Tim."

"It's just one way of looking at it, Adrienne."

"But how would the mantas infuse their psyche into that field?" asked Van. "I don't get it."

"In the same way it happened to all of you," said Tim. "Your experience, like ours, was a group thing—like the mantas themselves—powered by the synergy of several minds acting as one—even synchronized by chanting in your case—and aided and abetted by the mushrooms. It opened you to psychic contact in a very powerful way. I've got to wonder if the mantas' original contact didn't happen during a tribal ceremony held by the Kalapuya several hundred years ago. Maybe they'd eaten the mushrooms as well—who knows? And like you, they opened themselves up in a very powerful way to the astral plane or the spirit world or whatever you want to call it. And when the mantas took advantage of it, instead of creating a psychic channel to the Kalapuya—as they did with all of you—it was embedded in the mycelium, because there was greater kinship between the mantas and the mushrooms than with the humans. Judging from your drawings of their offspring, the mantas might actually be more flora than fauna."

"Yeah," said Ray, "when they got into us in the teepee, they got into everything—the dog, the cat, the chicken, the spider. Why not the mycelium?"

"Exactly. The mycelium grows several feet beneath the ground and spreads a network of thread-like roots out over several acres. As a living entity, it's bigger and older than a giant sequoia. Not everyone believes that plants or fungi have a consciousness or a psyche—but I do."

"And so do I," said Rain.

"Absolutely," followed Adrienne, "they don't think in words, but my plants definitely know when I've come into the greenhouse. I've learned to never underestimate the intelligence of a plant," she patted Moxie beside her, "or an animal."

"Imagine something larger than a tree and the psychic presence it must have," continued Tim. "It's significant. And now after many hundred years dwelling in the mycelium, because of the special circumstances that took place in your teepee, and with Ray, the mantas got a chance to conjoin with a higher life form—and did."

A long silence held, then Rain asked the question everyone was thinking. "Now that you've thrown us a series of curve balls, Tim, what do we do?"

"First of all, we're all just guessing about this and making up possible scenarios, which can't be proven one way or the other. So, my suggestion is to go with the flow. Do exactly what you're doing."

"But what if they stay with Ray?"

"Go with the flow," repeated Tim. "You've had some kind of transpersonal experience with an alien entity—regardless of its origin—another planet or out Route 45. You have no choice but to acknowledge the unknowable and see where it takes you. Hell, Ray, you can heal people. This is worth figuring out."

"And if it suddenly stops," asked Marsha, "does that mean the mantas are extinct?"

"Either that or someone plowed up the mushroom field twenty feet deep."

CHAPTER 142

Although Tim's observations about the mushrooms had opened a whole new set of variables to the group, and even alleviated some of the heartbreak from what they'd seen on the mantas' planet, they still had no idea what to do, other than go with the flow. And they did, returning to Glorium once a week to continue their research.

On a Saturday night in late June, with Janice upstairs in bed, struggling to get comfortable with her over-sized body, the other members of Blake College convened in the dining room for another excursion to Glorium. With anxious looks all around, they joined hands and closed their eyes. As in their recent visits, they flew with a dwindling number of mantas while the creatures traced their usual route—a trip to the mountain valleys seeking grass seed, followed by a dip in a lake, and, on occasion, a sentimental visit to the breeding grounds that had been stripped clean of their offspring. Except for the exhilaration of flying with the flock, the visit was much like their previous ones—each more disheartening than the last.

When they released their hands, they were a somber group. "There's less than twenty mantas," said Van, after collecting the bits and pieces of information they had brought back from the trip. "They aren't going to last much longer."

"And yet they're still with you, Ray," said Rain.

"Clearly they are."

"Maybe it's as Tim said, they've already transplanted to the mushroom field." Marsha continued talking as she went to the kitchen to heat water for tea. "And the mantas will remain with you long after what we imagine is their extinction."

"I don't know," said Ray. "Something tells me—maybe its them driving this thought—that I'm not their final destination. It just doesn't feel that way."

Rain was staring at one of the pressed flowers that she and Marsha had framed and hung in the dining room. They had pressed a few of the flower's seeds beneath the glass alongside the blossom. "If wild crafting has taught me anything," she said suddenly, "it's that life is maintained through the transmission of seeds, not pollen. So, if they need to propagate, wouldn't a female make a better carrier than a male?"

"But they don't need to propagate if they're already here in the mushroom field," said Tai.

"Unless what's happened with Ray—because of his suicide," countered Rain, "is something better. An evolutionary step up from the possession of an underground fungus. And now that they share a human mind, physical reproduction would be next."

Tai laughed. "Ah, yes, the beginning of a real alien invasion."

"Come on, that seems impossible to me," said Van. "And I'm not convinced it's in the mushrooms. Tim's idea about an element of time is intriguing, but I still believe when the mantas go extinct, it's over. They'll be gone, and Ray will be first to know."

Marsha spoke from the kitchen. "If Ray's possession is our working model, then the only way they could get into a woman would be if one of us committed suicide. Rain, are you going to volunteer? How about you, Adrienne?"

"Not funny, Marsha," said Adrienne, shaking her head.

"Maybe we should sacrifice Lena?" quipped Tai.

Lena, sitting on the sideboard, immediately jumped to the floor and darted out of the room.

This got a chuckle from everyone, but the moment of levity was abruptly shattered by a yowl from Janice. Rain bolted from the table and dashed up the stairs. Adrienne followed.

"Her water's broken!" Rain shouted down to the others. "We've got to get her to the hospital!"

Moments later, Adrienne and Rain were assisting Janice, wearing a nightgown, down the stairs. Tai was already at the door with Van, Marsha, and Ray. They were all going to the hospital.

When they clambered out to the vehicle, it was clear not everyone could fit into the van. Van and Marsha offered to stay at the school. Rain told them to call the hospital and tell them they were on the way.

Tai got behind the wheel. Ray took shotgun, and a moaning Janice stretched out on the van's bed with Adrienne and Rain kneeling beside her.

The hospital was only ten minutes away, but Janice was shrieking in pain before they'd gotten out of the driveway, and it was clear the baby wasn't going to wait. Rain had participated in two illegal homebirths with midwives and had little choice but to dive in. She quickly threw back Janice's nightgown and got her to spread her legs and bend her knees. "Jesus," cried Rain, "the baby's crowning. This is happening now!"

"Should I pull over?" shouted Tai.

"No, get to the hospital!"

"Go to the emergency room entrance," urged Adrienne, holding Janice's hand and prompting her to breathe.

Ray gave directions, while Tai swung the van wildly through three turns and two red lights. A squad car pulled up behind the van as they came to a stop at the doors to the emergency room—*and Rain withdrew the infant from between Janice's legs!* She lifted the baby by its feet and gave the little girl a whack on the fanny. An intern slid open the van's side door just as the baby took her first breath and let out a wail.

"Nice work, lady," exclaimed the intern as he climbed into the van to cut the umbilical cord and wrap the bloody infant in a towel. "You ever do this before?"

Rain was nearly as wound up as Janice, who was sobbing. "Not on my own. Is she all right?"

"She's just fine. Kicking and screaming."

While Tai explained the obvious to the police officers, the intern took the newborn into the hospital and sent a gurney out for Janice.

An hour later, they visited Janice in her room and got their first good look at the beautiful little girl with a few wisps of blond hair on the top of her head. An exhausted Janice even smiled when the others congratulated her.

Adrienne summed it up best. "What a school year! We helped our friend Gloria address the challenge of dying, we charted a distant planet, and we delivered a baby in the back of Tai's van!"

CHAPTER 143

Ray awakened Sunday morning and abruptly sat up. He looked around at the sun filled bedroom, then cocked his head in thought.

Adrienne roused. Lying on her back, she looked up at Ray. "What is it?"

"They're gone."

Adrienne sat up. "No way."

"I can't feel them at all."

They clasped hands and closed their eyes. Nothing happened.

Adrienne was relieved, but Ray was wistful. "Either I've lost my connection to the mushroom field or they have finally died off."

"Maybe there never was a way for them to leave their planet."

"Or as Tim suggested, they're already here." Ray sighed. "I will miss them. They gave me a profound glimpse into the nature of the universe and the extent of consciousness."

"At least you didn't go wild and do something stupid—other than confess to the FBI."

Ray laughed. "No, I didn't do anything stupid." He thought of Joey and all his trips to the Eugene Mission. "But I'll miss helping people."

"You did plenty, Ray. Feel good about that."

He shrugged. "Yeah, I guess so.

"Think we'll ever have contact with the mantas again?"

"Who knows? Maybe we need to try the mushrooms again."

"Please don't. Besides, we could never recreate the circumstances of our first contact—that was entirely unique."

"I just hope they have a new home and are not simply gone."

"We may never know. It's sad." Adrienne's somber face transformed into a smile. "But I really like having a boyfriend from the same planet."

Adrienne, Ray, Van, and Marsha were at the dining room table eating breakfast or sipping coffee, when Rain and Tai came in the front door. Tai had picked Rain up after she had spent the night at the hospital. "Both mother and child are in perfect health," she announced.

"How's the midwife?" asked Adrienne, standing from the table to hug Rain.

Rain opened up with a big smile. "Blown away and tired."

Marsha also stood to hug Rain. "When will Janice be back?"

"She's got two days in the hospital. Then she gives up the baby and comes home. We should all be prepared. She might have a hard time with this."

"I can imagine," said Ray.

"Give her some time and some space, and it will be fine."

"Does anyone know where the child's going?" asked Adrienne.

"No," said Rain. "That was part of the arrangement. The parents don't know the mother and the mother doesn't know the parents. I might not have done it that way, but I understand. In a way, it makes it easier."

"Was it a local family?" asked Marsha.

"The doctor wouldn't say."

After Rain brewed herself a cup of tea and joined the others at the table, Ray made the announcement. "The mantas are gone."

"Truly?" asked Van.

"Truly."

"I wonder what that means?" followed Tai.

"You know the options—either I've lost my connection to the mushroom field or somewhere out in the universe the last manta died."

"Wow, that's sad," said Rain.

Van stood up to get more coffee. "But seemingly inevitable."

"Isn't it also possible they found a better place to relocate?" asked Marsha.

Ray shrugged. "Maybe, but I doubt we'll ever know."

CHAPTER 144

John and Joyce Walters received a phone call from Doctor Rosenburg. Their baby had been born three days earlier. There had been no complications, and the mother and the baby girl were fine. The mother would release the baby that afternoon.

John and Joyce met Tom Rosenberg in his office at four. They signed the necessary papers, and a nurse brought the baby into the office.

"She could not be prettier," said the nurse, as Joyce took the swaddled infant into her arms.

Joyce peered into the baby's dark blue eyes, then showed her proudly to John. "Look, John. She's perfect."

Both of them fought back tears.

"We're naming her Stella," said John.

"Because the stars aligned for us to get her," added a glowing Joyce.

The nurse reviewed the basics of baby care then left the new parents with the doctor.

"Thank you, Doctor Rosenberg," said Joyce. "I don't know how we could have done this without your help."

Tom smiled. "No, it wasn't me. It was both of you. There are many children in need of parents and not nearly enough parents to adopt them. Thank you."

John and Joyce had already bought everything they would need for the child's first few weeks. They drove back to their farm and placed Stella in a cradle that had been Joyce's as a baby.

Maynard and Ann came over that evening to see Stella. John and Joyce stood back as the older couple went into the tiny bedroom. Ann picked up the baby and was instantly in love. "Oh, what a lovely girl," she said, holding her out to show Maynard.

"Oh, they always say that," muttered Maynard, who had never really gotten comfortable with the idea of adoption. "At least she's white."

Ann frowned. "Come on, Maynard. Let it go. A child is a child is a child. And this one is our grandchild."

Maynard reluctantly accepted the little bundle of love into his arms. He peered down at the infant and her thin wisps of blond hair. He couldn't help himself—he smiled.

Joyce came up from behind and hugged her father, while looking over his shoulder at Stella. "I can see her milking cows already."

Maynard chuckled. "If you start her too early, you might find her sucking at the working end of an utter."

Joyce laughed. "I have a device that allows her to suckle from my breast when she nurses. The milk comes through a tube taped to my nipple."

"Wonderful," said Maynard, just old-fashioned enough to wince at Joyce's use of the word nipple.

CHAPTER 145

Two months passed. Van and Marsha had both gone home to prepare for starting school at Stanford in the fall. Janice had moved into Gino's van (Gino now slept on the floor of the print shop), and the foxes had been introduced to the wild, leaving Rain, Tai, Ray, Adrienne, Lena, Moxie, and the chickens as the only holdovers from Blake College. They remained in the house, but the school was unofficially closed. Tai planned to leave for more globe trotting at the end of the summer, and Rain was still going out with Bob Yates, spending several nights a week at his apartment.

One afternoon, while Rain was selling her dried herbs at Saturday Market, she saw Joyce Walters pushing a baby carriage through the crowd. Rain did not know Joyce very well and had not seen the baby or even known Joyce was pregnant. Rain left her ten by ten booth and walked up to the mother and child.

"Hi, Joyce. I didn't know you and John had a new family member."

Joyce beamed. "We adopted her. Isn't she beautiful?" She pulled back the blankets so Rain could see.

Rain followed with all the standard comments about babies but couldn't help noticing the thin blond hair on the child's head and the bright blue eyes. *This has to be Janice's child,* she thought to herself.

"We couldn't be happier, Rain. Even my parents, who fought the adoption from the beginning, are in love with little Stella."

Rain leaned into the carriage to whisper and coo at the baby. To her surprise, she saw a tiny blue manta floating over the child's head. Rain nearly gasped at the sight but knew she was seeing what no one else could. She complimented the baby again and gave Joyce a hug, then returned to her booth, her head flooded with thoughts and questions.

Later that evening, while at the dining room table with Adrienne, Ray, and Tai, Rain told them what she'd seen. Upon finishing her story, Rain's face lit up. "My gosh, remember what Gloria told us. The life force or prana enters a newborn at the moment of its first breath and leaves the body with its last. Ray was there in the van when Stella took her first breath. That must have been when the mantas left Ray—in favor of a newborn girl!"

"That's right, I didn't notice it until the next morning," exclaimed Ray. "But they had left the night before. You must have had it right, Rain, the mantas were looking for a female."

"And who would have been better than Janice's child?" said Rain. "Stella was very likely possessed as a fetus in the same way we all were— and the mantas were there waiting all along!"

"What a thought," murmured Tai.

Adrienne looked around at the others. "Might have to keep track of that girl as she grows up. She might be something special."

"Unfortunately," said Tai, "we still don't know if the mantas' source was the mushroom field or their planet."

"Well," said Rain, "maybe we do have an answer."

She left the table and went upstairs to her bedroom. When she returned, she had the register for Saturday Market that listed the names of the vendors and their addresses. She sat at the table and ran her finger down the listing. "It's as I thought," she said looking up. "John and Joyce Walters live out route 45. Not far from that mushroom field!"

"That doesn't prove anything," said Van.

"But, man," said Ray, "it sure makes you wonder."

EPILOGUE

On July 22, 1971, Bill Bowerman was named the chairman of the Olympic Trials selection committee. Under his guidance, and despite the occupation of the ROTC building in May, Eugene was awarded the Olympic Track and Field Trials in October.

The Olympic Trials took place in June of 1972. Steve Prefontaine qualified for the Olympic Team in the five thousand meter, and Jon Anderson, the Mayor's son, prompted by the enthusiastic hometown crowd, surged past two other runners on the final lap of the ten thousand to finish third and earn a place on the Olympic team.

The tragic events four months later at the Olympic Village in Munich, Germany made all the excitement about Eugene's getting the Trials bittersweet. Bill Bowerman, who was the Olympic Track coach, was so distressed by what happened he retired from coaching following the conclusion of the games. He was seventy-one. Shortly afterward, Bowerman's waffle-iron running shoe and Blue Ribbon Sports blossomed into Phil Knight's multi-billion-dollar success, Nike, and the little college town in western Oregon, known as Tracktown, USA, would triple in size over the next fifty years.

ACKNOWLEDGMENTS

I could not have written this book without the love and support of my wife Judith. My thanks to her is always and forever.

Thanks is also extended to the contingent of readers who helped me with this novel: Tyler, Judith, Tim, Jim, Chris, Joshua, and Sean. Additional thanks to Sean for the scores of stories he told me about the creation of the counterculture community in Eugene during the 1970s.

Though I stated in the front matter that this book is fiction and not history, for clarity, the Hoedads did not exist in 1970; they were organized in 1971 and had grown into a significant co-op by 1973. Similarly, the anti-war tension between the Free Souls and Gypsy Jokers was my invention and not based on fact.

I should also note that "Stoopid" was a real person and a charter member of Eugene street life. He did not die in the bombing of Campbell Hall. That was a fictional embellishment. His death, however, was a result of eating toxic mushrooms that he had foraged and put into a stew.

454

THE AUTHOR

Dan Armstrong is the editor and owner of Mud City Press, a small publishing company and online magazine operating out of Eugene, Oregon. Information about his books, short stories, political commentary, humor, and environmental studies is available at www.mudcitypress.com.

Made in the USA
Middletown, DE
20 July 2019